"I cannot do this." Beth's heart beat so that she could speak only in a whisper.

"This?" he questioned innocently, passing his hand over her cheek, barely grazing the silken skin. His own heart was beating harder than he had ever known it to beat before. "Cannot, Beth?" he echoed. "Nay, never say cannot." His fingers twined with hers. "Let me show you the way of it."

Beth shook her head. "No, I—" Everything within her shouted "Yes," begged for it to be "yes." But she knew that if she gave in to him, to her own hunger, she would no longer be her own master. She would be tied to this man who could make her want things that should be beyond her reach.

It was a wicked battle that raged within her.

It lasted all of a few moments, but it felt like eternity. Determination triumphed, much to desire's sorrow. With a mighty cry, Beth pushed him from her.

Hitting his head on the bedpost, Duncan fell with a thud to the floor. Stunned, he rubbed his head and looked up at her.

Beth rose and ignored the desire to see to his head. "Though you make my body rebel against my mind—"

Duncan did not let her continue. Instead, he smiled in victory.

"Do I, Beth? Do I?"

TODAY'S HOTTEST READS
ARE TOMORROW'S SUPERSTARS

VICTORY'S WOMAN   (4484, $4.50)
by Gretchen Genet
Andrew—the carefree soldier who sought glory on the battlefield, and returned a shattered man . . . Niall—the legendary frontiersman and a former Shawnee captive, tormented by his past . . . Roger—the troubled youth, who would rise up to claim a shocking legacy . . . and Clarice—the passionate beauty bound by one man, and hopelessly in love with another. Set against the backdrop of the American revolution, three men fight for their heritage—and one woman is destined to change all their lives forever!

FORBIDDEN   (4488, $4.99)
by Jo Beverley
While fleeing from her brothers, who are attempting to sell her into a loveless marriage, Serena Riverton accepts a carriage ride from a stranger—who is the handsomest man she has ever seen. Lord Middlethorpe, himself, is actually contemplating marriage to a dull daughter of the aristocracy, when he encounters the breathtaking Serena. She arouses him as no woman ever has. And after a night of thrilling intimacy—a forbidden liaison—Serena must choose between a lady's place and a woman's passion!

WINDS OF DESTINY   (4489, $4.99)
by Victoria Thompson
Becky Tate is a half-breed outcast—branded by her Comanche heritage. Then she meets a rugged stranger who awakens her heart to the magic and mystery of passion. Hiding a desperate past, Texas Ranger Clint Masterson has ridden into cattle country to bring peace to a divided land. But a greater battle rages inside him when he dares to desire the beautiful Becky!

WILDEST HEART   (4456, $4.99)
by Virginia Brown
Maggie Malone had come to cattle country to forge her future as a healer. Now she was faced by Devon Conrad, an outlaw wounded body and soul by his shadowy past . . . whose eyes blazed with fury even as his burning caress sent her spiraling with desire. They came together in a Texas town about to explode in sin and scandal. Danger was their destiny—and there was nothing they wouldn't dare for love!

Available wherever paperbacks are sold, or order direct from the Publisher. Send cover price plus 50¢ per copy for mailing and handling to Penguin USA, P.O. Box 999, c/o Dept. 17109, Bergenfield, NJ 07621. Residents of New York and Tennessee must include sales tax. DO NOT SEND CASH.

MARIE FERRARELLA

MOONLIGHT SURRENDER

ZEBRA BOOKS
KENSINGTON PUBLISHING CORP.

ZEBRA BOOKS are published by

Kensington Publishing Corp.
475 Park Avenue South
New York, NY 10016

First Printing: June, 1994

Printed in the United States of America

To Charles,
who still makes
the magic
happen

Chapter One

Rain came down steadily, dolefully, playing wretched havoc with the dirt road. The storm made the journey even more arduous and vile than it already was. Nature had joined hands with the fates to attempt to prevent her from reaching Paris.

At least, it seemed that way.

Elizabeth Beaulieu wound her fingers around the worn leather coach strap and sighed as she stared out the window. The English countryside was dreary and bleak. Trees on either side of the road hung their heads as if in meek submission to the heavy drops that fell with monotonous regularity upon them.

She had always loved rain before this trip; now she hated it. The rain was slowing them down, presenting yet another obstacle in a long, frustrating series of hurdles. A storm was responsible for her being on this miserable road in this miserable country in the first place. If not for that storm at sea, she would be in Paris now and her mind would be at ease.

She truly hoped her mind would be at ease then.

A light buzzing sound like that of a mosquito in flight caught her ear. Sylvia was snoring. Beth glanced toward the only other occupant in the coach and smiled tolerantly at the heavyset matron.

Poor Sylvia. This was all so hard on her. Sylvia had stayed below deck during the typhoon, praying the entire time they were being tossed about like peas being shelled into a bowl. The older woman had nearly worn out the beads on her rosary, begging an indifferent God for a calm sea. When the storm finally passed, the merchant ship was afloat, but just barely. It was badly in need of repair. The vessel was too unsafe for them to attempt to continue the journey. Blown off course, they were forced to dock on the northernmost side of England.

The captain had offered to take Beth and Sylvia on the remainder of their journey when the ship was seaworthy once more, but that would take time. And time was something Beth didn't know if she could spare.

That was the frustration, not knowing. Was she too late? Would she be in time? Or was she concerning herself needlessly?

If only the letters had not stopped arriving.

The coach lurched like a drunken man as the wheels struggled over a rut. Sylvia ceased snoring for a moment, but kept on dozing. The gentle noise resumed. Beth folded her hands in her lap, mentally urging the horses on faster. There had been no ship ready to sail for France for days, so she had decided to take an overland route to Dover. Once there, she could easily cross the Channel and reach France.

More time spent . . . more time wasted.

I'll find you, Father, she thought. *I don't know how, yet, but I swear I'll find you.*

Sylvia's snoring grew louder. As she slept, the woman restlessly tried to find a comfortable position on the hard seat. The humid air hung about them, thick and moist. Sylvia had been unhappy about the journey right from the beginning. She had spent most of the crossing moaning, her face at times a shade of green that rivaled the very water they were sailing on.

There was no end to the sympathy Beth felt for the chaperone her mother had insisted accompany her on this journey. Beth was certain she would have fared better alone. As it was, she felt responsible for the other woman, though at forty-three, Sylvia was nearly twice Beth's age. Sylvia was at home amid her paintings, her books, and the garden. This was not a journey for a woman who considered a morning walk around the veranda strenuous exercise.

But Dorothy Beaulieu had insisted and Sylvia had acquiesced.

Beth had been more than willing to make this journey alone. To avoid taking any unnecessary chances, she had thought of disguising herself as a young boy, the way her neighbor, Krystyna McKinley, had once done on her initial journey to America. Mrs. Beaulieu had adamantly refused to hear of her daughter traveling alone, disguise or no disguise. It just wasn't done. Rather than waste time arguing, Beth had accepted a fidgety, nervous Sylvia as her traveling companion.

A smile lifted the corners of Beth's mouth as she looked at Sylvia again. It wasn't as if the woman could do anything to help her if something *did* happen. Unless, perhaps, she might strangle an assailant with her rosary beads, Beth mused, then hastily say ten Hail Marys as penance for gross disrespect of the holy object.

No, dear Sylvia would be no help at all to her in any perilous situation. It would be upon her own quick mind that she would have to rely, a mind she had inherited from her beloved father.

Dear God, she hoped he was safe, and that all this was for nought.

Beth sighed and blew out a long breath as she watched the branches point green-rimmed fingers toward the ground in supplication for the storm to end. The heavy rain had ceased; now there was only an annoying, continuing mist which did not alleviate any of the oppressiveness of the weather. Her traveling dress was sticking to her body like an uncomfortable second skin. Beth wiped her forehead with the back of her hand. She felt as if she was in a pot of water boiling on the hearth at home.

Home.

Virginia.

Longing burst through her like magnolia blossoms in spring. She was so terribly homesick. But staying safely lodged on the front porch of the lovely mansion, which her father had built for her mother, three sisters, and herself, would not help solve the mystery.

Her father had seemed to have vanished. There were no letters from him, no responses to their written supplications for a word to quell their fears . . . nothing.

Dr. Philippe Beaulieu was missing in Paris, in the land of his birth. He had disappeared just as a revolution had threatened to break out and engulf the country in fire. What filled Beth with apprehension was that the revolution on everyone's tongue, in everyone's mind, was a revolution of the poor pitting themselves against the rich. Philippe Beaulieu was descended from a very old, revered line. He was an aristocrat at a time when his former countrymen held aristocrats suspect and looked upon them with envy and hate.

If only he hadn't been moved to return. If only he had been content to stay at Eagle's Nest, enjoying the fruits of his new life in a brand-new land, a land he had helped to form.

But the whispers of revolution that had drifted across the sea concerned him. He was worried about his family in Paris. Added to that, he felt an overwhelming sense of compassion. If there was a revolution, he felt he could be of some service. He was a trained physician with years of experience. Revolutions always needed physicians to tend to the injured. And to close the eyes of the dead.

Another man would have been gratified to rest upon his laurels, to enjoy his well-earned retirement by the time he had entered his fifth decade. But Dr. Philippe Beaulieu was not like other men.

As concerned as Beth was, this selflessness, this ability to put everyone else above himself, was what she had always loved best about her father. He was always so willing to give of himself. The Beaulieus of Paris had been wealthy for generations. Dr. Beaulieu used his money to provide his family in Virginia with all the comforts they could possibly want. But his wealth and his respected position in Virginia society did not stop him from ministering to the sick. It was his calling. Being a physician, he had told his tearful wife on the eve of his departure, was who and what he was. Without his work, he was nothing.

Fourteen years before, he had fought in the American Revolution, caught up in the cries of freedom and liberty. He had fought beside his countryman Lafayette to bring independence to the Americans—and to heal their wounds when it was necessary.

Now it was more personal. But the cry had an uglier

tone this time. His beloved homeland was threatened by hatred and fear. Foremost in his concern was the welfare of his old mother and a maiden aunt who lived with her. He had no choice, he informed Beth privately, but to go.

Beth understood. Of all his children, she was the most like him. His feelings, his beliefs, were hers. When Philippe set sail, he left things, he told her, "in your capable hands."

Beth looked down at them now as her fingers twisted together. "Capable hands." "Capable Beth." "Sensible Beth." How many times had she heard those?

It was to her that her mother had turned one night to pour out her heart and reveal the fears she didn't voice before the others. Dr. Beaulieu had promised to write home faithfully each week. And he had. The news in his letters painted a grim portrait of a world he no longer recognized. But he had vainly tried to be optimistic about the situation, writing to his family that this cloud would pass. The letters arrived regularly, just as he'd promised. Each merchant ship from France that docked in the Virginia harbor had a letter for Mrs. Beaulieu, if not two.

And then, nothing.

A whole month went by. Then five weeks, then six. And the news from France, when they heard it, grew steadily grimmer. The *Virginia Gazette* editors, Riley O'Roarke and his sister, Rachel Lawrence, always attempted to keep abreast not only of local events, but also of world events, when information was available. There were articles in the *Gazette* that told horrible stories of aristocrats in France being threatened, of ancestral homes being taken over, of people imprisoned. And worse.

And still there was no word from Dr. Beaulieu.

Beth had quietly listened to her mother as the frail, regal woman had echoed Beth's own fears about her father's welfare. It was a cool evening. Beth stared into the flames of the dying fire in her hearth and made up her mind to travel to Paris. She told her mother that she would go to her grandmother's home and see for herself why there were no more letters arriving from her father.

Perhaps there was a simple, logical explanation. If not, she would deal with that when the time came.

Dorothy Beaulieu clutched her daughter's hand, wanting to rely on the girl's strength, yet afraid for her. "Oh, Beth, you can't go."

But Beth's mind was already made up. "There's no one else to go, Mother," Beth pointed out softly. "The others are too young." Garnering her father's favor, Beth had always felt much older than the others, even though Anne was only two years younger than she and the twins a year younger than that.

Dorothy blinked back tears as she looked at her eldest child. "What if something happens to you?" Dorothy knew she couldn't live with herself if something terrible came to pass.

Beth never worried about things that hadn't happened yet. It was a waste of time and energy. She covered her mother's hand with her own. "Nothing will happen, Mother. I have always taken care of myself."

Dorothy shook her head. "Yes—here, in Virginia. But France is a foreign country, and you're—"

"An American whose father taught her well," Beth concluded. "And remember, I speak the language. There's nothing to worry about." She smiled as she kissed the older woman's soft cheek. "It's settled. I'll go on the first ship sailing for France."

Mrs. Beaulieu rose and restlessly began to pace about

her daughter's bedroom. She was torn between a mother's protective love and a wife's growing concern. "Elizabeth, I really don't believe that you should go. These are dangerous times, especially for a young woman. And I—"

Beth placed her hands on her mother's shoulders. As Dorothy looked into Beth's eyes, the young girl shook her head.

"You've nothing to say about it, Mother, so please don't trouble yourself with arguments I won't listen to." A resigned smile lifted the corners of Dorothy's mouth. As with her father, when Beth's mind was made up, there was no changing it. "Someone has to find out what has happened to Father."

Beth let her hands slip from her mother's shoulders as she took a deep breath. "I'm the logical choice." They both knew that Dorothy's health had been failing for the last few years. "You're not well enough to endure the journey, and we've already dismissed the girls as being far too young. That leaves me." Beth smiled warmly at her mother to assuage the fears she saw in the other woman's eyes. "And I'm equal to the challenge."

Dorothy smiled. With light fingers, she touched Beth's cheek. Sometimes, Dorothy wondered who was the daughter and who the mother. Beth had always seemed so much older than the others, so sure of the path she was taking. It grieved Dorothy deeply that Beth hadn't gotten married and started a family of her own, the way other girls her age had. Perhaps it was her fault, Dorothy thought. She depended on Beth far too much.

"I never really told you before, but you were everything your father ever wanted." Dorothy smiled, remembering. "He used to look at you when you were a little girl while you slept and say to me, 'This one, she will do great things. Wait and see.' " Tears filled Dorothy's eyes once again and threatened to choke away her words. "He loved you very much."

Beth refused to accept such a fatalistic attitude.

"Loves, Mother, he *loves* me very much. Father is alive." She squeezed her mother's hand tightly, making a promise. "And I *will* find him for you. For *us*. And bring him home."

She knew her father would not be pleased about the request, the demand, really, but there were things he owed to his family ahead of his native country.

"The noble cause can go on without him." Beth had been barely eight years old when her father had fought in the American battle for independence, but she remembered it vividly—waiting up by candlelight, wondering if tonight was the night her father was coming home. "I think that one revolution is more than enough for any man."

Dorothy nodded. She knew that look on her daughter's face. It mirrored one she had seen on Philippe's time and again. They were a stubborn pair, she and Philippe. "All right. But you'll take Sylvia with you."

Beth thought of her former tutor. The woman had stayed on to teach the twins. Alone, with no family, Sylvia resided now at the Eagle's Nest as her mother's companion and confidante. Beth was horrified at the thought of taking Sylvia with her. Protests sprang to her lips, mingling until they merged into a single strangled sound of protest.

"Mother."

But Dorothy Beaulieu could be just as stubborn as her daughter and husband if the situation required it. She shook her head.

"I won't hear of anything else, Beth. You must have

someone with you to protect you." Dorothy watched Beth's mouth open in protest. She held up her hand to stem the flow of words. "Please. I will feel better about letting you go." She looked into the deep blue eyes that reminded her of her husband's. "For me?"

Beth sighed deeply. If nothing else, she had learned that there were times when concessions had to be made. "All right, for you."

But she wasn't going to like it.

And she didn't. Sylvia was a dear, sweet woman who was afraid of almost all of God's creatures. They both knew that she belonged back home in Virginia, not aboard a merchant sailing vessel, nor on a swaying coach bound for yet another seaport. Rather than a help, Sylvia had been a hindrance, requiring more than a little care on Beth's part.

Beth would have preferred not to have to worry about the woman, her seasickness, her queasiness on the coach, her fearful start at every noise. She wanted her mind free to concentrate on rescuing her father if he indeed needed rescuing. In the single trunk she had brought, tucked away inside the false bottom, was enough money in gold to ransom Philippe, if ransom was what was necessary. And within her breast was enough courage to face any challenge she might encounter while attempting to free her father.

Sylvia's snores droned on as the horses' hooves plodded along the muddied road.

Faster, Beth thought impatiently, staring at the land through a curtain of fine mist. *Faster.*

Beth prayed that she would not arrive too late.

Chapter Two

The coach jolted to a halt a moment before the crack of a pistol being discharged rang out in the stagnant summer air. Beth stiffened, her body tense, rigid with nervous anticipation. She heard a guttural moan, followed by a sickening thud. Something had fallen from the top of the coach and had hit the ground.

Sylvia's tiny black eyes snapped wide open, darting from side to side like loose berries as she attempted to comprehend what was happening. Her earbobs swung back and forth like huge silver pendulums in the wind.

Frightened, Sylvia grasped Beth's arm tightly. "By all the saints, what was that?"

Highwaymen. The single word echoed in Beth's mind like a dark, foreboding chant. Her heart began beating madly in her chest. Yet she gave no outward sign of agitation as she looked at Sylvia. One of them had to keep her head.

"It wasn't any saint, I can guarantee you that much."

A deep, raspy voice that sounded as if it was coming from the depths of a whisky barrel sliced through the air and dispersed any further speculation. "You there, in the coach, step down."

Sylvia's eyes were opened so wide, they appeared ready to pop out. "What are we to do?" Fear surrounded each whispered word.

Beth fervently wished now that she had kept her pistol with her, instead of packing it in her trunk. Her father had taught her how to load and shoot both musket and pistol, but the skill was meant for sport, not protection. Never in his wildest dreams had Philippe imagined that his oldest daughter would need to know how to protect herself. He believed that all his daughters would always be safe, nestled in the midst of a genteel Virginia society. The physician had felt confident that all the horrors which had been unleashed by the war for independence were over. Nothing ugly would ever touch his family again.

She glanced about the coach for a weapon, something to throw, to gouge with—anything.

There was nothing.

"Step down," the man ordered again, "or the next bullet will be through the coach, instead of your driver!"

The driver. He had shot the driver, Beth thought, filled with horror. Her concern immediately shifted away from the money at the bottom of her trunk. Had he mortally wounded the man? She had to see if she could do anything to help him.

"We'll step down," Beth called out.

Sylvia trembled. Huddling, she looked as if she was vainly attempting to shrink into her seat. Beth opened the coach door and stepped out. The heel of her shoe sank into the mud.

She was not unaware of the highwayman's appraisal, singeing her skin like hot coals. His eyes all but ravaged her where she stood. Struggling to ignore him, she looked around for the driver. The man was lying on the ground a few feet away, his face smashed into his tricornered hat. Beth swallowed the gasp that rose in her throat. With determination cloaking her, she took a step toward the driver.

"Don't bother, he's dead." The highwayman's smug words assaulted her ears. "And so might you be, if you don't mind what I say." The man leered. "Be a pity, though, to shoot something as comely as you." He ran his tongue over his greenish teeth in anticipation. "Right away, at any rate."

Beth struggled to keep the cold shiver from sliding down her spine. She couldn't let this man see that she was afraid. Raising her head, she kept nothing but contempt in her eyes as she looked up at the man.

The highwayman was attired in filthy clothes, with a ragged cloak slung over one shoulder. In each of his large hands he held a pistol. Looking down at her from atop a large bay, he brandished the left pistol as he spoke.

With her trembling hand wrapped about the door for support, Sylvia slowly descended from the coach. Her eyes never left the man on the horse. Horror was imprinted on her broad, open features.

"My Lord, it's the devil himself." Sylvia pressed a hand to her large bosom as her very breath felt as though it was backing up within her lungs.

Oh Mother, why did you force me to bring this woman with me? "Don't you dare faint," Beth hissed between her teeth, hoping a sharp warning would jolt the other woman into gathering her senses together.

The highwayman used the tip of his pistol to push his hat further back on his head. He wanted a better look at the young prisoner. His eyes all but glowed as he mentally tore the woman's clothes away from her shapely form. He licked his lips, completely ignoring the quaking cow behind her.

"It's a fair treasure I see I've found today." His lascivious look grew as the grayish stubbled cheeks spread in anticipation. He leaned forward, his elbow on the pommel of his saddle, his gaze burning into Beth. "What is it that you have for me, wench?"

"Nothing but the utmost contempt." Her cold demeanor belied Beth's growing fear. She spat on the ground before the highwayman's horse.

His laugh, dark and evil, tainted the air. "Oh, a spirited one. Those are the best for bedding. Usually." There was a warning in his words. He motioned to her with his pistol. "Come closer."

Beth raised her chin, her sapphire eyes darkening. "No."

Duncan Fitzhugh looked over his shoulder at the snow-white horse calmly following in his wake. "Fine time to throw a shoe, you miserable nag. We must be five miles from the manor. Couldn't you at least have done it when we were closer?"

The horse snorted.

Duncan had the distinct impression that the animal was laughing at him. He had to admit that despite these last few years, which he had spent landlocked, he had never gotten used to horses. A ship was the only thing he felt comfortable traveling on, not a four-legged nuisance that ate hay and did what it wanted to, *when* it wanted to. A ship knew who was master.

Duncan sighed as he fondly remembered his privateering days.

But all that was behind him now. He was the acting

agent for the absent Earl of Shalott. In exchange for his duties, he had the run of the manor, food and shelter for the extended family he had come to care for during his years on the London streets and on the high seas, and more comfort than he had ever dreamed of.

A little too much comfort, actually. It was all a bit too tranquil for him, too easeful. Duncan couldn't help yearning for his old life. Trapped within a respectable position, he felt a longing burrowing through his innards, a longing for the excitement he had once known. There was no danger to pit himself against, no test of courage to endure.

It could easily turn a man soft, he thought disparagingly.

He pulled his shoulders closer. His wet shirt stuck to him like a leech beneath the vest he wore. It was too hot, too wet. Duncan's humor was fouler than the weather.

His trip into the small township just beyond the manor had been far from satisfying. These last few months he had been keeping company with a pretty slip of a thing. Elaine. Elaine, of the ripe hips and the ruby lips. She had informed him this morning that they were either going to come to an agreement about their future together, or he could just take himself and his smooth tongue away.

Duncan smiled unconsciously, remembering how she had looked, her hands fisted at her waist, her dark hair thrown back as she waited for his answer. Elaine, he knew, had been confidently counting on his capitulation. She had warmed his sheets more than once and proved to be a very satisfying bed partner.

But it would take more than a warming of the blood for him to give up his freedom. She must have been a little daft to think that he would willingly place his head in a noose to be led around like some lamb by a woman with shapely hips and a sharp tongue.

Only honey dripped from Elaine's lips. Until this morning, of course.

He laughed to himself. This morning, after his refusal, she had shown her true colors, reviling him with a razor tongue she had kept hidden till now. All women developed sharp tongues; it was a basic law of nature. They developed sharp tongues just as surely as they developed breasts, and while he enjoyed the latter, the former was too great a price to endure for being allowed to fondle them.

He had left her rather quickly, letting the rain soothe his fevered brow—and various other fevered parts of him as well. Freedom, he had learned long ago, often came at a high price. But high or not, it was dear, and worth *any* sacrifice.

The crack of the pistol in the not-too-far distance brought Duncan instantly to life. It was like the explosion of warm whisky in an empty belly. All his senses immediately sprang to attention; he was alert, eager.

He'd never reach the scene on foot quickly enough, he reasoned. With an oath, he swung himself into the saddle. "Come on, you useless horse, something's afoot, and I've no intention of missing it. You can hobble a bit for a good cause."

Anything taking place on or near Sin-Jin's manor was Duncan's business. He owed it to his employer to look into the disturbance as quickly as possible.

Beyond the obvious necessity of employing speed, if there was trouble, Duncan knew he cast a more imposing image astride a horse than he did walking it. He kicked his heels into the horse's flanks and urged the animal on. At the same moment, he drew his pistol from his waistband. There were highwaymen about, and he had never taken any unnecessary chances.

With renewed spirit, his foul temper all but forgotten, he rode in the direction of the pistol shot.

Though his lust was raging in his loins, business always came first for Jeremy Jones. That meant counting riches before mounting bitches.

He chuckled to himself at his own cleverness. He had been quick to spy the trunk atop the coach and order the women to take it down. He'd been treated to a glimpse of long-stockinged leg as the pretty one had struggled to bring the trunk to the ground.

The trunk now at his feet, he looked down and found it locked.

He raised a brow toward the young one. "Open your trunk for me," he ordered.

She had brought the trunk down because the highwayman had threatened to shoot Sylvia, but now enough was enough. The money in the trunk might be the only hope she had of rescuing her father. She wasn't about to lose it because of the likes of him. Anger got the better of her common sense.

Beth fisted her hands on her waist. "I've lost the key."

Dismounted, the man stood barely half a foot taller than Beth. His eyes became small slits as he regarded her. He didn't want to be wasting powder and ball shooting off a lock if there was a way around it.

"Don't sass me, you little bitch, or it'll go harder on you." To make his meaning clear, he raised the pistol that hadn't been fired yet and aimed it at her breast.

"Would seem a pity to ruin such a fine pair. But I will. Make no mistake about it."

"Tell him, Beth!" Sylvia bleated, hanging on Beth's arm. "For heaven's sake, where's the key?"

Beth shook her off. When she made no answer, the highwayman cocked his pistol slowly. "If you kill me, you'll never find it."

"On the contrary," he countered. "If I kill you, I'll have the pleasure of searching your person without getting scratched for my trouble." His eyes narrowed as he looked at the hint of soft cleavage that peered out from her bodice. His fingers itched. "I'd wager the key's being kept nice and warm."

Beth raised her chin stubbornly, then gasped as a shot rang out. Her hand flew to her breast, but there was no sticky trail of blood, no fiery pain, nothing. She was unharmed. It was the highwayman who crumpled in a ragged heap, his bloodcurdling scream piercing the air.

Stunned, confused, Beth stared down at the bleeding man. When she looked up, there was another man on horseback approaching. This one was far better dressed, his golden mane flying in the wind as he rode toward them. He held a smoking pistol in his hand.

Two of them in one day, she thought in disbelief. The country was crawling with highwaymen. Quickly, she wrenched the pistol from the man on the ground. Holding it in both hands, she stepped forward and took aim at the rider.

"Hold," Beth ordered. "Sylvia, get behind me."

Duncan pulled up his horse. The short, squat woman scurried behind the pretty one with the pistol. It was like a bear trying to hide behind a sapling, he thought. A very beautiful sapling. He wondered why he hadn't seen her before.

Duncan stayed where he was, but he nodded at the weapon she held, his amused smile mocking her slightly. He surmised that the pistol in her hand was the one he had heard discharge a moment ago.

"You have to load it again before it works."

The green eyes were mocking her, she thought, annoyed. Beth cocked back the hammer with her thumb. "This one hasn't been fired."

She realized that in her haste, she had picked up the wrong pistol. It was the other one that hadn't been discharged. But luckily, this man had no way of knowing that.

She hoped.

His first inclination was to lean over and push the pistol she was holding away from him. It made him exceedingly uneasy to be staring down the barrel of a firearm. But she looked as if she would fire it at him with no qualms. It was prudent to keep a safe distance, for the moment.

"I've just saved your life," Duncan pointed out.

He swung one leg over the pommel and dismounted, his eyes never leaving hers. His men had often said he was capable of talking the down off a duck and the virtue out of a saint. But he was never foolish when it came to firearms and a woman's freshly raised ire.

Beth relaxed marginally, though her thumb was still on the hammer.

"True, but are you a good samaritan?" She studied him cautiously with eyes that looked far older than she, "Or a lecher?"

"I've been known to be a little of both at times," Duncan said truthfully.

He glanced toward the highwayman. The man was motionless. Dead, no doubt. But he wasn't in a position to verify his supposition. The girl raised the pistol higher, its muzzle aimed directly at his chest.

"A samaritan at the moment," he added, hoping that would placate her.

He assessed the situation quickly as he smiled warmly at Sylvia. The older woman hesitantly returned his smile. "We'll need to bury these two." He nodded toward the two bodies that were in close proximity. "And it appears that you'll need a driver."

She gave him no opportunity to volunteer. There was something about the look in his eyes. Beth wasn't certain she could trust him. There was too much amusement within them to make her feel comfortable in his company. "I can handle the horses myself."

An independent wench, he decided. A rarity indeed. "Good. As it happens, my horse has thrown a shoe and I need a ride to my manor." Taking up his reins, he took a step toward the rear of the coach to tie his horse to it. "You can take me. It's due east. You can't miss it."

She didn't trust him. He smiled too quickly, too broadly. His manner was too smooth. She turned, pistol still cocked, its target still his chest. One look at the barrel had Duncan halting in his tracks.

"Sorry, I'm on my way to Dover. I've no time to take you anywhere." Beth motioned Duncan away from the coach. "Sylvia, get in. And as for you," she addressed Duncan, "you can make yourself useful by loading our trunk on top of the coach. I—"

The whine of a bullet cut into her words.

Duncan's eyes widened in surprise a moment before he crumpled at Beth's feet. Beth whirled and saw that the highwayman had momentarily rallied. He had fired his pistol at Duncan, then fallen back motionless into the blood that had flowed from his mortal wound.

Behind her she heard a thud, and knew without looking that Sylvia had finally fainted.

Chapter Three

The rain began to fall from the heavens in earnest again, the clouds shedding horrified tears as they witnessed what Beth saw.

Beth stood alone in the clearing. Waging a battle to blanket her anxiety, she stared at the bodies surrounding her. They were strewn about like so many cast-off, tattered dolls. Broken dolls in need of attention.

Indecision tore at her. She did not know who to turn to first.

Friendship would have had her hurrying to see to Sylvia. But her traveling companion was in the least need of Beth's skills. Sylvia had only fainted and would be all right. The rain would undoubtedly revive her, by and by. And there appeared to be no rocks nearby upon which she might have hit her head.

Compassion would have dictated that Beth see to the driver to ascertain if he was truly dead. Or, at the very least, it would have her directing her attention to the handsome samaritan who had come galloping to their aid. Instead of being rewarded, misfortune had fallen upon his shoulders.

But as much as Beth wanted to be in all places at the

same moment, she knew that the highwayman was the one in most urgent need of her attention. Not because she feared for his life, but because she feared for hers and Sylvia's. And quite possibly the others', if they were still alive.

If the spineless blight on society—even for England, she thought vehemently—was not dead, if he was only wounded, then the highwayman was a danger to them all.

A danger only she, at the moment, could protect them from.

Beth glanced at the pistol that lay a few feet from the highwayman's hand. Its muzzle was partially embedded in mud. She lifted it, then carefully cleaned it with a corner of her skirt. She sighed a little as she watched the deep green material darken as it absorbed the filth. This was no time for vanities.

Her eyes never left the highwayman as she watched for signs of life. For a moment, thinking of the grief he had caused, she contemplated quickly reloading the pistol and discharging it once more. She knew her inclination would have shamed both her parents. But then, she knew quite well that she was too willful and far too aggressive to suit the norms of the day. She had certainly heard it said and been directly told as much by enough people in her time.

Beth tightened her hand around the hilt of the weapon and walked toward the would-be thief. With pistol cocked as if it were loaded—for how was he to know the difference?—she nudged the man's side cautiously with the toe of her shoe. Beth took care to keep out of reach of his hands, should he be only pretending.

The wound in his chest oozed, the blood mixing with the rain as it flowed into the puddle forming just beneath his body. The mud reddened as the blood soaked its way into the earth.

Beth swallowed and told herself not to think on it. The man was a scoundrel and deserved what he had gotten.

The grizzled man didn't move. Unconvinced, cautious by nature in some avenues, Beth watched for precious seconds more. Her eyes were on his chest, waiting for some telltale rise and fall.

There was none.

Gathering her courage to her, she leaned closer. Hesitantly, her hand hovered over his mouth. Though the rain beat down on the surface, there was no breath to warm her palm.

The man was dead.

With a sigh, she pulled the pistol from his frozen grasp, yanking it from his stilled fingers. Quickly she turned toward the driver.

She found no cause for hope there. The small, round hole in the old man's head was exuding blood. Were it not for the rain, it would have covered his face in a macabre mask of scarlet. Rather, there were thin red strips running along it, tiny tributaries dripping along his cheeks to the ground beneath.

Beth shuddered, feeling her stomach lurch and knot at the sight.

Quickly, as she had seen her father do countless times, she made the sign of the cross and commended the man's soul to a higher authority than any found on earth. She could only hope that he had not suffered.

The deep groan had her starting. She immediately swung around, her heart lodged in her throat. But the dead remained dead. It was the man who had fallen at her feet who moaned.

Mud was adhering to the bottom of her shoes as she made her way over to him now. He had a bullet wound in the shoulder, but he was still alive.

Crouching down, the hem of her dress absorbing the mud, Beth quickly examined the younger man. She placed her fingertips to his throat to feel for a reassuring sign of life.

Mixed with the raindrops, Duncan felt something soft feathering along his skin. His eyes fluttered opened and he tried to clear his vision of the heavy mists that clouded it. He blinked twice in hopes of better discerning the form next to him.

Beth saw the man's lips move, but heard nothing. She leaned closer, trying to make out the words.

"What?"

His head was filled with the smell of his own blood and the odor of wet wool that clung to the air. But above this was something lighter, something stirring. The scent of a beautiful woman.

Duncan felt his mouth curving, though he wasn't quite certain how he had managed it. "So I've finally reached it, have I?"

The man was obviously out of his head. "Reached what, sir?"

"Heaven." The single word floated out on the last of his breath. As he drew in another, his ribs ached. Fire burned through him, hurting his shoulder, his ribs, his belly. "For you're surely an angel." This time, he was sure he smiled. He wanted to die smiling, if that was the way of it. "Strange! I had never envisioned angels dressed in dark green. I suppose it makes you easier to find, amid the clouds."

The man was flirting with her. Bleeding like a pig prepared for a feast, and he was showering her with words she knew he felt would turn her head. Obviously he couldn't be in as bad a condition as she first had surmised, not if he could bandy words about like some shameless miscreant.

She leaned back on her heels, tottering slightly as the ground softened beneath her.

"No, this is decidedly not heaven. And you are exactly where you were five minutes ago, on a Godforsaken road in a Godforsaken country."

He would have laughed if the fire in his shoulder had let him. "You're not English, I take it."

She was American born, with a rich French heritage to fall back on. Neither country called the English "friend."

She frowned as she looked at his wound. The ball, she would wager, was still lodged there. It needed to come out. But not here.

"No, thank God, I am not. And neither will you be within a short amount of time, if I don't find a way to bind that wound. You're liable to bleed to death out here."

With effort, Duncan raised himself up on his uninjured elbow. He turned his head slightly as a thousand marching militia pounded across his shoulder and arm, making them throb even more. He managed to look down at his shoulder. The hole, he was certain, was small. It felt as if it was a huge chasm. He'd never been shot before. His wounds, and there hadn't been a significant number, had always been from the sword or the dagger, weapons of choice in his former line of work. This was something new, and he couldn't say he cared for it.

A cough welled up within his throat. He cleared it to

no avail. His throat continued to feel as dry as parchment.

His eyes turned toward Beth. The tables were reversed for the moment. His fate lay in her hands. It wouldn't be the first time that his life was in the hands of a woman. He had managed to survive until now. Confidence combined with growing weakness curved his mouth.

"I would say that if you are of a mind to do something, do it quickly. I've grown very attached to my blood and would like to keep it within the vessel where it currently resides, if at all possible."

She needed to get him to someplace dry. Beth hissed slightly between her teeth as she glanced in Sylvia's direction. The woman was still unconscious, despite the rain falling on her wide, pleasant face.

Curse the fates. She would have done better to bring Stephen along with her on this journey. But their youngest stablehand at the Eagle's Nest was far too lusty and virile for her mother's pleasure, Beth thought. Stephen was exactly what Dorothy Beaulieu wanted to protect her daughter from.

Lusty or not, Beth could have certainly used his strong back at a time like this.

No use wishing for things that could not be.

Beth looked into the stranger's eyes. She faltered for a moment, as if she had looked into a glass and had seen something she didn't want to see. A tiny bit of the future. Her future. She shook the thought away. She did not believe in premonitions or visions.

"I need to get you out of the rain," she murmured.

Duncan nodded. "Can't very well lie here and drown," he agreed.

But when he leaned forward, sweat burst forth on his

brow, mingling with the rain, as a weakness bit into him, devouring a large chunk. The response angered him that much more because he feared it. The weak were swept under, swept away by the strong and the ruthless. He had learned that lesson years ago. During his youth, spent in the streets of London, he had seen strong men laid low by fate and an enemy's sword in a moment of weakness. They were quickly snuffed out.

He had vowed then that it was never going to happen to him.

Biting off an oath, he struggled forward.

The fool was going to do more damage to himself, straining this way, Beth thought, annoyed. She quickly laid a hand on his arm to stop him before he fell at her feet again.

"Wait, put your arm around my shoulders—"

Were he better, he would have liked to have placed his arm around something more supple than her shoulders. The smile that lifted the corners of his mouth made promises that he couldn't hope to keep in his present state.

"That is tempting, mistress, but I'm afraid that I wouldn't be able to satisfy you at the moment—"

The conceited oaf. Did he think she was looking for a quick tumble? Exactly how disheveled and wanton did she appear?

"You will satisfy me, sir, if you lift your mind from the level of your boots and your loins and concentrate on getting yourself into the coach." She took a deep breath as she positioned herself beside him. "Now, your arm, sir." It wasn't a request; it was a direct order.

"As you wish, General." Even in his weakened state, the man's wide, sensuous mouth mocked her.

Let it. It was nothing she wasn't accustomed to. Even her sisters, who loved her, always teased her about her ways. They called her the queen, or the dictator. Only her father seemed to understand that she wasn't meant for needlepoint and starched caps. Only her father indulged her and let her mind flourish when all the others around her wanted it to remain shut up behind closed doors, like a fragile flower that couldn't exist in the light of day.

It was from Philippe Beaulieu that she had learned the basic skills for caring for the sick.

Beth nodded at the man's cryptic salutation as if the title was her due. "That's better."

She shifted until her side was pressed against his. Carefully, she lifted his good arm and brought it around her shoulders. Holding it firmly in position, she tucked the other around his waist. It made her think on a grotesque minuet.

Beth braced herself. "All right, on the count of three, we will rise."

Wounded, wet, and weak, Duncan was still not oblivious to the warm body next to his. "Aye, and perhaps even sooner than that."

She turned to look at him, her hair plastered to her head, her eyes a bright, knowing blue. Her first estimation was correct: good samaritan or not, the man was a lecher. "You are not taking your condition seriously, sir."

"On the contrary, mistress, I am taking it very seriously. It is not every day that a beautiful woman wraps her arms around me." He only wished he was well enough to do something about it. As wet as a field mouse straggling in from the river, the young woman beside him still put Elaine to shame.

Beth's breasts rose in impatient indignation as she drew another breath. To her growing annoyance, the man's eyes were fastened there as if she was the hole and he the lacing.

She gritted her teeth together. "One, two, *three.*" The last word was ground out as she rose wobbly to her feet, pulling him up with her as she straightened.

Perspiration joined hands with the rain, but she managed to bring him to his feet. The next moment, they almost went down again and would have if Beth had not braced herself quickly.

Duncan struggled to gain his footing on the wet, muddied earth. His head spun violently and he fought to hold onto it as red flares discharged in his brain, threatening to overtake him and drag him under.

For one embarrassing moment, Duncan sagged against the young woman. He felt her waver unsteadily beneath his weight and thought that they were both doomed to fall. But he managed to right himself at the last moment. The movement brought her closer to him, crushing her to his side.

A pity he couldn't really enjoy it.

Duncan forced a smile to his lips, though he knew it was a thin effort. "You caught me unawares," he murmured against her hair. "I never learned to count past two."

This was harder than she imagined, but determination stiffened her back and strengthened her aching arms. "Let's see if you learned how to walk."

With small steps, she succeeded in guiding him toward the coach.

Duncan groaned. The coach looked to be in the next county. "I'll do my best, General."

Her arm tightened around him as he mistepped. "See that you do."

In her soul, Beth cursed the rain, England, and the highwayman. And the wounded stranger at her side.

Chapter Four

If the rain had not plastered her hair and clothes to her body, the effort of guiding the man to the coach would have easily brought about the same result. The man she held onto was making an effort to help, but he was losing blood quickly and was a good deal weaker than she'd wager he was content about. He was certainly a great deal heavier than she had first thought. She was fairly staggering beneath the burden.

Beth gritted her teeth and muttered under her breath as she forced one foot ahead of the other. Passage was hindered by the fact that her heels were sinking into the muck with each step she took. How quickly dust turned to mud, she thought. Her eyes strayed toward the driver on the ground. And how quickly flesh turns to dust.

With renewed determination, her eyes fixed on the coach door, Beth concentrated on getting the man beside her to her destination.

"Don't drag your feet so," she panted.

"I shall remind you of that someday, General," Duncan promised, a weak smile on his lips.

The man was delirious, she thought. He was obviously confusing her with someone he knew. Someone

he intended to see in the future. Someone whom he undoubtedly would share his muscular body with. If she
managed to save it, she thought wearily.

If they both didn't drown out here.

From where he had fallen, it was no more than four
yards to the coach. It felt as if it were a long, tedious
journey. She was breathing heavily by the time they
reached it.

Beth swallowed and braced the man against the side
of the coach.

"Stay," she muttered breathlessly, as she struggled to
open the door while holding him upright.

It was only the sweet scent of the woman that had
him leaning so heavily on her arm, not the encroaching
weakness, Duncan thought. It was a thin lie, but he held
onto it as if it was a raft in a turbulent sea.

He blinked, fighting to keep his mind awake. He
spied the wide figure on ground, dressed in black. Had
the woman been shot as well?

"Your friend?" As he asked the question, Duncan
fought to remain above the waves of scarlet that reached
up to pull him under like a violent sea assailing the
sides of a ship during a storm.

His concern surprised her. "She only fainted."

Duncan heard the thinly veiled disgust. "She sleeps
heavily."

"Yes," Beth agreed, far from happy about the matter.
"I know. My mother sent her with me in hopes that she
would protect me."

Duncan sagged against her once more, this time
partly by design. The woman was soft in body, if not in
temperament, and he required very little at the moment.
"I would venture to say that you were in no need of
protecting, General. You seem very capable."

That was both her strength, and to some, her failing, she thought. But what was, was.

"I would hold that thought and my tongue, if I were you." She looked into the interior of the coach. But in order to gain it, he would have to walk up two steps, or be dragged up. She certainly couldn't carry him. "You need your strength."

As she turned, her breasts rubbed against his arm. He would have to be dead and buried not to feel them and not to react.

"It takes very little strength to talk."

She knew she had absolutely nothing to fear from this man. He was as weak as a kitten. But there was just the smallest prick of nervousness weaving through her. Anticipation, perhaps. Uncertainty.

But of what? And why?

"Nonetheless, I wish you wouldn't." She addressed herself to the immediate problem. "Can you manage the steps?"

He shifted so that he was leaning on her and not the coach. His eyes sparkled with more feeling than he had at his disposal. "It will be a sad day when I cannot lift a leg, mistress."

Beth nodded, trying not to think of how physically close she was to this man. And of the effect it was having on her. He was wounded and needed her skill, not some detached flights of fancy.

"Good, then get in."

He cocked his head, unable to resist despite his condition. "What was that?"

"Get in," she repeated, gesturing toward the coach as she braced herself, her hand splayed on the side. "Get in, get in." He was rapidly growing too heavy for her.

"Oh." He clutched to the side with one hand, the

other still draped over her shoulders. "I thought you'd said get on."

Beth all but pushed him into the coach, then climbed in after him. "Your lust far outshines your ability at the moment, sir."

"I would like to show you otherwise someday." He chuckled to himself, the sound low in his throat, and completely unsettling to Beth.

She was just angry, Beth thought. And rightly so. She was trying to save this heathen's life, and he was after a way to get under her skirts.

With tentative fingers, she probed the wound carefully. It was not clean through. The bullet was still in there. Damn.

"Quiet," she snapped at him. "Or I shall forget that you have rendered me a favor and that I am obligated to you."

He tried his best not to wince as she touched his shoulder. It felt as if a torch had been placed at its root. "Are you now, pretty lady?"

She raised her eyes to his. "I am obligated to save your life as you have saved mine, nothing more."

As gently as possible, she tore away his shirt from the wound. She could see that even the slight movement inflicted pain. His jaw tightened as he clenched his teeth. It amazed her that his smile never wavered.

"Your eagerness would please me more at another time, General." Duncan barely ground out the words.

Exasperation sapped her patience. He was wounded, perhaps severely so. Didn't he know the danger he was in? "Will you hold your tongue?"

Never let it be said that a Fitzhugh whimpered before pain. Duncan reached for her, but even his good arm dropped weakly at his side. His strength was rapidly leaving him.

"I would rather hold yours. Gently," he whispered, not from intimacy, but from ebbing strength. "Between my teeth." For a moment, he locked them together. "Like so."

Something hammered within her chest like a hummingbird hovering over a morning glory. She knew it was born in her indignation and anger, not by the image his words aroused in her mind. She succeeded in ripping the shirt further, a little less gently this time.

"Does everyone in this Godforsaken country prattle on so?"

It was as dark and dreary in the coach as if it were twilight instead of midday. Yet her hair gleamed before him. Or was that just his eyes playing tricks as his soul whispered away?

"Only when inspired."

"Or when half mad, I wager." Beth stood up in the coach and lifted her skirt. She saw interest glow in his eyes as she began to tug on her petticoats.

His vision was beginning to blur. Duncan nodded feebly toward her skirt. "Isn't that something I should be doing?"

Beth ripped at the petticoat a little too hard and rent it completely. "If you don't shut up, the first bandage will be applied to your mouth, sir."

Damn the man's eyes, did he think her flattered by this? Did he feel he had to play a role for her? She wanted only to get him to his home, tend to his wound, and be off, her debt repaid. She didn't want her feelings stirred, or this strange, nameless warmth seeping through her body.

"Duncan," he corrected her. "My name is Duncan Fitzhugh."

She swiftly tore the petticoat into strips, then seated herself next to him to apply her handiwork. "Well, Duncan Fitzhugh, if you don't take this seriously, you will shortly be the late Duncan Fitzhugh."

He watched as her fingers worked swiftly, capably. She'd done this before, he thought, and often. "You do this well."

Beth continued binding his wound, taking care to make the bandage just tight enough to stem the flow, but not so tight as to cut it off completely. "I've had practice."

How did a young woman become versed in bandaging wounds? "Men dueling over your favors?"

She raised her eyes for a moment. "No, I've shot men who have been after my favors, then felt moved to prevent them from bleeding to death, much like you."

Duncan laughed at her serious tone, then groaned as pain seared through his shoulder.

"Be still, sir, or it'll go hard on you." He had no sense at all, she thought, with a shake of her head. She inspected her work. "There, that'll have to do until I take the bullet out."

"You—?" He drew his brows together. The closest he'd come to being ministered to was by Samuel. The man, his mentor and surrogate father from his street urchin days, after his mother had died, lived in the manor with him now and was originally a barber by trade.

She didn't know whether to be insulted or amused by the astonished expression on his face.

"Me," she replied. "I will have to get you to your home. A shot of whisky might help the pain."

"A shot of you might do the same," he guessed. This

one would be an adventure, he'd wager. An adventure on a path he would like to explore.

Before she could respond, a bloodcurdling scream echoed just beyond the coach. It jarred Beth's very bones.

Duncan looked startled. The cry sounded as if it was only half human.

"That would be Sylvia," Beth told him with a sigh. Poor thing had probably awakened befuddled to see the carnage about her. "Sylvia," Beth called over her shoulder, her voice stern. "Calm yourself. It's all right. I'm in the coach."

The next moment, there was the sound of clawing at the door, sounds made by a frightened animal seeking to escape. Beth opened the door and looked at Sylvia's face. It was paler than a sheet.

The shock she felt intensified when Sylvia saw Duncan lying sprawled on the seat. Her breath hitched in her throat as she tried to speak. Sylvia pointed behind her, her hands shaking.

"There are—there are—"

Very deliberately, Beth bracketed the woman's wide shoulders between her hands. She spoke in a measured cadence to calm Sylvia down.

"Yes, I know what 'there are.' They're both dead. This one," Beth nodded toward Duncan, "is obviously not. Bleeding like a stuck pig, he insists on behaving like a rutting one instead."

Duncan felt himself sinking and fought against slipping away into a numbing darkness. He hadn't the strength to sit up. With a sigh, he resigned himself to his position for the moment. "You wound me, mistress."

"Not I. 'Twas the highwayman's sights you were in, not mine," she said pointedly.

It was not wasted on Duncan. He smiled. "It is 'mistress,' isn't it, and not 'madam'?"

The man's nerve staggered her. Here he was, bleeding badly, a bullet lodged in his arm, and rather than think of his wound, he had attached his thoughts to that part of his anatomy that was, in all likelihood, less than useful at the moment.

Sylvia was quick to stop her when Beth opened her mouth to reply. "Don't tell him anything, Beth."

"Beth, is it?" Her name was Beth. It was a beginning, Duncan thought.

She was far from afraid of a wounded man. One well-placed blow would leave him unconscious. Beth saw no harm in answering his question. "To satisfy your curiosity, it is Elizabeth Beaulieu. *Mistress* Beaulieu."

The smile was arrogant and cut to the heart of her, mocking her bold stand. "That only whets my appetite."

Beth glanced outside. The rain, once again, was abating. It seemed as if it would continue this way indefinitely, surging and retreating like a band of marauding Indians.

"I was speaking of your curiosity, not your appetites, sir."

" 'Duncan,' " he urged, wanting to hear his name on her tongue.

"Sir," Beth repeated obstinately. "All right, I've done what I can with you at the moment." She needed fresh water, preferably boiled, and fresh bandages, as well as a knife to remove the bullet with. "Did you say you lived somewhere close by?"

"Yes." He was going to lose consciousness, Duncan thought with growing alarm. He gripped it tightly, like a beggar his only coin.

He was growing pale, Beth observed. The ball had to

come out. And she needed poultices before a fever began to claim him. She leaned closer to him. "Where?"

His voice was growing faint and he cursed himself for it. "Three miles from here, due east."

"East?" Sylvia bleated, as she peered out of the coach. Directions were all one and the same to her. Despair began to grow. All was lost. The driver was dead, and the only man who could help them looked as if he was going to die at any moment.

The poor, silly goose, Beth thought. She would have been infinitely happier at home, talking to her pets, tending to her garden.

"I know which way east is, Sylvia," she assured her gently.

"Somehow, I knew you would," Duncan breathed, his world shrinking quickly to a small, rounded spot.

"But how will we get there?" Sylvia wailed. She caught herself, knowing she was whining. But her look implored Beth for reassurance. "He can't drive us, and the driver is—" She covered her mouth suddenly as her stomach rose to her mouth.

"The driver is past helping us," Beth agreed. She bit her lip. The last thing she wanted to do was leave the man out here. It wouldn't be right. He would be fodder for animals. She motioned Sylvia out of the coach. "Since you're awake, you can help me with him."

Sylvia nearly stumbled as she climbed out. "Help you do what with him?"

"Get him into the coach."

Sylvia's eyes grew large as she shrank back against the side of the coach. It was slippery with rain. "But he's—"

She wasn't getting anywhere by coddling the woman. Beth took a sterner tone.

"—Most likely a Christian who deserves a decent burial. I can't bury him here. I've no tools to do it with. But perhaps he has a family, people who need to mourn him and place him in his final resting place." *Please God*, she thought, *don't let it be that way with Father.* "At any rate, we can get him to Mr. Fitzhugh's house. Once there, someone can contact the proper authorities about this and our consciences will be clear."

Sylvia knew it was useless to say that her conscience was clear now. She glanced toward the driver. The man was dirty, bleeding, and dead. She cared for none of that, least of all the last. In her heart, Sylvia bewailed the timidity which had prevented her from resisting Dorothy Beaulieu's request to accompany her eldest on this journey. Much as she loved Elizabeth, Sylvia had no illusions as to her influence over the young girl. Traveling with her would only bring one chaotic disaster after another.

Tiny black eyes looked at the young girl in supplication. "But how—?"

Beth could only shake her head. Sylvia was always defeated before she ever began. "Between us, we can do this, Sylvia." She stared at the dark haired, faint-hearted woman as if willing some of her own determination into her. "Now."

The last thing Duncan remembered thinking was that, wounded or not, he shouldn't just be lying here. He was a man and Beth was just a wisp of a thing, though she possessed a tongue as sharp as any cat o'nine tails. He should get up and help the headstrong little vixen before she hurt herself dragging the driver to the coach.

Duncan got as far as reaching for the coach door before darkness slipped over him again. It consumed him.

"Damn," he muttered, as he pitched into blackness.

Chapter Five

Getting the driver into the coach proved to be a far more arduous endeavor than bringing Duncan to the same destination. The other man was built like a barrel; because he was dead, he was about as maneuverable as one filled with lead. There was no way they could carry the man between them. Though it seemed irreverent, Beth finally resorted to dragging the driver by his feet until she reached the coach.

Uttering a cry low in the back of her throat, Beth managed to right him and pushed him into the coach, but his lower body still dangled without. She circled the coach and climbed in from the other side. Grasping his hands, she struggled to get him completely inside. It was as if she were pitting herself against a boulder.

"Push, Sylvia," she growled at the inert woman. "For pity's sake, push. He can't feel you doing it!"

Hesitantly, moaning under her breath, Sylvia laid her hands on the man's posterior and pushed as Beth had instructed her.

"It doesn't seem right," Sylvia clucked, shutting her eyes more against the immodesty of the act than against the rain that was falling with renewed vengeance.

"It seems less right to leave him here in the mud," Beth pointed out as she struggled.

There. Done.

Sylvia looked over her shoulder at the last body on ground. She shuddered. "Are we taking that one with us, too?"

Still squatting beside the body within the coach, Beth rested a moment before getting down to join Sylvia. She shook her head.

"No, that one deserves to lie and rot here until Saint Peter comes looking for him."

"Lucifer would be more the way of it," Sylvia pronounced.

Beth shrugged. "Whomever." Shielding her eyes, she looked up at the sky. There was no sign that the rain was going to relent today. "We'd best be on our way quickly." She nodded toward the highwayman. "He might have had confederates."

Sylvia hadn't thought of that. She drew closer to Beth, then turned to board the coach. She stopped abruptly, a fresh dilemma presenting itself to her. Both feet on the ground once more, she turned toward Beth and bleated, "But where'm I to sit?"

Beth saw no problem. She gestured toward the interior of the coach. "The other bench is empty."

She looked around for Duncan's horse. It was still standing where he had left it. The horse was well trained, she thought. With slow, measured steps, she approached it, holding her hand out. When he didn't back away, she stroked the fine, silken muzzle.

"Oh, you're a handsome one, you are." Taking his reins, she led the stallion to the back of the coach and tied him to it. She had no intention of leaving the animal out here. In all likelihood, the horse was probably the only thing Duncan owned.

Sylvia shadowed Beth's steps, taking three for each of Beth's. To a distant observer it would have appeared to be a nervous little dance.

"In there?" She pointed behind her. "You want me to ride with a dead man and a scoundrel?"

Beth tested the reins to assure herself that they were securely fastened. Satisfied, she rounded the coach and looked inside. Duncan was still unconscious. It was better that way; less pain for him. Sylvia tugged on her arm for her attention.

"That scoundrel," Beth reminded Sylvia, "saved our lives."

Sylvia remained unconvinced. She had lived twenty more years than Beth and had seen much of man's lasciviousness. It had never, of course, been directed at her, but she was aware of its existence nonetheless. She pursed her lips. "For himself, not doubt."

Beth gathered up the horses' reins. "He's badly wounded, Sylvia. He can do you no harm."

That was the trouble with this child, Sylvia thought mournfully. Elizabeth knew nothing of the wicked world. A man could always find a way to have his way with a woman. Sylvia raised her chin.

"Any man can do you harm."

There was no time to stand and argue. Beth shrugged. "Fine, then you can ride with me." She placed a hand on the coach wheel to steady herself as she judged the distance to the top.

Sylvia watched her young charge wide-eyed. "You're driving the coach?"

She said the words in the same tone she would have employed questioning Beth's sanity if Beth had announced that she was going to throw herself from the Liberty Bell tower in Philadelphia and fly.

Poor Sylvia, such a mouse. "The coach cannot drive itself, and the horses don't know the way."

Wrapping the reins around her hand, Beth hiked up her skirts and placed a foot on the first step. The horse closest to her snorted, moving slightly. The coach shuddered as Sylvia squealed, prepared for the worst. Beth held fast and gained the top.

Sylvia released the breath she'd been holding, amazed that Beth hadn't fallen and injured herself. Agility of this sort, like a common cat's, wasn't seemly. Didn't the girl see that? As for her suggestion, that, of course, was preposterous!

She attempted to reason with her, knowing it was hopeless. The girl was as headstrong as a wayward mule. "But it isn't seemly for a young woman to be driving a coach like some common peasant."

Images and illusions had never been important to Beth. "Neither is remaining here, shivering in the rain helplessly while he bleeds to death," she nodded toward the interior of the coach, "and we catch our death of cold." Bracing her foot against the brake, she balanced the reins in her hand and then looked down at Sylvia. The woman remained stolidly stationary. "Well?"

There was no response. Neither choice was good. Sylvia looked from one unsatisfactory place to the other as she wrung her hands.

Though she had vowed to be patient with the woman, Beth felt that Sylvia had well exceeded her allowance for the situation.

"Sylvia, we haven't all day, and the rain is beginning to fall heavily again."

Still the heavyset woman remained where she stood, her face a mask of indecision. "I—"

Beth had had enough of this foolishness. *"Get in the coach."*

Distress at the notion of being in a confined area with a dead man seized her. Religious to a fault, Sylvia still believed in the existence of ghosts.

"But—"

Beth gripped the reins. "Now! Or I swear I shall leave you here."

Horror stamped its imprint on the round face. "You wouldn't."

No, she wouldn't, even though she was sorely tempted. But Beth was secure in the knowledge that Sylvia was too fearful to risk the chance. Beth raised the whip in her hand as if to snap it over the horses' heads. She looked down at Sylvia one last time.

"All right, all right, all right," Sylvia cried. As if a pack of wild animals were snapping at her heels, she scrambled into the coach. Fear thickened her throat as her eyes bounced from the dead man on the floor to Duncan and back again. "But your mother shall hear of this. This I swear to you upon my immortal soul."

Beth was counting on it. "Fine. Then perhaps the next time I need to make a long journey, my mother will refrain from sending you with me." She glanced down to make certain that Sylvia had closed the door.

Sylvia dug her wide fingers into the coach door, holding on for dear life. "Nothing could please me more."

Beth snapped the whip and the horses were off. "And neither me."

With a quick forward lunge they were off, heading due east.

Duncan had been drifting in and out of a dark, formless world. He was aware of a body being deposited into the coach and of a faint buzzing about his head that turned into a caterwauling. He opened his eyes just as Sylvia was struggling into the coach.

"She's a virago, isn't she?" His eyes drifted toward the ceiling.

Smarting at being ordered about by a mere chit of a girl, angry at the indignities she had been forced to suffer, Sylvia sniffed.

"A hellcat from the day she was born, they tell me." It suddenly occurred to Sylvia who she was addressing. She shrank into her seat, not an easy matter, given her girth. "Keep your distance, sir."

He couldn't have risen up if the coach had been on fire. Her order struck him as humorous. "Your wish is but my humble command, madam."

"Mistress," she corrected primly.

"I rather thought that," Duncan muttered softly, a moment before he slipped away again.

Samuel ran his hand through his hair, causing a ripple in the thick, silver mane. There was no getting away from it, he thought, as he paced about the small tower room. Old age was besetting him. Together with unnecessary, unwanted aches along his lanky, thin-boned body had come a change in temperament.

He had transformed into a worrier.

Fifteen years ago, this would not have transpired. He'd been too full of life to worry about its possible ramifications. Where once nothing had concerned him except the next meal, the next full wind, and the next wench, and not always in that order, now concern would gnaw at him with the annoying persistence of a galley rat.

It was Duncan's fault, all of it. Nothing but Duncan's fault. Duncan had been the one who'd taken him away from his element, taken all of them away. For Duncan had been the leader since before the time he had reached full manhood.

Samuel sighed. The rain increased the ache in his bones, fouling his mood further.

It had been too long since they'd been at sea, living by their wits, their fates in the hands of Neptune, he mourned. He ran his hand lovingly along the smooth, cylindrical spyglass as if it were the long, supple limb of a willing woman.

Much too long.

The land did things to a man. It civilized him, for one. The very word left a bad taste in Samuel's mouth. The land made a man think of things such as harvests and tax collection. On the sea, the only harvest was one they'd reap from another ship and the only tax collector was fate, not some flesh-and-blood man with too much kidney pie and spirits in his belly.

Samuel spat on the dusty wooden floor. Then, as an afterthought, he rubbed it in with his foot.

He leaned out the narrow window, the wind covering his face with rain.

Damn it, where was that boy?

The storm was growing too intense for him to see very far, even with his spyglass. He wrapped bony fingers around the instrument again in frustration. Duncan had promised to be home before the noon hour, and now it was more than twice past that.

As if to verify his assumption, Samuel glanced at the pocketwatch that Duncan had given him last Christmastide. As he had looked down at the gift all those many months ago, Samuel had scoffed at it as a symbol of a landlocked man. But truth be known, he had admired the gold case around it and the fine craftsmanship on the face.

Samuel had always loved fine work and pretty objects.

He closed his hand about the watch as he pocketed it in the pouch at his baggy trousers. Touching the watch only reminded him of things, made him long for the life he'd once known. A life of privateering on the high sea; a life of danger and excitement, where a man felt alive.

Before then, he and the crew had lived on the streets of London, seeking their fortunes in other men's lapses. But Samuel preferred the sea, even though it was on the streets that he had first found Duncan. He'd been a young, angry whelp of a lad then, in danger of being devoured by the bands of miscreants who roamed the dark alleys, plundering and taking from those weaker than they.

Duncan was his. He had given him life, though his loins had not produced the boy. Samuel had rescued Duncan from meeting his maker that fateful day, jumping in beside him when there were four to his one. Then there were two, and the odds had turned drastically.

Samuel smiled fondly, remembering. He had been a fine one with a sword in those days. None better. He could slice the hairs from a peach without bruising the skin. He sighed longingly. That was when his eyes were clear. Now he squinted when cutting Duncan's hair, secretly fearful of cutting his neck instead.

Old age was a bastard thief that mercilessly stole the most meager possessions of its victims.

He sighed more deeply, then raised the glass to his

eye again, vainly sweeping the road that led to the doors of Shalott.

Silly name, that, he thought, fruitlessly attempting to make out the figure of a horse and rider when there was none to see. Shalott . . . it sounded as if a fop lived here, instead of Duncan, the former terror of the English sea. Not that this estate was Duncan's, of course. It was only his to oversee for that former British transplant, Sin-Jin Lawrence. But it felt like his, and they had the run of it. The arrangements Lawrence had made were generous. Food and shelter for Duncan and the crew and money to line their pockets with amply.

So they had remained and continued to do so. And grew soft in the bargain, he thought with a trace of bitterness. He thought of Duncan. Soft enough to fall prey to things that they wouldn't have before.

Something appeared on the road, materializing out of the shadows. A large, dark shape. It was moving, and moving quickly.

Samuel started and leaned forward. Rain thudded against the end of his glass as he strained to make out what was approaching.

A ghostly apparition.

His heart stopped.

He forced himself to look again. It was a coach from hell, the horses' hooves pounding the earth as they came straight for the manor. The very earth trembled as they grew larger.

"Sweet Jesu." He crossed himself the way his mother had each time she'd uttered the oath.

His breath caught in his throat as he made out the form of a woman, her rain-lashed hair flying about in the wind as she urged the horses on.

It couldn't be real.

Samuel took an instinctive step back away from the window. The spyglass nearly slipped from his icy fingers. He could see the coach now without benefit of the glass.

A moment later, he came to life and fled the room.

Chapter Six

He was turning into an old woman, Samuel upbraided himself, as he hurried down the narrow stairwell that eventually led to the second floor. That wasn't a ghost coach approaching, no vehicle from hell searching for a passenger to take over the River Styx to the netherworld. That was a woman driving the coach. A ripe, wet, flesh-and-blood woman. It was the weather that had disoriented him so.

That, and his damnable concern.

Well, Duncan be damned. He was probably holed up with some tart, acquainting himself even now with what she had hidden beneath her skirts.

He thought of the woman driving the coach. Maybe he'd do some acquainting himself, tonight. It was high time, too. All the women in the manor were either spoken for, babes in nappies, or toothless old hags. The manor needed young blood, and so did he.

"Rider approaching!" Samuel shouted.

He hurried down the long, darkened hallway to the front stairs that led into the large sitting room. Candles flickered as he passed, striving vainly to hold onto their flames.

Grasping the banister to aid his quick descent, Samuel saw two of the crew at the game table below.

Hank, with his thatch of strawberry hair hanging in eyes the color of sand pebbles, looked up at Samuel's cry, barely interested.

"Duncan back?"

His gaze returned to the cards he held. Another poor hand, he thought, disgusted. Jacob was going to win this round as well.

He glanced at the younger man sitting across from him. That would make four in a row. Hank frowned thoughtfully as he studied the deck. Jacob was his brother, but that didn't absolve him from cheating.

"No," Samuel announced, as he reached the bottom. "It's not Duncan. There's a woman driving a coach as if the very hounds of hell are snapping at the horse's hooves."

Hank dropped his cards, coming to life. He had heard only one word Samuel had said, but it was the only one he needed.

"Woman?"

"Yes," Jacob said easily. He flipped over his brother's hand and smiled. Beaten him again. Too bad they weren't playing for real money, instead of pebbles. "You know, those creatures who like to wash themselves more often than you."

Samuel laughed as he passed them. "The cat likes to wash itself more often than Hank does."

Hank frowned, his face looking even more pinched as his lips drew together. "Don't hold with taking me skin off to satisfy some giggling wench."

Samuel laughed, the sound reminding the others of a hen cackling triumphantly after laying an egg. "Yeah, only his britches."

Jacob pushed away from the table. The day had been long and monotonous, just like the day before it.

"Let's have a look-see on what the fates have sent to Master Sin-Jin's door." He hurried after Samuel.

Hank trailed behind both of them, still muttering about what foolishness it was to wash more often than each full moon.

Samuel unlocked the heavy oak doors. His fingers ached as he grasped each handle and turned it. With a mighty shove, he threw both doors open in unison. The courtyard before him was slick and dark as he took a step out.

A shift in the wind's direction had the rain lashing out at the trio, sending them momentarily retreating to the shelter of the house. Angry waves of rain fell on the ground as if the sea had suddenly been upended and hurled pell-mell into the sky. It was determined to return back to earth.

Beth felt as if her arms were being pulled out of their sockets. She'd been struggling with the reins from the first and now yanked hard on them, attempting to bring the horses to a halt. It wasn't easy, after the full gallop she'd allowed them. She'd needed no whip to spur them on their way. The rain and the thunder had driven them far faster than she could have. It was controlling them that was the trouble.

That, and stopping them.

If she didn't manage to bring them to a halt soon, they were going to run straight into the house, Beth thought in mounting despair. A house as fine as any she remembered seeing in Virginia.

Apparently, she thought, as the distance between the horses and the house decreased at an alarming rate, she'd misjudged the man within the coach. He didn't live in some small hovel with his wife and twelve children.

Unless, of course, the manor wasn't his.

Straining, struggling to hold onto the reins even as they bit into her palms, Beth saw an old man appear in the doorway as the dark doors suddenly yawned open.

Dear God, she was going to run him down, she thought in horror.

"Hold, you horses, hold!" she ordered, shouting the command at the top of her lungs.

Bracing her foot against the brake, she tugged on the reins with all her might. Her entire body was straining against the horses' will.

"Is she real?" Hank spilled out into the doorway, crowding Samuel.

Jacob was instantly aroused. Blessed with better eyes than the others, he saw the way her breasts were straining against the wet fabric of her dress. More than two handfuls. His mouth watered and his young loins began to burn in anticipation. At nineteen, he hadn't had what he deemed his fair share of women. This one would make up for it nicely.

"Real or not, she's mine."

Hank turned and looked at him sharply. "I saw her first."

"And last; if we don't stop those horses of hers," Samuel snapped.

He hurried into the courtyard, leading the way. With hands that were still nimble, hands that had once taught Duncan how to lift a purse without the owner feeling so much as a light flutter, Samuel caught hold of the harness on one side.

Hank mimicked his actions on the opposite side while Jacob clambered up onto the driver's seat. The woman moved quickly aside as he snatched the reins from her. Of the three, it was Jacob who was most at home at the manor. The youngest of the three, he had an affinity for animals and counted horses as among the most beautiful of God's creations, second only to women.

Straining manfully, his young body like a sturdily rooted sapling, Jacob stood and pulled mightily on the reins, saying something to the horses in a native tongue Beth had no familiarity with.

Within a moment, and a heartbeat away from the front doors, the coach came to a halt.

Proud of himself, Jacob looked down into the woman's face. What he saw there temporarily made him forget his lust as a higher emotion transcended it. He was looking down into the face of an angel.

Jacob was instantly smitten.

"They're stopped, mistress." He very nearly tripped over his tongue as he raised his voice to be heard above the howl of the wind.

Beth struggled to gather herself together. She let out a long breath of thanksgiving. For a moment, as the horses were thundering across the cobblestones in the courtyard, she had the horrible impression that they were going to crash through the front door and trample to death the old man who stood there.

"Yes, I see," Beth whispered, then raised her voice and repeated herself. She smiled as warmly as she was able. Jacob was hers for the asking. "Thank you." She pushed the wet hair from her eyes, relief still spilling through her veins.

Jacob remained where he was, gazing at her, completely unmindful of the rain that was coming down.

"I'd like to get down, now," she coaxed, when the

young man continued sitting there, staring at her like an eager puppy.

"Oh, yes, of course." Jacob leaped down fluidly, then turned, waiting. He raised his hands toward her, anxious to be of any assistance. "Here, let me help."

Hank was behind him, ready to elbow Jacob out of his way. But Samuel placed a restraining hand on the other's shoulder. The grip was firm, the warning clear: no fighting. Though they laughed and teased Samuel, in Duncan's absence, the man maintained order.

She would have rather refused the young man's offer, but she was tired, so she allowed him to wrap his wide hands about her waist and guide her down.

"Thank you again."

Belatedly, awkwardly, the man withdrew his hands from her waist. She smiled at him. He had to be the twins' age, she guessed. She looked around at the dreary surroundings. Beth had no way of knowing if she had reached her destination. The weather had made it all too easy to lose her way.

"Have I reached Shalott?"

Samuel stepped forward. "Yes, mistress." He inclined his head in a formal bow. "Have you business here?"

Thank God.

"No," she admitted. "But I believe he might."

The three men followed her, curious, as she moved to the coach. Beth opened the door. The three were momentarily struck speechless as they stood gaping into the interior.

Samuel recovered first. His heart beat quickly at the sight. The lad looked far from well.

"Duncan!"

Then he *did* belong here, she thought, surprised and relieved at the same time. Beth stepped back, out of the way, as the taller of the men climbed into the coach. "He was shot saving us from a highwayman."

Yes, that sounded like Duncan. A regular do-gooder he'd turned into, Samuel thought. Not that he'd ever been a cutthroat, of course. They'd never killed anyone who hadn't deserve it, he liked to boast. But of late, the edge had been taken off. In private moments, Samuel referred to his former protégé as "Saint Duncan."

Hank took hold of Duncan's feet as Jacob eased him from the coach.

"Steady, boys, steady. Be gentle with him, now," Samuel instructed. "Don't drop him on his head, it's the softest part."

Conscious, Duncan gave him a woeful look. "After that ride, anything would seem gentle by comparison." He looked at Beth and smiled wanly as she stepped forward. "Next time, I'll drive."

He was continuing to make the assumption that she was going to remain somewhere on the perimeter of his life, she thought, annoyed. Besides being egotistical, it was foolish. She had no time for the foolish.

Samuel was staring into the coach. "The other is the driver," she explained. "There's no help for him in this world, I'm afraid."

Samuel nodded solemnly. He was vaguely acquainted with the man. There would be a new widow in town tonight. A new widow and three or four fatherless children. He shook his head at the waste. Samuel would send someone to tell her.

"I know the man's wife," Samuel attested. "Donovan will go in the morning to fetch the poor woman."

A noise that sounded like an animal whimpering had his attention reverting to the coach. It was then that

Samuel saw her, a cowering shadow in black. He turned toward Beth.

"Your mother, mistress?"

Her mother was younger, Beth thought fleetingly. And undoubtedly as worried as Sylvia was at this moment, with far more cause.

"My traveling companion," Beth corrected.

Though she knew that Sylvia's nerves were on the verge of causing her to faint again, she had little time to soothe the woman now. All through the journey here, she'd heard Sylvia's cries and shrieks of fear with each crash of thunder. Ebbing and flowing, they had echoed even above the sound of the thunder and the horses' galloping hooves.

"We're here, Sylvia. You can come out now," Beth urged, trying to curb her impatience.

The dark head peered out. Sylvia looked around timidly. "Here?"

"You are at Shalott, madam," Samuel said, bowing low. "Welcome."

"It's mistress," Sylvia corrected hesitantly, color rising to her damp cheeks.

"Then doubly welcomed you are," Samuel said, extending his hand toward her.

Sylvia took it and something akin to a smile fluttered across her lips as she stepped down.

"It'll be all right," Beth assured her.

Then, having no further time to coddle the older woman, she turned on her heel and hurried after the men who were carrying Duncan into the house. She still had a wound to tend to.

She slowed down as she fell into step beside Duncan. "I need fresh boiled water, clean sheets—" she began telling Hank.

Her words brought a smile to his lips as well as to Jacob's. Both men envisioned the woman languishing in a tub of water, washing away the grime of the journey from her supple body. They exchanged looks. They'd lead her to the east bedroom. There were knotholes in the door.

"And a clean knife," Beth continued as they entered the house.

They'd almost dropped Duncan then.

Hank looked at her wide-eyed, trying to fit her request in with the scenario he had been painting eagerly in his mind.

"For a bath, mistress?"

Were they simple-minded? "No, to remove the lead from his shoulder, of course." She gestured toward the bandage on Duncan's arm. "I couldn't see to it before, there was no time."

Samuel followed, shaking his head. "Of course." Entering, he called for Donovan to see to the horses and to have someone dispatch the driver's body to the cellar until the morrow. Then he looked at the beautiful disheveled woman giving orders, and wondered what manner of woman had Duncan run afoul of this time.

Chapter Seven

Donovan emerged from the depths of the manor at the sound of Samuel's voice. Quickly he hurried past him to do Samuel's bidding. He stopped only to glance curiously over his shoulder at the inert form Jacob and Hank were carrying. His eyes hovered on the two women, then returned to Duncan.

"He ain't—?"

Horror prevented the shallow-faced man from finishing his question. Duncan was their leader, their protector. Unable to make his way in the world alone, Felix Donovan had always been in need of a protector, someone to tell him what to do and make certain that he was provided for.

He had suffered a great deal at the hands of bullies and opportunists before he had had the good fortune to fall under Duncan's wing.

Behind him, a slight-built youth of no more than twelve or thirteen scurried in from the kitchen, drawn by the noise and the clatter. Tommy's mother was the cook, and he made himself useful by scouring the pots and pans and hoping someday to prove himself indispensable to Duncan. He dreamed of being his right-hand man, like Lancelot had been to Arthur. He was too young to know the end of the tale.

"He's not dying, is he?" Tommy cried, his eyes so wide, they took over the whole of his face.

"He'll be fine, both of you, just fine. Don't you be worrying none about Duncan," Samuel snapped, a little too quickly, worry taking the polish from his tone. He gestured forward for Hank and Jacob's benefit. "Take Duncan up to his room, boys."

Tommy fell in step quickly behind him, hovering about his hero. Samuel turned. "Tommy, fetch my basin and fill it with water. Bring towels, if you can find them."

As quickly as he had appeared, the small boy whirled on his heel and ran off to do as Samuel asked, eager to help in any way that he could.

"Clean towels," Beth called after Tommy. She had a feeling that the request might be hard to fill. With a sigh, she raised her skirts to hurry after the men carrying Duncan. "Your grandson?" She addressed the question to Samuel as she followed him up the steep stairway. Heavy breathing informed her that Sylvia was laboring up the stairs behind her.

Samuel spared Beth a glance, his mind elsewhere. He'd snatched up a lantern when the men had crossed the front room and now held it high to guide them. The light shone on Duncan's face.

"Tommy belongs to all of us." The answer came matter-of-factly as fresh concern washed over him. Samuel didn't care for Duncan's color. It was white and pasty. "Just as Duncan does."

Beth tried to make sense of the reply. "Then he's Duncan's son?"

They'd reached the landing now. The narrow hall

stretched out before them, its corners solemn and secretive. The candles that lined the walls cast long, mournful shadows on the floor. It was as if they knew of Duncan's danger and sought comfort in reverence.

Samuel shrugged. "In a manner of speaking."

He was hardly aware of his reply. Samuel worried his lower lip as they entered the bedroom that Duncan had selected as his own. Samuel had never liked it, not from the first. It had belonged to the late Earl of Shalott, Sin-Jin's brother, Alfred Lawrence.

There was the stain of death in this room, Samuel thought, as he crossed himself now to ward off the curse. The earl's wife had poisoned him, and he had died lying in this very bed. He'd asked Duncan not to take it, but Duncan had only laughed at Samuel's fears. Duncan had never been one for omens.

The long, velvet portieres hung open at the windows, moving restlessly, swaying like penitent nuns at vespers as the wind nudged them. The room had suited Duncan because it bade farewell to the setting sun long after it could not be seen from the other rooms. Duncan had always favored the setting sun. While they had sailed the seas, Duncan could always be found standing on deck, dusk after dusk, watching it make its departure.

Samuel fervently hoped that the tables were not turned and that the sun would not now be watching Duncan's departure.

"Set him down gently, now," he ordered the two men, his voice no longer teasing. He hurried to the window and closed it. In deference to Duncan, he left the curtains as they were.

As he turned, Samuel looked at Beth. Her companion was hanging back, but the young woman had moved Jacob aside and was now at Duncan's side. Duncan had obviously plucked another flower, he mused. Another one smitten by the young man's prowess.

Samuel approached and laid a gentle hand on her arm. "Mistress, I think you'd best be leaving now."

Tommy came hurrying into the room. Water splashed wildly on either side of the basin's lip as he approached. He brought two towels with him, one tucked under each arm. Neither looked clean, from what Beth could see.

"Here, sir, like you asked."

Beth had no intention of leaving, not after what she had seen. She looked up at Samuel. "And I think it's best not."

Samuel's mouth fell open.

Beth turned toward the boy and then frowned at the remaining water in the basin. Fire from the hearth cast a bright glow through the room. It easily illuminated a dark speck floating in the basin. She raised her eyes to Samuel's.

"There's a fly in the water."

A breath hissed through the space in Samuel's teeth. Samuel dipped his finger into the water and then flicked the offending speck away. "And now there's not."

She was far from satisfied. Beth looked at the boy. "Have the water boiled."

Tommy turned his large blue eyes to Samuel, clearly undecided as to whom he should be obeying.

Samuel laid a restraining hand on the boy's shoulder, but his eyes were on the young woman. Just who did she think she was, coming into their midst, issuing orders like the Queen of England?

"The water don't need boiling, mistress." The words were polite but firm. "He ain't going to be eating anything now."

Beth shook her head. "For his wound, sir. To clean

it." Patience was the best way to handle this, even though impatience tugged at her soul. "Believe me, it's best done that way. You want him well, don't you?"

After a moment, Samuel nodded at Tommy and released his shoulder. The boy hurried off, back to the kitchen.

Samuel knew that the other men were watching him to see what he'd do. He wasn't about to surrender his position to a mere slip of a thing, no matter what manners might dictate. After all, she was a mere woman, and he was Duncan's second in command.

His eyes narrowed as he appraised her. "All right, we'll boil the water. Now, you can stay, but keep out of my way."

He meant to elbow her aside, but Beth held fast to her position. She was certain that she could do Duncan far more good than this grizzly beanpole of a man, no matter where his heart lay.

"No, sir, I think that you will have to keep out of mine."

Hank snickered until Samuel gave him a black look. Jacob merely gaped, his mouth open in awe. He'd never seen a woman stand up to Samuel before, not even Amy, the cook, who put the fear of God into the rest of them.

Samuel squared his shoulders. "I've always tended to his wounds before."

She glanced toward Duncan. His eyes were shut, and she wondered if perhaps it was already too late to help him. There was so little to be done. But as little as it was, she knew she could do it better than this man.

"And I'm sure there have been many of them." She turned and pinned him with a look that made him want to squirm, though he hadn't the faintest notion as to why. "Are you a physician?"

The word sounded as if it had something to do with relieving himself. He took umbrage, especially since Hank was giggling again like some silly young wench being taken for the first time.

"I am not, indeed," he said, with all the dignity he had at his disposal. "I'm a barber."

"A barber," Beth repeated. She should have known. There were sections of the country, both here and at home, she'd heard, where a barber doubled as a healer, cutting both a man's hair and his life short with one careless pass of his instruments.

Beth looked down at Duncan's finely chiseled face. It was as white as the pillow it lay against.

"Well, when he needs his hair cut, and it appears that he does, you are welcome to tend to that. But he sustained his wound helping me, and I cannot stand aside and simply let you make the matter worse, bathing him with fly-infested water and drying him with towels stained with spittle."

Hank stared, confused. He looked at his brother. "What's she talking about, Jacob?"

"Foolishness," Samuel bit off.

He and the interloper stared at one another, a standoff in the making.

Sylvia moved forward and placed a hand timidly on the man's bony shoulder.

Samuel turned, his face a mask of annoyance. He tried to subdue it for the older woman's sake. It was not her fault that her companion was more headstrong than the ancient mule that was stabled below.

"Yes?"

Suddenly aware of the intimate contact she had initiated, Sylvia dropped her hand to her side. She was not accustomed to touching strange men.

"She's a little sharp-tongued, but her father taught her well, though the why of it none of us ever understood." It had always seemed to Sylvia a rather shocking thing for a man to teach his daughter about things that had to do with the human body.

Samuel was attempting to exercise patience. He glanced and saw that the young woman was beginning to remove Duncan's bandage. She appeared to know what she was about. "And her father would be—?"

"A doctor. A healer," Sylvia added, for good measure.

When Samuel pressed his thin lips together, they had a tendency to disappear altogether. "I know what a doctor is, mistress."

Samuel always knew when he was outmatched, and he knew it now. There was no reasoning with the wench, short of tossing her into irons. And she seemed sure of herself. Perhaps she *could* help Duncan. Duncan was, after all, his main concern.

His *only* concern.

Frowning, Samuel scratched his head, as if that could help him perceive things more clearly. Duncan had always been his to care for, and if the truth be known, he loved the man like no other.

He watched a moment longer as Beth carefully removed the bandages from his arm. "You won't hurt him?"

Beth didn't believe in making promises she couldn't keep. "I'll try not to." A small smile flickered over her lips. It was the best she could offer.

Duncan pried open eyes that felt weighed down. He had heard the exchange between Samuel and the girl.

As it heightened, he had struggled to sit up, but to no avail. He was as weak as a day-old pup, and it fed a fury within him he hadn't the strength to display. But he finally mustered enough to speak.

"I'm not the last piece of meat on a plate in prison. Stop fighting over me, and dig out the ball. My arm feels as if it's being burned off."

Beth looked at the wound. The hole in his shoulder was angry and red. His arm would swell up soon.

"Whisky." She looked at Samuel over her shoulder. "I need whisky."

Samuel stared at her. Was she daft? " 'Tis a bad time to be drinking, mistress."

The old man was a fool. She gestured to Duncan. "For him. This is going to hurt like the devil."

"Jacob, fetch a bottle," Samuel ordered. The younger man began backing away, his eyes still fixed on Duncan's face, like a servant looking to his master.

"Hold, Jacob," Duncan cried weakly. He meant to put his hand out to stop him, but it remained at his side. Duncan looked at Beth. He wanted his senses clear. Above all, there was to be no display of weakness before his men. "All I need is to gaze at you and I'll be drunk enough to stand whatever you turn your hand to."

Samuel shook his head. "Half out of his head, and he still talks that way." He leaned forward, looking at Duncan over Beth's shoulder. "Women'll be the death of you, Duncan." His small, dark eyes slanted toward the young woman. "If one hasn't been already."

Guilt grew, chewing away at her conscience. He had taken the wound because he had come to her aid. If he hadn't been talking to her, he would have readily seen the highwayman raise his pistol. This was her fault. And her responsibility to right, if she could.

She looked around at the men surrounding her. "The knife?" she asked impatiently.

"I've one here." Hank hastily produced the one he wore sheathed at his side.

Beth took it from him and carefully turned the knife over in her hand. She examined both sides. There was no rust on it, but it was far from clean. Tommy had returned with a fresh basin of water. She dipped her hand into it quickly and sprinkled water on the blade, then handed the knife to Samuel.

"Place it in the fire for a moment."

Samuel stared at her as if she was speaking gibberish. "Why?"

If he questioned everything she requested, they would be standing here all night debating while Duncan lay dying.

"I've not time to explain to you, sir; please, just do it." Beth paused, then changed her tone. "It'll be better for him if you do."

Because her voice had softened, Samuel nodded. He brought the blade to the fire Duncan always wanted kept blazing in the hearth and poked it toward the flame. He moved the knife quickly, tempering it. The metal turned dark.

"That's enough," Beth called. "I've need of it now, not tomorrow."

Samuel swallowed an oath about women knowing their place and turned from the hearth. As he passed Sylvia, he shook his head.

"Bossy, that one is." He dropped his voice to a whisper.

Sylvia smiled, knowing full well how he felt. Still, loyalty was second nature to her. "Her heart's in the right place."

By now Samuel wasn't certain that the wench had a heart at all.

"I'll be taking your word for that, mistress," he murmured. He crossed to the bed and presented the knife to Beth, bowing with a flourish. "Will there be anything else, Your Highness?"

Beth saw the tall man she'd sent out returning with a bottle. She was glad he'd come back. She'd probably need all three to hold Duncan down as she worked. She doubted the old man had much strength, certainly not enough to manage half the task himself.

"Yes." Her fingers wound around the knife's hilt. She'd watched her father do this before, but had never attempted it herself. Fear tightened its hold. "I'll need you to help hold him down."

"There'll be no need for them to lay their sweaty hands on me," Duncan murmured. " 'Tis only a whisper-thin needle you hold in your hand."

Bravery was all well and good, but it wouldn't hold him still when she needed it, Beth wagered. She nodded toward the men.

"Hold him," she ordered grimly.

Hank gripped Duncan's good side and Jacob placed his hands on the other. Beth bit her lip as she watched Duncan wince. She wanted to cry out that Jacob's hold should be gentler, but she knew that it couldn't be. If Duncan bucked, she ran the risk of cutting him severely and doing far more harm than good.

When she was certain that the men held Duncan down securely, Beth raised the knife.

A prayer flashed through her mind.

Chapter Eight

Perspiration, warm and sticky, slowly slid down a spine that was already damp as Beth gingerly placed the knife to the wound. Tension gripped her arm like the tightening jaws of an attacking wild boar. Her heart drummed in her ears. She watched Duncan's nostrils flare as she probed, but he made not a sound, stirred not an inch beneath the men's firm hold.

She hated the fact that she was hurting him with each slow, painful turn of the knife. An apology burned in her throat, but she knew it would be an insult to him if she said it aloud.

She felt nothing. The knife came in contact only with flesh. The ball had eaten its way more deeply into Duncan's shoulder than she had first suspected. She had been afraid of this, afraid that once she started, more would be required of her than she was capable of providing. Beth held her breath and probed deeper.

The flame grew in his arm, turning hot, then cold, then hot again. Duncan stared at the ceiling, searching for the words to dirty songs Samuel had taught him in his youth, trying vainly to cast his mind somewhere else. Someplace else.

The words wouldn't come. The pain seared through him like a thousand flaming arrows.

Duncan felt his blood flowing. He knew it was staining his chest and the woman who was hovering over him, delving into his flesh. There was blood on her hands and on her clothes. His blood.

That bound them.

Duncan's breath hitched in his throat, bursting to be set free in a lusty scream. He kept it prisoner, clenching his jaw so hard, he thought it would shatter at any moment as cleanly as a pitcher being thrown down on a floor made of stone.

He lowered his eyes to watch her, his mind winking in and out, seeking a darker, cool place to be, one where there was nothing. By an act of sheer will, he managed to remain conscious. Sweat was gliding down her forehead, clinging to her lashes. The firelight shone there, making her glow until he thought she was not real, but only some figment of his imagination.

A spirit.

Where is it, dear God, where is it?

The frantic question beat in her brain like a thunderous tattoo. She couldn't continue digging in his shoulder like this, but she had to get the ball out. It *had* to be here somewhere. The wound was not clean through.

There was no noise in the huge bedroom. All held their breath, waiting, as they watched Beth's hand move slowly, turning the blade in Duncan's flesh. Those who knew how prayed.

Time dripped, slowly, relentlessly, as if there was no beginning and no end.

And then, Beth felt the tip of the knife hit something hard. She became aware that her lungs were aching, exploding. She released the breath she'd been unconsciously holding.

It rushed out with her words of triumph and relief. "I found it."

She looked up quickly and saw that Duncan was watching her. His eyes burned into hers. For a moment, all her thoughts fled, save one.

His life was hers to save.

Quickly, she looked back to her task. "It won't be long now," she promised.

"It's already been too long," he snapped from between clenched teeth.

"I'm doing the best I can."

Biting down on her lower lip in empathy, Beth moved the knife swiftly. Within moments, the ball slid out in a river of red. Beth caught it and held the lead in her fingertips. There was no way to describe the relief she felt.

"There." She sighed as she deposited the offending sphere of lead on the night stand. Then she raised her eyes to Jacob and Hank. "You can let him go now." They were quick to release him.

Tommy picked up the ball and stared at the tiny bit of metal in wonder. "Just this?" he asked, looking up at Samuel.

" 'Just that' can kill a man," Samuel answered gruffly. Tommy flushed and set the metal down.

Beth washed the blood from Duncan's shoulder. She turned toward Jacob. "I'll take that whisky now."

Jacob looked at her sheepishly. "I couldn't find the whisky, but I brought some rum—"

It was the alcohol that was important, not the type. "That'll do. Give it here." She extended one hand, the other pressing against the wound to keep the blood from flowing.

Jacob placed the bottle in her grasp, then stood watching, curious to see what she would do with it. Tommy's eyes grew wide as he watched her pour a liberal amount over the wound she'd just been probing.

Taken by surprise, Duncan started. He caught a shout of pain before it could emerge from his throat, strangling the sound. His eyes reddened and filled with it.

"The devil take you, woman," he yelped. "What are you doing, pouring spirits over me like some pig about to be roasted?"

Beth set the bottle down on the night stand. "Very possibly saving your arm."

Suddenly very weary, Beth brushed the perspiration from her forehead with the back of her hand. She sank back for a moment, gathering to her what was left of her strength. The worst, she hoped, was over.

She looked up at Hank and Jacob. They were far more manageable than either the old man or Duncan. "I need to bandage his shoulder now. Take the rest of his shirt off, please."

Jacob and Hank were swift to follow her instructions.

"She said the shirt, not my skin," Duncan hissed between his teeth.

His arm hurt worse now than it had before. The room began to swirl before his eyes and he blinked hard to steady it once more. He saw Beth tearing something white into strips. A sheet. She was tearing a sheet.

"I would prefer your petticoats next to me again," Duncan murmured. Damn, he was drifting, he thought.

"I imagine you would."

As gently as she could she bound his wound again. Blood insisted on seeping through each layer. She wound the bandages she'd made as best she could. "There, is that too tight?"

She raised her eyes to his. But his eyes had slid closed once more.

Just as well, she thought; he needs his rest. She dusted her hands one against the other as she looked at him. His was a strong body. It should mend.

"Well, I've done what I can. The rest is in God's hands." She glanced at Samuel. "I doubt if He would want to see him so soon." She fervently hoped not. Not on her account, at least.

"More than likely," Samuel laughed, trying to shake off the grip that fear had upon him, "it would be the other place." He gestured toward the basin, its water now darkened with Duncan's blood. "Tommy, take that back to your mother."

Hank raised his eyes until his thick black brows formed a single dark line across his forehead. "Are you done with that, mistress?" His hand hovered over his knife on the night stand.

"Yes, thank you." She sighed wearily as she said it and offered the weapon back to him.

Hank cleaned the blade against the back of his trousers and then sheathed it once again. He saw Beth watching him. He shrugged shoulders that moved uncomfortably in a shirt that had always been too small.

"I'll wash it later," he mumbled.

"A very good idea," she agreed, knowing that despite his words, he would forget.

Beth rose from the bed, but as she turned, Duncan caught her wrist. Surprised, she stared at the link between them. She would have taken an oath that he was unconscious but a moment ago.

Duncan had circled her wrist weakly with his fingers. "Stay," he murmured.

The next moment his eyes had slipped closed once

more, as if he had no more strength to keep them open, as if the last of it had gone into his words. Beth could have easily slipped her hand from his. There was nothing to make her remain.

Nothing but his petition.

She sat down again.

Samuel looked down at her in surprise. Why hadn't she taken her hand from Duncan's? The man was clearly as weak as a newborn lamb. He cocked his head and studied her more closely, now that the danger had seemingly passed. "Will you be eating, mistress?"

Beth shrugged, disinterested. Hunger had been her companion earlier. Now, she was oddly past that. "Perhaps later."

She had done her best for Duncan. It had earned her a place in Samuel's esteem. Earlier hostility at her territorial invasion was now nudged aside by sympathy and compassion, two sentiments he'd have cut out a man's tongue for accusing him of possessing. "Surely you need to rest."

Rest.

It had a lovely sound to it. She was exhausted and miserable beyond belief. Her clothes adhered to her body uncomfortably, and she longed to strip and wash herself. But she had not come on this long, arduous journey to surround herself with niceties. She had known, when it had all started, that the road which lay ahead of her would be a hard one.

And she did owe this man a great debt. Beth looked down at the slumbering face. She had always believed in a debt for a debt, a life for a life. She would stay to see him through the night. By the morrow, if all went well, he should be on his way to mending.

If not . . .

She found herself unwilling to dwell on it.

Her gaze drifted toward the window. The weather was just as inclement now as it had been half an hour ago. As it would undoubtedly continue until dawn. They could not travel far in this had they the means, and she yet to arrange for that.

No, she and Sylvia would have to remain here for the night.

Beth looked toward the large scarlet chair standing at the ready by Duncan's desk. "I can rest here."

She slipped her wrist from Duncan's grasp. His hand lay open, fingers lax, against the dark cover. Beth rose and crossed to the chair. It was a cumbersome, heavy piece of furniture, and it resisted as she tugged on it.

Jacob was quick to rush to her assistance. Smiling shyly at her, he placed his hands where hers had been. His brother was a shadow's breath behind him, taking up the other side. Determined to win exclusive favor, they tugged one against the other. It took but a look from Samuel to have them working together.

"By his bed, please." Finding herself amused, Beth stepped back as they maneuvered the chair toward Duncan's bed. She nodded at both men. "Thank you."

Heads bobbing like will-o'-the-wisps in the wind, Jacob and Hank stepped away.

Clearing his throat, Samuel motioned them all out of the room. Sylvia, swept up by his authority, retreated, but hovered hesitantly in the doorway.

"He'll sleep now," Samuel told Beth gently, trying to urge her away.

"Yes, I know." She pressed her lips together as she stared at the sleeping face. "But there yet might be a fever."

"And you can fix that?" Genuine curiosity lit his eyes.

Would that she could without fail. But her father had shown her things that could help. Nature had provided aids that men passed by without suspecting.

"There are herbs and potions and poultices that can help at times. I can tell you what to pick, if it comes down to that."

Samuel stepped forward where the light was better and studied the young woman intently. She was fair of face and hair, and though her tongue was sharp, her dispositon seemed kind. And magic, he knew, took on many forms.

"Are you a witch, mistress?" When she looked up sharply, he leaned forward in the manner of a confessor . . . or a conspirator. "You can tell me."

The laugh that rose to her lips was genuine and light. "If I were a witch, I wouldn't have needed the knife, now, would I? I could have simply cast out the lead and healed him with but the pass of my hand."

Samuel nodded slowly. What the girl said was true, of course, but that did not change the fact that she had certainly bewitched Duncan. He had seen the look in the man's eyes. Beyond the pain, there was something more. It was a look a man wore when gazing upon his first treasure.

Perhaps she was a witch, at that.

A movement at the door caught her eye. Sylvia. Poor woman, she thought, to endure all this. Beth looked at Samuel as she settled into the chair to wait out the night and the fever that might yet come.

"I would appreciate it, kind sir, if you would find a room and supper for my companion tonight."

Samuel smiled. " 'Tis already done." But his concern,

for the moment, was the young woman by his Duncan. "I'll be bringing your supper here, then."

She smiled, grateful. Eventually, her hunger would return. "That would be very nice."

His eyes slid over her and the way her clothing clung. "And a change of clothing?"

Beth glanced down. She smiled ruefully. There was mud and blood on her dress, and it was torn in several places, ruined. But there were others, and she had no time to mourn something so insignificant as cloth. She knew her mother would differ with her on that, but apparel had never been important to her.

"I do look like something that the cat might have brought in when she was mousing, don't I?"

Samuel laughed, pleased at her humor. Pleased to see her smile. "A very fortunate cat it would be."

Flattering words seemed to come easily to this crew. Because he was her father's years, she found herself at ease.

"You've a tongue on you, sir." Beth laughed softly.

"Aye, and an eye to match." He winked. "I'll have Jacob bring your trunk up here. And Amy makes as fine a soup as any could want."

Despite the warm weather, there was a chill in her bones. She nodded her consent. "That sounds wonderful. And you will see to—"

He nodded. That would be his personal pleasure. "The lady will be well looked after, mistress. This much I can promise you. Do not give it a care." He cast one last look at Duncan. "Thank you for taking care of my boy." The words were said softly.

She had surmised as much, though there was no resemblance to look upon. "He is your son, then?"

Pride swelled Samuel's thin chest. "As sure as if I had given him seed."

With a nod of his head, Samuel withdrew quietly, urging Sylvia along with him.

Sylvia cast one uncertain look toward Beth, then followed.

Settling back once more, Beth shook her head. This was a very strange place fate had flung her to, she thought.

Without, the wind howled its agreement.

Chapter Nine

Left alone with only Duncan in the room, Beth felt restless. Like a book whose open pages were being rustled by the wind, she couldn't find a place for herself. She could not guess at the reason for it, but there was no denying that an unease had seeped into her.

Annoyed with herself, Beth scoffed at her unease as being as baseless as being afraid of things in the dark. That she had outgrown long ago.

She glanced at Duncan as if he was the cause of her trepidation.

He was just a mortal man, after all. A wounded mortal man. Perhaps fairer of body and limb than most, but still a man. There was no reason for her disquietude. It made as little sense now as when Sylvia had voiced it earlier, before entering the coach.

With renewed determination, Beth leaned forward, her outstretched fingers brushing against his forehead. It was warmer now than it had been just minutes ago. She didn't like it.

"Where shall I put it, mistress?"

The voice had caught her unawares. She looked toward the doorway and saw Jacob dragging in her trunk. It "shooshed" along the boards as he pulled it inside.

Beth gestured vaguely about the room. It mattered not to her where he placed it, so long as it was here. She wanted to be close to the ransom money she had brought with her.

"Anywhere will be fine, thank you."

Taking her at her word, Jacob left the trunk exactly where he had stopped. His brows drew together like light-haired caterpillars huddling for warmth.

"You're frowning," he noted, as he straightened. He took her look to reflect on him. "Somewhere else, perhaps?" He pointed at the trunk.

As if that could possibly make any difference. "No, it's not the trunk." She looked over her shoulder at Duncan. Her concern deepened her frown. "He's warm."

Jacob nodded his head vigorously. This was nothing new to his ear.

"Aye, so I've heard many a lady say." He saw the startled expression cross Beth's face and realized his error. "Oh, you mean something else."

He blushed for her and his own mistake, not wanting to offend.

She wondered how young the man was and how he remained that way, considering the company he maintained. She nodded toward Duncan. "He has a fever."

This was not good. He had to inform Samuel. Late last year, two of their own on the manor had died of a fever. The very word brought fear to Jacob's heart. "Samuel will not be happy."

" 'Tis not Samuel I am worried about." She sat down again beside Duncan upon the bed. The fever had to be brought down. "Could you fetch me more water?"

"You wish to bathe?" he asked eagerly. He moved quickly to the doorway.

Yes, oh yes, Beth thought longingly. But that was a luxury for another time, not now. Now there was something more urgent to concern herself with.

"I wish to bathe his forehead," she clarified. If Duncan awoke in the night, he was going to need nourishment. "And Samuel said something of sending up some soup?"

She had no sooner finished her question than a woman, wide of hip, with tawny hair bound up religiously by a battalion of pins, came marching in. She was carrying a large bowl of soup before her, balanced on what appeared to be a knight-errant's shield.

When she heard that there was company, Amy had taken the shield from the weapons room and pressed it into service as a tray.

"Right here, mistress," she clucked, as chipper as the weather was gloomy. "Hot and nourishing it is, if I must say so myself."

Beth turned to find herself looking up into a smile as wide as a garden gate.

Amy had brought up the meal herself, rather than send her son or someone else with it. She wanted to see the woman they were all whispering about downstairs. Her bright blue eyes, the mirror image of Tommy's, appraised Beth as swiftly and as thoroughly as Samuel had. But she saw a strength there, beneath the weariness, that Samuel had missed. It was a determined chin the woman possessed, and those were keen eyes. Amy smiled to herself knowingly.

Without question the woman was a match for this rowdy house she found herself in, Amy mused.

She smiled at Beth genially, and a maternal note was struck in her breast.

"Where will you be wanting this?" Her eyes shifted questioningly to the soup that tottered unsteadily on the rounded underside of the shield.

It was more for Duncan that she wanted the soup than for herself.

"Here, on the stand." Beth gestured toward it.

The young man was still standing in the doorway, gawking at her as if she was some sort of eighth wonder. "The water—"

"Jacob, mistress." He inclined his head, waiting to hear her repeat his name. "My name is Jacob."

Beth had laid the back of her hand against Duncan's cheek. It was hot. "The water, please, then, Jacob. And hurry."

She needn't have bothered adding the last words, for he had dashed off before she was done, the sound of his name on her tongue providing the wings beneath his feet.

The bowl safely on the table, Amy held the tray against her wide bosom. "Leaping around like a puppet, you have him," she noted, with no trace of envy or malice. "The other one, too."

Beth looked at her, confused. Which one was she referring to? "The other one?"

"Hank. His brother." Amy jerked a thumb at the doorway through which Jacob had disappeared.

She was talking about the taller one, Beth thought, the one who had given her his knife. She wondered if her presence threatened the woman.

"I mean to have no one leaping," Beth told her. "I only want to pay my debts and go."

Amy was silent for a moment as she weighed the import of Beth's words. "Do you, now?"

Beth guessed at the woman's thoughts. The slight smile on her face reached her eyes, but there were many in Virginia society who laughed and smiled into your eyes while they readied a dagger to use on your back. The world was not as simple a place as her mother believed or her father would wish.

"Yes," Beth said firmly. "I do."

Beth was weary beyond words. She needed to be off, to find her father and bring him home. She longed to have this whole business behind her. Instead, here she was, sitting in a darkened room—a man's sleeping chamber, no less—ministering to him while a parade of his servants came by, one by one, to look at her.

Amy cocked her head. "You look tired." Any fool with half an eye could have seen that, she judged. Why hadn't Samuel? "I can send Tommy in to sit with Duncan and watch him. Tommy's my son," she added proudly.

So the boy actually did belong to someone. Beth shook her head. "No, that's all right. I'm not tired."

The bloody hell she wasn't, Amy thought. She made up her mind about Beth. A warmer smile rose, creasing into the folds of her cheeks and transforming her round face into a beatific one.

"My name's Amy. Mind you eat that." She indicated the bowl with a short, stubby finger. "It's better hot, but not so bad cold." With that, Amy shuffled out of the room. There were still things to do before she could see to her own needs and Tommy's.

"I'm sure," Beth agreed absently.

The woman was forgotten before she even left the room. Beth feathered her hand across Duncan's brow again. It was too warm, much too warm to please her, even for such a warm night.

Beth sat back on the bed, her eyes skimming over Duncan as if she hadn't seen him before. He was lying on his covers, stripped to the waist with only the bandage she herself had applied to divert the eye from a chest that undoubtedly had many hearts beating fast. It was smooth and hard, and as she passed her hand lightly over it, urged on by curiosity, she felt a tingling sensation cross her palm.

Of course she was unaffected by such things, Beth thought stoically. She saw him only as a human being in need of aid, nothing more.

"Nothing more," Beth whispered under her breath, as if to reinforce the sentiment in her mind.

Still, she thought, as the tips of her fingers glided along a muscular ridge, it would be a pity to see any harm come to him on her account.

"I brought the water."

Beth sucked in her breath, startled. She instantly dropped her hand to the bed, upbraiding herself that it had a guilty appearance to it where none was warranted.

She drew a breath to steady her voice. "Thank you, Jacob."

The basin he carried was the same one she had used to wash Duncan's wound. He'd filled it to the brim and somehow managed to carry it up the stairs that way.

"Set it here." She pointed to the opposite night stand. There were still strips left from the rented sheet she had used for Duncan's bandages. She took one up now and rose to wet it.

Jacob twisted his hands together. "Will there be anything else?"

She smiled at him as she drew closer to reach the basin. Jacob didn't step back. "No, thank you, I can manage from here."

He took a deep breath and thought he could smell something sweet, like flowers. He could stand here near her all night. "I could stay, spell you, perhaps."

She appreciated his offer, but she truly wanted to be alone right now, to go about her task and gather her thoughts.

"Thank you, but I'm fine."

When he didn't move aside, she gently nudged him away from the basin.

Jacob nearly tripped over his own feet, attempting to get out of her way, yet remain close. "Need someone to talk to?" he asked hopefully.

She didn't want to be rude. He had been helpful, but she did want him to leave. "I'm too tired to talk."

He raised his brows comically in one last attempt. "To sit in silence with, then?"

"Thank you, but no," she said firmly. Her words all but pushed him out the door.

With a huge, reluctant sigh, Jacob withdrew, easing the door shut behind him.

Finally.

Relieved, Beth soaked the strips of sheet in the basin. Carefully, she placed the first on Duncan's forehead and then tied the other two about his wrists, hoping to lower his fever. Later, perhaps, if he was awake, she'd coax a bit of liquid between his lips, but for now it was best if he slept.

Impulsively, Beth cupped her hand to his cheek. A bittersweet sensation she took to be fathered by guilt flittered through her.

"You can't die on me, Duncan Fitzhugh. I can't have you on my conscience."

He remained sleeping.

With a sigh, Beth rose. She turned her back on him, not seeing his eyes flutter open.

Renewed restlessness rushed through her. Beth wandered to the trunk and opened it. Temptation had her removing one of her simpler dresses, something her mother hadn't deemed suitable for traveling. Beth, ever headstrong, had brought it with her nonetheless.

As she held the light blue garment against her, she remembered the last time she had worn it. She'd been in the garden at home, discussing her father's proposed trip with him and silently imploring him with her eyes not to leave.

But he had.

And now she was here, in a foreign country, nursing a stranger in his bed. Beth glanced toward Duncan as if to assure herself that this was real, and not some fanciful dream.

But there he lay, in the grip of a fever.

Because of her.

She sighed and stretched. The dress she wore felt scratchy against her tender skin. Grime, blood, and dirty rainwater had stiffened it until it felt like the bark of a tree, rubbing against her.

Beth bit her lip, debating.

In all likelihood, it would be a long time before Duncan regained consciousness. And she did ache to rid herself of this filthy garment. If she moved quickly, she could have another on in a matter of minutes.

She glanced toward the bed again. There was no movement. She made up her mind.

Swiftly, with sure fingers, she undid the lacings at her back and shed the dress. It fell to the floor like a leaden weight. Stepping gingerly out of it, she kicked it aside.

She felt dirty down to the very core, but there was no remedy for that now. Fresh clothes would have to do until such time as she could adequately bathe herself. Hands flying, she unearthed undergarments and spread them out for herself.

Duncan, unable to move, not at all convinced that a heated delirium hadn't seized his addled brain, still had the good sense to bite back the groan that rose to his lips as he watched the woman in his room begin to peel her clothing from her body a layer at a time.

Chapter Ten

He had died.

There was no question in Duncan's mind. He had surely died and gone to heaven.

Or perhaps this was hell, with temptation pricking him, being just a hairsbreadth out of reach.

Heat consumed him.

God knew he was burning enough for this to be hell. There was a fire on his brain and another burning in his shoulder.

But neither was a match for the one he felt flaming in his loins.

He made not a sound, afraid to breathe, lest she vanish like smoke into the night; vanish like the apparition she was.

His eyes were fastened to her as if they had been created that way. Though she moved with grace and speed, he saw all that she did transpired slowly.

The chemise she wore left her torso, then floated down like a leaf in the summer breeze, until it touched the floor beneath her shoeless feet. The petticoats, the ones, he vaguely recalled, she had ripped for him, slid down from hips that made his mouth water. She wore no corset, no stays to reinforce a waist that was hardly more than a whisper and a prayer. Stockings followed, exposing calves that were whiter than milk.

She wore nothing now but a thin, translucent undergarment. White pantaloons, and something equally as thin covering her breasts. She was so close, he swore he could see the rigid profile of her nipples straining against the fabric.

Time hung suspended on a spider's single thread.

Would she remove these last articles as well?

Please God, I've been good. Well, fairly so, he amended, praying fervently that this dream that pulsed through his brain would not end abruptly, depriving him of the last look, the last bit of paradise.

And then, with her face turned toward the fire's glow, the angel within his room carefully slipped the last of it from her body, first the pantaloons, then that last shred covering her breasts.

She was nude.

Her limbs were golden, gleaming invitingly in the fire's light. Fresh perspiration rose on Duncan's brow. As she turned now to reach for the garments she had spread out, he greedily filled his gaze with her. His loins pulsed as if they would burst. She was the most beautiful woman God had ever created.

The moan had Beth starting. She snatched up the last garment she'd cast off, pressing it against her. It did a woeful job of covering her.

Turning wide, accusing eyes in Duncan's direction, she saw that his were still closed.

He was still asleep, she thought in relief. It was just the wind, she realized. Only the wind moaning mournfully.

Beth tossed the garment on top of the heap of discarded clothing and stretched. There was a horrid ache in her neck, in her very body.

Duncan pressed his lips together, barely able to withstand it as he saw her thrust her ripe breasts forward through slitted eyes. It was as if she was offering herself to him.

And he longed to take the gift.

His eyes traveled slowly, longingly over the length of her body and he ached.

Haze began to blot out his mind again, creeping in like a low-lying fog at sea. If this *was* the netherworld, he was glad to be here, even if there was to be no fulfillment. Just to gaze on her was enough.

But the next moment, she was slipping on accursed clothing, hiding her supple body from him, and Duncan knew that he had been pitched headlong into hell, deprived of that which he sought most desirously.

Within a heartbeat, he slipped back into the arms of Morpheus.

Beth dressed as swiftly as she could, afraid that at any moment Samuel or someone else in his stead would be knocking. Or worse, walk in unannounced. She hastily kicked aside the clothing she had shed, then thought better of it. Gathering it up in her arms, she deposited the soiled, stained garments in her trunk. She would wash them when she found the time.

Or perhaps, she mused, as she drifted once again to the casement and gazed out, she would merely set them outside in this accursed rain. It was falling in sheets now, blotting out the very land from her view. It gave no sign of ending soon.

Murmuring a lusty curse that would have turned her mother's hair white, Beth crossed to Duncan's bed. With a light sweep of her hand, she removed the compress and then touched his forehead. She hesitated, then leaned over and pressed her lips to it in her hand's stead. It was still hot.

She shook her head, knowing that she was being anxious and getting ahead of herself. Fevers didn't vanish instantly, they ran a course and his had just begun. Dipping the compress into the water, she then rung it out and placed it upon his head once more. Though it was useless and foolish, she silently wished his fever away.

With a sigh, she settled into the chair, determined to wait out the night at his side, should he wake. The soup remained where it was, forgotten.

"Mistress."

There was a persisted buzzing about her head, an annoying fly that refused to go away.

Beth's eyes fluttered open.

Disorientation greeted her as it had each morning she had been on this journey. A moment later, she remembered where she was. And why.

Duncan's room.

An ache speared through her shoulders, working its way to her neck. She had fallen asleep, she realized ruefully. With a sigh, she ran her hand through her hair. It loosened from its pins, tendrils raining down at will.

As her eyes cleared, she saw that Samuel was hovering over her solicitously. Instantly awake, she sat upright. "Duncan?"

Had he taken a turn for the worse? Had she slept through the night and not heard his cry?

Samuel smiled, his lips exposing faintly yellowed teeth and reddened gums.

"Seems to be better." He was well pleased when he

had slipped into the room barely two minutes ago and touched Duncan's forehead. It was cool. "You slept here all night with him."

It would have been a lie to say he wasn't surprised at her vigilance. He had been sure that she would have sent for one of them during the night to take her place. Her dedication pleased him.

The ache in her back attested to the fact that she had spent the night in the chair. She rotated her shoulders, seeking to shed the stiffness.

"Yes, apparently I did."

And what would her mother say when she heard that piece of news? Beth had no doubt that the woman *would* hear. Sylvia would make a lengthy report as soon as they returned, and perhaps even write of it before they ever reached France. But she had no time to dwell on that, or on the effect it would have on her mother.

Beth moved forward and touched her hand to Duncan's forehead. The compress had slipped down and was about his chin now.

"It's cool as a witch's—" Samuel stopped himself with a gulp. "As a baby's bottom," he amended for her sake with a sheepish grin.

She withdrew her hand, greatly satisfied. "The fever's broken." She said the words to hear them aloud.

Samuel beamed at her as if Beth had performed some sort of miracle. "All Duncan needed was the laying of your hands."

She merely laughed, thinking that he jested with her. "Sylvia?" She suddenly remembered that the woman's welfare was her responsibility, or at least, that was the way it had evolved.

"She's well, mistress." Samuel's smile widened, so much so that it aroused her curiosity. "Very well, indeed." His eyes swept over her, approval registering in them. The morning dress became her. "You've changed your clothes, I see."

She recalled the eerie feeling that she had had last night when she was changing, a feeling that she was being watched. "Yes."

Samuel looked around for the pile of discarded clothing. "Might I have the others washed for you?"

Beth shook her head. "I don't intend on staying that long."

Samuel nodded toward the window to bring her attention to the rain.

"The weather intends otherwise, I'm afraid." He looked at the sleeping man in the bed. "And Duncan is not full well yet. I know he'd want to thank you himself for what you've done."

She didn't want to waste time, waiting for thanks. And she had an uneasy feeling that she had no desire to be around Duncan when he was at his full strength and well.

"There's no need," she assured Samuel.

He eyed her knowingly. "Just as there was no need to repay him for saving your life."

He had her there.

"I see your point." She sighed, frustrated. "Well, given the weather, I suppose we're not going anywhere just yet." Beth hesitated, then opened her trunk again. Scooping up the garments she had bundled on top, she handed them to Samuel. "Here."

Samuel tucked the lot of them into a ball under his arm. "A wise decision. They'll be cleaned and ready for you when you leave us."

She nodded as she turned toward the window. "Does it always rain like this, for days at a time?"

"Sometimes weeks." His comment had her looking at him sharply. "But not now, I'm sure," he added hastily, lest she decide to leave while rivers ran from the sky. Duncan, he had a feeling, wouldn't forgive him if he let the young woman leave before he had a chance to speak with her.

With the clothes tucked safely under his arm, Samuel quietly removed the untouched soup. "I'll be sending breakfast up to you shortly. Or will you be taking it downstairs?"

It sounded like a very good idea. She'd spent too much time sitting here, looking at that face last night. A change would do her a great deal of good.

"Send someone to stay with him," she instructed. "I shall be eating downstairs." Her first order of business, she decided, was to ask Sylvia the meaning of Samuel's broad, satisfied smile.

"Right away, mistress." Arms loaded down, he began to back out of the room the way one would in the presence of a ruler.

"One more question, if you please?"

Samuel came to an abrupt halt. "Yes?"

"The driver. Have you—?"

Samuel nodded. There was no need for her to continue. "Donovan's gone to fetch his widow even now. Will that be all?"

She nodded. As he backed away, Beth laughed to herself. What a curious place this was! One moment Samuel was eyeing her as if she were an interloper, the next he was treating her as if she had raised Duncan from the dead.

"You *are* real."

Beth gasped as she swung around at the sound of his voice. Duncan was sitting up in bed, weakly propped up on his good elbow. His long, flowing golden hair fell riotously about his rakishly handsome face, brushing against the tops of his bare shoulders. Beth felt a tightening in her chest the likes of which she hadn't experienced while he lay unconscious. Awake he was twice the man he was when he lay sleeping.

Her mouth felt as if her father's cottonseed had fallen into it. She coughed and cleared it, or tried to. "Excuse me?"

He smiled, one corner of his mouth lifting higher than the other. Her stomach turned to undercooked porridge. "Last night, I thought I dreamt you."

She thought he was speaking of when she was trying to probe the lead from his shoulder. The words he had heaped on her head returned to her and she smiled. "Do you always curse your dreams?"

Feeling weakened, he was forced to lay back against his pillow again.

"Curse you?" he echoed, confused. "If I remember correctly, I was completely lost in worship."

Now it was Beth's turn to be confused. She stared at him. "Sir?"

Trepidation created uncertain ripples within her. His smile was too familiar, too unsettling. Apprehension began to consume her.

The smile widened further as the memory returned, vivid and clear. "I have never gazed upon a woman as perfect as you."

"You hardly saw me last night," Beth pointed out nervously.

Anxiety dried her mouth. She remembered the moan she had heard when she was changing and vehemently denied the source, clinging to her belief that it had been the wind.

"You were out of your head most of the time as I was removing the ball from your shoulder. And then," she insisted in isolated, measured words, "you slept."

"Aye." Duncan's eyes touched her body as if he knew what it looked like without her morning dress on. "And dreamed."

"Of what?" she barely whispered.

Please God, don't let him say what I think he's going to say.

"Of a wondrous, supple-limbed woman in my room, as unclothed as the day she was created." The familiar smile grew only more so. His eyes held hers. "Like a goddess rising from the sea, ripe and beautiful."

Though she thought herself far beyond it, Beth blushed from the roots of her hair to the bottom of her soles. Fury seized her. After all she'd done for him. . .

Her throat was hoarse when she spoke. "You, sir, are no gentleman. You are a rogue."

"Aye, perhaps," he agreed. "But I'm a very blessed one."

Chapter Eleven

She didn't know which inflamed her more, his words, or the wide grin upon his face. In either case, she whirled on her heel, wanting to put distance between them as quickly as possible.

"Wait," Duncan called after her.

Against her better judgment, she stopped. Curiosity, she knew, would one day be her undoing. She stood still, not deigning to face him, feeling that he deserved no more than to talk to her back.

"Stay. I meant no harm."

The man meant more than harm. He was a heathen. She had no idea why she even bothered to converse with him. She would have fared better talking to her horse.

Still, Beth fisted her hands at her side and turned around. "If you meant no harm, why didn't you close your eyes, or give me a sign that you were awake, instead of watching me like some blackguard pirate?"

She'd hit upon the truth without suspecting it, he thought, as he watched the way her bosom rose and fell, fueled by indignation. It made him think on the way she had been last night, supple and inviting.

He lifted a shoulder and then let it fall, shrouding himself in innocence. "At times, old ways are hard to part with."

Her eyes narrowed. He was admitting his shamelessness? "Then you are a blackguard?"

"Was," Duncan amended, as he inclined his head. "At least, there were some who called me that." He saw curiosity highlight her eyes like beacons shining upon the darkened waters. "I was a privateer."

That was merely a title to hide the bearer's true intent.

"A thief, you mean." There was no difference between a pirate and a privateer, except that one held an allegiance to himself and the other could be publicly bought.

Duncan held up a finger to halt her verbiage before it spilled out. "An honorable one."

As if there was honor among thieves. Did he think her a brainless dolt to believe in such prattle? "Who sold himself to the highest bidder."

Duncan smiled as he leaned back against his bed. That was not the way of it. It had been allegiance that had bought him. That, and the need to provide for his extended family.

But if he told her that, she would call him a liar. So he told her what he knew she would readily believe that *he* believed.

"Money is an honorable institution."

He was having sport with her. Did he think, because he had seen her without a stitch of clothing, that she was entirely without a mind as well? Or scruples? "I won't remain here and be mocked."

"Not mocked, Beth." He shook his head as his mouth curved. "Worshipped." She had a body that invited worship, and he possessed hands which he would readily raise in prayer.

They hardly knew one another, and he was speaking to her the way a man would after asking permission to court her. No, she amended, not even then, for she would have had his tongue cut out for being so forward. "You are too familiar."

Her umbrage made Duncan laugh, though it hurt his shoulder to do so. "Ah, not nearly as familiar as I would wish."

She had had enough. Beth turned once more on her heel and aimed for the door.

Now you've done it, he thought. She looked intensely angry this time.

"Wait," he called again, but she didn't bother to stop. "Would you walk out on a wounded man?"

She gained the door and pulled it open. The words were thrown over her shoulder. "I would if that man were a rogue and a base scoundrel."

"A rogue and base scoundrel who saved you from a dishonorable fate." He saw her brace her shoulders and knew that he had guessed correctly. She was the kind who felt honorbound to repay her debts.

Beth spun around, her eyes flashing. She crossed the room to his bed, as if to engage in battle. She saw through him well.

"A fate that you would wish now to bestow upon me, no doubt, *if* you were able." She poked a hard, angry finger at the center of his chest.

"I am more than able for that, Beth." As her hand rose to strike him, his eyes met hers and held. Duncan grew serious, his voice softening. "But never that way, Beth. That much about me you must believe. If we *were* ever to come together, it would be strictly by your wishes."

Duncan saw that he had her and continued. He told her nothing less than the truth.

"I see no joy in taking a woman against her will." He smiled at her, his words moving like warm waves upon her skin. "The joining of two bodies is truly a wondrous thing. It should never be marred by curses and pain."

Did he really believe that? she wondered. Once more he had caused the very breath within her to be stilled. To hover in her throat, moving neither up nor down as she stared at him.

Beth shook herself loose of the spell he cast upon her. The man had the tongue of the devil, she thought, not completely grudgingly.

"So you mesmerize your victim instead, like a serpent with a helpless mouse."

He laughed once more, then groaned as he clutched at his wound. "You are no mouse, Beth, and you are as far from helpless as heaven is from hell."

What was she doing here, bandying words about and talking of bedding with a man who wasn't her husband? Yet her feet remained where they were, held fast by she knew not what.

A fascination spun through her, though Beth resisted it.

She pressed her lips together and tried to think of other things than the unsettling effect this man was having upon her. Her eyes fell upon the way he clutched his shoulder.

"Do you feel better?"

"Looking upon you has helped me do that." He heard her quick intake of breath, saw the angry flash rise to her cheeks. He rather liked it, but knew he was treading in dangerous waters. "Yes, much." He regarded the neatly bandaged arm thoughtfully. "You did this?"

He vaguely recalled her ministering to him, but it was far less vividly imprinted in his mind than her supple silhouette had been.

"Yes."

He obviously didn't remember. Perhaps he had been out of his head with pain after all. She brushed her fingers over it now as if to straighten it. It was, she knew, but a shameless excuse to touch him again. She dropped her hand, annoyed with herself.

She raised her eyes to his. "How could you tell?"

Duncan felt himself warming again as fresh desire stoked the fire within him. There would come a day, he suddenly swore to himself, when he would have her.

"Samuel would have left something three times as large in its stead. His handiwork is not nearly so neat."

"Wait, you're undoing it," she chided, batting his fingers away. Carefully, she tucked the end of the bandage about again.

Duncan scented her. Here was a woman, he thought, to stir a man's blood to unimagined heights. She was so close, he had but to spread his hand and his fingers would brush along her face.

He reached to her.

Beth's eyes grew wide as she felt his fingers slowly sliding along her cheek.

"Smooth," he murmured. "So smooth." His fingers feathered along the gentle slope a moment before they slipped into her hair. He cupped the back of her neck, drawing her mouth closer to his.

She could feel his breath on her lips and was aware of her heart hammering. She knew she could flee, she *should* flee, but all she could think of was that she wanted this, wanted to feel his mouth on hers. Wanted to know what it would be like to taste a man.

For none had ever dared to want to kiss her. None, at least, had ever tried.

Beth's eyes fluttered closed.

"Duncan!"

Jacob crowed out his name as he hurried into the room like a puppy who had not yet grown into his feet. Beth sprang away, praying that the flame within her had not risen to her face.

But Jacob did not seem to notice, if it had. His eyes were on his leader. "You are well!"

The man's timing could not have been worse if he purposely sought to undermine him, Duncan thought in frustration, as he looked at the distance that had suddenly sprung up between the girl and him. The opportunity was missed. But there would be others. He swore to himself by all that was dear to him, there would be others.

"I am sitting," Duncan corrected good-naturedly, lest Beth take his wellness as an excuse to leave.

Jacob clapped his large hands together. "'Tis wonderful."

Belatedly, Jacob remembered the reason he had entered the room in the first place. He turned toward Beth and his tongue immediately thickened in his mouth and became clumsy.

"I've come to take your place, mistress. That is, of course, no one could take your place; but I will stand here while you go below. Or perhaps sit." His meaning was becoming more tangled, like a skein of yarn being chased by a cat.

Jacob took a deep breath and tried once more. "Samuel said you wished to eat with the others."

He had cut cards with his brother for the privilege of coming up and telling her this. He'd left Hank grumbling at the table. It wasn't until he was halfway up the stairs that he'd realized Hank would be the one to be sitting with her, while he took her place with Duncan.

She had need to get away, Beth thought. She had very nearly kissed the man. Though she thought of herself as not bound by her mother's prudery, this was too bold a step even for her.

Beth nodded, beginning to leave. "Yes, thank you. I shall only—"

"She'll eat here," Duncan ordered, his voice reinforced with the authority he had become accustomed to wielding ever since he was sixteen. "With me."

All the softness she had felt but a moment before vanished like morning dew. Beth turned, her face a mask of controlled fury. How dared he? How dared he presume to have authority over her?

"I shall eat where I wish, sir, when I wish, and with *whom* I wish. I'll not be ordered about like chattel. Especially not by the likes of you!" Gathering her skirts up to facilitate her steps, struggling with her anger, Beth turned her back on him and prepared to do just as she'd pronounced.

His own anger unfurled, but he collected it to him like a flag that would only invite enemy fire if flown. Shouting now would not yield the result he sought. Duncan was a shrewd judge of human nature. And what woman couldn't be drawn with honey? Even one whose eyes shot daggers, like those of Diana the huntress.

"Please."

The single word had her foot hovering over the doorsill as indecision reared its shaggy head. She wanted nothing so much as to leave his presence. But to do so before his man after Duncan had humbled himself for her sake would be unduly cruel and willful. She might be stubborn, she readily admitted, but it was not in her nature to be cruel, or to humiliate a man intentionally— unless he deserved it; and as yet, Duncan did not.

At least, not to this degree, and not before his man.

With a great sigh, Beth released her skirts. As the hems whispered seductively against the floor, she turned slowly around and faced him, aware that Jacob was still there, hanging on every word.

"Very well. I shall stay. For but a meal," she added purposely, lest Duncan misunderstand.

Duncan only smiled in reply, as if he knew more than she. He inclined his head in a slight bow. "Thank you, Beth."

Jacob knew not what to make of the scene, save for the fact that he felt his chieftain's interest in the woman. That mean he could not dare to approach her. It was just as well, he thought sadly. She was out of reach, in any event. He'd take himself to town and soon, lest his manhood dry up for lack of activity.

But Samuel, he knew, was waiting below, as was Amy. And Hank, he suddenly thought with a smile. Poor Hank, he would be disappointed. "Then you'll be taking your breakfast here?"

Beth nodded, resigned to her fate for the moment, and not altogether saddened for the excuse. "Apparently."

"I'll fetch it!" Jacob declared, eager to win another smile from her. Duncan's brand upon her notwithstanding.

"I'll be in your debt," she murmured without thought. Her words brought a huge smile to the plain face. "And bring a bowl of soup for Duncan," she added. As if his feet had wings, Jacob was off.

That was not so hard, Duncan thought, well pleased with himself. He wondered what words it would take to talk her into his bed.

Beth turned away from the doorway and crossed to Duncan's bed. To satisfy herself about his condition, she touched his forehead. It was just the way it had been earlier, which was promising.

She saw him raise his eyes to hers, waiting for her to speak. "'Tis cool still."

He took her hand and pressed it to his cheek. His intention was to kiss it. The palm of a woman's hand was a sensitive place, as sensitive, some said, as their very core. But Beth pulled her hand away.

His eyes followed her, teasing. "But I burn."

As discreetly as she was able, Beth rubbed her hand against the folds of her dress, trying to rid her palm of the strange tingling sensation she felt.

"No, that you did last night," she told him seriously. "I feared your fever would consume you."

"It did."

The words hung seductively in the air. Beth could not believe the gall of the man. If he meant to seduce her, he was going to be sorely disappointed. She was not some common tart ripe for the plucking, to have her head turned with a few words.

"Sir, if you continue this way—" Beth took a step toward the door, her meaning clear.

He raised his hand in a solemn promise. "I shall behave."

"I find that difficult to believe." But she took no further steps away.

"I will," Duncan swore, "but only if you offer me a trade."

She regarded him suspiciously. This was a man who had earned his money by his wits, and he was still alive. She would not make the mistake of underestimating him. "Which is?"

His smile could have coaxed birds from trees. And women, she'd wager, from their virtue. "Call me by my given name."

She raised her brows innocently. "Scoundrel?"

He laughed lustily and paid dearly for it, for every sound vibrated through his body. He pressed his lips together and held his arm to him. "Duncan."

But Beth shook her head at the suggestion. "It is far too familiar."

His eyes played upon her face, whispering secrets to her. "Just as are we, now."

She looked at him sharply. "I warned you, sir, that if you continued—"

He spoke as if she had not begun. "We have saved one another's lives," he told her smoothly. "Would that not make us familiar in the eyes of God?"

It was not his true meaning and they both knew that, but she let his words pass. He seemed to be a master at them. She was willing to concede, for the moment and in silence, to be sure, that she had met her match.

"Very well, then, Duncan." She said his name as if it left a bitter taste upon her tongue.

If he noticed, he gave no sign. "'Tis much better. I do not care for formality and airs in my guests."

Oh no, he wasn't going to trap her that easily. "I am not a guest, merely a passerby."

He let that argument die for the moment, curiosity spurring him onward. "And wither are you bound?"

"To France." And to whatever destiny had in store for her, she added silently.

She could not leave now; the roads were impassable. "Not while these floods overtake us," Duncan responded.

Beth sighed as she looked out the window at the monotonous rain that fell with no end. She could not continue to let time slip through her fingers in this manner. Her father needed her.

"I've no choice."

Chapter Twelve

Duncan studied her in silence for a long moment. What could induce a young woman like Beth to cross the ocean and find her way to a foreign land during dire times like this? Was it a lover who goaded her to take such chances with her life? It was dangerous to travel at all times, but especially these.

"Then I shall give you a choice," he proposed quietly. "Remain with me."

Beth turned away from the window, her eyes dark and dangerous. Did he mean to insult her honor further? Had he not learned yet what kind of woman she was? Not some child to be led astray, but a woman who knew her own mind. And knew what it was that she had to do.

He could read her as easily as any parchment. It was all there in her eyes for him to see. She was not like Elaine or any other common chit. To win her to his bed would be a challenge. One with many rewards, he'd wager.

He smiled easily. "As my guest," he reiterated. "Or my nurse, if you will. For as long as you wish." Duncan glanced down at his shoulder. "I've a feeling that I shall be in need of tender care for a while, yet."

If he meant to play on her sympathies, she saw through him readily. He was more than capable of mending without her. And the only tender care he really required now was to another portion of his anatomy. A portion she had no wish to render service to.

"There's Samuel," she pointed out carelessly.

He shook his head. "Samuel is not known for his gentleness."

Beth laced her fingers together and smiled prettily. "Then Amy, perhaps."

She could easily envision that. And Duncan yelping in pain as he suffered beneath those wide hands of hers. Like broadswords, they were.

Duncan shuddered as he cast away the thought. "Her hands would be capable only if I were a sack of flour." He reached for Beth and managed to capture one hand in his. He laced his fingers through it. "No, 'tis your hands I seek. What do you say, Beth?"

She disengaged herself from him, not quite as firmly as before. "I say that I have a journey to complete, and as soon as the rains leave, so shall I."

He tried to guess at her purpose. Only one came to mind. "To join your beloved."

Her father held her heart safely in his hands. She'd never loved another, for no other had ever understood her. Or withstood her, for that matter. She lifted a slender shoulder and let it drop.

"In a manner of speaking."

Duncan edged forward in his bed, his interest aroused more than he thought was warranted. "In what manner of speaking?"

She hadn't meant to share any of this with him, not

her name, not her destination. Most assuredly, not her purpose in being here. She moved around the room restlessly. In the gray daylight, she saw the crossed swords that hung above the fireplace. His? she wondered. Or merely some ancestor's?

"Do you mean to extract all my secrets?"

He could not help smiling at that. "I've been gifted with the most blessed of your secrets, Beth." He saw her blush and knew that she understood well his meaning. "The others are all lesser in comparison."

She meant to give him as severe a tongue-lashing as he had ever received, but Jacob crossed the threshold just then, the same shield that Amy had carried the night before in his hands. Atop it was another bowl of soup. And what looked to be a goodly portion of ham, eggs, sausage, and kidney pie for her.

She bit off her retort. It would only serve to amuse him, no doubt. She decided to ignore his ribald remark and give him an answer to his query. There was, after all, no reason to keep it from him. It mattered not one way or the other if he knew.

"I'm bound to Paris to find my father."

And find him I will, she swore to herself. He was alive. In her heart, she knew he was as alive as she.

"Paris?" Duncan's expression became grave as Jacob quickly busied himself with arranging the plates upon the small table in Duncan's room. Duncan propped himself up in the bed once more. "'Tis not safe in Paris. Or in France, for that matter. Madmen roam the streets."

She felt her heart quicken at the description. "Yes," she said softly, "I know."

He watched her face. Jacob withdrew from the room, but Duncan took no notice. "But yet you wish to go there?"

"Yes. I must." She took a breath. There was no comfort to be found. "I have no choice, as I said. My father is there somewhere." Her voice lowered. "I know he is."

He reached to take her hand again, this time as a friend. "Tell me."

She shrugged, the words tangling hopelessly in her mind. What was she doing, telling all this to a stranger? She was by nature her own confidante, unless it was to her father she spoke. No one else had the patience to listen and to understand.

"'Tis a long story."

But he would not permit her to extract her hand this time. "Tell me," he coaxed again softly. Then a smile chased away the somber expression. "While you feed me."

"Feed you?" she echoed incredulously. He looked no more in need of being fed than she did.

He nodded in reply. "Yes, feed me. The spoon is heavy and I am weak." His green eyes sparkled like June bugs in the wind. "I need nourishment."

Nourishment her foot. "What you are sorely in need of is manners."

His eyes teased her, and she found them hard to resist. "You may teach me that, too, while you are about it, if you wish."

Beth placed the bowl of soup on the stand next to his bed. When she sat down, she saw his smile widen. "You really are infuriating."

His eyes watched her, committing each movement to memory. "And your humble servant."

She seriously doubted that the man beside her had ever known a humble day in his life. Pride was etched into his features. Not a false pride, but one that spoke of his knowing exactly what he was capable of. Exactly how far his reach extended.

Carefully she dipped the spoon into the steaming broth and raised it to his lips. They remained closed, spread in an amused smile.

A bit of soup dripped into her cupped hand that hovered beneath the spoon and she winced. She should have let it just drop on his belly. It would have served him right. "Open for me."

"Gladly." His eyes shone with a jest he did not share with her.

It was a mistake to remain, Beth thought.

She dipped the spoon into the broth again.

As she coaxed the soup into him, he coaxed the full story from her. It emerged in jumbled bits and pieces, but he had the whole of it by the time the bowl was empty and she had pushed aside her own plate.

Finding himself with an appetite, Duncan reached over her to take up her half-empty plate. The meat was cold, but he could remember a time when he had chewed on rotting crusts of bread and been grateful for it.

He cut a piece and studied it with the way of a man who loved his food to the last morsel. "So you are determined to go."

"I *am* going," she retorted.

If he hadn't understood that by now, then he hadn't really been listening. What did she expect? She cleared away the bowl from the stand, leaving it on the table where Jacob had placed it when he had brought it in.

She frowned as she looked up at Duncan. His britches

had slipped a little and now clung tightly to his hips. Trim, narrow hips well suited to riding a horse.

Or a woman, a small voice whispered perversely in her head.

She averted her eyes and purposely looked at his face. "Really, it is no business of yours what I do."

He waved that away with his good hand. "We can talk of that later."

"Later," she echoed in disbelief.

Just how long did he think she was planning to stay? She had already informed him of her hurry. Was he deaf? Or merely mule-headed?

Finished, he moved the dish aside on the bed. "I shall make you a trade, Beth."

Though she loathed the role of servant, she loathed slovenliness even more. Lips pressed together, she took up the plate and placed it next to the other with a bang.

"And that would be?"

"Stay and tend to me." Duncan saw her brow raise and hurried to continue, "Just until the rains cease."

There was more to his tone than that, unless she missed her guess. "Yes? And what am I to get out of it if I remain?"

Her very countenance forbade him to be bawdy, although he was sorely tempted. The woman was made for loving, and he had made up his mind to wear her down at first opportunity. He had not lied before. The idea would be hers. But there was nothing to stop his whispering it into her ear until she believed it to be her own.

"If you remain, when they have ceased, I shall provide you with a coach and someone to drive you to Dover." He looked at her pointedly. "And accompany you across the Channel."

Someone else who saw her only as a weak woman, in need of protecting. She drew herself up, her shoulders braced. "I need no company."

He was swiftly becoming convinced that she was the most stubborn woman on the face of the earth, but then, he had never encountered real opposition before. Women had a tendency to cleave to him.

"You are a woman alone," Duncan pointed out patiently.

She remained silent about her abilities to ride and shoot a pistol close enough to a man's head to part his hair without harm. There was no need to inform him of that.

"I have Sylvia."

The manners she claimed he did not possess prevented him from laughing aloud. "As I said, you are a woman alone. That makes you a tempting target for some hot-blooded reprobate."

She arched a knowing brow. "And you would be the one to know about reprobates."

He was amused at her accusation. "It takes one to know one," he agreed. Dramatically, Duncan placed a hand to his breast, though he would much have rather placed it on hers. "But I am reformed."

She would no sooner place her fate in his hands than she would attempt to swim across the Channel to France. "I seriously doubt that."

But he was not one to give up easily. 'Twas the fight he enjoyed. The victory was but an added boon. "Put me to the test."

Her eyes narrowed accusingly. "I unwittingly did— last night."

The soulful eyes that turned to Beth's asked for her to

grant him another chance. "One lapse does not a reprobate make."

There was something there in his eyes that spoke to her, that touched a portion of her soul she had not known existed. Uncomfortable at its discovery, Beth sighed and shook her head.

"I have to be mad . . ."

"But—?" he urged eagerly, knowing that he had already won.

Beth felt it best to keep her distance from him. She paced about the front of his bed.

"Since I have no coach and no choice, as you have pointed out, I shall take you up on your offer. All but the companion. He can turn back with the coach, once Sylvia and I are aboard ship."

Crossing to him, she placed her hand in Duncan's. "'Tis a bargain." Hopefully, not with the devil, she added silently.

He was surprised at the gesture. The women he knew did not shake hands. America had to be a very interesting country, he decided. No wonder Sin-Jin had wanted to return.

He curved his fingers about her soft flesh. "You shall not regret it," he promised.

Something small and nameless within her warned Beth that she already had cause to.

Slowly she removed her hand from Duncan's. But the warmth generated there refused to leave even after their hands no longer touched.

She pinned him with a look that had often sent her sisters scurrying for shelter. "That remains to be seen, Duncan."

This would be a woman who would meet him thrust

for thrust. She would not disappoint him when the time came. And the time, he hoped, would come soon.

Mindful of his shoulder, he allowed himself only a short laugh, but it was filled with a lustiness that brought a shiver of anticipation to her spine.

"I like your manner, Beth. You have spirit."

If he meant to flatter her into dropping her guard against him, it would not succeed. "I would not test how much, if I were you. You might just find that you have received far more than *you* bargained for."

He could hope, Duncan thought, settling back in his bed as content as a cat in cream. For that he could truly only hope.

Chapter Thirteen

Samuel had placed her, Beth discovered, in the bedroom right next to Duncan's.

It made the task of moving her trunk from one room to the other an easy one for Jacob. But even if it had meant taking her trunk to another floor, Samuel remarked and Beth would have had to agree, Jacob would have willingly followed her to the ends of the earth, dragging the trunk in his wake like a weight that had been tied to him by decree.

Beth moved slowly about the room, taking in its measure. She was not certain yet if it appealed to her tastes or not, though she would not be here long enough for that to matter very much.

The room was smaller than Duncan's, but far more ornately decorated. Duncan's room had the look of a man's place about it, its furnishing sparse, but what there was in it was massive. Much like the man himself.

In her room, there was so much, either hanging, or lying, or scattered, that Beth felt oppressed.

Oppressed by the tapestries on the walls and the heavy draperies at the casements. By the portraits of ancestors long gone to their reward, looking somberly down at her as she paced about.

The room had been perversely bedecked in shades of scarlet, as if whoever had had a hand in it had feared that it might all go unnoticed if the colors were muted. Samuel had informed Beth as he'd brought her to it that the room had belonged to the former mistress of Shalott, the late earl's widow.

The late earl's subtle executioner, it was believed by many.

She was to sleep in a bed that had once cradled the body of a murderess, Beth thought. A shiver sliced through her.

Though she was far more aware that there was evil in the world than were her mother or the other women in her family, Beth could not bring herself to understand why one person would be intentionally wicked to another.

Why a person would kill another for what he carried in his pouch, or because he did not care for the way another person looked upon him.

She did not understand why, she thought, as she fingered the draperies, a woman would intentionally poison her husband if she no longer wished to be with him.

Or why countrymen turned on each other because they stood on different sides of a question, different sides of a privilege.

It made less than no sense to her.

The sound of grunting coming from the doorway behind her scattered Beth's thoughts like so much corn thrown on the ground before chickens in a barnyard. She turned in time to see Jacob and Hank struggling as they carried a cumbersome oblong tub between them.

"Steady now, men," Samuel warned. "If you drop it,

there'll be a dent in it for sure and Duncan will not be pleased about it."

"Damn it, old man, you have the easy part of it, flapping your lip while we put our backs to it. This thing is heavy," Hank grumbled, as he shuffled, moving backward over the doorsill.

The reproving look that Samuel shot him was black. "If you put more of that energy into your back and less into your mouth, you wouldn't be struggling with your end of it like some fresh-faced girl. No offense, mistress," Samuel amended quickly, slanting a look toward Beth to see if he had angered her.

"None taken," she assured him as she crossed to him. Now, what was all this about?

With a heavy sigh, Jacob and Hank deposited the tub in the center of the room. Samuel impatiently waved them out again.

"Well, get on with it," he instructed. "You're not done yet, you know."

Beth drew her brows together as she stared at the metal object. Bemused, her question tumbled out with no thought behind it.

"What is it?"

Samuel looked at her, surprised. Surely they had tubs to bathe in where she came from. "Why, it's a tub for bathing, mistress."

She wondered if he thought her that naive. "Yes, I realize that, but what I meant was, I didn't ask for any to be brought."

Samuel smiled. "Duncan thought you might want to refresh yourself after the long night you spent at his side, tending to his wounds."

It was a thoughtful gesture, Beth readily conceded, one she would not have immediately attributed to him.

As she looked upon it, people began filing in behind her, carrying kettles and pots of water before them. Steam rose seductively from each and every container. Beth looked quizzically at Samuel, taken aback by the unannounced parade.

He gave a slight shrug of his even slighter shoulders. "What's a tub without water? Hey, you there." He wagged a bony warning finger before Tommy's face. "Mind you don't spill any."

Pot after pot was emptied into the metal receptacle. The level within it climbed ever higher. Beth watched, mesmerized. To be clean again, after endless days of travel, to wash away dust that had become almost a second, unwanted skin upon her ... it seemed like a blessing too precious to wish for.

Beth sighed without realizing it.

Samuel smiled to himself. He clapped his hands together, calling for the line to move more quickly. Those who emptied their pots retraced their steps back to the kitchen and the twin cauldrons that were boiling water on the hearth.

There was a lag and Samuel stepped to the doorway. "Be quick about it, or it will be too cold by the time the mistress uses it," he called down the stairs.

In response, two more women hurried into the room, a large, black pot supported between them.

Beth wanted nothing more than to immerse herself in the tub and let the waters work their miracle upon her. But she recalled last night, when her desire had led her to be less than utterly cautious. The smirking look in Duncan's eyes was the price she now had to pay for her haste. She was not about to commit the same error again.

"Samuel." She laid a hand on his shoulder, not knowing quite how to modestly phrase the question that sharply arose in her mind like the lightning that had streaked across the brow of the summer sky last night.

From her tone, he gathered that there was a secret to be imparted. Samuel liked nothing better than being privy to secrets.

"Yes, mistress?"

She began slowly, searching for the proper words, ones that would not frame her in the wrong light. "This is the former duchess's room, is it not?"

He had told her as much not more than half an hour past. Surely she remembered. "Yes, mistress, that it is."

"Is it—connected to the other room, by any chance? To the earl's?" Beth couldn't bring herself to call it Duncan's room. It made her question much too intimate.

Her eyes swept over the wall which separated her room from Duncan's. She saw no door, but old manors were known for secret passages that lovers might use in the dead of night for trysts.

Samuel shook his head vigorously, the straggled gray locks whipping through the air like tiny gray serpents.

"Oh, no, mistress. I heard that she was a virago. Beautiful, but deadly." He inclined his head, his voice lowering even more. "She went about her own way a great deal." His expression sobered. "Had lovers, so the stories went."

He'd heard tell of that in the town. The barkeep there liked to number himself among the woman's lovers, but Samuel had his doubts. No woman could have had as many as they said she had, but he would have dearly loved to verify that on his own.

"A woman like that would not have permitted her room to be connected to her poor, cuckolded husband's."

It made perfect sense. Still, would a husband with a wife like that not want somehow to confirm his suspicions discreetly?

Beth bit her lip, knowing that Samuel might take umbrage for Duncan.

"And there are no . . ." she waved her hand airily, ". . . knotholes, perhaps?"

Samuel cocked his head. Was she asking him if there was a way to observe Duncan without being seen?

"Why? Were you hoping to—?" He saw the shocked expression seize her features. Quickly he retreated. "Oh, you mean the other way of it?" He shook his head, the picture of piety. "Oh, no, mistress. There's no way that anyone can look in on you." He crossed his heart, as if that was the end of it. "Unless, perhaps, it might be a bird." With a flourish, he gestured toward the partly open window. "Though there'd be none flying in this sort of weather, I'd wager."

He nodded benevolently as Jacob deposited the last bit of hot water into the tub.

"You'll have your privacy, mistress, I swear it upon my mother's grave. And I'll even post a guard for you at the door, so none can enter by accident." He winked at her. "Or by design."

She was a winsome lass, and he could well see her concern. There were those in the house who would profess ignorance of the room's occupation and pretend to stumble in just for a look at her pleasing form. Were he younger, he might have used the same excuse himself. As it was, the more settled, ample figure now tempted him. A man enjoyed having something to hold onto. He thought of Sylvia and smiled to himself.

She breathed a sigh of relief. "That would be greatly appreciated, Samuel."

He beamed at her words of thanks. "Consider it already done, mistress." A stubby finger beckoned Jacob forward. The younger man had been loitering in the room, searching for an excuse to remain a little longer. "You, there, Jacob. You'll stand at the lady's door until such time as she wishes you to be gone."

Jacob straightened his shoulders like a soldier standing to attention. His obvious pleasure at being singled out was evident in the foolish expression he wore.

Beth wondered if perhaps it was a little like having a fox guard the henhouse. She leaned toward Samuel, lowering her voice.

"And he won't—?"

There was no need for her to finish her question. He understood her meaning. Samuel moved his head solemnly from side to side. "Not unless he wishes to have his eyes put out."

It was a gruesome image, but it did make Beth feel safer. "Thank you."

He didn't want her to misunderstand. Samuel would never rob Duncan of his due. "'Tis Duncan you should be thanking, mistress, not me. While you are here, you are under his protection."

Yes, she thought, but what or who was to protect her from Duncan?

Beth pushed the thought from her mind as she looked down at the tub. The water called to her seductively. Her inclination toward caution began to slip away, lulled by Samuel's promise.

She'd been won over, Samuel thought, reading her expression, and he was pleased to have her trust. She had done well by Duncan, and thus had earned his loyalty. He clapped his hands together once, signaling that the others were to depart from the room.

He herded them out, then turned and backed away himself. He gave Beth a reassuring smile as he placed a hand on each of the open double doors.

"Anything you need, you've but to ask," he reminded her, a moment before he rendered the doors shut.

"This'll do very well, thank you," she murmured.

Hurrying to the door, she locked it, then tested its strength. The lock was secure. But to put her mind at ease completely, and to prevent Jacob from taking any action they might both regret, Beth dragged a heavy chair over and set it against the door.

That done, she surveyed the room slowly with a critical eye. Walking toward the wall that separated their two rooms, she pushed aside tapestries and ran her tapering fingers along the frames of the portraits. But there were no suspicious indentations in the walls, no knotholes that might be unobstructed at will.

It appeared as though she was indeed safe from prying eyes.

The water had cooled somewhat as she had conducted her search, but her heart was finally at ease.

Quickly, not to waste any more time, Beth shed her garments and then eased her body gratefully into the tub. A sigh that was nothing short of ecstasy escaped her lips as the waters embraced her.

Without, standing guard at her door, as Samuel had instructed him to do, Jacob smiled to himself. He wished with all his heart that he were braver. If so, he would crack the door but a little and steal a glance at the woman.

As it was, he had to content himself with the multitude of fantasies that were racing through his young mind. Though what Samuel had told the lady was a lie—for Duncan would never put out an eye for such an offense—Jacob still knew that if he did look upon the woman's form, even for half a breath, there would be consequences to face. Duncan did not look favorably upon the breaking of one's word, especially not if it involved his as well.

To incur Duncan's displeasure was enough to trouble the heart of any of his men. Jacob's most especially, since he worshipped the man.

So he sighed in secret and stood his guard. And let his mind drift.

In the next room, Duncan smiled to himself as he stretched out on his bed. He had heard Beth's sigh as well. Both of their windows were open, despite the rain, and the sensual sound that had escaped her lips had carried. Someday, and soon, she would sigh that way beneath him, a moment before she cried out his name. A moment before they were joined.

Anticipation heated his blood.

For now, Duncan told himself, he would act the genial host and proper gentleman.

Or perhaps, not too proper. He would render to her no less than she required. And no more.

The hunt, he smiled, had assuredly begun.

Chapter Fourteen

Duncan hated the idea of being weak, even temporarily. The very thought imprisoned him in a state of mind in which he did not wish to be.

While Beth took her bath in the room beside his, Duncan pushed himself out of bed, restless to test his strength. It was in shorter supply than he had been given to believe. Grasping the bed post with a sweaty palm, he forced himself to take a few steps.

His head spun like a downy-faced lad taking his very first swig of ale. Gritting his teeth together, sweat pouring from his brow, Duncan forced himself to make an incomplete circle about the border of the bed, going from post to post and then back again. His legs felt a bit steadier, but his head still spun, and he cursed it for its lack of loyalty to his command.

With a mighty sigh, he dropped back against the pillows, taking care not to unduly jar his shoulder. An invalid. He felt like a bloody invalid.

"Damn!"

Though he was in charge here at Shalott, in charge anywhere his men were with him, the ghost of years past rose up now to haunt him. Years past when he had been but a young whelp of a lad, to be ground under any gentleman's boot if the whim took the man.

The way it had the man who had given him seed within a night, his mother had recalled, filled with great suffering and pain.

The very memory of the man who had sired him had Duncan clenching and unclenching his hand at his side in controlled rage. It did not help quell the rage to know that the man had paid, paid dearly for his brutality, both then and later, to the woman he had raped ... Duncan's mother.

This frustration drumming within him would aid nothing, Duncan told himself, willing the hot blood from his veins. He would be up and about soon enough. He needed but dip a little into the pot of patience Samuel was continually babbling about.

His dipper, Duncan thought with a rueful smile, had a hole in it.

Once more about, he thought, his bare feet touching again upon the dark wooden floor. He'd push himself a bit more, and then be done with it for a while. He needed his strength to return if he was to be of any use as a man to the fair creature that the winds of fate had seen to blow his way.

"God damn Dorchester's bloody eyes," Duncan gasped, as his knees suddenly buckled beneath him.

Had he not been holding onto the post, he would have surely found himself eye to eye with the knotholes on the boards in the floor.

Beth stifled the urge to run to his aid. She had just now come to see him, to thank him for the tub, and been in time to witness the display of weakness on his part. Men were such prideful creatures, and though it made little sense to her, she knew accepting her help, except under the most dire of circumstances, or upon his own conditions, would shatter that fragile shell known as manly esteem.

She purposely hung back in the doorway and made her presence known. "You're up, I see."

Her voice floated to him, as sweet as any spring breeze scented with blossoms. He turned to look in her direction.

"Not nearly as much as I would like."

Silently cursing his legs, and the wound that had rendered them to the consistency of Amy's runny gruel, Duncan lowered himself upon the bed. Pride or no, he held onto the bedpost. It would be far more embarrassing to fall before her than to admit to a need for assistance.

Sitting, he turned and arranged himself on the bed, then looked in Beth's direction. He regarded her with intense enjoyment. She had changed again, and wore a dress of light pink. Pink, like the color which rose so easily to her cheeks.

"Do you always enter a man's room unannounced?" Amusement highlighted his ruggedly handsome face. "If so, you might just see more than you bargained for." His eyes glinted as a smile entered them as well. "Unless, of course, that *is* what you bargained for."

It seemed, she thought, her mood still deliciously mellow from the bath, that she could not readily expect a leopard to change its spots.

"I see your tongue seems none the worse for your injury." She spread her dress as she took a seat on the chair beside him. "And to answer your question, I knocked."

"I did not hear." Though in truth he was not listening

for the soft rapping of knuckles upon his door. He was too busy silently chastising his own weakness.

"I shouldn't wonder," she agreed. "You were grumbling too loudly to hear anything but Gabriel's trumpet, and perhaps not even that."

Duncan shrugged, letting it pass. He hadn't been aware that he was speaking aloud at all.

Beth leaned forward, curiosity poking rigid fingers at her. He had worn a particularly angry expression when she had entered. "Who is Dorchester?"

He was not about to let her pry into his affairs. "No one you would want to hear of."

She hated that firm, distancing tone, that tone that separated men from women, the very young from the old. She always had. It was a tone that meant to keep her from opening knowledge's door.

Her face hardened with an accusation. "I see. My secrets are open for examination, but yours are not."

Their eyes met. There was no room for argument within his. "Exactly."

He was like all the others, save her father. Anger flashed in her eyes at being so dismissed.

"That is not fair, sir."

He meant to divert her from the subject that was hurtful to him, even after all these summers had passed.

"The only fair thing in this room is you." His tone belied his intense feelings. Duncan's eyes swept over her in delighted appraisal. "You seem refreshed."

Beth locked her temper away. It served no purpose, arguing with the man. What did she care if he shared his thoughts with her or not? They meant nothing to one another and never would.

She inclined her head in acknowledgment of his words. "That is why I came, to thank you for your kindness." Because it felt too confining to remain so close to him, she rose once more and moved about the room, though there was nothing to take her attention there, save him. "It was unexpected."

He watched as she moved, sheer poetry embodied in a supple, tempting body.

"It should not have been. I can be very kind." His voice was gentle and coaxing, whispering promises without forming any. "But you will come to learn that."

Why was it that a single glance from him could make her mouth so dry and the rest of her body hum with anticipation? She drew herself up and turned toward the window. The scene had not changed. Rain, nothing but monotonous, annoying rain.

"That will take time, sir, and I do not have that to spare." In her heart, she cursed this foul weather. "It cannot rain forever."

The laugh was deep and sultry. It pleased him that it no longer hurt to laugh. "The English countryside might surprise you."

She looked at him over her shoulder. "The English surprise me."

"How so?" He leaned back against the pile of pillows and patted the place next to him. After a moment, Beth crossed to him. She took the chair again instead, just as he knew she would. He smiled as she seated herself. If the challenge was easily met, then it was not a challenge.

Beth looked at him, her words earnest. "The war we fought between us is not that far in the past. Why would you *want* to help me?"

He ached to slip his fingers along her face, to acquaint himself with the feel of her lips, and weave his touch so that his hands could memorize her body.

"I fought no war with you, Beth." A cynical look crossed his brow as he thought of those years. "Wars are for old men to plan for gain."

That wasn't why they had fought the Revolution. She was proud to have been born in a country that had forged a singular place in history. "There were principles involved in our war."

Our war. She was a rare woman, indeed. Like none other he was acquainted with. "And I see that they were important to you. But you are too young to remember what it was like."

He couldn't be that much older, she judged, yet he spoke as if he had wisdom and she possessed but childish notions. "Freedom is something one is never too young to savor."

Her answer pleased him to a degree that surprised him. "Ah, we think alike. I've no great love for the men who wish to keep others beneath their yoke." He could see by her dubious expression that she needed convincing of that. "I am English by the very whimsical happenstance of birth, not affiliation. Or choice. My loyalty is to my men and to those I serve." His eye narrowed as he thought of his past. "Whom I *choose* to serve. I have no love of aristocrats." He spat the last word.

His sentiments confused her. "An odd thing to say, for a man who owns all this." She waved her hand about the room, then looked at him, suspicion entering her gaze. "Or did you steal it?" That would seem more than likely, given the man's beliefs.

"Neither." Her confusion heightened and he all but laughed to see it. "I am but overseeing the manor and its lands for a gentleman presently residing in the Colonies. The States," he amended, "I believe they are called now, out of earshot of the King. Saint John Lawrence is the present Earl of Shalott, not I."

"Sin-Jin?" she asked, her eyes wide. Could they be speaking of the same man?

"Yes." He leaned forward, intrigued. "You say his name as if you know him."

"I do," she affirmed quickly, stunned at the coincidence. Fate, she was beginning to perceive, was a very odd thing. "He is a neighbor."

Duncan's smile was wide in his pleasure. "Then that makes us neighbors as well." He reached for her hand. "By association."

She moved her hand before he could fold his fingers about it again and send her heart racing. "By very limited association."

His laugh was lusty, then tolerant by turns. "As you wish."

Her curiosity returned as she looked upon him. Eyes the color of the sea he professed to love, hair like a golden flag unfurled about his broad shoulders. And still he wore no shirt, a fact that was playing very badly with her reserve and her nerves.

"What I wish is for you to tell me who you are."

Her quietly voiced question rippled along his skin. "Why?"

She sought refuge in but part of the truth. "You are my host. My well-being has temporarily been placed in your hands." She drew herself up. "I would like to know to what manner of man I have entrusted that welfare."

Here was a woman who could probably outtalk the devil. Had she been Eve, the serpent would have been induced to take a bite of the apple himself. "You turn an argument well."

"As do you." He was attempting to flatter her away from her purpose. She stood by it. "I am waiting."

Duncan shook his head in admiration. "Would that my mother had your fire and tenacity." His mother had been a sweet-faced woman, kind of soul, with no more backbone than a flea. "I would have, perhaps, had another father than the one who begat me." He spoke the last of it to himself rather than to Beth.

"Dorchester," she guessed, and saw his eyes darken again. She guessed correctly.

Duncan nodded grimly. "Yes, the late Earl of Dorchester."

There was something in the way he said it that aroused her unease. "He died?"

"Aye, by my hand." He could see it all even now, if he but closed his eyes.

This was too heinous a fact to comprehend. Surely there was some mistake, or barring that, an explanation that would absolve him in some way, though how, she did not see.

"You killed your father?"

He would not lie to win her, not about this. "Yes, but not by design, though in my heart a thousand times I had done the deed in as many ways. But that evening, when I went to him, it was only to talk, to ask for a share of what was mine by rights for what he had done to my mother."

Duncan looked at her and saw no reason to sugarcoat the words. If she would know, then he would tell her. "He raped her." He saw the horror enter Beth's eyes, just as it must have his mother's. "She was the stablemaster's daughter and he took her there, in the stables, with no gentleness, no love, not even a kind word.

He took her by the right of ownership." The words left a foul taste on his tongue. "It broke her spirit."

Duncan had never known her any other way, except with a sadness in her eyes. She had loved him as best she could, but there was only a part of her left to give the young boy, only a small part to show him the way.

"I was twelve when she died. Dorchester would have none of me after that. An hour after the funeral, he had me cast from the estate, to find my way on the streets of London." Bitterness twisted his mouth as he recalled the event. "He had a wife and two foppish sons. He did not need to look upon a bastard."

Beth's heart ached for the motherless child he had been. Her own life, though filled with impatient trials, had always known love. There was not a day she was without its comforting arms.

"Samuel found me." A smile rose at the memory. "He cut a finer figure then. He took me in and taught me a trade. Not a noble one." A smile curved his generous mouth. "But one that helped me survive long enough to return to my roots."

Beth held her breath, though he had already told her the outcome. "And what happened?"

"I was eighteen when I finally confronted my father with my claim. I was young and angry, and still a little idealistic, perhaps. That had been my mother's doing. She always waited for things to become better. She died waiting. I was not about to.

"But Dorchester was no more of a mind to accept me then than he had been six years before. Less. He threatened me. That failing, he tried to stab me with his dagger. It was not the best of homecomings." His breath caught as he recited the events dispassionately. "I meant only to deflect the blow, but he fell. And the dagger found a different target."

He took a breath as he looked out the window. In a way, it seemed as if all this had happened to someone else in another lifetime. "I went to sea that night, a price upon my head. I took the others with me and we learned another sort of trade."

Duncan turned to look at her. Beth had taken his confession in silence, but there was no condemnation written across her brow.

"So there you have it, my life spread out before your feet. Do you wish to trample it with those delicately fashioned shoes?"

Is that what he was expecting from her? Had some other woman voiced her contempt for him because he had been born on the wrong side of the blanket?

"No," Beth answered quietly. She raised an encouraging smile to her lips. "How did a privateer come to be living in a manor like this?"

It amazed him how easily she passed over his story, as if it was no more than that. As if there was no oppressive weight to it.

"I saved Sin-Jin's wife's life, though she was not that at the time." He spread his hands wide. "It was another matter of debts being paid and repaid. I am a great believer in repayment of debts." He owed Samuel more than he could ever repay, but he could try in some small measure. Duncan took a deep breath, pushing the memory all away into the past once more. "Sin-Jin and Rachel wanted to live in America, but there was the manor to see to. He left that for me to do. So now me and mine live here, reformed men all."

He reached over and snared a curl that had come loose from its pins. He toyed with it, winding it about his finger, his eyes on hers. "Have I satisfied your curiosity, Beth?"

"Yes," she lied, her breath gathering once again in her throat.

He had satisfied her curiosity about his origins, but had not even begun to explain why it was that he stirred her so; why he managed, with but a look, a promise of a touch, to arouse emotions so violently within her.

That was something, she knew, that would have to go unexplained. Curiosity had killed the cat, and Beth had no desire to join its legions.

Though the way he looked upon her now did give her pause.

Suddenly alerted, Beth gathered her skirts together and rose abruptly.

"I must see to Sylvia," she announced. "I have not seen her since last night."

"Samuel tells me that she has been well taken care of," Duncan called after her.

"That is what I'm worried about," Beth tossed over her shoulder as she hurried out.

Chapter Fifteen

Beth hurried from Duncan's room, her skirts whooshing along the floor, announcing her passage. Suddenly, she had need to turn to a familiar face.

Where had Sylvia gone to?

She had not looked upon the other woman since last night, when they had brought Duncan in. What had become of her since then? The woman was such a mouse, it seemed odd that Sylvia had not sought her out before now. Beth hoped that nothing bad had befallen her.

Determined to find an answer to this puzzlement, Beth went in search of Sylvia. The first to cross her path was Jacob.

He brightened immediately when he saw her approaching, ready to be of service once again.

"Is there anything you require, mistress?" He wanted nothing more than to prove himself to her, to win but a small corner of her regard and esteem.

"Yes." The emphatically voiced response echoed down the long, darkened halls that were somber even in the brightest of days. With the weather so dreary, the halls were cast into mournful shadows. "Have you seen Mistress Sylvia?"

Jacob looked at her blankly. The name meant nothing to him.

"The older woman who came in with me last night," Beth pressed.

Enlightenment washed over his face. "Oh, the one who's taken such a fancy to Samuel, you mean?"

Beth blinked, astonished. "Has she?"

She couldn't envision Sylvia raising her eyes from the floor long enough to take a fancy to any man. The woman always kept to herself, guarding her person and most especially her maidenhead as if it were the Holy Grail. She feared having anything to do with *any* man. She had even been shy with Philippe Beaulieu, and everyone knew, Beth thought, that a warmer, kinder man God had never created.

Beth was convinced that Jacob had made some mistake. Yet Jacob appeared to know who she was asking for by this description.

"Oh, yes, mistress. Like two peas, they've become, sharing the same pod." Suddenly realizing that he had said too much, Jacob closed his mouth abruptly. His two large lips flapped against one another like freshly laundered sheets spread out on a line to dry in the April wind.

Beth stared at him, completely stunned. "What do you mean, the same pod?"

"Mean?" Jacob cleared his throat, his eyes lowering to the floor as if he were searching for some response there. He looked as guilty as a cutpurse caught with his hand around a pouch. "I mean nothing." A weak smile spread his lips. "Always talking too much, Samuel says I am."

He began to shuffle away from Beth, hoping to get

away before she questioned him further. It was not his place to tell her anything.

"He's right, you know, but that's only because I never know when to stop." And he should have ceased now, Jacob thought, by the look of the shocked expression on Beth's face.

She could sooner believe that women had been granted a say in their government than she'd believe that Sylvia had taken up with a man. Her expression softened and she placed a supplicating hand on Jacob's arm. She felt the muscle there tighten.

"You can tell me, Jacob," she prodded softly. "Did they share the same room?"

The young man looked torn between telling the woman he clearly worshipped what she wanted to know and keeping a confidence he knew he should. Loyalty to Samuel won out of his eagerness to please her.

"You'd best be asking the lady that yourself, mistress."

Frustration mounted within her. Beth maintained a rein on it. "And that I shall. But where is she?"

A hint of the patience she was losing was in her voice. Were there no straight replies in this Godforsaken place? Was everything here a huge riddle, spun for their enjoyment and at her expense?

Jacob's shoulders eased as if he felt the inquisition had passed. "With Samuel, I'd wager. The last I saw of them, they were going into the weapons room."

"I see."

Sylvia, who averted her head and shivered whenever someone swatted a fly, who fainted at the sound of discharging pistols, was in the weapons room. The world had indeed turned upside down.

"And that would be where?" Beth prodded, when Jacob said nothing further.

He could easily tell her, but that would be sending her away. He meant to keep her company a moment longer, if he could.

"Come, I'll show you."

"Please." It was not so much an entreaty on her part as an order.

Jacob, his ear trained for instruction, did not miss the intent. He took her down the hall quickly, the sound of his boots preceding him.

"There." Jacob waved a large hand toward the open doorway, but took not a step further. He valued his peace and his head, both intact.

Beth looked in. She found Samuel and Sylvia with their heads together, the gray one inclined against the dark one with flecks of white in it. They were whispering to one another over broadswords like two young children suddenly discovering that their bodies had been newly reformed for procreation.

She stared in silence for a moment, unobserved and speechless.

When Beth finally stepped into the room, she was aware that Jacob had remained without. Obviously, chivalry did not extend itself to incurring Samuel's wrath, she thought vaguely.

But she didn't need Jacob at her side. She needed Sylvia there. Preferably within a coach, its horses galloping towards Portsmouth. They needed to make plans to be gone.

Another sound, almost like a giggle, pierced the air. "Oh, you," Sylvia tittered, as coquettishly as any girl a third her age.

"Sylvia," Beth cried, unable to decide whether she

was bemused or amused. What she was, however, was plainly confused. This was not the Sylvia she knew.

Sylvia sprang away from Samuel with an agility that surprised Beth. A look of guilt flowering on the woman's broad face. Her hand flew to the bosom that had been heaving for another reason only a moment before. "Beth, you startled me."

Beth's gaze never wavered, her expression unreadable. "And you me."

Sylvia flushed and looked down at the floor, her silence saying far more than any words could.

Could it possibly be? Beth thought. Sylvia? Her Sylvia? And Samuel?

Samuel was quick to step forward, his body shielding Sylvia's as much as he was able. "'Tis all my fault, mistress."

"And what fault would that be?" Beth asked, feeling her way around the subject slowly. She did not know if what Jacob said was mere speculation on his part, sheer gossip, or the uncoated truth.

Samuel glanced over his shoulder to offer Sylvia a smile. She had been a surprise for him last night, one of those pleasant ones that did not happen often at his advanced state in life . . . one he valued.

He turned toward Beth again. "Why, keeping her from you all this time, of course." Samuel's expression was as innocent as that of a babe on its first day. "I've just been showing her around the manor." His smile broadened, spreading freshly shaven cheeks. "There are a great many rooms in Shalott."

Beth looked at Sylvia. The woman's shoulders were hunched, as if huddling from any censure she might garner from Beth, but she was clearly smitten with the old rogue. Beth felt a smile creeping to her lips. Who would ever have thought it?

"Might I have a word with her, Samuel?"

"But of course."

Sweeping a hand before him and bowing grandly, he then stepped away. With his back turned to the women, Samuel pretended to occupy himself with a set of matched pistols that were hung in a case upon the wall, a gift from the King to the fourth Earl of Shalott.

Beth crossed her arms before her. Her expression softened and Sylvia smiled hesitantly. One would think, Beth mused, that their positions were reversed, and that she was the chaperone.

"How are you faring?" Beth asked gently.

Sylvia slanted a look toward Samuel and all but sighed her answer. "Wonderfully."

Amusement lifted Beth's lips as she arched a brow. She nodded at their surroundings. "Weapons, Sylvia?"

Like a child caught in a lie, Sylvia drew herself up. "A mind should always be open to an education, Beth. I have always told you that."

Now Sylvia was playing with words. "You have also said that a woman's education should extend only to gardening, needlepoint, and reading poetry."

With a stubbornness that had been foreign to her nature until this moment, Sylvia insisted, "Weapons are far more exciting."

Beth looked at Sylvia knowingly. She lowered her voice to keep Samuel from overhearing. "You mean Samuel, don't you?"

To Beth's utter surprise, the woman laughed behind her hands. There was not even a hint of a blush. Only pleasure splashed her cheeks. "Yes, there's that, too."

"Sylvia, what's come over you?"

In reply, Sylvia sighed deeply as she laced her fingers together. "Love, I think."

Beth stared at Sylvia dumbstruck. Finally the word struggled to her lips. "Love?" Her eyes narrowed.

There was not a trace of hesitation as Sylvia replied, "Yes."

Was she mad? Had she eaten or drunk something here that had affected her mind?

"In one day." Beth's tone, far from amused, was now mocking.

Sylvia turned on her, angry at the show of disbelief. "Romeo and Juliet knew immediately."

Beth attempted to lay a gentling hand on the woman's arm. Clearly the woman was ill. But Sylvia shrugged her off.

"A play, Sylvia. 'Tis but a play."

Sylvia had spent her whole life shut up with books. "Works of fiction are based on life."

Beth took a breath. There was no point in arguing with the woman. The madness would pass. It was up to her to take the lead. As always.

"When the rains cease, I have made arrangements for us to be taken to Dover." Sylvia's expression, rather than become contrite, only grew more obstinate. "Or would you have me leave you here?"

Sylvia addressed the row of muskets upon the wall behind Beth, unable to look at the expression on Beth's face any longer.

"Perhaps, until you are ready to return."

She could not believe what she was hearing. Beth opened her mouth, then shut it again. It would be hypocritical to remind Sylvia of her duty, or of the fact that her mother had placed Beth in her care. Not from the first moment had Beth ever thought of Sylvia as anything but a person she had to protect.

With renewed patience, Beth asked gently, "You are that taken with him?"

Sylvia thought of last night, of the comfort she had found in a man's caring arms. And the passion. That was something she had only dreamed about. Something that she had always thought had passed her by on the steadily narrowing path to old age.

"Yes, oh, yes."

Mystified, Beth only shook her head. "Then I wish you well, though I truly believe that it's madness to remain here."

Perhaps it was only the work of the rain, she mused. Many acted in a disoriented fashion after being trapped within a house, waiting out an endless storm.

Yes, she reminded herself, but it had only been a single night.

Apparently, she glanced at Sylvia's face, a very productive, interesting night.

"Is there anything else?" Sylvia asked, impatient to return to Samuel.

"No." Beth shook her head. "We'll speak more later." The words had hardly left her lips before Sylvia had flown back to Samuel's side.

She was completely oblivious to Beth's presence.

Well, whatever Sylvia chose to do or not to do, Beth had her path clearly cut out before her, she thought. She needed to reach Paris as soon as it was possible. With or without Sylvia at her side.

Perhaps it might even be better this way, she decided, as she crossed the threshold, leaving Sylvia to her newfound adventure. Without Sylvia at her side, Beth would not have cause to worry about her. There would only be herself to watch out for. It would be a comfort, leaving Sylvia here, safe and secure.

As she left the room, Beth heard the sound of soft laughter. She turned to look and realized that it was floating from between two rows of armor. She could not see either Sylvia or Samuel, but she could well imagine why Sylvia was laughing.

A shaft of envy touched Beth as she closed the door once more.

[illegible faint text from previous page showing through]

Chapter Sixteen

The rains continued for two more days and nights. During that time, the different members of the household took it upon themselves to make certain that Beth was never bored or without diversion.

Evenings were the best, when they all gathered together after the day's work.

Even when she was away from Duncan, Beth never found herself at a loss for sources of entertainment. The conversations she had with Hank, or Samuel, or any one of the handful of people whose names she had learned, were edifying as well as amusing. Beth had long ago learned the benefits and joys of leaving her mind open to a myriad of influences. The former privateers who lined both sides of the table each night as they partook of dinner were as lively a group as ever she'd hoped to encounter.

Far from the bedraggled band of thieves and cutthroats she would have imagined them to be, Beth discovered that they were all eager to earn their way on the manor. Some farmed, others tended the livestock, still others worked within the house itself.

As she listened to them tell their tales to a willing

new set of ears, she learned that, to a man, they had been driven by despair to feed and clothe their own by any means possible, fair or foul. If that meant cutting a purse now and again, or ramming the side of a ship for precious cargo, so be it.

But none of the privateers welcomed the dark title of "thief."

This new turn in their lives suited all but the most restless of the crew. Those, Duncan had been quick to make clear, were free to leave whenever they desired. If they remained, they earned their way, same as always, but in a different fashion, one that did not run afoul of the Crown.

As for Duncan, this was the bargain he had struck with Sin-Jin, and stand by it he intended to, until such time that the wanderlust moved him again.

As of yet, it had not urgently wished in his ear.

He was content enough to remain here, the whole of his extended family fed and taken care of, with a roof over their heads and their needs met. It was, he told Beth, a good life.

She believed that he truly meant that, and was impressed.

Not only with stories was she entertained, but with slights of hand and bits of "magic" that had her laughing and begging to be shown the trick of it.

Duncan placed his long, tapering fingers to one side of his plate and leaned back, studying her as Hank made a coin appear from behind her ear. Beth seemed, Duncan thought, to be fitting in well here.

Again he wondered how she would fit against him. The thought was never far from his mind. Each time he looked at her, he burned a little more intently, longed a little harder. He supposed, in a way, it was a sign that he was mending.

He wanted her to remain for a little while longer, he thought. But the rain had ceased as of late evening, and that meant she would be pulling at the bit, eager to go at first light. He could not keep her with feeble protests of needing her to tend to his wounds. He was recovering amazingly well. The sling he wore to house his injured arm was more for her sake than his. Strength had returned with speed.

As it should have, he thought.

He smiled at Amy as she took away his plate. "Excellent, as always, Amy."

"Of course it was," Amy retorted, but it was easy to see she was pleased at his words.

He rose, his chair scraping along the smooth floor. Duncan made his way to Beth. Hank was on one side of her and Jacob on the other, each vying for her attention.

When Duncan extended his hand to her, the others moved away.

"Will you walk with me?" He smiled at her invitingly.

"Perhaps."

"If I make coins appear from your pretty ear?"

She hadn't even had to look up to be aware of his presence. She had sensed him as he had crossed to her. Like a rabbit that knew a fox was nearby. But she was no rabbit. She was his match, not his prey.

Beth returned his smile as she withheld her hand for a moment. "Only if you show me how."

He closed his hand over hers and brought her to her feet. His smile never shifted, but it was just a shadow darker around the edges.

"After my secrets again, Beth?"

She shrugged as she crossed to the terrace. It was the first clear night since she had arrived, and the doors were opened to admit the stars into the manor.

Beth walked out and leaned against the wall that surrounded the outer rim of the terrace. She looked out upon the fields.

"Those secrets are not yours," she pointed out quickly. "They belong to any magician."

He did not wish to address her back, unless it was to peel away her clothing and then press kisses to the soft skin he'd glimpsed beneath.

With his free hand, he turned her around to face him. "Magic," his breath whispered along her skin, "belongs to anyone who can seize it."

There was nowhere to turn. The wall came up to her waist and she was pressed against it. She had thought she might be able to sidestep his efforts. She had been wrong. Beth read his meaning clearly in his eyes, eyes so green she knew she could easily drown in them if she didn't hold fast to the shore.

"I am not magic, Duncan."

"Ah." He smiled, and suddenly there was nothing else in the world for her but him. "There we have a difference of opinion."

Duncan slipped his hand from the sling. Taking her into his arms, he lowered his mouth to hers before she could utter a single protest to stop him.

It was magic suddenly to have her pulse racing and her mind galloping out of control like a horse frightened by the crack of thunder. Magic he had created within her.

There was only blackness without and a host of colors within.

Beth had no idea that when two people came together, when they touched lips in this manner, it could be so glorious, so breathtakingly stunning. The very air had left her, as if she had run a long way to fall into his arms this way.

His hands were roaming her back, pressing her more urgently to him as his mouth slanted over and over again on hers, draining her, renewing her, bringing something dark and thrilling to her that she feasted on.

She felt the urgency of his desire as he moved against her. Startled, she gloried in it the next moment, absorbing the heat she felt pulsating there. It created a twin within her very core that would have had her ashamed, if she could but think clearly.

Or at all.

He banished her thoughts, her very will, with the hot, savory taste of his mouth.

Duncan found his appetite growing, rather than abating, as he kissed her sweet mouth, her cheeks, the tempting hollow of her throat. He wanted to strip her bare where she stood and take the body that he had become enamored with that first night in his room.

But Beth was not one for a quick tumble in the loft. She was to be wooed and won. That was why she had to remain here with him. So that he might wear her down.

He only prayed that the waiting would not undo him, and that the event would not be too long in coming.

He gathered her closer until he felt her heart against his. His shoulder ached, but it was nought compared to the other ache he felt, the one throbbing so urgently in his loins.

Sweet God, but he wanted her.

Excited, thrilled, frightened, Beth felt his hands hot on her, curving, touching. His fingertips brushed along the swell of her breasts and she struggled to draw back. The fear that beat within her was not that he would take her, here, like a common tart, but that she would let him. More, that she wanted him to.

She wedged her hands against his hard chest and cursed the fact that they were trembling. Her heart was beating as quickly as if she had run the full length of the manor and back again.

Perhaps she had.

She waited a moment until she found her breath. Her eyes held him at bay. To her satisfaction, he looked as disoriented as she, though this was far from his first time, as it was hers.

"Sir," she swallowed, steadying her voice. "You presume too much."

He passed his hand over her hair. Like dark honey, he thought, soft and shimmering when it caught the light. And tempting. He wanted to see that honey spilled out on his pillow.

"I think, sweet Beth, that I presume just enough." He stood now, with his back blocking her only course of retreat. And barring any prying eyes that might look upon them, should they be thus inclined.

"I will not mince words, Beth. I am a simple man with simple wants." He framed her face with both his hands, the sling hanging abandoned and useless about his neck. "And I want you."

To divert his attention from the hammering of her heart, she tugged on the sling a bit too hard, as if she meant to choke him with it. "That much is obvious."

But she could not break his concentration. "More than I have ever wanted another woman before. More than I wanted revenge upon my father." His eyes held her prisoner as he uttered his promise. "And I shall do what I must to have you."

She struggled to gather the shreds of dignity that his kiss had stripped from her, for surely he must have tasted the hot desire beneath . . . just as she had tasted his.

"I am not a treasure to be stolen from the hold of some merchant ship, Duncan."

He shook his head. "No. You are far dearer than any treasure I have ever discovered."

She forced herself to swallow. The laugh she uttered was meant to put him off, but it rang nervously in her ear. Still, she could read him well.

"And you are not a simple man, not with that tongue."

His laugh enveloped her, touching her as if she stood before him nude again. "I can show you what this tongue can do."

She was sure he could. Things a girl with her breeding would never have dreamed in her wildest fantasies. Her cheeks colored. What did he think of her? What *could* he think of her? He had almost dissolved her beneath the heat of his mouth. Worse, she had almost jumped upon him rather than slapped him for the insult he had rendered.

"Enough, sir." With her eyes daring him to touch her again and her back still resting against the wall, she moved aside. With a hand she willed to remain steady, Beth gestured behind her. "The rains have ceased."

He nodded slowly, knowing where this road was leading him. "So they have."

She pressed her lips together, still tasting him. It dampened the ire she was attempting to raise against him. "And our bargain was that you would provide a coach and driver for me and my companion when they had ended."

He glanced over his shoulder. Sylvia was still at the table, deep in conversation with Samuel. The old goat was behaving like a young ram, Duncan thought fondly, pleased at the turn of events. Every man needed to feel alive that way.

"I think that Sylvia would rather remain here," he said as he turned back to Beth. "With Samuel."

"He is amusing himself with her." Her voice was harsh. She did not wish to see the woman hurt.

"He is making her happy," Duncan corrected, as he placed his hands on her shoulders. "As I could you."

Beth shrugged off his hands, knowing full well that if she let them remain, she would be undone. A battle raged within her, none the less potent for its invisibility. Not all of Beth wanted to resist Duncan's advances, only the part of her that clung to honor.

"If she wishes to remain, that is her choice and she is free to make it." Beth stepped into the room once more. "I, however, am bound by honor to make mine, and I choose to leave."

"In the morning," he reminded her.

"Yes." He was too close. Standing behind her, he was much too close for her to successfully continue resisting.

"But for tonight—?"

The question whispered along her body, tempting her, drawing to something within her that was completely unknown to her.

"I shall be packing tonight," Beth answered, her very words sticking to the roof of her mouth like dried bits of oats.

His hands slid once more to her shoulders, but the

pounding she heard this time was not her heart, but the sound of a fist beating against the front door.

"See who that is," Duncan ordered, annoyed at the distraction. If she meant to leave tomorrow, he meant to have her in his bed tonight. His sense of decency warred with a hot, surging desire.

But the next moment, a boy came running into the room, his eyes wild and unseeing as they scanned one and all.

"Where's Master Duncan?" he cried, his voice struggling with hysteria. "I need Master Duncan."

Concerned, Duncan released Beth and made his way to the boy. "Here, Jamie."

Beth quickly followed.

Jamie almost fell to his knees as he stumbled toward Duncan. "Please, you must come. Now. It's Mother!"

All thoughts of seduction and Beth warming his body left him. "Has her time come?"

The flaxen head bobbed vigorously. "But it's not like the others," he wailed. "Mother says it's wrong. Something's wrong."

He did not understand. All Jamie knew was that he was frightened. His mother was shrieking in pain and his father was becoming undone.

"My father's afraid and he wanted me to fetch you. Come help, Master Duncan. Please." Frantically, the boy tugged on Duncan's arm, pulling him to the door.

Amy saw the confusion cross Beth's face. "They come to Duncan with everything."

"Apparently," she murmured. It earned her a reproving look from Amy. But Duncan was the furthest thing from a midwife Beth had ever seen. "What are you going to do for the poor woman?" she wanted to know, as he began to follow the boy.

His link was forged with these people in a chain the likes of which Beth could never hope to understand. "Whatever I can."

Beth bit her lip, tasting him again. She was torn. On the one hand, she could not allow herself to become more involved with these people than she already was. She wanted to leave on the morrow.

But what did Duncan know of helping a woman with child?

"I'll be back, my love," Samuel told Sylvia, giving her hand a squeeze. "Duncan, wait," he cried. Duncan turned at the door. "I'll go with you."

Beth could not believe her eyes. "A barber and a 're-formed' privateer," she scoffed, with a shake of her head. "To assist at a birthing."

Duncan's eyes challenged her, daring her to throw her lot in with them. "Well, what of it?"

Beth closed her eyes. She was being a fool again. Their troubles were not hers. Still, her father had taught her well. With a huff, she raised her skirts and hurried to the door.

"Wait, I'll go with you."

Duncan suppressed his smile of triumph. "Haven't you packing to see to?"

He was mocking her, but she let it pass.

"There's not that much to pack." She pushed past Duncan and took the boy's hand in hers. She gave him a reassuring smile. "And I shall not be able to live with myself if I let you two go and tend to that poor, de-fenseless woman on your own."

Jacob thrust a lantern into Samuel's hand to lead the way. Jamie had stumbled to them in the dark, with but the moon to mark his way. The old man looked at Beth, taking insult at her words.

"Mistress, I've been tending to these people's complaints for longer than you've been alive."

"It's a wonder, then, that *they're* still alive." She murmured the words under her breath, but Duncan heard and laughed.

"Let's be off," he urged, ushering Beth out before there could be further words between them. There was a woman lying on a straw bed who needed them at her side. "Don't you worry, Jamie, everything is going to be all right."

Beth looked up at Duncan as they hurried into the night, wondering how he could make such promises when they weren't his to keep.

Chapter Seventeen

The cottage was outlined by the light cast from Samuel's lantern as they rushed across the meadow. Though it appeared to be small, it had the look of warmth and comfort about it.

She felt a sharp prick of nostalgia. The cottage reminded her of the slaves' quarters back home in Virginia. But those were whitewashed, and neatly arranged in two long rows, like dancers at a reel. Here, the little building stood alone, with gray stones surrounding its foundations like rocks about a rose garden. A thatched roof sagged sadly overhead, worn and the worse for wear from fending off the rains. It would have to be mended, and soon.

Beth heard the loud keening before they were even close to the door. It ripped across the darkness like a sharp dagger.

"Mother!"

Terror echoed within Jamie's voice and left its mark on his face. He tried to break free, but Beth kept her hand tightly about his. He tugged at the link between them, his eyes accusing as he looked at her.

"Birthing is a hard thing on a woman," Beth told the boy softly. "'Tis only natural for her to cry out."

Beth raised her eyes and saw the look in Duncan's. These cries, they both knew, were not natural. They went beyond the realm of what was expected.

It was as if the forces of hell were trying to rent the woman in two.

When they reached the door, there was no need to knock. Beth doubted that any within would hear. The woman's cries smothered every other sound.

Duncan pushed the door open with the flat of his hand, impatient to help, not knowing how.

As soon as they entered, the square man pacing before the fireplace like a hunted beast all but fell upon them. He clutched Duncan's arm with the desperation of a man who knew he was drowning. "Duncan, you're here. Saints be praised."

If he was unsure of himself, Duncan gave no indication to the man. The look he gave him was confident and comforting.

"I'm here, John." He smiled at the cluster of children who were quick to collect around him. Beth counted five in all, including Jamie. Duncan nodded toward the other room. "How is Enid?"

"Not good, not good." John scrubbed his hand over his face. Sweat gleamed. "It's been this way since before sunset." John rung his beefy, wide hands, which were better suited to tending a plow than to aiding his wife with the delicate task of bringing a new life into the world. "The baby feels all wrong to her."

He looked toward the room as if something unspeakable was happening there. Another shriek came like a volley of musket fire. One of the children covered his ears, hiding behind his brother.

"You know how easy the others came. Like eels sliding out of the water." His hold tightened on Duncan's arm. "Can you help her?"

Duncan pressed his lips together. There was nought that he could do but offer words of comfort to the woman until the deed was done. "I—"

Beth shifted impatiently. He might be the master here, but she had no time to wait until he gave leave for her to act. The next cry that arose from the bedroom had her pushing him aside to enter the tiny bedroom where the woman lay.

The sight that greeted her eyes made Beth gasp. The woman, haunted and small but for the mound formed by the child, was writhing on the bed. Her hands were red and bleeding.

Her heart in her throat, Beth crossed to the bed and lifted one bloodied hand to examine it. "What is this?" she asked in a hushed whisper.

John pushed his bulk past Duncan into the room. With the five of them in it, there was no room to move. "She's been biting on them when the pain grows to be too much to bear."

"She'll gnaw off her fingers like a trapped animal. Get her a stick or something to bite down on." Beth tossed the command at Samuel.

She touched the woman's head. It was burning from the heat and the strain.

Authority rose in Beth's voice. "I want a basin filled with hot water and another with cool to bathe her forehead." As she spoke, she pushed the sleeves of her dress up past her elbows. It looked to be a long night ahead for all of them.

John shook his head as Samuel returned with a stick

he had pared down. "You'll get one or the other, we haven't two."

Beth took the stick from Samuel as she looked over her shoulder at Duncan, impatience on her brow. Duncan was quick to understand her meaning. "Samuel, fetch another basin from the house."

"Done." The word hung in Samuel's wake as he hurried away.

It was a hot, moist night. There was precious little air in the room to breathe as it was. The press of bodies made it intolerable. Beth turned to the remaining men and the children who looked in at the doorway.

"Now, clear the room, all of you." She gestured with her hands as if to chase them from the small space.

"But I'm her husband—" John protested. Fear mingled with a desire to flee, shaming him.

Another scream from the woman had Beth raising her voice to be heard.

"Yes, I know," she said kindly. "But I don't want you getting underfoot. See to your other children, and calm their fears."

Rather than leave, John turned questioningly toward Duncan. "Who *is* she, Duncan?"

Despite the situation, a smile touched Duncan's mouth. He had been wondering that himself tonight, after he had kissed her. Beth had managed to catch his soul off guard. "That all depends on who you ask. Jacob thinks she's a goddess brought to earth. Samuel regards her as a meddlesome fairy sprite."

"And you?" It was the only opinion that mattered to the man.

Duncan's expression softened as he looked down upon a man who had fought by his side for the better part of ten years. He could trust his life to John.

"She's a woman, John. One who, I would wager, can help your Enid. Come." With his arm around the short man's broad shoulders, Duncan ushered him out of the room.

There had been a myriad of faces in the outer room, but they had swum together for her as she had hurried to the woman. Beth looked up now. "Do you have a daughter, sir?"

John's head popped up when he realized she was addressing him. "Yes."

She was going to need help here, Beth thought, a woman's help. And Sylvia's stomach was too weak. There was no point in sending for her.

"Of age?" She wanted no child weeping and moaning at her side.

"Soon." He nodded vigorously, his eyes upon his wife. "She's thirteen summers old."

She'd been twelve the first time she had stood by her father to help. Beth nodded. "Send her to me, with the basin."

Duncan leaned in for a moment. "Hot water in it, or cold?"

"Cold, for now." She wanted the woman's forehead bathed. The girl could do that, while she saw to the rest. "When Samuel comes, have the one he brings filled with hot water. Now, get out."

"Yes, General," Duncan said, a touch of humor mingled with respect.

Beth had turned her back on the lot of them. They ceased to exist for her. There was only the woman now, writhing on the bed, her face as shallow as the cloth upon which she lay.

Enid's lashes, weighed down with sweat, fluttered open. "Who—?"

She could not even manage a single question, her breath stolen from her by the continuous onslaught of pain.

Beth gave the woman her most reassuring smile. "My name is Beth. My father's a doctor, and I've helped him at some birthings." She squeezed the woman's damp, bloodied hand in hers. "I'll do what I can for you."

Enid heard only part of what Beth said. She was drowning in a sea aflamed with agony. *"Am . . . I . . . to . . . die?"*

It wasn't in Beth's nature to lie, but she could not bring herself to deny the woman some small token of hope, even if she felt there was little to give. "Not tonight, you won't."

"Aaaaii!"

The shriek that tore from the woman's lips vibrated within Beth's very chest.

"Enid?" John cried from the other side of the door, afraid of the answer.

"She's still with us, John, giving it the good fight," Beth called in response.

The door behind her opened.

"I said, stay out," Beth snapped, as she turned toward the offender.

A young girl with hair the color of wheat stood hovering in the doorway, a basin in her hands. She was trembling so much, the water was spilling from either side. Her ice-blue eyes were wide with fear.

"They said—" She couldn't finish, her eyes frozen to her mother's pain-wracked body.

"No, not you," Beth beckoned. "I thought your father was entering."

When the girl remained standing where she was, Beth

took her arm and gently ushered her into the room. She closed the door again.

"Set it there, please." Beth nodded at the chair by the bed.

The girl did as she was told, then began to back out of the room once more, her hand clawing for the latch behind her.

Beth had pushed the sheet from Enid's swollen body, intent on examining her. She looked up as the girl retreated.

"No, I want you to stay." The girl froze, as if she was afraid to move in either direction. "What's your name, child?"

"Jane." The name dribbled from the girl's lips, her eyes never leaving her mother.

"It isn't always this way for a woman," Beth assured her gently. "I want you to bathe your mother's forehead, Jane."

The girl nodded slowly, and did as she was bidden.

Enid's heels were moving quickly against the mattress, as if she were attempting to scramble away from the pain that wracked her body.

Beth's eyes were on Enid's, her voice calm. "I'm going to see where the baby is, Enid."

"In me. Dear God, in *meee!*" Enid pulled the sheet free beneath her, fisting it in both hands.

Jane jumped at the scream, almost overturning the basin. She was quick to catch it before it tipped.

"Yes, I know," Beth's voice was low, soothing, belying her own agitation. "But I need to see exactly how it lies within you."

As gently as she could, Beth felt the outline of the swell. Her heart began to hammer quickly. Dear God, the child was sideways. Dropping her hands, she stood back.

Another wave of pain seized her and Enid stuffed her hand into her mouth. Beth grappled with the woman and pulled her hand out once more. She quickly gave Enid the stick to bite on in its stead.

She'd seen this before, a breech baby. The child would never pass. The woman would die unless the child could be turned. Or taken from her.

Pushing her sleeves further up her arms once again, Beth began to talk to the woman, her voice steady, never varying above the screams. She tried her best to turn the child.

And failed.

Disheartened, Beth moved toward the door and cracked it. "Duncan."

In the lull that followed the last scream, Beth's voice was hardly above a whisper. Duncan still appeared instantly. He'd been listening for her.

He didn't like the look upon her face when he entered. "Yes?"

She motioned him to the side, away from Jane and her mother. The words did not come easily. "I need to take the child from her."

He stared at her, not understanding her intent. "What do you mean, 'take?' "

Beth fought to keep the wave of hysteria from her voice. Giving in would do none of them any good. Still, she could taste it in her mouth. It was bitter as bile.

"It won't pass the normal way. The child is within her sideways."

The news numbed him. Women died giving birth. He thought of John. And the children. "What are you going to do?"

There was nothing else she could do. "I have to cut her. To operate."

Her words stunned him. What manner of woman was she? "You know how?"

Beth placed a hand to her throat as if to calm herself. She nodded slowly. "I've seen it done. If I don't try—" She hated the sound of that word, it was so weak. Try, not succeed, but merely try. "If I don't try," she repeated, "we'll lose them both. If I do, there's a chance of saving them both. Or at least the child."

Duncan looked over her head at the woman in the bed. The cry that came from her wasn't human. Duncan's jaw grew ridge.

"Do it."

Beth looked up at him in surprise. "The decision isn't yours to make."

The look in his eyes silenced her. He didn't take the decision lightly, but there was more to think of than just the immediate situation.

"It can't be John's if it goes wrong." He knew that John could not live with himself if he agreed to this and then Enid died. Duncan accepted the burden, and the outcome that might go with it.

Duncan looked down at Beth's face. He was placing his faith in her hands, hands that had worked to make him well. "What do you need?"

Quickly she enumerated the tools she would need to try and save not one life, but two. "A sharp dagger, cleaned well." He nodded. "A needle no less sharp, strong thread, and whisky to cleanse her with."

Beth took a breath and it hitched within her lungs. There was no denying the fact that she was frightened. And there was no denying the fact that she knew of no other way. "And prayers, if you know any."

The prayers he remembered were few, and none had ever received an answer. His expression hardened. "I'll fetch what you requested."

Beth turned to look at the woman and said her own prayers as another scream ripped through the heavy air.

Chapter Eighteen

Duncan wouldn't leave her side.

Though Beth had instructed him to go and calm the others, he handed that task over to Samuel. It was Samuel who stayed with John and kept him from breaking down the door when Enid's screams swelled and intensified. Duncan remained with Beth.

It was Duncan who held Enid's frail arms down when Beth made the first painful cut in the woman's belly. Enid's scream tore from her lungs, even though Duncan had encouraged her to drink liberally from the whisky bottle to help numb her.

"She's fainted from the pain, thank God," Beth whispered, glancing up as Enid fell back against her flattened pillow. There were times, she thought, when God was merciful.

Beth worked as quickly as one who was uncertain of what to do was able. The lantern that Samuel had brought with him to guide their way now stood on the chair next to her, guiding her hand instead. She'd sent Jane away. Only she and Duncan were in the room with Enid.

There was not a part of Beth's body that wasn't held

fast by tension or drenched with oily sweat as she moved the tip of the dagger along the faint brown line upon the woman's swollen belly.

Duncan felt his own stomach turn more than once as he watched Beth's hand move steadily downward. Blood dripped like mournful tears along the whitened skin as the stroke lengthened.

Every prayer that Beth knew filled her head and her lungs. This had to work. It had to. What if she lost them both, mother and child? How could she face the woman's husband? His children?

How could she face herself?

Please God, please. Let me remember the way, and guide my hand.

The incision was finally completed. Her hands covered with the woman's blood, Beth reached into her belly and took Enid's baby from her. A lusty cry filled the air as the infant took his first breath. Trembling within, her hand sure and firm without, Beth severed the chord that joined mother to child.

One was alive, she thought. One more to save.

Quickly she handed the infant to Duncan. There was no time to look at his expression or say more to him than, "Give him to his sister to clean off. I have need of you here."

Every moment counted.

Beth knew she had to close the opening she had made quickly, before there was too much blood gone. So much had been spilled already, and the woman's breathing did not please her.

In her hurry, her fingers began to get in each other's way. She took a long breath to calm herself, then swabbed the area with a bit more whisky. The skin along the sides shrank and danced in fearful spasms, as if it had a will of its own.

Exhausted, clinging to shreds of hope, Beth swiftly sewed the flaps of skin together, first one layer, then the other. Her motions imitated her father's the time she had seen him perform this same surgery on the young slave on their plantation. Angel and her child had lived.

Please God, so would Enid and the boy.

She was not certain just when Duncan had entered the room again. She just knew he was there, offering words of comfort, of encouragement. As he spoke, as he soothed, there was a deep reverence in each word.

"Shine the light here," Beth instructed, and Duncan lifted the lantern so that it cast its light lower. "Almost done," she murmured, more to herself than to Duncan or the woman who could not hear her. "Almost done."

Duncan was in awe as he watched Beth's fingers move skillfully. It was like watching St. Peter spin a miracle, he thought. "Will she live?"

I don't know.

"I don't know," Beth muttered, when she realized that she had answered silently the first time.

She was close to tears, the tension wrenching them from her. She wished her father were here. With all her heart, she wished that it was he who was working upon this human flesh and she the one who held the lantern.

Would she ever see him perform surgery again? Would she ever see him?

No, there was no time for that; the woman needed her complete attention. She could not allow herself to lose her heart to sorrow now.

"But at least the child will live." Beth let out a long, ragged breath. "There, I've finished."

With shears that had been used to shear a sheep only

a week ago, Beth cut the last bit of thread away. She brushed her hair aside with the back of her wrist, smearing more blood on her face.

The woman needed to be cleaned better. Her body and bedclothes were all filthy with blood. Beth glanced at the basin. Its contents were dark with blood she had washed from Enid.

"Is there any more clean water?" Beth asked hoarsely.

Duncan nodded. He cupped her chin in his hand and slowly rubbed the blood away from her cheek with his thumb. "I had Jamie fetch a bucket from the well." He glanced toward the window. There was a lightening cloak of gray about the world outside. "'Tis almost morning."

"Is it?" she asked vacantly, too tired to know the difference. Or care. She stood over Enid and watched as the woman's chest rose and fell. Still alive, she thought. Enid was still alive.

Fresh water was brought in. Beth lost no time in cleansing Enid as best she could. Sometime during the night, Amy had come from the manor with food for John and the children. She had brought a fresh change of bedclothes and another nightshirt for Enid. Beth recognized it to be Sylvia's.

Beth smiled to herself. So, in her own way, Sylvia had joined this crew as well. Beth slipped the nightshirt on the woman.

Enid had not awakened since she had fainted earlier. Beth did not know if that was merciful, or a sign of something much worse.

"Please live," she murmured.

Duncan heard and was moved. She was not just a woman to be bedded, but one to be prized as well. He watched as Beth's fingers touched the woman's brow. No woman could have been gentler, even with her own mother, he thought.

The forehead was cool, Beth thought, relieved. Her pallor was the color of day-old porridge, but at least the woman was breathing.

With a sigh, Beth settled into the chair where the basin had been but a few minutes ago. The seat was damp, but she did not care. If felt as if she hadn't sat down in a fortnight.

She saw Duncan looking her way, his brow raised in question. "I'll stay with her 'til she wakes."

He wondered if saints were perverse and tried the patience of their Maker. He knew Beth tried his.

"Beth," Duncan said sharply, "you're tired. It's been a long night. I'll take you back to the house."

Beth gripped the arms of the rickety wooden chair, holding fast. "I'll stay with her," she ground out stubbornly, between teeth that were clenched. Her nerves frayed, she was far beyond reason now. If he argued with her, she would surely hit him with what little strength she had left.

"As you wish."

Duncan knew the signs. She was past exhaustion, and would fight like a wildcat. The only way to remove her would be by force. It was easier to let her stay. Perhaps she would fall asleep where she sat and he would carry her back.

The thought appealed to him.

Meanwhile, he closed the door and left her.

By and by, the woman's eyes fluttered open. Pain returned, an ever-present bedfellow, but it was a different sort of pain, like the time she had cut her hand with the carving knife. It was like that, but multiplied a thousandfold.

"Oh, God, the pain," Enid cried. Her hand flew to her belly. Her eyes widened as her fingers spanned the flattened mound. "Where—?"

Beth scrambled forward, falling to her knees beside the bed. Her heart was bursting with relief. "You had a son, Enid. A beautiful, lusty boy."

"A son," Enid whispered. Another darling baby boy to love. Then her eyes narrowed as the memory of the long night returned. "He's alive?"

"Yes," Beth breathed, her fingers laced with Enid's, gratitude flowing through her veins. "And so are you."

She remembered, through the haze of pain, hearing words. The baby was turned wrong. She knew two women who had died because of it.

"But how—?"

Tired though she was, Beth couldn't help smiling. It spread from ear to ear.

"I had to take him from you. There's an ugly cross on your stomach, but it will heal," she promised. "And I can give you something for the pain you feel." There were herbs easily found in the meadow that could be used and brewed to deaden the worst of it. Her father had taught her much, as had Callie, a wizened old slave who knew the ways of the land. "And best of all, you've a son to show for your wound."

"I want to hold him. I want to hold my son," Enid begged, a mother's love washing away the pain coursing through her.

Beth nodded. She rose, her body feeling like lead, and moved from the room to the doorway. She opened it and something felt as if it had been set free.

"John, your wife wishes to see her newborn son. And you," she added for good measure, when she saw the sudden fear in the man's eyes.

"She's not—?" John choked upon the word as Samuel and the others crowded around.

"No," Beth smiled, content, as she shook her head, "she's not dying."

The door of the cottage was opened and Beth could see the sunrise from where she stood. Long, golden fingers were reaching out across the meadow, nudging aside the darkness.

As if drawn by the sight, Beth moved to the doorway and leaned against the doorjamb. Behind her, the others filed into the tiny bedroom to see Enid.

She had to remember to tell Samuel to gather the herbs she needed, she thought, too weary even to form the words now.

Duncan moved out of the way of the others. Enid would be fine and the burden of her life lifted from his shoulders. By the grace of Beth's skillful hand.

He crossed to her. When he slipped his arm around her, Beth leaned against him. He smiled, content just to hold her.

For a moment, Beth allowed herself to lean into the strength she felt emanating from Duncan. Her own was depleted, like a rain barrel with a hole in it.

"Have you ever noticed how lovely the sunrise is?" she asked softly.

"Not nearly so lovely as you."

She raised her eyes to look at him and for a moment, she thought he was going to kiss her right here, in the midst of all this activity. It was not a thought that met with resistance, though she knew it should.

"You were magnificent in there."

Far from magnificent, she had been frightened beyond belief, but there had been no choice open to her, save the one she had taken. She felt his arm tighten around her. It felt better than she could say to have him here with her like this.

She smiled at him. "I'm too tired to fight off your advances, Duncan."

He knew she was right. He could easily have her now. But it would not be fair. When they came together, he wanted her fully alert and awake. Aware of everything. For the experience was one to be shared by them both, not just him alone.

"For now," he told her, as he began to guide her out the door, "there'll be no advances." She looked at him in surprise. "I give you my word," he promised. "Come, I'll take you home."

She was too exhausted to correct him. It wasn't her home, but his he was taking her to. But for now, anyplace would do.

When she sagged, he lifted her easily into his arms. "Your shoulder," she protested.

"Is well, thanks to you, as are my friends. Now, hold your peace for once, woman, and let me take care of you."

The protest died on her lips as she lay back in his arms. "Just for now," she murmured.

She fell asleep a moment before her body touched the bed and she slept the whole of the day away, too exhausted even to turn.

When she awoke, the first thing her eyes rested upon was Duncan. He was sitting, dozing, in a chair beside her bed, just as she had sat beside Enid, and before that, beside him.

But she was not in any need for medical aid.

Beth looked about. Dusk was entering the room. Had she truly slept so long?

As she stirred, she saw Duncan's eyes open. "Why aren't you in your bed?" She struggled to clear the cobwebs from her mind.

A smile slowly curved his mouth. "The view there is not nearly so beautiful." Now that she was awake, there were questions he wanted to ask. He shifted from the chair to her bed. "How did you know what to do? Last night, how did you know?"

Beth sat up, dragging a hand through her hair. "My father's a doctor. He took me with him when he tended to his patients. At times he let me help. He would always let me watch him when he worked." She pulled her knees up and hugged them to her as she wrapped her arms around them.

Duncan frowned slightly. "'Tis a strange thing to let a daughter do."

So many people thought. Beth shrugged. "He has no sons. I think I fill that space for him."

Duncan laughed softly. "If he thinks of you as a son, the man's eyes are not what they should be." His eyes seemed to touch her everywhere at once. And burned what they touched. "I've never seen a less likely boy."

She averted her face. His eyes were too intense and her resolve too weak. "I am not like my sisters. I have no interest in 'womanly' things."

"Your training, odd as it is, was very fortunate for Enid." He cupped his hand about her cheek. She was forced to turn her eyes to his. It was her downfall. "But you don't speak the truth."

"What?"

"You have an interest in some womanly things, Beth." He rubbed his thumb over her lip. Instantly, the last vestiges of sleep fled. Every fiber of her body was awake.

Waiting.

He saw desire bloom in her eyes, and it aroused him to a fever pitch he didn't think possible. Very deliberately, he gathered her into his arms.

Alarmed, she pulled back, knowing she possessed no strength to fight him. Or herself.

"Duncan, you promised."

"Aye, that I did." He smiled, knowing full well the words he had spoken. "But that was this morning, at dawn," he pointed out. "And I kept my promise then. But this is now."

The next moment, his mouth found hers as if it was the other half of a whole. The other half of his soul.

Chapter Nineteen

This is what it must be like, Beth thought, to be drunk on wine. To be so hopelessly intoxicated that you do not know of anything beyond your own senses. And even those were not to be trusted. Everything seemed to be so much larger, so much brighter, so much more overpowering now. There was nothing outside of herself, save for the haven created by this man.

A haven within a storm.

A haven that had its own storm.

As Duncan's lips moved over hers, coaxing, stirring, hot and moist, Beth became aware of a hunger within her, a hunger she did not understand, for things she did not know of.

Unable to stop herself, she wound her fingers into his hair. It was as if her body had parted company with her mind, as if it had deserted her will completely and was now rushing recklessly toward something she sensed was wondrous. Though she fought against it, her body was attempting to drag her along with it in its wake.

She could not surrender. There was too much at stake and no time to indulge herself, even if it was proper and without sin.

Trembling, she shifted until she managed to wedge her hands to Duncan's chest and push him back. Her heart pounded so that she could speak only in a whisper, a whisper that tempted and aroused him.

"I cannot do this."

"This?" he questioned innocently.

Gently Duncan passed his hand over her cheek, barely grazing the silken skin. His own heart was beating harder than he had ever known it to beat before. Beating hard from wanting her.

From knowing that he was not to have her.

As hot as his blood surged within him, Duncan would not force himself upon her. He wanted no accusations in those blue eyes when they looked at him, for they would haunt him all the days of his life.

Just as she would now.

Even the lightest of touches ignited flames within her. Beth tried to draw away, but there was hardly anywhere to go upon the bed.

"You know what I mean."

"No." His breath tantalizing her face, Duncan softly pressed a kiss to the slender slope of her neck. "Tell me," he whispered.

He knew very well what she meant. And what he meant for them to do. What she longed to do. "Coupling," she breathed.

"Cannot, Beth?" he echoed. "Nay, never say cannot." His fingers twined with hers. "Let me show you the way of it."

Beth shook her head. "No, I—"

Everything within her shouted, "Yes," begged for it to be "yes." But she knew that if she gave in to him, to her own hunger, she would no longer be her own master. She would be tied to this man who could make her want things that should be beyond her reach.

It was a wicked battle that raged within her.

It lasted all of a few moments but felt like eternity to her. Determination triumphed, much to desire's sorrow. With a mighty cry, Beth pushed him from her, from the very bed.

Duncan fell with a thud to the floor. He hit his head against the bedpost as he landed. Stunned, he rubbed his head and looked up at her.

Beth rose and ignored the desire to see to his head. "Though you make my body rebel against my mind—"

Duncan did not let her continue. Instead, he smiled in victory. "Do I Beth? Do I?"

His words hung about her like a beckoning siren's song. It was easy to see that he had made his life upon the sea. The rogue.

"You know you do." Her hands upon her hips, she looked down at him. "And I cannot say that it is not—" She searched for a word that would not incriminate her. "—Pleasant."

Duncan leaned on an elbow, his brow arched in amusement. "Only pleasant?"

"Yes." She ground out the word. The man was as far from being a gentleman as Virginia was from France. "Pleasant," she repeated. "I cannot dally with you any longer. I must go to Paris."

Dally was it? Perhaps the woman needed a lesson after all. "To save your father," he quoted patiently.

She didn't care for the condescending tone in his voice. Did he think her a child on a fool's mission, to be patiently humored until she lost interest?

"Yes, to save my father."

Duncan shook his head. They had been over this

ground before. It was a stubborn breed that God had put into skirts.

"You are a woman," he pointed out patiently. "I would not use the word 'mere,' for there is nothing mere about you, but the fact remains that you are a woman, and subject to the lascivious desires of any man."

Her eyes narrowed as she looked down upon him. "I can care for myself."

"Can you, Beth?" Had she listened for it, she would have heard the warning note in his voice.

But as it was, she was too busy taking umbrage at Duncan's presumption to notice. Beth lifted her chin stubbornly. "Yes, I can."

The smile on his mouth mocked her. "You could not with me."

Her smug look was meant to silence him. "You are on the floor, are you not?"

The next moment Duncan's arm darted out and he struck her on the calves. He caught her unawares, and Beth shrieked in surprise as she tumbled down onto him.

She landed so that her body covered his much as a blanket does a horse. Duncan was quick to catch her hands so she could not rise.

"And now, so are you." His laugh was lusty as it filled the air. "See how well we fit together, Beth?"

She struggled against him, but it only served to arouse him more. And her as well.

When his tongue touched but the merest hollow of her throat, it made her ache for him once again.

With a little cry, Beth brought her mouth down to Duncan's.

The kiss, of her own volition, was the beginning of

her undoing. The room and all within it seemed to spin into a deep, rimless darkness.

She gave herself up to the sensation for a moment, savoring, delighting, mourning for what was not to be. She swore to herself that the control, the reins to this ride, were still in her hands.

To prove it, she pulled back from him with all her might. Her weight was balanced on her palms, which were spread out on the floor. Her body hovered over his, her breasts, full and ripe, straining to fall free. She was aware that his arms were around her. Still, she could get up, if she wanted to.

But did she want to?

Her breath was not easy to catch. She forced it to steady within her breast before she spoke.

His eyes were fastened to the tempting cleavage as it rose and fell before him.

"I was not questioning the fit, Duncan, merely the propriety of it."

He knew better than to laugh at her words. Propriety could go to bloody hell. Duncan cupped his hand at the back of her head so that she would not draw too far away from him.

"Then do not question anything at all, sweet Beth. For I am long past questions and words. Feel, Beth." The word rippled seductively along her bare throat. "Here." He drew a tiny mark across her breast, where her heart beat wildly. The tip of his finger singed her. "Feel here."

The very sound of the words brought a cry from her. More than anything in the world, she wanted this man.

Now.

"This changes nothing," she warned, as her eminent capitulation shimmered before her.

"Oh, no," he contradicted, his eyes on hers. "This changes everything."

The next moment, the debate dissolved in smoke as the last of her will deserted her. With a cry of surrender, Beth descended into the fires that were waiting for her.

The clothes were cumbersome. He was desperate to have her free of them. Duncan burned for all of her, for every taste, every look. More than anything, he wanted to satisfy his curiosity if the goddess he had dreamed of that first night truly existed or if she was just a worshipful creation of his mind.

As his mouth reduced her to the purest form of passion, he undid the laces at her back with hands that were well suited to their task. Bridling his impatience, he tugged the unwanted material from her shoulders and slid it down hips that were ripe for a man's hands.

He thought himself in heaven, just as he had that night.

Beth moved slightly as she realized that the material was leaving her body. She had no idea that he was removing her dress until it was gone.

For a moment, her eyes held his. "You have skill at this."

"Purely a beginner's luck," he murmured against her mouth. The taste he found there excited him. The wine within Sin-Jin's cellar paled in comparison.

Her fingers spread upon his open white shirt, she looked at him, undecided as to whether to be insulted or not. "What kind of a fool do you take me for?"

He was hungry for another taste, not words. "No fool at all, Beth. Merely my salvation."

The words echoed from his mouth into hers as he kissed her once more.

The words were pretty, but she would not let them cloud her head. It would be her undoing entirely if she did. Beth knew that what was to happen now between them Duncan had done many times before. It was only for her that the mystery existed.

Only for her that the excitement pulsed.

Pushing her uncertainties aside, Beth placed herself in Duncan's hands and let him lead her to a land she wanted to enter.

Her desire grew, becoming boundless. The fire within her grew to incredible portions, like a bonfire struck within the meadow that the winds suddenly whipped out of control.

She felt his hands hot upon her fevered skin, felt him tug away her chemise and the pantaloons she wore, felt his touch as it skimmed and explored and caressed her nude, pulsating body.

The touch of his hand was as gentle as it was urgent.

His hands were everywhere, claiming her, making her yearn, creating a woman she did not recognize.

She groaned as she felt Duncan's lips at her breast, suckling there like the child she had delivered yesterday.

And yet not like the child at all.

She had no idea that a man could do this to a woman.

Eager, her hands wild, she tugged on Duncan's shirt. Duncan swallowed the pleased laugh that echoed in his throat. It was just as he had thought, just as he had hoped. Beneath the cool words beat the heart of a wildcat.

And for this moment, the wildcat was his.

He took her hands in his and rose, bringing her to her feet as well. She was as nude now as she had been that first night, that night he half thought he created her in his delirium.

His gaze swept over her, warming her blood. "You are more beautiful than you were that first night."

Even now, she blushed. "I thought you were asleep."

"And I thought myself in heaven." He stripped his shirt from his body and threw it aside. He was eager to feel her flesh against his, eager to savor every tiny shred that he could, every tiny bit she had to offer. He almost laughed at himself. He was behaving as if this was his first time as well.

Perhaps, in a very strange way, it was.

Chapter Twenty

She did not know what madness overtook her. She only knew that it *was* madness, and she was glad of it.

With hesitant, questing fingers, she dipped her hands down to his britches. They formed a barrier she wished to breech.

"You are dressed and I am not," she protested. Heat seemed to flow from her fingertips, warming his very skin, though she touched but the cloth between. " 'Tis not fair, Duncan."

Fair? No it was not fair, he thought. It was not fair that the hunter became the hunted. And yet he had, and gladly so, if it meant having her this way.

"I shall always be fair to you, Beth. Always."

The promise, delivered with a smile, held more truth than she could ever have hoped for, far more than she would have believed. It frightened him to feel the depth of emotions that were coursing through his veins like the force of a river swollen with the rain from a deluge. He had always been in control of all his feelings, even that night at his father's manor. Never once had there been a need to struggle in order to maintain a tight rein.

There was need now.

For in his heart, in his very soul, he felt emotions straining to break free. Emotions that would shackle him more tightly than any iron chain forged in the bowels of the Tower of London.

He wanted her, forever. Exactly the way she was this moment.

What would she say if she knew?

Rather than aid her, Duncan let Beth undo his britches herself. He sucked in his breath as her long, tapering fingers slid along his hips, urging the fabric down. And by the same stroke, urging him up.

The britches fell to the floor and he kicked them aside carelessly, leaving them scattered with the rest of the garments they'd taken from each other.

He burned to plunge himself into her, to feel that hot burst within his loins which would allow him to renew himself.

But rather than race to the end he knew was waiting for him, Duncan took her hand and softly kissed the palm. He felt her shiver, not from the cold but from the heat, and his heart was made glad.

It would be worth the trouble and the wait. *She* would be worth the trouble.

"Come, Beth, let me show you what it is like."

Fear had entered her heart.

Fear of going forward. Fear that he would cease now, before she reached journey's end. She was torn, confused, and needy beyond her wildest expectations.

But as his mouth touched hers, as his body pressed against her in all the points that God had created to join them eternally, and they fell together to the bed, all doubts fled from her mind. No thought was left, save that she wanted to follow to where this man led, not two steps behind, or even one, but at his side.

When he touched her, his palms gliding along her sleek body, she groaned, but held fast to that one thought, that one goal. She would make him hers as much as he made her his.

Determined, Beth matched him touch for touch, stroke for stroke, passion for passion, until the leader became the follower, the jailer the prisoner.

And then the tables were turned again and they began from the beginning.

Duncan had long ago lost count of the women he had had. In their time, they had brought him endless pleasure. He could not now remember a one. Indeed, there might as well have been none, for all the impression they had left upon his mind and soul. Their very memory was burnt away in the trail this woman forged now.

The embers this small chit of a woman stirred were something new, something completely beyond the scope of his imagination.

She humbled him, made him want to fall to his knees in worship and thanksgiving. He feasted upon the banquet she offered him. And with each new secret he imparted to her, she showed him one in kind.

It was as if he had lived all these summers with a stranger and did not know himself.

They tumbled about the bed, dragging sheets and bedclothes in their wake until all was a tangled mess, kicked off to one corner.

She was passion, she was fire, she was beyond his wildest hopes and dreams. She left him weak and empowered him as well.

Beth could not begin to describe what was happening to her. There were no words that were fitting. She felt ablaze with passion, with wants, with cravings. The more he touched her, the more she wanted to be touched. The more he kissed her, the more she sought out his mouth.

And all the while, she felt as if she was rushing to some end.

When Duncan knew that he could hold himself back no more, he rolled her onto her back, his body ripe and poised over her.

The time had come.

He looked into her eyes, smoky with passion, and yet still so innocent. A moment from now, she would no longer be innocent. He imprinted her face, as she was this moment, upon his heart. She was forever his, no matter who loved her in years hence.

His weight on his elbows, Duncan framed her face for a moment with his hands.

"This will hurt, Beth," he whispered, wishing it could be otherwise, wishing he could be her first and not have the fact outlined in pain, "and for that I am truly sorry."

She was lost in his eyes, she thought, drowning in that green sea, just as she had once feared she would be. Except that there was no fear now. She had never felt as sure of herself before as she did now. A smile lifted the corners of her mouth.

"It will hurt me more if you do not do it."

As of that moment, Duncan was completely lost.

Murmuring endearments to her, making promises he knew she did not hear, Duncan entered the citadel in triumph and remained to become a prisoner himself.

Beth stiffened as the pain he promised came. But it faded, eaten away by the raging fire that consumed her. The raging fire ignited the moment Duncan began to move within her.

Afraid to be left behind, Beth began to move with

him, and their bodies melded in a hymn that the morning doves sang at sunrise.

The hymn became a wild sea chanty, its tempo increasing like a storm at sea. Finally, they rode the crest of the highest wave together. Beth cried out his name, the sound muffled against his shoulder.

Spent, Duncan tumbled to earth once more, dazed, disoriented and fearful that he had been, at the end, too rough with her.

He felt the rise and fall of her soft breasts beneath him as they rubbed tantalizingly along his flesh. Even now, exhausted, she stirred him. He felt himself quicken within her. What manner of woman was she, who could raise him up so high so quickly and do it all with no design on her part?

With his last shred of energy, Duncan forced himself up upon his elbows and looked at her.

"Beth?"

If she tried, she was certain that she need but reach out her hand and capture a fistful of stars. He made her feel as if she could do anything.

"I am still here," she murmured, her eyes shut, the wonder pulsating within her.

Duncan moved slightly and a smile curved his mouth as the soft impression of her body rippled against him. "Yes, that much I know. But—"

Beth's eyes opened. Was he going to say something to spoil all this for her? Would there be words to wash away the happiness she felt at this very moment?

"There is no 'but.' " Beth laid her finger to his lips to silence him. "I want no words to pass between us, Duncan."

Humor entered his eyes as it curved his mouth. "Ever?" he murmured beneath her finger.

She felt the heat of his breath and it excited her. "No," she laughed, dropping her hand. "Only for the moment."

He waited a moment as she requested. His amusement faded, to be replaced with something far more tender. "Forgive me, but I must ask. Did it hurt?"

She stretched like a cat sunning herself in the afternoon sun. "Yes."

He knew it would, yet he could not help but wish it hadn't. "Much?"

She curved her hand about his cheek, moved at his concern. Whatever his lips said, she saw his feelings in his eyes. "No, not much. The price was small for the goods that were purchased."

He said nothing, but gathered her to him on the bed and held her. The contentment within her rose until it filled her completely, leaving no space untouched.

Suddenly, there were words he wanted to offer her, words that sprang to his lips like a bubbling stream, from somewhere within him that he had never known existed.

But he kept his silence as she had bidden him and as prudence dictated, more for his sake than hers. Though he understood not the immediate origin of the words nor the emotion that rendered them into existence, he only knew that he had never voiced these feelings to another. Had never felt them about anyone. And saying them aloud would shackle him forever.

So he held her, content to run his fingers along her arm, content to feel the warmth of her body as it lay against his.

And said nothing.

* * *

They spent the night in lovemaking. And dawn came too quickly.

Beth stirred, then awoke. Guilt came. Not from the deed, but for the time she had wantonly lost. She needed to be off. Shifting gently, she sat up.

Duncan caught her wrist in his hand. "Stay with me, Beth."

Beth looked at him over her shoulder. She knew he was not speaking of the moment, but of longer. Far longer than she was now free to give.

She shook her head and slipped from the bed. "I still have to go. I told you before we began that this changes nothing."

But it had, she thought silently. There was an ache in her heart that was not there before. And it was there because she had to leave him.

How often had he said those same words to other women? How often had he felt that himself? Yet when she said it, an anger rose in him that was not easily banked down.

He sat up. "Very well, if you are determined to go, I will go with you."

He had said he'd send someone with her. She had not thought he meant himself. "Why?"

Perverse woman, always questioning everything he said. "Because."

Duncan rose from the bed and crossed to her. He was a magnificent specimen of a man, his body fresh from loving her.

Beth, her chemise held in her hand, met his gaze boldly. And felt her pulse beat rapidly.

Duncan placed both hands upon her shoulders and brought her to him, trapping her garment between them. Did she really need answers?

"I have a weakness for lips that taste like raspberries and for eyes the color of sapphires."

There was more. He did not want to let her go from his life, but he cared too much to keep her prisoner. Knowing her, she would have found a way to leave even if he were to chain her in his room.

Duncan grew more serious. "Would I be overstepping my bounds if I said I want nothing harming you?" These times were perilous and no one knew that better than he. "That I could not bear it if you were killed?"

Her eyes dipped down for a moment. When she raised them again, there was a smile on her lips. "I would say that you have overstepped more than just bounds, Duncan. But you needn't concern yourself. As I said before, I can care for myself."

When he thought of another man's hands on her, his blood ran cold. "Like last night?"

She turned from him and casually retrieved her garments one by one. "Like last night." She arranged them on the bed, which looked as if it had been in the path of a storm. Her eyes held his. "If I had not wanted it, it would not have happened."

He crossed his arms before him, as comfortable with his nakedness as if he were fully dressed. "You are a bold one, Beth Beaulieu."

She laughed, but kept her eyes to his face. "I also know how to shoot a pistol and hit what I aim for. Firing it in such a way that a man could never trouble a woman again."

His hands moved to cover that which her words had plainly targeted. "Ouch."

A smugness touched her lips. "Exactly."

He grew somber once more as he took her hand. "Still, I cannot have you go."

She tugged to take her hand away, but he held fast. "You have no say in it."

"—Without me," he added. "If you try to leave without me at your side, you will find yourself a prisoner in the very place where you were an honored guest." He drew her closer. "There are ways to keep you here, Beth. Don't force me to show you."

Her face darkened. "I do not care for ultimatums, Duncan."

That, he did not have to be told. In spirit, she matched him. "Then consider it a forceful suggestion. Consider it whatever you will, but you are not leaving here without me."

Despite her bravado, Beth knew she would be a great deal safer if Duncan accompanied her. And if the truth be known, she did not want to be parted from him so soon.

With a sigh, she nodded. "Very well."

"Good, that's settled." He looked out the window and judged the hour from the position of the sun. " 'Tis at least an hour before we break fast. What would you suggest we do until then?"

Beth smiled.

He did not wait for her to answer.

Chapter Twenty-One

It was less than an hour after breakfast that Beth asked Sylvia to walk with her in the garden.

Though afraid of what might come, Sylvia hesitantly agreed. Beth did not miss the fact that the older woman touched Samuel's hand before leaving the dining hall to follow her outside.

A multitude of flowers, freshly washed off by the rains, perfumed the air on either side of Beth as she walked slowly, gathering scattered thoughts to her. Her mind had been so organized only a few days before. Now she found it difficult to think.

Several minutes passed. Sylvia walked beside her in uneasy silence, waiting. Finally, Beth turned toward her. "Sylvia, I am leaving for France today."

Sylvia nodded, twisting her hands together before her. "I suspected as much."

Beth looked at Sylvia's face, but the woman's eyes were cast down. "And you will remain here?"

It was not really a question. Beth knew that Sylvia wished to remain. She merely wanted to assure herself of it.

Duty and longing fought within the ample breast. Fingers knotted more tightly. It matched the feeling in her stomach.

"I know I promised your mother, but—"

Beth placed a gentling hand over Sylvia's before the woman tore her fingers from her hands.

"I do not care what you promised my mother, Sylvia. What is in your heart?"

That was an easy thing to answer. Sylvia looked toward the house. Samuel was standing in the doorway, watching her.

"To stay here."

Beth glanced up and saw Samuel there. He smiled in their direction. "With that man?"

Sylvia could not tell if there was censure in Beth's voice or not. She was a timid soul, easily influenced by a lift of a brow, a carelessly thrown out word. But for this one time, she held her ground.

"He makes me happy, Beth."

Beth smiled and nodded. "Very well, then you are fortunate." It was in her nature to always look upon the brighter side of things, and there was a large one to this. "'Tis well. If you remain here, I shall not have to worry about you."

Sylvia's face darkened as guilt pricked at her conscience with pointy lances. "'Tis I who should be worrying about you." She took Beth's hands into hers. "And I do."

Beth smiled as she squeezed Sylvia's hand in return. "There is no need. I am more than able to look after myself."

But Sylvia held fast to her hand. "In Virginia," Sylvia insisted. "This is not Morgan's Creek, or even America."

Beth eased her hand from Sylvia's. She looked off

into the distance, seeing things with her mind rather than her eyes.

"No, 'tis not. 'Tis supposed to be more civilized."

"Supposed to be," Sylvia echoed pointedly.

A bee buzzed by her head and Beth waved it away. She looked at Sylvia, touched by the concern she saw there. "At any rate, there is nothing to fear. Duncan is coming with me."

Sylvia breathed a huge sigh of relief. "Then you will be safe."

Beth inclined her head slightly. "Perhaps."

Perhaps not. He made her feel safe from harm, but not safe from him. The man had made her lose her will, her precious feeling of independence. She had never wanted to cleave to a man before, never wanted to be beneath his yoke, and while she did not go so far as to say she was willing to do that even now, Beth knew she would go a long way to have Duncan with her.

For that she resented him, for he was changing her and she did not want change. She did not want to become some dewy-eyed girl who lived and died on her beloved's whims and sighs.

Sylvia frowned at the sound of Beth's singularly worded assessment. It was all well and good for her to be with Samuel, for they were both to poverty born. But it was another matter for Beth to be with Duncan. There was a class difference.

"I fear your mother would not look upon Duncan as a proper match for you."

As if the man was interested in matches. Coupling was all that took Duncan's fancy. This she well knew, and at least she was well forewarned. If she lost her heart to him after that, it would be but sheer folly on her part, not due to any doing on his part.

Beth laughed. "There is little about him that is proper."

Sylvia's eyes grew huge as she remembered the nights that she herself had spent with Samuel. Had Beth's honor been sullied?

"Oh, Beth—"

Beth's eyes narrowed. She wanted no preaching. There was no shame in her for what had happened. And she was not inclined to share anything that had gone between her and Duncan with someone else. That was private and would remain so.

" 'Tis past time to be saying, 'Oh, Beth.' " Beth drew herself up, and though there was no more than an inch that separated them, she cast the more formidable shadow. "And 'tis best you look to your own house, Sylvia, before you point a condemning finger at mine."

Sylvia shook her head. Beth had misunderstood her meaning. "I was not about to point, merely to offer comfort if it is needed."

Beth stared at the woman dumbfounded. This was something new. "Sylvia?"

The older woman smiled, understanding Beth's surprise. She scarcely recognized herself these last few days.

"Aye, I've changed, have I not?" She looked toward the doorway. Samuel was still there and her heart swelled at the sight of him. "Samuel has made me want to change."

She raised her face toward the sky and laughed aloud, happy to be alive. If Beth would not have thought it strange, Sylvia would have hugged herself.

Sylvia took Beth's arm now and tried to make the younger woman see it through her eyes.

"I feel like a flower, Beth, having spent the whole of

my life in the forest, beneath the shadow of some giant oak tree. And now suddenly, the tree has been cut down and the sun has found me." Her eyes held Beth's, imploring her to understand. Perhaps to even give her blessings. "I never knew how warm the sun could feel."

Beth saw nothing but sheer joy in the kindly face. With all her heart, she wished that it could always be so. "I wish you well, Sylvia."

Her steps were already taking her to Samuel. "And I you."

She passed Duncan on her way to the house. Her newfound happiness gave her the strength to say, "Treat her well, Master Duncan, for she deserves no less."

"Aye." He nodded. "That I know." He crossed to Beth in several large strides. "I'm glad you've finished with Sylvia."

Beth nodded vaguely, watching Sylvia as she joined Samuel. Like two young lovers they were, she thought, even though there was more than a century between them. She did not realize that there was a sad smile playing upon her lips. "She is not coming."

That much he suspected. "In that event, I must ask you a question."

Impatience tugged at her. Was he going to attempt to talk her out of it once more? "No, I will not change my mind."

He did not care for the defensive tone in her voice. Why did she assume that there was always to be a war between them? "And you will not display patience, either," he replied.

She looked up at him sharply, then contrition washed over her features. "Pardon, my temper is a little sharp at the moment."

He laughed. "That is nothing new to me." He hurried

on, lest she begin to take offense anew. "I was not about to ask you to stay. I know that your mind is set upon the journey and cannot be budged any easier than an anvil can be carried off by a newborn babe. My question is a far simpler one. Can you ride a horse?"

Though they were alone in the garden, he inclined his head toward hers and added in a whisper, "For I know full well that you can ride a man."

Startled at his boldness, she quickly looked around, afraid that someone might have overheard his words. There was no one, but it did not help to cool her anger.

Beth fisted her hands at her waist. "Have you no shame?"

"No, none with you, or because of you." Unable to resist, he satisfied his yearning with a quickly stolen kiss. She pulled her head away, "We are past pretenses, you and I. From now on, there is nothing but the truth between us." He had judged that it would be easier for her than for him. Perhaps not. "So tell me, you did not answer my question. Can you ride a horse?"

"Yes." And then, for good measure, she threw in "Astride, not sidesaddle."

The habit gave her mother much distress, but she refused to do it differently. Riding sidesaddle had always seemed awkward to her.

Duncan nodded. "Somehow, I envisioned you that way in my mind, though there are sidesaddles in the stable." If she rode astride, it meant she rode well. "Good." It facilitated matters for them.

Beth's eyes narrowed. It seemed a strange question to pose. "Why do you ask?"

He had given the matter some thought over their meal. The sooner they were there, the sooner they would return. He looked at her and longed to hold her in his arms. But he knew that she would not allow it in the open. At least, not yet.

"I thought that since you are in a hurry and I was the one who caused you delay, riding horses to Dover would be much faster than going there by coach."

Now that she didn't have to worry about Sylvia's comfort, the idea of taking horses, rather than a coach, seemed inspired. She smiled her approval. "Wonderful. When can we leave?"

He needed to take very little with him. And Samuel knew how to run the manor as well as he. "As soon as you are ready."

She thought of the gold in the false bottom of her trunk. She had checked it just after Duncan had left her room this morning.

"I need but an hour."

Admiration shone in his eyes. "You are a rare woman." He slid his hand along the curve of her cheek. "But I already knew that."

She willed that her heart not beat so quickly at his touch. Her heart refused to obey. "You said there would be no pretense between us."

Why was it so difficult for her to accept what was true?

"And there is not." Her hair was held back with pins. He longed to free it, to run his hands through it again. To run his hands along all of her again. "Why Beth, did no one ever give you pretty words before that you deserve?"

Her sisters were the ones men paid court to. She was too much like her father to attract any of them. Not that she wanted their attention. She had no time to simper and roll her eyes and pretend to have no thoughts in her head save the ones that were "seemly."

And if any had been attracted, the sound of her tongue soon drove them away.

"None but you."

He nodded knowingly. "Then they are right."

She had no idea what Duncan was referring to. "About what?"

His mouth curved with teasing pleasure. "When they say that the States are populated by fools. Had I lived near you, I would have given you pretty words each day."

She had no doubt that they came as easily to him as breathing. "And meant none of them."

He toyed with a tendril and watched her eyes grow dark with feeling. It aroused him. It aroused him just to look at her.

"On the contrary, I would have meant every one."

She refused to be fooled, to make more of it than it was. She was well aware of the only reason for his flattery. "Because they will get you closer to your goal—the inside of my pantaloons."

He laughed and hugged her to him. She was indeed a rare woman. "Only in part, Beth, but you must admit, it is an admirable goal."

Beth turned her back on him so that he would not see her blush. "I need to prepare."

He shook his head as he watched her walk toward the house. "And it seems that I shall never be prepared enough," he murmured.

Beth made sure that she did not see him before she hurried to the stables with her saddlebags. She struggled not to bow under the weight. There were but a few garments within it. The bulk of the space was taken up by the gold she'd brought, the gold she hoped to ransom her father with.

"Here, let me help you."

Beth jumped when she heard Duncan's voice behind her. She braced her shoulders. Curse the luck. She had hoped to elude him until she had placed the bags across the horse's saddle.

"No, 'tis all right."

The woman was the embodiment of stubbornness. Anyone could see she was struggling with the bags. He reached across her and took them up in his hand.

"I can—" He stopped. The weight caught him unawares and he all but listed to one side. Duncan stared down at the saddlebags he held. "What manner of clothing did you pack, woman?"

"None of your business." She tried to snatch the saddlebags from him, but his hand tightened about the leather.

He lifted the flap, curious as to her odd behavior. "I have seen you without them, surely I can see them without you."

So saying, he plunged his hand in and moved aside the garments. He felt something hard against his fingers. Bewildered, he curved his fingers about it and lifted the object out.

The gold bar gleamed in the sunlight.

Chapter Twenty-two

Duncan's eyes were dark when he lifted them to look at Beth's face. He saw unease mingled with defiance there. He held the bar up higher.

"What is this?" he demanded.

Beth lifted her chin. She held her ground and had no idea why she felt as if she had done him an injustice. This was not personal; it went beyond what had passed between them earlier.

"Money to ransom my father."

Duncan dropped the bar into the saddlebag once more. It strained the leather with its weight. His voice was low and all the more frightening for it. His men knew the extent of the anger that boiled just beneath the lid. It rarely occurred, but when it erupted, it was a fearsome sight to see.

His eyes pinned her. "You weren't going to tell me about it, were you?"

She felt her pulse quickening, still she could not retreat. It was not him she was afraid of, but something else she could not name. Something in his eyes. "It did not concern you."

"On the contrary, it concerns me very much." In disgust, Duncan threw the saddlebags to the ground. The next moment he swept her up in his hands, his palms bracketing her shoulders. He restrained himself from the urge to squeeze her between them and vent his anger. "Were you afraid that I was going to steal from you, Beth?"

Bitterness traced his chiseled features until he almost looked malevolent as he shouted his anger into her face. "Did you think I was going to rob you somewhere along the trail and then abandon you?"

Her breath caught in her throat. She saw the angry, accusing hurt in his eyes, and for reasons beyond her understanding, it stung her heart. Her secrecy was to safeguard the gold for her father, not to hurt him. Angry now at his tone, she raised her face to his defiantly, defending her action. At the very least, she had not wanted to place temptation in his path.

She matched him, tone for tone, anger for anger. "You said yourself you were a privateer."

He could have shaken her until she swooned, but what good would that have done?

"Were, Beth, *were.* And I told you why I took to that life—because I had no choice. I *have* a choice now. I have a life now. Somewhat maddeningly tranquil at times, but it *is* mine by choice."

Duncan gestured toward the house. "There is nothing that I require that I cannot have here." His face hardened. Her judgment of him wounded him far more than the highwayman's discharging pistol ever had. It made no sense to him, but that was the way of it.

"Greed was never in my nature, Beth—except when I look upon you." For a moment, his hands upon her softened as he remembered the night. "You are the only thing that ever aroused my greed, Beth. Wanting you."

His eyes traveled over her face and he knew he was lost. And a fool. "Having you does not seem to be enough. You prey upon my mind worse now than before."

And then his anger rose again like a flame in the wind, fueled afresh by the hurt she had done him. His hands tightened on her shoulders so that her very breath was stolen. His eyes were dark, like the sea during a storm at midnight.

For just a moment, she felt herself afraid at what might lay just beyond.

"Do you really think I would steal from you?" He shook her then. "Do you?"

She winced and tried to pull from him. "You are hurting me."

He released her then, pushing her away from him. She fell back against the horse's flanks. The bay whinnied in protest. Beth stared at Duncan with stunned eyes.

"No more than you are hurting me," he whispered harshly. "More fool I." He turned his back on her and began to stride away from the stable.

She had wronged him, she thought. Dear God, she had wronged him. It flashed across her mind like a bolt of lightning creasing the brow of the sky.

"Duncan, wait."

He stopped, though he knew he was being a dunderhead for doing so. Waging a battle with his common sense, Duncan remained where he was. But he did not turn around to face her.

"Why?"

She desperately searched for words that would make him understand and not take offense. She had not only wronged him, but she knew now that she *was* wrong. If he had wanted to take the gold from her, he would have done so now, not cast it aside and walked away.

"Place yourself for a moment in my position." She drew a long, shaky breath. "Pretend you are a woman, not a 'mere' woman," she repeated his words to him, smiling nervously to herself, "but a woman nonetheless."

She watched his shoulders. Anger was not holding them as stiffly now as it had a moment ago. She hurried to continue.

"A woman who, in all probability, is all that stands between her father and eternity. You have with you enough gold to purchase his freedom, if that is what is required." She licked her lips, remembering him as he was last night. "And suddenly, there appears on the horizon a golden-maned, golden-tongued *ex*-privateer, with the devil in his eyes and honey on his lips."

Beth thought of the passion that had exploded between them, of tasting his lips. "A man who has turned your head, made your body rebel, and dissolved your very limbs with his touch."

Her voice grew quiet. "But you know nothing of him save what he has told you, and all these could be lies. Would you trust him with your father's life?"

Duncan turned around slowly, his temper suddenly cooled as a blacksmith's hot iron plunged into a bucket of water.

"You trusted me with your body."

She swallowed as he took a step toward her. "I had no choice."

Did she really think that? Their hearts had met for a brief instant. Could she now not see into his? "You always had a choice, even at the end."

She was not well versed in men, but there had been

stories she had heard. What manner of man was he, to be so different?

Beth lifted a brow. "I did?"

He laid his hands on her and the touch was as gentle now as it had been rough before. It grieved him that she winced, bracing herself, before her shoulders were lax once more. That was no one's fault but his.

"Did you think I would take you like some rutting sheepherder if you said no?"

She smiled ruefully. "The time for 'no' was before my clothes were gone." No man would have held back after that.

Duncan curved his fingers along her arms. "You could always have said no."

Beth looked at him in wonder. "And you would have listened?"

He laughed softly. "Torn out my hair, perhaps, and railed. But I would have listened."

Beth looked into his eyes and saw that he spoke the truth. Truly he was an unusual man. Her heart softened immeasurably. She pressed her lips together.

"I'm sorry, Duncan. I should have trusted you."

Now that she relented, he allowed himself to see it all through her eyes. "No, you are right, you do not know anything of me, save what I have said."

No, there was more to it than that. Signs she should have noted. "I have seen the way your men look at you as if you were a god."

False praise he held suspect. True praise made him uncomfortable. He lifted his shoulders and let them drop. "Ex-privateers as well."

Beth shook her head. "Not the women. Not the old ones." She laced her hands together. "This is hard for me, Duncan—very, very hard." She looked down at the saddlebags nestled in the newly scattered straw. "I do not trust easily and I am afraid for my father's life. My mind is not clear. I no longer know which path to take."

Duncan put out his hand to her. "The one beside me, Beth." She placed her hand in his. "For I know the best route."

Releasing her, Duncan walked over and picked up her saddlebags. The weight was more than passingly heavy. "We need divide this between us, Beth, 'lest your horse become swaybacked before we reach our destination."

Crossing to his horse, he patted the dark stallion's muzzle.

"And we will have need of swift horses before this is over. For I have heard dire things about what goes on in France." He looked at her and wondered how much she knew of the horrors that were rumored. "I mean no offense to your ancestors, Beth, but these French peasants are a mad lot. They cry for freedom, yet they strip it from anyone in their path they do not like."

He opened his own saddlebags and transferred several of the bars from hers into it. The others he left untouched.

But as he placed the saddlebags across her horse's saddle, he looked down at Beth's face. His heart quickened. He did not want to risk her.

"Are you sure, Beth? Are you very, very sure?"

She gave him a brave smile and nodded. There was no turning back for her.

"Yes."

Duncan expected no less from her. She was stubborn, honorable, and foolhardy—always a dangerous combination. It served heroes well, but made life difficult for the rest.

He draped an arm about her shoulders. "Well, then,

we will be off within the hour." He guided her from the stable and toward the house. "Come, I have a few last things to settle. And Amy is packing provisions for us. Hunting along the way may not be easy."

And like as not, they would probably become the hunted before long, he thought.

Beth turned in surprise. Jacob hailed Duncan as he rushed toward him in the stable. A saddlebag upon his slender shoulder, Jacob looked ready for travel, same as they.

Jacob hurried to the horse the stableboy had saddled for him and placed his saddlebags across the horse's rump. "I have everything as you asked, Duncan."

Beth looked at Duncan, her brow raised in question. He had not mentioned anything about Jacob to her. "He is coming with us?"

Duncan nodded as he took up his horse's reins. "We will have need of an extra sword beside us. And another pistol as well. And though I have your word for it, I have not seen how well you shoot."

She had not oversold her abilities, but harbored no desire to point the weapon at a man. "Perhaps there will be no need," she whispered.

Jacob was tying down his saddlebags but looked up to stare at her as he recognized the voice. "Mistress? Mistress Beth?" His face looked as if he had seen an apparition.

"Aye."

It was Duncan who answered and Beth who laughed at the surprise on the young man's face. His bewilderment was due to the clothing she had donned. Skirts were far too cumbersome for a long journey on horseback. She had borrowed a shirt and pair of britches from Tommy, making his heart glad by trading him a gold coin for the worn clothes. He had run off, crowing, to show his mother his booty.

" 'Tis I, Jacob."

Jacob circled her slowly in wonder, as if to convince himself that it was truly her. "Why are you garbed like Tommy?"

She saw the amusement in Duncan's eyes. He had said nothing when she had entered the stable, as if he could expect nothing less from her than the unexpected. She wondered what he thought of it. She had received severe criticism for dressing this way before.

To her it made perfect sense. "Skirts are made for sitting in parlors and long strolls on moonlit nights. They are not made for riding quickly, for stealth and a long journey atop a horse."

As she spoke, Duncan's eyes swept over her form. The britches adhered to her posterior in a very pleasing way. "There is much to be said for this new fashion you have taken."

His gaze made her warm and she looked elsewhere, afraid that Jacob would see more than he should.

They brought their horses out into the courtyard and found that many people had come to see them off.

Sylvia tearfully kissed Beth goodbye, then fell back into the protective shelter of Samuel's arm.

"I charge you with her safety," Beth told Samuel, and he but laughed, pleased.

"It is my first concern, I swear it," he vowed, looking down into the older woman's face.

As she turned to mount her horse, Beth found that

John had come to see them off as well. "How are Enid and the baby?" she asked.

"Well, both well, thanks to you." He pressed something small and wooden into her hand. "Here."

"What's this?" Beth looked down and genuine awe took her features. In her hand she held a small, delicately carved cross. It hung upon a long, thin gold chain. Beth raised her eyes to the farmer's. "I cannot accept it."

She tried to return it to him, but he would not accept it. He pushed her hand away.

"Please, 'tis but a small token for what you have done. May He protect you on the journey you undertake, mistress." John crossed himself piously. "Your name is sainted in our home."

Beth hung the chain solemnly about her neck. "Thank you."

"'Tis I who should be eternally thanking you." He bowed as he backed away.

It was time to go, if they were to make good time before evening. "Beth?" Duncan asked.

"Ready."

She swung into the saddle with such grace, it filled Duncan with pride just to watch her. She was a magnificent figure of a woman, he thought, and woe to the man who tried to tame her.

Duncan gave the signal. "Let's be off."

Chapter Twenty-three

If there were any doubts that still existed in Duncan's mind about Beth's ability to keep up, they were quickly dispelled when he saw her ride.

Holding the reins tightly in her hands, Beth leaned into the big bay. She and the horse were as one as they galloped across the lush British countryside. The wind was hot as it whipped through her long hair. It flew behind her like golden brown streamers.

Duncan urged his horse closer to hers and raised his voice. "You seem to the saddle born."

Though they were moving swiftly, she heard the note of awe in his voice. Beth smiled.

"It always caused my mother much grief to see me ride thus." She sighed as she thought of it. "Everything I did caused my mother much grief." Though they loved one another, mother and daughter had no common ground upon which to meet. Dorothy Beaulieu could not begin to understand her daughter's strange ways. And her mother's wishes to remain hiding in the shadows of life often mystified and annoyed Beth. "She is far happier with my sisters."

He had not thought of her as having more of a family

than just her father. Since he was his mother's only child, he had given the attribute to Beth. "Are there many like you at home?"

She guided her horse away from a low-hanging branch that would surely have tangled in her hair.

"None." She flashed Duncan a smile when she saw the confusion on his face. "But I have three sisters, if that is your question." Beth looked forward and continued, as if reciting, "All comely, obedient, and well versed in womanly arts."

And hopelessly boring and dull, she added silently.

And very all different from Beth, Duncan thought. He laughed and the sound echoed from the trees that surrounded them like green, shaggy sentries as they made way.

"I'd wager that the entire lot of them is not worth one of you."

If she meant to suppress the pleased smile that rose to her lips at the sound of his pronouncement, she failed miserably. Her mouth curved deeply. "You would be the first of that opinion."

He looked at her. If that were true, then he was not only the first to make love to her body, but the first to kiss her lips as well. The idea pleased Duncan beyond measure.

He nodded. "Good." With a kick of his heels, he urged his horse ahead of hers.

Beth pressed her heels harder into the bay's flanks, refusing to be passed. She did not ask what he meant by his comment. It undoubtedly had something to do with his manly pride. She knew that men enjoyed being the first to have a woman, and Duncan had been her first.

And, she thought, though Beth locked the secret away deep in her heart, he would be the last. She did not have to look over an entire field to know when she had seen a rare flower that had no match. So it was with Duncan. She did not need to look upon the faces of all men to know that there were none like Duncan.

Beth had never been one to accept second best if there was something better in the offing. Rather nothing at all than settling.

And that, she thought, as she slanted a look at his face as they rode, would be what she would have in end. Nothing. For Duncan was not one to be shackled to a single woman. Like a bee that was meant to go from flower to flower, to gather honey where he might, Duncan would always remain free. This was something she knew in her heart to be true just as plainly as she knew herself.

The weather smiled upon them and the journey went swifter than Duncan could have hoped for. He knew the countryside well, knew the shortest paths to take. They stopped only to rest the horses. Beth would not allow them to stop on her account. After so much delay, she was anxious to reach journey's end. Beth feared that the weather would turn foul once more and prevent their crossing the Channel.

Far from worrying that Beth could not keep up with them, Duncan found that he and Jacob had to press hard so that they could keep up with her.

Though she seemed tired, there was an unmistakable urgency that pushed her onward.

She was a complete puzzlement to him. She looked like a dove and behaved like a falcon. He spurred his horse closer to hers again, the way he had done a dozen times since they had set out. "You ride as if the very devil is at your back."

Her breath was being stolen by the wind, and she had to husband it in order to be heard. "No, up ahead, from what I have heard."

So she knew more than he had told her, he thought. "And what have you heard?"

She tried to separate the words from her thoughts about her father, from her fears about her father's safety. She pretended that she was reciting something that she had seen printed in the *Virginia Gazette* back home.

"That there have been killings and lootings. That there are bands of self-righteous people reclaiming things that never belonged to them to begin with, that they had never had a right to, under King nor God."

Jacob, who had ridden silently by them for the better part of two days, suddenly turned toward Beth, a question shining in his eyes. "Why did your father go to a place like that?"

She was surprised that Jacob had been listening. He had been so quiet, she had all but forgotten that he was with them. She turned slightly in her saddle and the wind whipped her words to him.

"Because he is a good man." *And good men do things that get them killed.* "Because his mother, my grandmother, and his maiden aunt are still in Paris, and he was worried for their safety."

Beth looked ahead, unseeing. Before her eyes was the last time she had seen her father and the conversation they had, the one in which she entreated him not to leave, all the while knowing that for her father there could be no other way.

"And because he thought he might be able to help. Whenever people take up the sword, he thinks himself needed." Beth turned toward Duncan. Her voice softened and perhaps there was even a hint of an apology there, because he had chosen to help her. "He fought against you in the Revolution."

Duncan shook his head. She was still not clear about that, he thought.

"I did not fight in the Revolution, Beth." He saw her open her mouth in protest. He was quick to clarify the difference as he saw it. "I plundered American ships for English advantage which was clearly in my family's interest."

Her brows drew together as she tried to understand the words. Had she misheard him? He had said his father was dead, as was his mother.

"Your family?"

Duncan nodded. There was no other way to think of the people who populated his life. "The people you saw on the manor and at the house. Samuel, John, Amy. Tommy." He laughed as he caught Jacob's eye. "Even that one."

It was an unusual sentiment, and a charitable one. "You think of them as your family?"

Since the moment he had found his way to the London streets and been rescued by Samuel. " 'Tis the only one I have now."

She thought back to the story he had told her about his father. "You mentioned half-brothers."

His face hardened, as different from a moment ago as day was from night. "They are strangers." He turned his eyes toward Beth. "Blood does not always make family, Beth. Feelings do."

She believed he meant that, and it made her heart glad. She had been right in her estimation that he was

MORE PASSION AND ADVENTURE AWAIT... YOUR TRIP TO A BIG ADVENTUROUS WORLD BEGINS WHEN YOU ACCEPT YOUR FIRST 4 NOVELS ABSOLUTELY *FREE* (AN $18.00 VALUE)

Accept your Free gift and start to experience more of the passion and adventure you like in a historical romance novel. Each Zebra novel is filled with proud men, spirited women and tempestuous love that you'll remember long after you turn the last page.

Zebra Historical Romances are the finest novels of their kind. They are written by authors who really know how to weave tales of romance and adventure in the historical settings you love. You'll feel like you've actually gone back in time with the thrilling stories that each Zebra novel offers.

GET YOUR FREE GIFT WITH THE START OF YOUR HOME SUBSCRIPTION

Our readers tell us that these books sell out very fast in book stores and often they miss the newest titles. So Zebra has made arrangements for you to receive the four newest novels published each month.

You'll be guaranteed that you'll never miss a title, and home delivery is so convenient. And to show you just how easy it is to get Zebra Historical Romances, we'll send you your first 4 books absolutely FREE! Our gift to you just for trying our home subscription service.

BIG SAVINGS AND CONVENIENT HOME DELIVERY

Each month, you'll receive the four newest titles as soon as they are published. You'll probably receive them even before the bookstores do. What's more, you may preview these exciting novels free for 10 days. If you like them as much as we think you will, just pay the low preferred subscriber's price of $3.75 each. *You'll save $3.00 each month off the publisher's price.* (A postage and handling charge of $1.50 is added to each shipment.) Of course you can return any shipment within 10 days for full credit, no questions asked. There is no minimum number of books you must buy.

GET
FOUR
FREE
BOOKS
(AN $18.00 VALUE)

a rare man. "Then you would get on well with my father, for those are his sentiments as well."

Duncan laughed shortly as he saw Dover emerge on the horizon. Beyond that, the harbor waters shimmered, beckoning to him as the sea always did. "I do not know how well I would get on with him. I do not think he would take it lightly that I have brought his eldest daughter into danger."

Because they were almost there, she spurred her tired bay on.

"I think that he would not smile," she agreed readily, "but he would understand that you had no choice in the matter." Beth raised her eyes to his, a pleased smile lifting her lips. "I am my father's daughter, not my mother's."

Duncan could only nod. "I am truly looking forward to meeting the man."

With all her heart, Beth prayed that he would be able to.

Duncan dispatched Jacob to discover which ship was leaving across the Channel for France at the earliest scheduled departure. In the time it took to secure that information, Duncan ushered Beth to an inn, though Beth protested that she was neither hungry nor thirsty.

"Then you are even rarer a woman than I thought. But I am only a mortal man, and I require both if I am to continue on this journey."

So saying, he chose the closest inn that did not look as if it contained the dregs of seafaring society within it. Dressed as a young boy or not, even with her hair now fastened and tucked beneath a cap, Beth was most assuredly womanly in form, and he wanted no more battles upon his hands than were absolutely necessary.

He nodded at the man behind the bar as he entered the Boar and Cock and quickly ushered Beth to a table. When the barmaid drifted to their table, he ordered three full meals, keeping Jacob in mind.

"Hungry, are you?" the young woman asked knowingly.

The dirtied blouse she wore barely clung to the swell of her more than ample bosom. Her face was worn, her smile eager; and her eyes were swift to measure the length and breadth of Duncan. She found him well worth her trouble.

"I've ways of satisfying men with large—" her full mouth curved more, "appetites."

"Then you'd best be on your way, doing it," Beth said evenly. The woman turned to look at her haughtily. "Because his appetite will be satisfied by what he can find at this table." The look in Beth's eyes challenged the woman to say anything further.

Though she was clearly angered, the woman retreated. "Very well, I'll bring your supper."

She turned on her heel and stalked away.

Duncan lifted his tankard of ale to toast her. "Fighting to defend my honor, Beth?" Duncan asked, amused.

She pretended not to take note of his smug manner. "Merely assuring myself that I will leave with exactly what I entered with." She leaned closer, her voice lowered. "If your head can be turned by something like that, you're of no service to me."

He set his tankard down, his eyes on hers. "On the contrary, Beth, I think that I shall be of great service to you."

Beth knew he meant it in more ways than one.

Jacob found them before they were finished, to tell them that he had found a ship leaving within the hour. There would be no others for more than two days.

Hastily wrapping what remained, as well as Jacob's meal, they left the inn and made their way to a ship whimsically called the *Bard's Honor*.

They were to sea within the hour.

The crossing, with a strong wind to assist them, took a little more than a day, and went smoothly. Jacob looked overjoyed to be back upon the water, even for such a little while. And as for Duncan, Beth could see that he clearly loved being on deck, feeling the water's spray in his face as he leaned at the railing. He'd been standing there for hours and she couldn't help but wonder what he was thinking.

Was the sea a woman to him, with endless allure?

Beth joined Duncan and Jacob as they stood at the railing in comfortable silence. She studied Duncan for a moment. "You look as if you are reborn."

There was something about the sea that spoke to him. He knew he would always be half in love with it, though she could know no master. A little, he thought, like Beth. "Do I?"

"Yes." She leaned forward so as to get a better look at him. "Your eyes have the look about them of a man who has come home."

With a trace of nostalgia gliding through his veins, Duncan ran his hand along the railing. The salty air had eaten into it, and rather than feel smooth, it was full of tiny holes. Just like his own galleon had been.

"I spent five years more upon the sea than on the land." He shut his eyes as the wind feathered long fingers through his hair and dipped into his soul. When he opened them again, he looked down into Beth's up-turned face. "For some, that feeling of belonging to the sea never leaves."

"For some," she repeated. "Such as you?"

Enough of these feelings, he thought. He laughed softly.

"I can make my home anywhere I must. I am adaptable to many conditions." His past life attested to that. "I remember someone once standing over me in prison, after they had flogged me, and saying that I was too wicked to die."

Beth's mouth had dropped open. "Flogged you? In prison?"

He wondered if learning that he had been in prison changed her opinion of him.

"Does that shock you, Beth?" he asked, his voice soft. "That I was in prison?"

She weighed her words carefully. They mattered dearly, she realized, looking up into his eyes. Though he scornfully laughed at danger, she had already learned that the man's heart could be easily offended.

"It shocks me that anyone could capture you."

It was the right answer. His mouth curved. "I am mortal, Beth."

He took her hand into his and gently stroked it with his thumb. He could see desire flowering in her eyes. Just as it flowered in his soul.

"You have proved that, if nothing else." He brought her hand to his lips and kissed it softly, his eyes holding her prisoner, just as the Tower had once held him. Jacob had secured one cabin for them to take their rest. It was all the captain had to spare. "Will you go below with me?"

She wanted to, but now was not the time. She turned to look toward the other man at the rail. "Jacob—"

With the crook of his finger, Duncan brought her eyes back to his.

"—Knows only what I tell him, thinks only what I tell him to think." He saw the look blossoming on her face. She was taking offense for Jacob's sake. But it was not a matter of Jacob being a lackey. There was another reason for Duncan's words. "Jacob is an innocent, Beth. He sees the world through eyes only children are blessed with. There is no condemnation within them, or in his simple soul."

Perhaps not, she thought, glancing at Jacob again and receiving a wide smile in return. "But the captain will know."

The captain was on the other side of the ship and cared not about his passengers' affairs if they did not affect him. "Only if we tell him."

Still she resisted. Her heart was not free to join her body. Not when they were so close to her goal. "Duncan, I cannot."

He smiled as he toyed with the outline of her ear, brushing his fingers along it. "The last time you said those words, you did."

She sighed as she shook her head. She was weakening and had to struggle to keep her resolve. "You have a silver tongue."

His laugh was warm and lusty. "You would be the one to best know the texture of it."

Beth bit her lip. "Truly I am tempted, but—"

He took her hands and placed them against his chest. Against his heart.

"It is very tiring to try to resist temptation, Beth," he

told her solemnly. "Do not tire yourself out. You need your strength for the journey."

His persistence was tinged with amusement, as if it were a game, one he knew he would not win this round. "Laying with you does not create strength, Duncan, it takes it away."

He released her hands and pretended to sigh. "You've an answer for everything."

Except for these feelings I have for you, she thought helplessly.

"Very well, I shall let you win your argument this time." Standing behind her, he placed his hands on her shoulders. "But 'tis a lonely thing, being a winner, Beth. Sometimes, it is best to lose."

She closed her eyes, struggling. And losing.

"Land, Duncan," Jacob cried excitedly.

Beth's eyes flew open and she stood on her toes, peering over the railing. There was but mist for her to see.

"There always is, at the end of the sea," Duncan answered, with a resigned tone.

And what, he wondered, was at the end of his sea? He had never wondered before, never taken more than a moment at a time. Perhaps this was what came of being landlocked for so long, he thought. Suddenly eternity shimmered before you and your thoughts turned stale.

He looked at Beth's face and decided that perhaps his thoughts were not quite stale after all.

Chapter Twenty-four

Duncan could feel Beth's anxiety growing as she stood beside him on the dock. They were waiting for their horses to be brought off. The captain had at first refused to allow the horses on his ship. His mind had changed when he'd seen the color of the gold coins Duncan crossed his palm with.

The animals' passage had cost them dearly. But Duncan did not want to trust his fate, or that of Beth's and Jacob's, to horses he was not familiar with. Though he might grumble about the animal, his stallion was sure-footed and swift as the wind. Duncan had chosen two more horses of equal ability for Jacob and Beth.

Destiny was a difficult sea to navigate blindly, but he did what he could to prepare for this adventure that stretched before him, this adventure that involved a woman he had come quickly to regard as as necessary to him as the very air he took in.

After a young sailor coaxed the animals down the gangplank, Duncan slipped a coin into his hand. The dull eyes brightened and widened. The boy bowed. "Anything else, Your Grace?"

Duncan laughed. Clearly the boy had his titles confused. "There is nothing of grace about me, boy." Duncan looked past the boy's head at the vessel. "I was a captain once, on a ship three times this size." But it was better not to speak of those days. There were enemies still alive, enemies who harbored grudges and a need for revenge. "No," he said, "there is nothing else."

Duncan turned to Beth as he handed her the bay's reins. "Do you know the way to your father's house?"

She nodded. "I was there once, years ago."

His eyes narrowed. She had not mentioned that before. "How many years?"

She thought back. "Fourteen."

He looked at her, stunned. "You were a babe in arms," he scoffed.

She raised her chin in a gesture he now saw whenever he closed his eyes. "I was eight."

"And you remember," he mocked.

Her eyes did not waver from his. "I remember. Every path, every tree," she insisted willfully. "My grandmother's home is on the outskirts of Paris. The northern outskirts," she added, for good measure.

His skeptical look was replaced with concern. "That is the center of the trouble, Beth."

She nodded, their differences momentarily aside. "I know." She looked up at him, a troubled daughter, her heart heavy. "That is why I am so worried."

Duncan motioned Beth and Jacob away from the docks. It was not the most reputable of places and he wanted to put distance between them and the sailors who were milling about there.

"How long since you have heard from him?"

She had it down to the moment, but gave him a rounded answer. "His letters ceased arriving two months before I left Virginia."

The skeptical look returned for a different reason, perhaps her alarm was baseless. "That is not that much time, Beth." Perhaps letters had arrived after her departure.

She would have agreed with him had the times been different. "Without a revolution around it, no. But under the circumstances, there is much cause for concern. My father was a faithful writer. A letter or more came upon every ship that arrived in port. Without fail, Duncan. Without fail."

Duncan led the way from the harbor, his expression thoughtful as he turned toward Beth. She was in many ways an innocent still. And she did not know of the darker side of men, no matter what she professed.

He broached it as delicately as he could, knowing how well she loved the man. "Beth, perhaps he did not want to return."

Her eyes filled with anger at the insult. Then, just as quickly, her emotions simmered down. She shook her head as they left the town behind them. "You do not know my father, or you could not say that. He loves his wife and daughters, his home in Virginia, and the life he has made for himself there."

"Then why did he leave?" Duncan pressed.

"I have already told you that: to help. He is a selfless man," she said fiercely.

She would not believe that her father chose to lose himself, to desert his wife and family. That might be the way for other men, but not Philippe Beaulieu. Tears gathered in her throat, formed by fear.

"No, something has happened to him." She turned her eyes to Duncan. "I know it."

He reached across the pommel to place his hand reassuringly on hers for a moment. He believed that *she* believed what she said. Whether it was true was another matter, but he would act as if it was, until they discovered otherwise.

"Do not think on it until we know. Worry never helped a cause."

Beth knew he was right, but she could not help the thoughts that crowded in her mind, trying to win possession of her.

"It'll be all right, mistress," Jacob chimed in, unable to remain quiet in the face of her distress. His voice rose like that of a young skylark singing praises of the rising sun. "If anyone can find him, Duncan can."

Sometimes it was hard, Duncan thought, taking the lead. He smiled once more at Beth and prayed that the situation was not as black as he feared.

They journeyed more than two days to her grandmother's estate. Rather than look for proper shelter at an inn, they slept upon the road. Duncan felt it was safer that way, and Beth saw no reason to contradict him. She blessed the God who watched over her that He had formed her so differently from her sisters. Otherwise she could have not endured the hardships she faced.

When they arrived on the grounds of the Beaulieu estate on the morrow of the third day, Beth was appalled by what she saw. The sight warred with the treasured memory she had retained in her mind. Frayed around the edges, touched with nostalgia, the estate, in her memory, was a thousand times better in appearance than what she looked upon now. The grounds were sad and sagging, like an abandoned widow left to die alone, overrun with weeds and the poison of neglect. The building was in disrepair. This was not the house of sunshine her father had told her about and that Beth remembered.

Yet she knew that there was no mistake. This was her grandmother's house. There was much for her to recognize and grieve over.

"Are you sure you are not mistaken, Beth?" Duncan prodded. She had been, after all, a child the last time she had walked here.

She slowly shook her head, numbed.

"I'm sure." The words were a whisper, not from fear of being overheard, but from disappointment. "It looks so sad, so forgotten."

Her father could not be here, she thought. He would not have remained and let his birthplace look like this.

"Many lose the will to smile in a revolution," Duncan told her practically. He slid from his horse and handed the reins to Jacob, who was quick to jump down from his. "Jacob, I want you to remain here with the horses until I come for you."

His words dissolved the aura of sadness about her. She looked at Duncan from atop her horse. "We are not riding up to my grandmother's door?"

"It may not be your grandmother's any longer," he told her matter-of-factly. "And it may not be your grandmother who waits now within." He looked toward the house. He saw no one at the windows, no one on the grounds. But that did not mean it was empty. "I've heard that many of the mansions belonging to the aristocracy have been seized and now each house many families rather than one. If that is the case here, I do not want to alert whoever is within that we are approaching."

The thought of the house where her father was born, where he had spent so much of his youth, defiled in this manner appalled Beth and stirred her indignation. Quickly she dismounted and handed her reins to Jacob.

Duncan caught her arm before she could take a step forward. "I would rather that you remained here with Jacob."

She glared at him. Did he think he was going to stop her so close to the threshold, after she had come all this way? "And I would rather that you remembered that you are with me, not I with you."

The only way to win this argument would be to tie her up and he had no time for that, though the thought tempted him.

Duncan hissed through his teeth, "Very well, but be quiet."

Her temper was short. "I was not about to trumpet my entrance."

His concern for her welfare had his own temper cut in half. He struggled to keep his voice low. There was no knowing who might be within hearing. "With that mouth of yours, I can never be certain."

She opened her mouth, then shut it again. Arguing would not get them anywhere but at each other's throats, and they needed to be allies now, not opponents. She waved him on.

Softly they stole across the overgrown grounds and slipped up to the house. They made their way not to either door, but to a window that looked out upon an overgrown section of the once beautiful gardens, gardens Beth recalled roaming with her father and grandmother.

Her heart hurt just to look at them.

When Duncan approached the window, she looked at him with wonder. This was, after all, the home of her ancestors, and thus her home as well.

She placed a hand on his arm to stop him. "We are to enter like common thieves?"

His hands upon the casement, he stopped only long enough to answer. "There is nothing common about you, Beth, and we are not here to steal. I am doing this to guarantee our safety as best I can. Now, would you argue with me over every step?"

She sighed and shook her head. He was right.

Duncan eased the casement opened. His hands braced, he easily vaulted into the somber-looking house and completely disappeared from her view.

Beth's heart quickened. She looked over her shoulder to where they had left Jacob. But she saw neither Jacob nor the horses. They were well hidden. She might as well have been alone.

"Duncan?" she whispered urgently, rising up on her toes to peer inside. She saw only shadows. "Duncan, are you in?"

In reply, Duncan suddenly raised his head into the window, startling her. "Well, I'm certainly not without, now, am I?"

This was no time for humor. "Give me your hands, you frightened me."

"Why?" With strong arms, Duncan swiftly pulled her inside the house. "Did you think something had happened to me? Were you worried?" The thought entertained him greatly.

She refused to give him the satisfaction he sought. "No, I was afraid I would have to rescue you." She rested her hand on the hilt of the pistol that she had sheathed in the belt at her waist. "And that would take up more precious time."

She took her first look around the room in fourteen years and grew silent. It was the library. There was a mournful layer of gray upon everything, as if nothing had been touched for a long, long time.

Without knowing, she placed her hand on Duncan's arm. "Do you think it's been abandoned?"

He lifted one shoulder and let it drop. "It has that look about it."

It didn't make any sense to her. "But my father arrived here more than eight months ago. He should be here now." She looked around as if searching for something that would prove her wrong, that it hadn't been abandoned. Only darkness met her gaze, despite the sun that shone without. "He would not allow it to deteriorate to this extent. He often told me that this was his favorite room."

Duncan moved slowly about the room. The outer door, leading to a hall, he presumed, was closed. "Perhaps he had no say in the matter. Perhaps he was not free to do what he wished."

Beth swallowed, knowing what Duncan was delicately skirting around. This was not the time for niceties, only the truth.

"You think he is a prisoner, don't you?"

He spread his hands slightly. "Or in hiding. The highborn are not loved here these days."

"But he came to help." How could anyone want to harm a man like her father?

Duncan draped his arm around her shoulders and pulled her to him, offering comfort.

"Madmen with a cause do not listen to simple words, Beth. They claim to hear a voice no one else hears." He had come up against a few in his time, but they were of a singular bent. Here, in France, there were bands of men like that. Duncan felt his blood run cold. "They

cannot have their hearing cluttered by logic and reason."
He looked down at her face. "Or goodness."

Beth looked slowly around the shadow enshroud
room. "Do you think that he is—?"

"Dead?" Duncan whispered softly.

She could not bring herself to form the word, but
merely nodded.

"No." It was a lie, but for a good cause. "Come, let
us move softly through the house and see what there is
to discover."

So saying, he pushed her behind him as the door began to open.

Chapter Twenty-five

The door opened very slowly, as if the person on the other side was hesitant to see what was within the room. The woman in the doorway was dressed in black from head to toe. It made her fragile frame appear only more so. Her slight shoulders were stooped with age and the oppressive weight of sorrow. Her white hair was wispy, and what there was of it was pulled back in a tight twist she wore fastened close to her scalp. It made her head appear almost skeletal.

There was not fear in her eyes, but outrage. The sound of her voice surprised them, for instead of cracking, it was full-bodied and angry. The words she shouted at the intruders she saw were in her native tongue and full of indignity.

The old woman shuffled forward, ready to do what little harm to them she could with the cane she leaned upon, the cane her nephew had brought her as a gift.

"Be gone. Out with you, vultures. We are not dead yet!" she cried in French.

She wielded the cane like a sword and caught Duncan about the shoulder and head as he moved quickly to shield Beth.

"By God, what matter of old crones do they grow here?" Duncan cried as he lifted his hands before his face. The woman countered by hitting him soundly across the ribs.

"Thief, cutthroat, away with you and yours!" the woman cried breathlessly in her native tongue.

The bit of light that was struggling in through a tear in the draperies shone on the head of the cane. Beth recognized it as the one her father had had especially made for his aunt. She had seen him pack that very cane in his trunk before departing.

"Aunt Cosette!" she cried out, as she stepped away from the shelter of Duncan's body.

Her arm raised to strike again, the old woman stopped abruptly at the sound of her name. Thin brows drew shrewdly together and she cocked her head like a bird examining the ground. She lowered the cane to the floor, then turned toward the window. With small steps, she arrived at her destination and pulled the draperies back. There was only silence in the room.

The silence, Beth thought, of the dead.

Cosette returned to the two in her library and examined the girl closely. Her small, dark eyes squinted, as if that would somehow rouse a memory for her and resurrect it.

The girl before her looked the way her sister had, almost three-quarters of a century ago.

Beth took a step forward. Duncan laid a restraining hand on her shoulder. He nodded at Cosette's cane. "I'd mind that stick, if I were you."

But Beth only smiled and stretched out her hand in greeting. "'Tis I, Aunt Cosette. Elizabeth."

The eyes that looked upon her were blank for a moment. Perhaps what had happened here had been so hard on her, it had wiped her great-aunt's memory away with it, Beth thought in despair.

"Elizabeth?" the old woman repeated between dried, thin lips. She said the name as if it was completely unknown to her.

Beth could feel her heart beating wildly in her breast. *"Oui."*

Duncan felt the end of his patience drawing near. It was obvious that the old woman didn't recognize Beth or her name. "Beth, what the bloody blazes is going on? I don't understand a word of their language."

The old woman raised her eyes slowly to his face. Rather than appear vacant, Duncan knew that he was looking into eyes that had seen too much, eyes within a woman who had lived too long.

Cosette inclined her head regally. "Then I shall speak in yours," she replied, a queen making a concession for a peasant. Cosette looked at Duncan rather than Beth. "You are not part of the Revolution."

It was not a question. She could differentiate him from the marauders. There was a scent to them, a wild look that was burned into her mind.

"No, madam, I am not." Now that he was no longer the recipient of her expertly wielded cane, Duncan bowed graciously. He took the gnarled hand into his and pressed a kiss to it as he raised his eyes to her face. "Duncan Fitzhugh, at your service."

The gesture pleased her. She always demanded and appreciated courtliness. Cosette smiled as she withdrew her hand.

She turned her eyes to her grandniece. "You have brought a charmer with you, I see." Then, with tears shimmering in her eyes, Cosette enfolded the girl in her arms. "Oh, you should not be here, but it is wonderful to see you one last time, Elizabeth." She pressed a kiss to her hair.

Beth placed both hands beseechingly on the woman's arm. It felt as if she was holding onto a mere bone. "Aunt Cosette, where is my father?"

Cosette sighed deeply. She could feel her heart breaking a little more within her thin chest just at the mere thought of that day. The day her fine nephew had been dragged away. If it were not for the fact that the vile scum were waiting for her to die, she would have gladly done so. She had seen enough of life, and she was tired. It had been a long life, and until the last few years, a life that had pleased her well. But to see her country torn this way, to see the destruction of so many things she had held precious, wounded her mortally, as it did her older sister.

Cosette felt the tears gathering in her eyes and willed them away. Tears were for the young and the weak. She was neither.

"Taken," she told them.

The word throbbed within her head. Beth exchanged a look with Duncan, afraid of what she was hearing, afraid of what it meant.

"Taken?" she repeated.

Cosette nodded heavily.

Duncan placed his hand on the woman's arm to gain her attention. "By whom?"

Cosette's pinched mouth twisted as she remembered the various titles they had bandied about.

"The 'friends of the people,' the 'enemies of the Crown.' " She shrugged helplessly. "Make your choice, they have many names they call themselves." Darkness entered her eyes as she spat out, "Assassins all." Her voice choked within her throat as emotion gripped it. "What have they done to my France?"

The woman's shoulders shuddered once, as if she were about to cry. Then they straightened slightly as she attempted to pull them erect again. But they would never be the way they once had been.

And neither would France.

"Grandmère?" Beth inquired hesitantly, afraid of the answer.

The smile was sad. "She is upstairs," Cosette assured her. "She never leaves her room anymore. I do what I can for her, but there is not much to do but wait, now."

They would want to see for themselves, Cosette thought and that was good. It had been a long time since Denise had had any company but hers.

"Come, I shall take you to her."

Cosette turned slowly, painfully, and retraced her small steps to the door. When Duncan offered her his arm, she took it gladly, but with the grace that befitted her station in life.

"It has been some time since we have had any visitors to talk to." She smiled at Duncan, and he could see, beneath the lines and leathery face, the handsome young woman she had once been. "It is a very unpopular thing to speak to the likes of someone like me."

Bitterness entered the old woman's voice as she remembered an incident from a week ago. "Women who would not have even dared touch the hem of my skirt now spit on the ground behind my back as I pass by them on the streets of Paris."

Duncan stopped at the foot of the long, twisting staircase. "You go out?"

The thin shoulders rose and fell carelessly. "Once in a while, I must." The look in her eyes challenged not him, but those who would dare to oppose her right. "And it is my city as much as theirs. More," she said fiercely. "We can trace our line back to the Crusades and Charlemagne. How far back can the scum go? It was formed but yesterday in the gutters."

Cosette shook her head reprovingly, hatred squeezing her heart in two.

She placed one hand on the banister, the other upon her cane. Duncan was tempted to lift her into his arms and carry the woman up, but he knew that while a ready arm was deemed gracious behavior, carrying her as if she was too feeble to walk would offend her delicate honor. The woman had nothing but pride left.

With measured steps, he walked slowly behind her. Beth trailed behind them, her heart bleeding at the sight of all this, yet warmed even in the midst by Duncan's thoughtfulness.

When they finally gained the top of the stairs, a long hallway stretched out before them. All was empty, all was solemn.

"Where are all your servants?" Duncan asked.

"Gone. Fled." She waved one hand dismissively in the air, before placing it once more on his arm. "They are cowards all." Her face softened. "Save Therese, who finds a way to smuggle food to us, despite the risks involved. But even she has not been here for a week," Cosette told them sadly. It was clear that she was worried about the woman. "It is not safe to help us. We are considered enemies as well."

Struggling, eschewing help, she opened the double doors and pushed them both aside. With dignity marking every step, she walked into the large, airless bedroom. There was a huge four-poster in the center.

Within it lay a small woman, dwarfed by the size of the bed.

Cosette laughed shortly. "This old woman and I, we are enemies to be feared." She shook her head at the nonsense.

"Cosette? Cosette, who is there?" Beth's grandmother called out feebly, in French.

Cosette moved forward and looked down upon the face of the woman she had loved for more than seventy years. "Elizabeth is here, Denise. Philippe's daughter."

Shock outlined the small, pale face framed by two long, thin white braids. Denise's hand groped the air futilely, searching for a hand to touch.

"Elizabeth?"

Cosette inclined her head toward Beth, "She cannot see," she whispered discreetly.

Her heart bleeding, Beth drew closer to the bed and fell to her knees beside her grandmother. She took the fragile hand reverently in hers and pressed a kiss to the translucent skin.

"Right here, *Grandmère.*"

The old woman felt the tears that were staining her hand. Very gently, she felt along the girl's face, trying to see her in her mind's eye. Blindness was only the last of a long line of indignities she had been made to suffer these last five years.

"You have grown to be beautiful. No, no tears, little one," she chided. "But why have you come here? It is not safe. Not safe."

Sorrow clawed at Beth's throat, but she forced the tears back for her grandmother's sake. "I've come for Father."

The old lips trembled as Denise fought back tears of her own. Too much, it took too much from her. She could not cry now, for she would fall asleep. And every moment lost to sleep was a moment closer to everlasting eternity. She did not want to leave Cosette to bear this all on her own.

The words were barley audible. "You are too late."

Beth's great-aunt had said he'd been taken. "Where did they take him, do you know?" Duncan asked urgently, as he stepped forward.

Denise turned her head at the sound of a new voice. "Who is this?"

"A young man who has come with Elizabeth," Cosette explained tactfully.

"Duncan Fitzhugh, Madam Beaulieu." Duncan touched Denise's hand.

She grasped it and his heart was heavy at the feeble strength he felt there. Her hold on life was but a thin thread now, he thought. He knelt beside the bed and allowed the old woman to glide her fingertips along his face.

"A fine man. A strong man," Denise pronounced, satisfied with what her hands saw. She dropped them to her side. "Your husband?" she asked Beth.

"Her protector," Duncan informed her easily, sparing Beth the awkwardness of attempting to explain why they were here together.

"Then you have your work cut out for you, monsieur," Denise said quietly. "For there is much here to protect her from." She turned her head in Beth's direction, and urgent expression on her worn face. "Go back, Elizabeth, go back."

Chapter Twenty-six

Her grandmother's softly voiced entreaty hung in the air between them, but Beth could not find it in her heart to obey.

"I cannot leave without Father," Beth told her.

Denise moved her head from side to side. "Stubborn, just like Philippe. I told him to leave, but he would not heed my words, either. And now," tears choked the very words from her, "it is too late."

Duncan looked from the frail woman in the bed to the one at his elbow. Of the two, he knew that Cosette would have the sharper mind. He asked his question once more, hoping this time to receive an answer.

"Do you know where they took him?"

Cosette could not tell him and her helplessness angered her.

"No. I have attempted to discover that, but I can find no one who knows." Cosette drew herself up as if to brace herself against the mere memory of that day. "The rabble came to our door one morning at dawn almost four months ago. Robespierre was at their head." Her mouth twisted as if she had tasted an unripened apple.

"The evil spawn of Satan seized my good nephew,

saying that he was to stand trial for his family's crimes against the people. Crimes." Her voice shook as she repeated the word. "It is *they* who are guilty of crimes, not we. We have done nothing against them."

Her eyes grew darker still. "The servants were given a choice of joining the Revolution, or going with Philippe." She struggled to keep her voice from breaking. "Andre chose to go with him. Robespierre ran Andre through with a sword before my eyes."

"Andre?" Duncan asked.

He restrained his inclination to draw the old woman into his arms and give her comfort. He knew she would surely lose the last of her strength if he did, and he could not strip her of that. So he remained where he was, and ached for her grief.

"Our steward," Denise replied, her voice filled with pity, with tears. "He had been with the family since my wedding day, oh, so many years ago." She sighed deeply, mourning the loss. "He should have not said what he did, but gone with the rest. Andre was a foolish, foolish old man."

Cosette waved a tired hand at the memory, at all the memories that crowded her mind, fervently wishing them gone.

"Now he is a dead foolish old man." Her eyes turned toward Duncan. "As they hope we will both soon be. They left us alive, my sister and me, hoping that we would starve to death."

She raised her chin proudly, and Duncan immediately thought of Beth.

"So far, we have not." Cosette looked from Duncan to Beth. "There is not much to offer you, but what we have, we will gladly—"

"No." Duncan was quick to silence the old woman

before her offer was completed. "Thank you, but we could not take a morsel from you, Madam Beaulieu," he took Denise's hand in his. "It was a pleasure meeting you."

"You are leaving?" she asked, pleased that he at least was heeding her advice after all and would surely be taking her granddaughter away with him.

"For a moment only." He took a step toward the door, aware that Beth had risen to her feet and was watching him intently. "Stay here, Beth," he cautioned when she crossed to him. "Jacob and I will go into Paris—"

Oh, no, she was not about to be left behind like so much baggage to be discarded at will. "If you leave, I will go with you."

She would only get in the way. He and Jacob could move more stealthfully without her.

"A little hunting venture, Beth, that's all." He saw that she was waiting for more. "I want to see for myself what there is to see and how the winds of war are blowing."

But Beth was not so ready to let him out of her sight. If there were dangers for her, they existed for him as well. And he had a further disadvantage. "You said you did not even speak the language."

That was not altogether true. He smiled at her confidently. "I know a few words."

And she knew exactly what words they were. "*Je t'aime* will not help you get by," she retorted knowingly, her hands upon her hips.

Duncan saw the way she fingered the hilt of her pistol and laughed. "Who knows? Perhaps Robespierre's first lieutenant is a woman."

"Then I will cut her heart out," Beth assured him. "One piece at a time."

"Stop, Beth, you are frightening me." He winked, then brushed a kiss quickly to her cheek. He noted that her great-aunt was watching them in reserved silence. "There are ways of gathering information that do not always involve long, flowing words. I am not a babe in the wood, Beth. Streets are streets and men with dark hearts and dark secrets are the same whether they speak English or French."

He saw the concern in her eyes and it pleased him. So she did care a little. "I shall return by dusk, I promise."

If something happened to him because of her, she would never be able to forgive herself. Beth bit her lip. "And what if you do not—?"

If they had not been in the presence of her great-aunt and her grandmother, he would have swept her in his arms and reassured her with a kiss instead of words.

"I will not leave you here alone, Beth." Duncan touched his hand to hers to seal the bargain. "That I swear to you."

Beth watched with a heavy heart as he kissed her great-aunt's hand and slipped out of the room. Worry became her pitiless companion even before his footsteps faded down the hall.

Beth forced herself not to think of all the things that could befall him while he was away from her. Instead, she looked upon her grandmother again. The old woman looked so lost within the bed, like a tiny drop of blood upon a snowbank.

Beth placed her hand upon her great-aunt's. Cosette's slanted toward her.

"What is being done for her?" Beth whispered.

Cosette shrugged helplessly. "She is eighty-six, Elizabeth. What *can* be done for her?"

The question only reinforced what Beth feared in her heart. "She is dying?"

Cosette knotted together her long, thin fingers before her. In her mind were many scenes. She remembered best when she and Denise were young. Her most treasured memory was the first ball their father had taken them to, and how they'd danced the evening away. The memory made the answer that much more painful.

"Yes."

Was there a sickness that was afflicting her grandmother? A disease, perhaps, something she could try to treat? "Why?"

It was a foolish question asked by the young of the old, Cosette thought, but she answered patiently. The child had come a long way and endangered herself because she still had ideals.

"*Because* she is eighty-six."

Cosette saw that Denise had fallen asleep. She leaned over her sister and tucked one cold hand beneath the covers, then lovingly adjusted them about the fragile body. It was summer, but somehow it felt cold. It always felt cold these days.

"Because her heart is broken," she continued in a whisper. "Because the France she knew has died, and her only son has been taken prisoner and perhaps died as well." She turned to look at her grandniece. "There are many reasons."

Cosette spread her hands airily, like thin, denuded branches swaying in a storm. "Which reason would you prefer?"

Beth drew her shoulders back. "I would prefer that she was not dying."

"Yes." Cosette nodded and pressed her lips together to hold back a sob that had risen to surprise her. "So would I." She adjusted the covers once more, though there was no need. "I will be alone when she goes."

Beth laid her hand on the old woman's arm. "Never again," she vowed softly. "Not while I am alive."

Cosette placed her hand over Beth's and smiled as she drew comfort from the young girl's warmth.

Dusk swept over the grounds with a dusty straw broom, covering everything in gray.

Beth looked out the window for the dozenth time. She was very near to leaving her mind. Where was he?

The question repeated itself endlessly in her mind like the stubborn staccato of the rain when it beat against a windowpane. But there was no rain now, no reason given by nature for his delay.

Only one, she thought, created by man.

"He will come," Cosette told her knowingly. "Your young man seems very capable to me."

Beth turned from the window and attempted to seem carefree. She was not successful, even in her estimation. "He is."

Cosette rocked slowly in her chair, the chair she spent most of her evenings in now. "But yet you worry."

"Yes."

Cosette sighed. "I understand. Capable or not, it makes no difference these days." Her face contorted with the memory of that morning. "They come and they come and they come and still there is no end, no rescue." She looked into the empty hearth as if she saw the ghost of flames there. "They come until we are no more."

There was a noise at the back door and Beth's pulse began to drum.

"What—?" Cosette began, her hands gripping the arms of her chair as she moved to rise.

Beth motioned her aunt to be silent as she listened for the sounds. Someone was entering the house through the kitchen. She drew out her pistol and slowly cocked it. But she could only fire once, and there might be more than one of them. Quickly, she caught up a poker from the fireplace and only wished that it was glowing red-hot.

Her breath lodged within her throat, Beth whispered, "Stay here," to Cosette and stole quietly out to the kitchen. Before she entered, Beth saw shadows upon the wall. There were two.

With a cry, she leaped into the room, ready to fire upon the first who would make a move toward her.

Her knees felt weak with relief. "Duncan!"

The look of surprise on his face quickly melted into amusement. He gently nudged the muzzle of her pistol away from him and looked respectfully at the poker. "Were you thinking of running me through with that?"

She placed the poker upon the wooden table. Though her heart was glad to see him, she looked at Duncan accusingly for he had startled her.

"I thought you were some of the rabble, breaking in." She glanced toward the parlor where she had left her aunt. "The stories my great-aunt and *grandmère* have been telling me have brought a chill to my blood."

Duncan could well imagine what they might have said. "And they probably don't know the half of it. It is just as I've heard, and worse."

But he did not want to talk of what was befalling the countryside tonight. There was time enough for that tomorrow. Tonight there were stomachs to fill.

"Here."

Duncan and Jacob opened the cloaks they held before them. Beth's eyes grew wide as she saw what tumbled out onto the table.

She looked at Duncan in wonder. "Where did you find all this?"

Jacob grinned foolishly at her as he bent to pick up the potatoes that had fallen to the floor.

Duncan shrugged carelessly, though he took pleasure in her look of amazement.

"We collected a little here, a little there. Surviving in the streets is not something that easily leaves you just because you have on a pair of polished boots."

Cosette entered the kitchen, drawn by the sound of Beth's voice. There were no angry shouts, no sound of a pistol being discharged. That meant, hopefully, that there was no thief here, but only Duncan returning, as he had promised.

Her eyes grew as wide as her niece's when she looked at the table.

"A goose, a chicken, vegetables. Carrots," she declared in wonder, as her hand passed over each item in turn. Cosette whispered the last as reverently as if she had said "rubies."

She looked at Duncan in amazement. "How did you find all of this?"

There was pride in Beth's eyes as she turned toward Cosette. "He has a talent."

Duncan shrugged it away. "I do not like being invited to supper unless I can bring something to add to the meal." He looked at the old woman's joy and it heartened him, wiping away some of the sorrowful scenes he had witnessed today. "I am invited to supper, am I not?"

She would have gladly married him if it had come down to that. "To supper and breakfast, and as many meals as you like." She caressed the goose as if it were a beloved friend come to visit.

"Oh, we'll have such a feast tonight!" Cosette promised gleefully, as giddy as a young girl once more. She turned and looked at the others. "Out of my kitchen, all of you," she ordered, tapping her cane on the floor. "I will call you when it is ready."

Beth looked at the old woman in surprise. She did not want to leave her to face all this work. "I did not know you could cook."

"Young ladies in my time were taught to do many things." Cosette regarded the pistol at Beth's side. "Of course, we had no knowledge of pistols, but that was a different time than now." She rallied from memories past and present. "Go, go!" Cosette shooed her out.

Duncan took Beth's arm and led her to the hall. "You were wonderful," Beth told Duncan.

He laughed and held her to him. "Ah, finally I am acknowledged for my true worth."

She hesitated, but she had to know. "Did you find out anything?"

He looked past her head toward the kitchen and watched the old woman working happily. "Much more than I wanted to know."

The breath caught in her throat. "About my father?" Beth pressed.

She looked to Jacob, for she could read his expression more readily than Duncan's. But there was nothing there for her to see.

"No, not yet." Duncan draped an arm around her shoulders. It felt good just to have her close. He inhaled deeply of the scent that always seemed to cling to her and felt himself renewed, cleansed. It would always be this way, he thought. "But I will return there in the morning, never fear."

"*We* will return," Beth insisted, lest he forget that she had a right to be there as well.

Impatience creased his brow. "I do not want to argue about this, Beth."

She nodded, pleased. "Good, then it is settled. I am going."

Duncan struggled with his patience, knowing that it would always be this way with Beth, one moment good and a hundred moments spent in aggravation. He arched his brow as he saw Jacob laugh behind his hand.

Duncan waved him on his way. "Go chop some wood for the old woman, Jacob. She'll have need of it. For God sakes man, make yourself useful to her." Jacob was already on his way. "And mind she's not to carry anything heavier than a carrot," Duncan called after him.

"Aye, Duncan," Jacob threw over his shoulder, as he hurried into the kitchen.

Beth placed a hand on his arm. "You are a good man, Duncan."

He smiled and winked. "Perhaps later, I will show you how good."

"In my grandmother's house?" she pretended to be shocked.

"In any house at all." He leaned and whispered in her ear. "And soon, Beth, soon, for I have great need of you."

Beth felt a warm shiver travel down her spine.

Chapter Twenty-seven

Duncan had not wanted to eat nearly as much as he did, but Cosette had urged food on him with the solemnity of a mother trying to fatten up her starving child.

Finally, he could eat no more. He pushed himself from the table with both hands and looked at her with a contented, sleepy-eyed manner of one who had eaten far more than his fill.

"The meal, *mademoiselle,* was heavenly."

Cosette inclined her head and took the praise as her due. But Beth could see there was a special glow in her eyes, one lit in response to Duncan's courtliness. It had been a long time since kindly words had been tendered to this dear old woman, Beth thought in sorrow.

"Yes, and the provider was heaven sent." She leaned over her grandniece to squeeze Duncan's hand.

Cosette looked over the dishes spread out on the table in the dining hall. She had taken a serving to her sister earlier, and they had all eaten well, but there was still much that remained.

"This is the most I have had on my table since before poor Philippe was taken from us." She wiped her lips delicately and then sighed as she folded the treasured napkin in her lap. She appeared annoyed at her own lapse. "But I am making noises like a bitter old woman." She looked at the circle of young faces around her, the sum of whom probably did not begin to equal her age. "I am, you know, but there is no point in making the noises to attest to that before the young."

She laid the napkin on the table and moved her chair back. Her eyes held Beth's.

"You have, God willing, a future before you. I have nought but the past." She raised her chin proudly, lifting the head that would never be bowed. "Which they cannot take from me. So, if you will excuse me, I will look in once more upon my sister and then this tired old woman is going to bed."

She struggled to her feet, leaning heavily upon her cane, eschewing the hand that Beth offered her.

Duncan rose quickly to his feet and indicated with his eyes that Jacob should follow suit, which Jacob did after an awkward moment.

Duncan bowed slightly upon Cosette's passing. "Good night, *mademoiselle*. Jacob and I will take turns standing watch."

His words brought a smile to her lips. "Then I sleep well tonight." With spidery fingers, she touched his cheek. "Thank you for all you have done." She glanced toward her grandniece. "And for all that you will do."

Cosette moved slowly out, like a shadow receding upon the wall.

Beth rose as well. "I will see if she needs anything," she told Duncan, as she hurried after the old woman.

Duncan nodded, then turned toward his companion. There was the business of details to see to. "Jacob, the table needs clearing, and it appears that there are but two of us left."

Jacob pouted slightly as he gathered Duncan's meaning. His small, bright eyes looked about the table sadly. He was more than happy to forage for the food and eat it, but to clear away the remains was another story entirely, and one not to his liking.

He raised his eyes to Duncan's face. "We should have brought a woman with us," he muttered.

Duncan looked over his shoulder toward the doorway through which Beth had gone only a moment before.

"We did." He laughed at the very thought. "But she would be no more inclined to do this sort of thing than you or I, Jacob."

Jacob heartily agreed. That was why he had bemoaned their not having brought someone with them to begin with. He could not envision Beth about a menial task such as cleaning.

Resigned, he gathered up the empty plates, stacking them carefully. He need not be told that they were delicate. "She is different, is she not? The mistress, I mean, not the old one."

Like a man with molasses in his veins instead of blood, Duncan slowly placed one dish upon another, his mind elsewhere. "So different, Jacob, that I do not even know where to begin to address the matter."

"But you like her," Jacob prodded, like a child who wanted to hear aloud the answer he already knew to be true. He scooped up the dishes and, bracing them against his breast, carried the lot of them into the kitchen.

If there were cats about, Duncan thought, shaking his head, they would be following Jacob about for the better part of the evening, just for the chance to run their coarse tongues along his shirt.

Duncan looked into the patient eyes and nodded. "Yes, Jacob, I like her."

Jacob stopped, three feet shy of the kitchen table. "A lot?"

Duncan pointed a finger at the work. "Scrub the pot for Mademoiselle Delacroix the way you would if Amy was here, and ask me no more questions I do not fully know the answers to myself."

The meandering reply puzzled Jacob. Duncan was always so straightforward with him and the others. Could it really be that he did not know?

"I like her a great deal," Jacob volunteered, his grin splitting his face in two.

"That is easy." Duncan clapped his hand on Jacob's back. "She has not railed at you."

"Yes," Jacob's voice was sad as he agreed. Amy had told him that if you aroused a woman's temper, you aroused her heart as well. "I know."

Her grandmother was already asleep when Beth and Cosette tiptoed in. Beth removed the tray, then left it in the hall as she accompanied her grandaunt to the latter's room. The old woman was tired, and Beth felt guilty at having kept her up so long.

"No, no, my child, it has been wonderful to speak with someone, with *something* other than shadows and memories. There was a time when I could have stayed up and talked to you until dawn, but those days are gone." She shuffled about the bed and with practiced moves, turned it down. "Now, I fear I must to bed, lest I do you the insult of falling asleep in the middle of one of your words. Good night, my dear. Sleep the sleep of the just."

With that, Cosette eased her door closed.

Beth stood for a moment, staring at the dark wooden door as if transfixed. She felt far too restless to go to the room her great-aunt had provided for her.

It was not worry for their immediate safety that pricked at her, but a despair for all that had happened here. Like a ghost, she roamed the hallway, examining portraits of ancestors whose names she did not know. Ancestors who would be as shamed as her great-aunt by the events that were transpiring.

Her father had spent many a night sitting upon her bed as the hour grew late, telling her tales of his childhood home in lieu of a fairy tale. He told her how beautiful it was. Eventually, her grandmother's house became almost like an enchanted land for Beth. And since she had seen it for herself when she was young, the magic was not dispelled.

It was now.

Now, it reminded her of the castle in the story of the sleeping princess, overgrown with brambles and weeds. And though it was not a witch who was responsible for the curse, the people who *had* caused all this to happen were far more frightening to Beth than any witch could be.

Beth sighed as she crossed the long, somber hallway once more, treading lightly so as not to wake the two old women. Restlessness stirred within her to even a higher pitch. She silently made her way past her room and to the backstairs.

She took care to make no noise as she descended.

Jacob had his back to Beth as she carefully eased by him in the kitchen. He heard nothing, grumbling softly to himself as he placed dishes into the water he had fetched from the well.

For a moment, she hesitated when she saw what he was about. This was her grandmother's house, and she should be the one doing what Jacob was occupied with. But needs greater than duty tugged at her.

She was not in the mood for conversation, even with a soul as simple and good as Jacob. For the moment, Beth wished to be alone with her thoughts and the ghosts of times gone by.

Quietly, she opened the back door and slipped into the garden.

Here and there, in the moonlight, she saw that a rose still bloomed upon bushes that were sagging. But by and large, the bushes had all either been trampled or cut away by cruel, hateful hands belonging to envious souls.

She thought of the rabble who had come here to seize her father and had killed the old servant as if he were nothing more than another flower in their path.

"Was it frightening for you, Father?" she whispered to the dark. "I wish I could have been here with you, to help defend you."

It was a foolish wish, she knew, but she was full of foolish wishes tonight. She wished for the power to save her father. She wished for a magical event that could make everyone lay down their arms and take up the plow in harmony.

Most of all, she wished for the tranquility she had known as a child, with her father by her side to guide her every step.

Beth felt tears weighing heavily on her lids, and since she was alone, she let them come, hoping to purge herself of this oppressive feeling of despair that was threatening to seize her.

* * *

He couldn't find her.

Duncan fully expected Beth to be in her room when he went upstairs. He had spent many precious minutes securing the house and checking the security of the windows. His mind was as much at rest as it could be, given the circumstances. He made his way to Beth's room, anticipating the faint scent of her perfume filling his senses.

The room was empty, untouched.

Since Beth was as unpredictable as any woman he had ever known, Duncan thought perhaps that she had taken the initiative and gone to his room. Smiling to himself, he hurried down the hall in the opposite direction.

But that room was empty, too.

His heart quickened. Perhaps she was still with her aunt or grandmother. Hoping that was the case, he listened intently as he passed before the rooms of the two old women, nestled together like two morning doves on a branch. He heard not a word. Though he loathed to disturb them, it was necessary.

Candle in hand, he opened the door to Beth's grandmother's room. The woman was asleep in her bed. There was no one else in the room. Quietly, he eased the doors shut once more, then went to the other.

Holding his breath, he eased the doors open a crack. Cosette surprised him by being on the other side, her hand on the doorknob. Her hearing still excellent, alerted by the sounds in the hall and room next to hers, she had gotten out of bed and was at the door when he opened it.

"Yes?"

He could not have been more surprised than if she had sprung up at him. Duncan took a breath to steady himself. "Pardon, mademoiselle, I did not wish to disturb you."

She looked at him shrewdly. "That is obvious, since you did not knock."

He did not want to alarm her, and said simply, "I am looking for Beth," as if he had merely lost his way within the intricate pattern of the house.

She had known his blood was hot the moment she had looked at him.

"Why, she is in her room, of course. Asleep, I trust," she said pointedly.

"Of course." Duncan nodded, already easing his way out. "Good night, mademoiselle. A thousand pardons. Sleep well."

The old head bobbed in acknowledgment as Duncan closed the door. "And you do the same," she advised softly. Then she chuckled to herself, something she had not done in more years than she could remember.

Where the devil had that woman gotten to? he wondered, crossing to the end of the hall. In frustration, he laid his hands upon the sill of the window that looked down at the deserted garden.

That was when he saw the slight form moving about the bushes.

Duncan's instincts were well honed from his years upon the London streets. His hand went to the hilt of the weapon that was never far from his side. He squinted, looking about the garden for signs that there were more than one about. He dared not lift the casement for fear of alerting the intruder.

There seemed to be only the one.

But there were many shadows in the garden, and he could well be mistaken.

Swiftly, Duncan took the backstairs two at a time. "Be on your guard, Jacob," he warned softly, as he went to the back door.

Jacob needed no more to silently lay aside the pot in his hands and to take up his sword.

Chapter Twenty-eight

Beth started at the sound and turned to see the drawn sword. She gasped as she saw the moonlight gleaming on the long blade. The next moment, recognition set in as the man brandishing the sword stepped out of the shadows.

"Duncan!"

Duncan did not know whether to hug her to his breast or give her the benefit of the back of his hand soundly across her posterior.

" 'Tis the mistress," Jacob crowed, a hooting laugh punctuating his words.

He put up his own sword and shook his head as if it was a grand joke on them all. But Duncan still had his extended.

"I do not think you need arm yourself against her, Duncan," Jacob prodded helpfully.

"Then you are most heartily mistaken." After a moment, Duncan sheathed his sword. "Return to the house, Jacob. You have the first watch at the front door. I will come in two hours to relieve you."

Jacob nodded, glad to be of the kind of use he was

accustomed to. This cleaning up was something he found far too demeaning.

There were many who thought him simple-minded, but Jacob knew when to withdraw his sword and when to withdraw his presence. This was such a time, even if he was not standing watch. He smiled at the two people before him.

"Aye, Duncan. Good night, mistress." He bowed grandly before her. "Pleasant dreams."

"The same to you, Jacob," she murmured at his retreating back.

Alone, Duncan gave vent to his anxiety. He grasped Beth by the shoulders with his steely hands, suppressing the urge to shake her. She had given him a turn or two, disappearing like that.

"What the devil are you doing here?"

She looked at him defiantly. Though he was here because of her, that gave him no authority over her, no right to order her about or question her actions.

"Walking."

Duncan knew that look. The woman was spoiling for another fight, and he was not. He released her. "I hunted the house for you."

She waved a hand and turned her back on him. "You had but to look out the window. I have been here all the—" Beth stopped and turned to look at Duncan, caught by the meaning in his words. "You hunted for me?"

"Yes." She had given him a start when he could not find her, and he meant to take her to task for that, for causing him anxiety, for being someone who caused him anxiety. He wished for his feelings to be free again, not entangled as they were.

If wishes were horses, beggars would ride, he remembered.

"And frightened your great-aunt in the process, I might add, as I prowled about."

Had he truly been worried about her, the way she had about him? she wondered. Her temper was suddenly at rest as her heart took over.

"I doubt that." She smiled sadly. "She is not easily frightened, that one; she has seen too much." Beth looked around the desecrated grounds. "As have the gardens." Unshed tears of regret rimmed her words. "This was a beautiful place once, Duncan."

"And it can be again."

She knew he was right, but it would be so difficult to restore what once was ... and it could never be completely accomplished. Nothing was ever the same after it was ruined.

"Yes, but—"

Duncan took her hands in his. "Beth, you have the look of a haunted apparition about you. We cannot resolve any problems out here tonight and it would serve no purpose to be so consumed with despair and worry. Neither has ever benefited any situation, to my knowledge." He took a step backward, urging her to follow him into the house. "Come to bed."

A knowing smile played upon her lips. "Yours or mine?"

She was a vixen, but he knew what lay just beneath the surface, and he would walk through fire just for a taste of her lips.

"It matters not, for I will join you wherever you are."

She withdrew her hands from his to fist them at her waist. "And I have no say in it?"

He sighed. He suspected that Beth probably liked to

argue more than she liked to eat. She clearly seemed to enjoy it more than having him make love to her.

"You always have a say in it, Beth. But I pray in my heart that the say will be 'yes.' "

There was so much in his eyes that she could not read, but this much she knew to be true. She cupped her hand to his cheek.

"Then set your heart at ease. For all you have done today, I could not turn you away."

But his eyes darkened. He did not want her body in trade for actions he would have rendered anyway. "I do not want your gratitude."

She lifted her shoulders and let them drop. "Nonetheless, you have it."

His eyes held her fast to where she stood. "I want something more. Something with a far dearer price attached to it."

As always, he had her heart beating quickly, hammering at her wrists and throat like a drummer boy in the militia, announcing a battle. But there were to be no battles fought tonight.

Tonight was for surrender.

"Perhaps you have that, too." He opened his mouth to speak, but she lay a finger across his lips to silence him. "But for the time being, content yourself with what there is, as you have bidden me to do."

Beth stood on her toes and twined her arms around his neck. Her body leaned into his in supplication. "Make me forget, Duncan. Make me forget what I have seen today and what I have yet to see."

He picked her up in his arms as easily as if she were but a small child.

"I will do my best."

His lips found hers in a rapturous kiss that began the

merciful process of numbing her senses as they ignited fires within her, fires that had never been completely banked from the first time.

Duncan pushed the back door open with his shoulder. Jacob was no longer in the kitchen. Duncan knew he was at his post before the front door. Balancing Beth in his arms, he paused now only to secure the lock on the back door. Duncan thought there was no eminent danger tonight, but he had not come to his present age by wantonly throwing caution to the winds.

She could have remained in his arms forever for the feeling being there spawned within her. She felt secure and on the brink of excitement at the same time. The man was a wonder.

"Jacob?" Beth looked around hesitantly as Duncan carried her up the stairs.

Duncan laughed softly to himself as he took another kiss from her lips.

"Will not save you tonight, my love. He is standing guard, and your grandmother and grandaunt are long asleep." He carried her to her room, as if setting her feet down upon the long, faded carpet would break the spell that was being woven. "There is but the two of us."

God help her, but she loved the sound of that. "For tonight, that is more than enough for me."

For tonight, he thought.

And what of tomorrow, and all the days that would follow? He knew he was having thoughts that were foreign to a manly breast, but he could not shed them any for the knowing. She had cast a spell over him, one he would have to work hard at overcoming when the time came.

"I have but two hours," he reminded her, as they

came to her room. The door stood open, just as it had
when he left it.

"Then we shall have to make the most of it." Without
waiting for Duncan to speak, Beth pressed her lips to
his once more with an urgency that Duncan found over-
whelmingly intoxicating.

His blood roaring through his veins, Duncan could
hardly wait until they were within the privacy of her
room. Her mouth, as it glided hot and questing along his
throat and lips, was driving him to the very brink of no
control. Beyond the perimeter were creatures he was not
certain he could contain.

Yet she easily pushed him beyond all that he had ever
known with her eager mouth and her grasping, slender
fingers. Even the sound of her breath as it echoed in the
room excited him.

Before he could successfully close the doors behind
them, Beth's hands were on his body, hot to touch, hot
to assure herself that here at least there was something
that had not been stripped away from her.

She sought the mindless ecstasy that only Duncan
could give her.

Setting her down, Duncan caught Beth's hands in his
and looked into her face. The moon provided the only
light within the room, and barely lit it.

"Beth," he breathed, his heart pounding, "there is no
race."

She shook her head, her hair flying loose. "Oh, but
there is. The world is spinning too fast for me to stop
now."

He pressed her to him, as if to absorb some of her
pain. He felt her heart against his, blending, melding.

"Then we will slow it down," he promised, against
her lips.

Though the fires of desire drove them both, Duncan struggled not to allow her questing hands and mouth make him lose what last shreds of control he still retained.

Clothes left their bodies quickly, so quickly that he feared some were torn. How would they explain that on the morrow, when Cosette eyed them?

But matters of clothing and reproving great-aunts soon faded from his mind as flames licked his body. She was nude before him and cleaving her body to his. He could think only of her, of wanting her.

Of dying within her.

With a sigh of absolute surrender, Duncan fell into the inferno that was waiting for him. It consumed him and he went to it willingly.

Anything to have her.

He worshipped her with his hands, with his eyes, with his mouth. Like a man possessed, he placed his brand upon her at every point that was exposed to him. He could not get enough of her.

Like a starving man, he feasted and was still hungry, drank and was still thirsty.

His mouth and hands played upon her as if she was a rare instrument, to be strummed reverently in order to make her body sing.

As Beth arched and moved beneath him, he discovered secrets that he had only guessed at . . . secrets of her body that Beth had never known.

He created waves within her. Waves, and unspeakably wonderful sensations.

Beth's eyes flew open as explosions rocked through her body, bombs discharging in her like precisioned musket fire, one after the other.

"Oh! Oh!" she gasped in surprise, immediately biting

down on her lower lip to still the cries that continued to rise up within her. Her body rocked to and fro as if it did not belong to her, as if it was governed not by her mind, but only by Duncan and his wondrous touch.

"Shh," he warned, "you'll wake them all."

But still his questing fingers did not stop. Nor could she have stood it if they had.

His tongue trailed along her quivering belly until he came to the very source of her heat, the very source of her passion. There was just a moment's pause, and that only to tantalize her with.

And then he plunged onward.

Beth felt his mouth touch her and struggled to bring him up. She did not know whether to be offended, or overjoyed. This couldn't be. This—

Was wondrous.

As she struggled to push him away, she succeeded only in driving him further in.

And then, as the heat of his mouth irrevocably claimed her, there was no strength in her body left to resist. He drove her upward, ever upward, and she found that she was thrown into the eye of the storm, tossed about from wave to wave until she was completely limp.

Her skin, damp with sweat, gleamed in the moonlight like that of a temptress. Duncan could resist her no longer.

She looked at him, dazed, as he raised himself up on his hands and slid his body along hers until their eyes met. Her body pulsed as rainbows crashed through her.

"What did you do?" she cried weakly.

He could still manage a smile, well pleased. "Made love to you, Beth. As I will do again and again."

"I can't—" she began to murmur, her voice scarcely a whisper, even to her own ear.

In the next moment, she discovered, as he began to kiss her ear, that she could.

And did.

Stunned, with a need to bring him into the swirling chaos he had created for her, Beth reached for Duncan.

As her fingers dipped low and touched the hardened shaft, she heard him moan her name in helpless surprise. Satisfaction curved her mouth. She knew that she had caught up the essence of his pleasure in her hand.

With instincts that came from she knew not where, Beth feathered her fingers over him slowly. His groan told her that her instincts had been correct.

Duncan caught her wrist to stop her before it was too late. Breath came heavily to him.

"Where have you learned these skills, Beth, to drive me mad so?"

She moved and felt him against her, heated and ready. "You have taught me everything."

"Then the teacher has become the student. And willingly so." Twining his fingers through hers as he held both her hands above her head, Duncan covered her mouth with his and entered her.

And then they were bound for glory, leaving far behind them a world gone mad.

Chapter Twenty-nine

Beth rolled over onto her side in the large bed. Slowly she dislodged herself from the tight cocoon of sleep that was wrapped around her. In the distance there were birds singing, greeting the day, just as there might be back home. It seemed, she mused, still hazy, as if all should be peaceful, rather than in a state of turmoil.

Her eyes still closed, Beth reached out for him.

But the place beside her was empty and cool. She opened her eyes to confirm what her fingertips had already ascertained.

A momentary pang of regret at being left alone drifted through her, to be nudged aside by the comforting warmth of memories.

She had fallen asleep in Duncan's arms, fallen asleep exhausted and contented after a night she would never forget. Never had she dreamed that it could be this way between a man and a woman. Her mother had never even hinted at the subject, and while she knew the basic motions and what was required within a coupling, Beth had not even fantasized about the emotions involved.

She would have never believed the incredible sensations had someone attempted to tell her.

Beth arched, and her body stretched along the sheets. They lay, rumpled and bunched beneath her, a tribute to last night's lovemaking. A tribute to Duncan and the power he could unleash within her.

Beth sighed and remembered, hugging herself.

Birds called to one another more urgently. It was past dawn, and time to be up. Time, she thought, to go about the business of why she was here to begin with.

Completely awake now, eager to be about, Beth rose and dressed quickly. It took her but a few minutes to arrange her hair and pin it up, out of the way. The clothes she donned were the same ones she had worn yesterday. Tommy's baggy linen shirt and britches were far more to her liking now than the skirts she knew her great-aunt would have preferred to see on her.

She wanted to be able to move quickly, if need be. Duncan could have no reason for leaving her behind today. If he hadn't already, she thought suddenly with a start.

Pulling her boots on, she made plans. She would greet her great-aunt and grandmother, then hurry to see about finding Duncan.

There was an unease in the air, and she knew not what it was, or why, only that she felt it.

The birds, she realized, had suddenly stopped singing.

Beth knocked on her great-aunt's door, but there was no answer. She knocked once more, then slowly opened it, only to find that Cosette was not there.

Though there was no reason for it, the feeling of foreboding grew greater, like a dark shadow spreading upon her soul.

She pulled the doors shut, attempting to calm her fears. Her father had said that his aunt was an early riser, often leaving her bed just when the moon retreated to its lair.

Still, the feeling that something was wrong persisted, gripping her heart.

Beth turned toward her grandmother's room as if she was being drawn there by some unforeseen hand. As she knocked, she heard a muffled sound from within. Beth took it to mean that she was allowed to enter. She pushed open the double doors and walked in.

Unlike yesterday, the draperies at the window were pulled back, admitting the dawn and the light. Denise had requested it.

Beth saw her great-aunt kneeling by the bed.

Her heart constricting within her breast, Beth immediately rushed to the other side of the four-poster. Anxiously, she looked from her great-aunt to the wan form in the bed.

Her grandmother's eyes were closed.

"Is something—?"

Cosette raised her bowed head and Beth saw the tears that stained the shallow cheeks. Beth placed her hand upon the withered shoulder in silent comfort.

Cosette sighed heavily, desperately fighting for control.

"It is her time."

Beth looked upon the face of her grandmother once more. It was so still, yet not devoid of life, though the eyes remained closed.

"Grandmère?"

The sightless eyes opened, and there seemed to be a lightness there, as if she could see what no one else was able to.

Her dried lips lifted in a smile. "Still here, little one,

waiting to say goodbye. I knew if I but tried, I would remain long enough for you to come."

Beth looked at her great-aunt. "Why didn't you send for me?"

But Cosette only shook her head, her eyes fixed upon the face of her sister. "I was afraid to leave, afraid that if I but turned my back—"

The shallow chest moved heavily with each breath. "I said I would wait."

Denise Beaulieu groped for her granddaughter's hand. Beth was quick to seal the fragile extremity within her own hands. The smile widened slightly, stretching skin across her cheeks until it looked as if it would tear.

"You said that you would find your father."

"Yes," Beth murmured, her voice thick with tears. "I shall. I promise, *Grandmère*. I won't rest until I find him and bring him home."

Denise nodded, though even the slightest action took much from her.

She sighed, relieved. "Then I can die happily, assured that you will." Her fingers tightened slightly. It was all she was capable of managing. "I know he is still alive. I feel it in these cumbersome old bones of mine."

The thin smile sagged into the corners of her mouth, unable to remain for long. The effort was too much.

"I will do what I can for you, once I have crossed to the other side." She said the words wistfully. "I will be much lighter then. And there are many I know who are waiting for me."

For a moment, she fell silent, gasping for air that would not come. A panic edged in Beth. She tightened her hold on her grandmother's hand, as if that would tether the old woman to life a little longer, to her a little longer.

Denise turned her head toward the direction of her sister's voice. There was not much time now. She knew it.

"Cosette?"

"Here." Cosette grasped the dying woman's other hand, her tears spilling freely and without pause. "I am right here, Denise."

Denise's lips moved once without sound. Cosette inclined her head nearer. This time, the words were aloud, a whisper in the wind. *"Je t'aime."*

"Je t'aime, aussi." Cosette replied, tears choking the words until they were almost unrecognizable.

But it was too late.

The old woman had slipped away from them as silently as smoke. Her hand slackened in her sister's. With the last bit of strength Denise Beaulieu had possessed, she had strived for dignity and willed her eyes closed before she left them.

A flood of tears rose within Beth, hammering at her throat and chest. But she could not indulge herself by releasing them. This was not the time to allow herself to give vent to the grief she felt. Her great-aunt needed her strength, not her sorrow.

Cosette buried her head in her arms upon the bed. Her frail body shook with sobs as grief sliced her heart in two.

Slowly, Beth raised the woman from her knees and held her to her breast. Cosette's grief was boundless, and Beth was at a loss as to what to do. She stroked the bowed gray head and murmured small words of comfort that she knew fell on deaf ears.

Perhaps it was more for herself that she said, *"Grandmère* will be better this way. Where she is now there is no more pain, no more suffering, no more sorrow or cause for it."

The words were muffled against her shoulder. So distraught was she that Cosette could not even lift her head to speak. "I know, I know, but I shall miss her so. There is no one left for me who remembers anymore. Everyone is younger, and now I am a stranger in a land I once knew."

She sobbed for a long time.

Duncan found them this way when he came to the bedroom to bid Denise good morning. He noticed it all in one sweeping glance, the draperies thrown open, as if to let a spirit free, the still woman within the bed, the sobbing old woman supported by Beth.

He crossed to them with no hesitation. He was no stranger to death, yet he could never meet with its handiwork easily.

Duncan placed a hand softly on Beth's shoulder. "She is gone?"

Beth raised her head, the tears she could not shed shimmering in her eyes and on her lashes. She nodded mutely.

He touched the shallow cheeks and felt the old woman's hands. They were still warm, but even now, they were cooling.

"When?"

Beth raised one shoulder and let it fall. "Just now. Within the half-hour." She shook her head helplessly. "I do not know." She looked down at the woman she held in her arms and pressed her lips together. "Time has slipped away from me."

As if her words touched off something within her

great-aunt, Cosette raised her head and pulled her shoulders back as far as she was able. Dignity returned as she wiped away the last of her tears, though her eyes were red-rimmed and deeply swollen.

She swallowed twice before she was able to speak. "We must bury her beneath the oak. It was her wish. And quickly."

"But why—?" Beth began uncertainly. She didn't understand why there was this sudden look of urgency in her great-aunt's eyes.

There was no time to explain.

"Just do as I say," she told them.

Cosette laid a hand to her breast. It was as if she felt a quake there. There was no time for sorrow now, only action. This, above all else, she owed to her dear sister.

"Quickly, quickly. There is no time to lose." She looked at Duncan as thoughts frantically collided with one another. "There are shovels in the shed at the far end of the garden. We'll have need of them."

Turning on the point of her cane, Cosette shuffled toward the doorway as if something vicious was but a few steps behind her.

Beth was completely mystified. There was a dignity to death, a tradition to follow. Her great-aunt, of all people, should know this. Had her grief somehow caused her mind to come unhinged?

"But a coffin, a wake," Beth began helplessly. "The priest—"

Cosette shook her head, cutting short the protest. "There is no time." Her hand braced on the doorjamb, she leaned forward on her cane and peered toward her grandniece's face. "Do you know what they do to members of our class when they find them dead?"

Beth slowly moved her head from side to side, unable

to voice any of the thoughts that were suddenly sprouting in her mind. They were all unspeakable and macabre, though she had heard some hints of it.

But civilized people did not behave in the manner she had heard whispered. That was for savages who knew no better—Indians, heathens, not people in a country centuries old.

Duncan knew what Cosette was driving at. He wasted no time in argument and saved her the trouble of explaining the indelicacies to Beth.

"They cut off their fingers and wrists to get at the jewelry."

Beth's eyes were wide with revulsion as her stomach turned. "How horrible."

"It doesn't end there," he assured her. "After they have what they want, they mutilate the bodies until no one can recognize them, doing unspeakable things with them. When they are finished, they burn what is left."

Duncan lifted the lifeless body into his arms. In death, as in life, Denise Beaulieu felt as if she weighed almost nothing.

Beth covered her mouth to keep back the gasp that screamed within her lungs. How could people do this to one another? She didn't understand and wanted not to believe, but Duncan wouldn't lie to her.

Cosette merely nodded as she moved into the hall. "Quickly," she urged again. "Quickly."

Beth grabbed up the sheet from her grandmother's bed and followed them out of the room.

Chapter Thirty

Jacob was in the kitchen, whistling tunelessly as he attempted unsuccessfully to brew some tea for the morning. He knew that Beth was partial to tea, and he was partial to Beth.

He looked up in surprise as the solemnly driven entourage came down the backstairs and poured into the kitchen.

The tea was forgotten as he looked upon the lifeless body in Duncan's arms.

Jacob bolted to his feet, upsetting the stool upon which he sat. "What's happened?" he asked Duncan.

"Madam Beaulieu has died, Jacob," Duncan informed him tersely. "Mademoiselle says that there are shovels in the shed in the garden. Fetch them. We have to bury Beth's grandmother quickly."

It was not in Jacob's nature to question why. It was enough that Duncan bade him do it. He hurried from the house.

They worked as swiftly as they were able, two men digging the hole that was to be Denise Beaulieu's final resting place.

As they worked, Beth solemnly wrapped the small

body in the sheet that she had taken from her grand-mother's bed. Beth's hands shook, but she managed to keep back her tears. They would not do her grand-mother any good now, and the show of despair might weaken her great-aunt's resolve.

"There, that should be large enough," Duncan said, vaulting from the hole. Jacob was quick to follow him.

"She is ready," Beth said, in a small voice.

Duncan began to pick up the body to lower it into the grave.

"Wait," Cosette cried.

With great difficulty, she knelt one last time by her sister's side. To the others' surprise, Cosette removed the single ring from her sister's finger. Kissing the life-less hand one last time, Cosette tucked it gently back into the sheet.

Duncan took Cosette's elbow and raised her up to her feet once more, not standing on ceremony or pride any longer.

It was past time for that now.

Cosette nodded her thanks as she brushed off her black dress. With difficulty, she uncurled her fingers from about the ring. The rays of the early morning sun seemed to flash a beam from the center of her hand. It was only the sun reflecting itself in the circle of dia-monds she held there.

"This was her wedding ring," Cosette explained to Beth. "In sixty-nine years, it was never off her hand for even a moment. She wanted you to have it when she died." Cosette offered the ring to Beth, but Beth did not move to take it from her. "She told me so last night."

Beth shook her head and took a step back from the outstretched hand.

"I can't," she whispered. This ring was her grandmother's, a symbol of her grandfather's love and fidelity. It should be on her hand in death, as it had been in life.

Cosette turned toward Duncan. She understood Beth's reasons. She could see them in the girl's eyes. But she had given her word to Denise, and that was what she was bound to honor.

The old woman took his hand in hers and placed the ring into his palm.

"Then you take it for her, and hold it until such time as she is ready to wear it. I charge you with its keeping, Duncan Fitzhugh."

Duncan nodded solemnly as he placed the ring within the pouch at his side. He knew the woman's words were not to be taken lightly.

The sigh that tore from her breast was ragged with emotion. She waved a spidery hand at the enshrouded body.

"And now, get on with it," she ordered, as she stepped back out of the way. "Cover her quickly so they cannot tell where she is when they come to look for her."

Following Cosette's instructions, Duncan and Jacob lowered the body into the grave and swiftly covered it until the hole where she lay was filled once more.

Resting the shovel against a bush, Duncan looked at Cosette. Her eyes were red, but there were no more tears. "Do you wish to say something over the grave?"

But Cosette shook her head. "There is no need for words. She had them all while she was still alive." With a critical eye, the woman looked over the grave. It was still too obvious. The earth looked freshly turned, and might arouse suspicions.

"Walk over it," she ordered them.

Beth's eyes grew huge. "Surely leaving it unmarked like this is sufficient."

"Mademoiselle, you cannot mean that we should actually walk on her grave—" Duncan protested.

Jacob's eyes were wide with fear at the mere suggestion of what Cosette Delacroix had asked. He did not separate the dead from the living so easily and feared haunts when the moon rose. The old woman's ghost might seek him out for the disrespect that her sister proposed.

"Walk over it," Cosette insisted more firmly. "I want no indications left for them, no signs. She understands." Cosette swallowed the agony that rose in her throat like bitter bile. "This is necessary, I assure you. And when I die, I want you to do the same for me." She turned her eyes toward Beth, silently demanding a promise.

Beth felt numbed. "I—"

Cosette clutched Beth's hand. "The same for me," she repeated. "Swear it."

Beth did not trust her voice to speak. She could only nod. She blinked back tears as she watched Duncan stomp upon the mound until it was almost flat beneath his heels. Jacob followed suit, though hesitantly, and with far less energy.

A noise seemed to rumble in the background, and Beth thought surely that it was thunder. For the heavens must be offended by what was transpiring here today.

Duncan stopped abruptly. His head jerked up and he turned in order to hear better. The rumbling seemed to grow louder.

The look upon his face alarmed Beth. She grasped his arm. "What is it?"

Cosette answered for him. "They're coming," she said solemnly.

Beth looked at her, confused. "They? Who are 'they?' " She looked off toward the town and could have sworn she saw a faint trail of fire drifting steadily toward them in the distance.

Fire?

Torches?

The look on Cosette's face was composed. This was what she had felt beating in her breast this morning when she arose. She had known they were coming.

"The rabble. I knew." She turned her face and saw them approaching on the hill. A swarm buzzing softly, carrying torches. Their noises would grow angrier as they came closer. "I awoke this morning and knew." She said the words more to herself than to them.

Beth and Duncan exchanged looks. Then Duncan picked up the shovels and hid them in the bushes.

"I never argue with omens that are so strongly felt," he told Beth. "Jacob, take the women into the house."

Jacob took Cosette's arm respectfully and reached for Beth's.

Beth pulled it away before he could wrap his fingers around her arm. "No," Beth protested.

"Damn it, woman, I have no wish to play the martyr," Duncan told her, a dry laugh punctuating his words. "I'll come, too. I just want to be certain that the traces are gone."

He nodded at the grave. He broke off a branch from the old tree and began to move it hastily about on the mound. "Take them, Jacob," he ordered, in a low voice that Beth was not familiar with.

But Jacob was. Duncan could laugh and joke with them, and there was no difference. But when it was time to lead, another Duncan emerged. And that Duncan was never to be questioned.

Jacob reached for Beth's arm once more. "Please," he urged.

"Take my great-aunt inside," Beth told Jacob.

She grabbed at another stray tree limb that hung low. Dried, it snapped easily in her hands. She began to follow Duncan's lead, swishing the tree limb and its scratchy branches along the ground.

By God, he was going to strangle the bloody woman someday. "You are going to be the death of me, Beth," Duncan snapped.

She raised her eyes long enough to flash a smile. "Two can do this faster."

In a moment, they were done. Casting the branches aside, they hurried into the house. Duncan hustled Beth into the kitchen before him and quickly bolted the door shut behind them.

The distance between the mob and the house was growing less.

Jacob stood in the room, waiting with Cosette. There was no light in the kitchen, save a beam that squeezed through where the shutters no longer met properly.

One hand holding Beth's, Duncan hurried to the younger man. "The doors and windows?" he asked Jacob.

"Are as secure as they were last night, when you retired," Jacob vowed.

Duncan knew there was no need to check again.

Jacob was always as good as his word, and Duncan knew he could trust him with his life. As he now did with Beth's and the old woman's.

Cosette shook her head solemnly. "They will not hold against them," she warned.

Duncan drew his sword. The sound set Beth's teeth on edge as metal left scabbard.

"They will not touch either of you while there is breath left in my body," he vowed.

Jacob's sword sang a muted cry as it left its sheath.

Cosette laid a hand on Duncan's arm. "Do not give up that fine body so quickly." When he looked at her quizzically, Cosette nodded toward the hall. "Come with me to the library. All of you."

Rather than follow her, to save time, Duncan sheathed his sword once more and swept the old woman into his arms. "This is more expedient," he promised her.

Cosette merely smiled indulgently and let Duncan take her where she bade him. Beth and Jacob followed quickly behind them.

Duncan set her down on the floor. He looked slowly around the room. There was more light available here, because the draperies were in disrepair. It was in the center of the first floor, but was easily gained by two doors, one on either side.

"This is not the best room from which to take a stand," he pronounced.

Cosette had moved toward the fine old desk her grandfather had brought with him when he had built the house. On it stood a lantern. Striking a flint, she lit it, then settled the cover over it once more. She saw the look on Duncan's face and knew that he thought the mob would detect the beam of light it cast. But it would not be here for long.

"We are not going to stand," she informed him. "We are going to flee. Take the lantern, please."

Beth did as she'd been asked. But she was not so ready to give up. Perhaps something could yet be negotiated. "But this is your home, and Father's as well. We just can't run away and leave it."

Her eyes were sad as Cosette shook her head. "Dying in it will not preserve it."

Beth dug in. "But if we talk to them—"

Duncan understood the old woman's words. "There is no reasoning with a mob, Beth, and they had the look of death about them."

It was time to leave, before it was too late. "That portrait there." As they turned to see what she meant, Cosette pointed toward the one hanging directly above the sleeping fireplace.

Jacob was quick to cross to it. He looked at Cosette over his shoulder, waiting for further instructions.

"Move the corner to the right, then step out of the way, lad." It had been a long time since she had done that. The last was some sixty years ago. Denise had been with her then.

He did as the old woman instructed. Jacob had no sooner touched the portrait than the massive fireplace began to move forward.

Yawning before them was a cave. There were stone steps leading down into darkness.

"Hurry," Cosette urged, breaking the stunned silence. "We haven't much time."

"Why didn't you take this passage before?" Duncan asked. Before she answered, he lifted her once more into his arms and hurried to the mouth of the passage-way.

Cosette placed her hand at the back of Duncan's neck to secure herself. "If we'd had the opportunity, we would have. But we were caught unaware. The mob was in our house before the sun had even risen. Touch that stone there."

Pointing, she indicated a gray rock that looked as if it had been there since God created the earth. When Jacob laid his hand on it, it shifted down and the fireplace closed once more.

"Hold the lantern high," Cosette instructed Beth. "There are many steps here and the way down is very narrow."

They began to descend. The light from the lantern cast eerie shadows on walls that had not seen a human form in decades.

Duncan tested each step as he walked down. "Where does it lead?" Duncan asked.

"Far from here," Cosette assured him. Despite every-thing, she had found that her hold on life was tenacious, and she intended to continue holding until God chose to take it from her.

"We will come out at the mouth of a cave. This pas-sageway was created when the Huguenots were fighting with the Catholics. My grandfather thought it best to have an alternate route from the house if he ever had need to escape. Hurry, hurry," Cosette urged again. "I do not think they brought the torches for light this time."

Beth blanched as she realized what her great-aunt was saying. "They are going to burn the house?"

"To the ground, I imagine." The stoic way Cosette said it gave no hint of the sorrow she felt. She turned her eyes toward Duncan. "Come, please hurry, Duncan. She is a Beaulieu as well as a Delacroix, and they will want her blood more than mine."

Jacob took Beth's arm and hurried her down the stairs before Duncan could bid him do it.

Chapter Thirty-one

The mouth of the cave at the end of the long passageway was obscured with brush and debris. Far more unkempt than the gardens at the house had been, it hid the entrance from view to the passing eye.

Taking great care, they stepped into the light, first Jacob, then Beth. Duncan soon followed with Cosette in his arms.

Cosette squinted, shading her eyes. The bright sunlight was almost too much for her to bear after the dimness within the cave. The lantern which Beth had carried to guide their way had cast only a minimal amount of light.

Beth extinguished the lantern now and set it down just within the entrance of the cave. Though she did not expect it, they still might have need of it and the secret passageway in the future.

Instinctively she turned in the direction whence they had come.

Because of the distance, they could not hear the noise of the mob as they overran the estate, but Beth swore that she felt it vibrating in her soul.

And they all saw the smoke.

It rose into the sky, an odious and ominous billowing plume. It was a symbol of the black death that had seized the land and would continue to hold it in its grip until such time as the madness passed and people, wearied, finally returned to their senses.

Until such time as the blood lust was at long last satisfied.

Though he had set her feet down upon the ground, Duncan kept his arm about the frail woman, offering her his silent support. She was erect, but seemed ready to sag at any moment; he feared that she would swoon.

But Cosette's mouth was set firm and her eyes were dry as she looked upon the frightening sight. She was, mused Duncan, incredible. He realized Beth had inherited both her strength and her courage.

Perhaps, Beth thought, as she looked at the stoic old woman, her great-aunt had no more tears left within her to shed.

The plumes multiplied, until they seemed to feather across the entire sky, darkening it. Red tongues were at the bottom, licking across the structure hungrily, consuming it in its entirety. Within the hour, there would be nothing left, only blackened ruins and the charred land beneath it.

"I lived all my life within that house," Cosette told them, in a gentle whisper. Her eyes never wavered from the horrific sight. She felt her heart being burned and cracked with each lick of the fire. "Every trace of me and mine is now gone."

"No," Beth insisted.

She moved so that she stood in front of the woman, forcing her great-aunt to look at her and not the wanton destruction. She took Cosette's hands into her own.

"I will find Father." Beth saw the look that Duncan

gave her, the one which sternly reminded her that she was not on this venture alone, nor would she ever be. "*We* will find Father," she amended. "And *you* still remain, as do I. A house is just a house, and possessions are not the mark or worth of a family; *people* are. You and me." Beth held the woman's hand fast. "And Father."

Cosette nodded slowly, grateful for the comfort the words brought, grateful for Beth. "He raised you well, Philippe did."

She looked around at the faces of the young people who had risked so much to save her and then slowly turned her back on the darkness in the distance.

"Come," she urged, placing her hand lightly on Duncan's arm. "I know of a place where we can be safe, at least for a while."

Struggling with her memory, Cosette gave them directions to her former servant's house. It was more than three miles from her own house. Duncan carried Cosette all the way, though Jacob offered to take his turn with her.

"It is an honor," Duncan affirmed, "that I would not pass on lightly." He was rewarded with the old woman's smile.

The journey took the better part of an hour. The sound of a barking dog alerted them as they approached the small cottage that looked so like John's had on the grounds of Shalott.

A small black-and-white mongrel advanced on them, barking fiercely as he danced from paw to paw, warning them to stay back.

"Nuisance," Cosette murmured, waving her hand at

the dog. "All animals are but nuisances. Call out to her," she instructed Beth, pointing to the cottage. "Her name is Therese."

Beth shouted the name above the dog's barking.

The front door opened a crack, enough to allow the person behind it view of the front yard. The next moment, the door flew open as if it was unattached and a wide-hipped, sweet-faced woman came bustling out. She wrung her hands in thanksgiving as she hurried to the visitors who stood before her house.

"Hush, dog," she chided sharply.

The dog whimpered and gave one bark for good measure before retreating.

Duncan gently set Cosette down once more. She gained her legs unsteadily and Duncan kept one arm discreetly about her waist.

"Mademoiselle!" Therese cried, as if she had seen a ghost. With hesitant fingers, she touched the thin arm. "It *is* you." She hugged Cosette's hand to her ample bosom. "You are safe. Praise God, you are safe."

Remembering her place, Therese dropped Cosette's hand and took a step back. Her eyes uncertainly searched the faces of the strangers with her former mistress. One never knew the face of a potential enemy these days.

"I have been hearing about such horrible goings-on!"

Cosette felt tired as she nodded. "All true. Anarchy has been visited upon us. My grandniece brought friends who came to my aid." She said the words in English for their benefit, since Therese understood a little.

With a regal gesture, Cosette indicated Duncan and Jacob.

Therese inclined her head to each in turn in a show of proper respect.

"Please, come in, come in," she urged.

She stood back until they were all inside and then, looking over her shoulder, closed the door firmly once more. She trusted her dog to warn her of anyone else's approach.

Duncan had ushered Cosette to a chair at the uneven wooden table that dominated the main room. Therese sat down beside her, then hesitated a moment before venturing to ask, "And Madam—?"

"Died this morning," Cosette said, each word weighing heavily in her mouth.

She saw the concern rise in Therese's eyes. Cosette allowed herself contact in a way she never had before this trouble had come to plague them. She squeezed the servant's hand. Therese had a good and faithful heart. She had been Andre's daughter and loyal to the last, and now Cosette realized she was a good friend. Maybe the strict lines between the classes could be blurred a little, she thought.

"There was time but to bury her before the vultures came, smelling blood," the old woman concluded passionately.

"Horrible times we are living in," Therese murmured, solemnly nodding. "Horrible times." She gestured about the meager two-room cottage. "I know that this is not even as large as your stables were, but what is mine is yours, as always." Her glance took them all in. "I would be honored if you would all grace me with your presence for as long as you wish."

It was not an easy offer to make, given the circumstances. If Therese was suspected of aiding the enemy, she could readily be tortured and put to death beside the very people she had given asylum to. They all knew this.

Duncan smiled and shook his head, refusing her kindness and her bravery. "We would not place you in danger thus. We cannot stay, but we do need a place where Mademoiselle Delacroix might safely remain. Can you suggest one?"

Therese knew of no safer place than here. There was a small network of people she could trust, people who were as heartsick over what had befallen France as she and her beloved Mademoiselle were.

"Here," Therese said readily, looking at Cosette. "She can pretend to be my aunt now, if it pleases her. Hopefully, no one will recognize her."

Cosette looked about the small room with its rough-hewn furniture and straw-covered dirt floor. Therese was right; it wasn't even as large as her stables. She smiled and ran spidery fingers along the woman's chestnut hair.

"It pleases me." She turned in her chair toward Duncan and Beth, concern etched into her fine lines. "But what of you? Where will you be?"

"In Paris," Duncan answered her. "We need to discover what has happened to your nephew." He glanced about the warm room. It reminded him of happier times at home. "We cannot learn that by being safe." He paused as he glanced toward Beth. "Would you consider—?"

"No, I would not," she retorted, knowing full well what he was going to ask of her. She rose to her feet to show her readiness to leave.

Duncan sighed. Beth's response had been a foregone conclusion. He lifted his shoulders and let them drop in the careless manner of one resigned to his fate.

"I thought that I might at least try. Very well, we've a need to make our way back to the estate to see if the horses have been taken. Perhaps they ran off and are not far away." That, too, he thought was worth a try.

"From there, we shall go to Paris." He turned his attention to Beth. "While there yesterday, I got the distinct impression that something was about to happen, but I could not discover what. Your knowledge of the language will be extremely helpful."

"Wait," Therese protested, as Duncan began to rise. "You cannot leave without something in your stomachs to see you through. I have a stew cooking." She gestured toward the large cauldron in the hearth. "It is almost ready. Surely a few more minutes do not matter."

They hadn't had breakfast. The events of the morning had driven all thoughts of food from them. Duncan nodded, seating himself once more. "That is a very good suggestion. We'll prevail upon your hospitality a little longer, then, Mistress Therese."

Though she was far older than Duncan, the woman giggled like a flirtatious young girl and went to fetch whatever serving bowls and eating utensils she possessed for her guests.

Beth leaned toward him at the table. "Too bad Robespierre isn't a woman. You could charm the Revolution right out of his head."

Duncan returned Beth's smile. "Too bad," he echoed.

The simple meal was filling, and over far too quickly. Fortified and well sustained, they needed now to be on their way. Therese told them of a man they might contact in Paris, should they need any help once they were there, a man who could be trusted to hold his tongue. His name was Louis.

Cosette remained seated at the table as they rose. The

day's events and travels had sapped her precious store of energy, though she loathed to admit it.

Beth bent down and hugged the old woman close to her. "I won't be back until Father is with me."

"No." Cosette shook her head. She was too old for dire promises. "You are as precious to me as your father. I wish to know what is happening, both to France and to you." Cosette looked up at Duncan, including him in her entreaty as well. "Send word to me if you can, return to me when you are able. With or without your father. Return." It was a mandate.

She squeezed her grandniece's hand. "God speed you and protect you, for He is the only one able to now."

Duncan and Jacob said their goodbyes and took their leave. As they departed from the cottage, Cosette made the sign of the cross over them, her thin hand cutting through the warm, moist August air.

Without thinking, Beth closed her hand over the cross she now wore at her throat, the one that John had pressed on her in thanksgiving for the lives of his newborn son and wife.

"God be with you as well, Aunt Cosette," she whispered, as she hurried from the cottage after Duncan. She knew that if she didn't keep up, he would force Jacob to take her back to her aunt.

To her surprise, Duncan paused a moment until she was beside him.

"Remember," Duncan cautioned, "when you see the rubble, it means nothing to you. There is no telling who is watching, or from where."

Above all, no harm was to come to her. No harm. He almost laughed at himself. He was taking Beth into the very heart of the devil's soul, and he was hoping she would return unscathed. His mother had always called him a dreamer.

What he asked of her was easier said than done, Beth thought. Could he really expect her to look upon her ancestral home and not feel remorse over what had befallen it?

"But—"

"It means nothing to you," Duncan repeated, more adamantly.

She nodded. "Nothing," she echoed, like a parrot repeating a phrase that had been taught to it. "It was just a house, no different from any other. Only larger."

But her voice shook with emotion and unshed tears as she said it.

Duncan silently linked his hand with hers.

It was worse than she could have imagined.

The fire was still smoldering about the remnants of the house. The once-proud edifice lay like a charred skeleton, a testimony of the hatred that had taken it down, the hatred that beat within the breast of the rabble who loathed anything that belonged to the aristocracy.

Duncan urged her away from the sight, though they were still not close enough to be noticed. His hands upon her shoulders, he ushered her toward where the stables had stood.

But those had been leveled as well.

This time, it was Jacob who was the more greatly distressed. His greatest joy had always been the animals he cared for.

"They've stolen the horses." He looked at Duncan as if to beg him to make it not so. "My mare, Duncan. They took my mare."

Duncan nodded. The three horses they had brought were the only animals that had occupied the stable. He laid a hand on Jacob's shoulder in comfort. "Perhaps we can recover her as well."

Beth was relieved that this changed nothing. "Then we are going to Paris?"

"We have no choice in the matter. It is in Paris that all the answers lie." Duncan looked down into her face. "And perhaps your father as well. If he is alive, he might very well be jailed in the Bastille, or on his way there from some other cell."

Given the situation and the times, it was the most educated guess he could offer. The peasants were eager to turn the tables on their masters. How better than to place the bluebloods in the very cells that had once been occupied by members of their own class?

Beth nodded, but she could not bear to think on what he had suggested. It seemed too horribly cruel, to envision her father in those surroundings.

From the charred remnants of the Beaulieu estate, they made their way to Paris. The path was slow and arduous, but none complained. They passed a few on their journey, men and women who looked upon them with suspicion and fear. Fear was now the companion of them all.

Duncan's scowl, when looked upon, was fearsome, and since the shadow he cast was long and powerful, there were none to challenge the three on their way.

An hour after they had left the estate, Jacob saw something in the distance that made his heart sing.

"Duncan, look," Jacob cried, excited, as he pointed

toward a clearing. " 'Tis my Megan. My horse. And the others. I swear it."

Duncan smiled broadly as he looked in the direction Jacob pointed. There, below them, were four men gathered around a fire. Not far from them were three horses, secured to bushes.

Duncan recognized his own stallion, and Jacob's beloved mare.

The last had the same coloring as the horse he had selected for Beth.

Duncan looked at Beth, well pleased at the turn of events. "It looks as if the God your aunt has charged with looking after us is smiling upon us after all."

His words brought a question to Beth's mind, but now was not the time to ask.

Now was the time to act.

Chapter Thirty-two

Duncan motioned Beth quickly back behind the tree. Though there was brush in the way, he wanted her well hidden from the men below.

"Stay here, Beth."

Her head snapped up to look at him, instead of at the men in the distance. He couldn't be thinking of leaving her behind. She had made it clear that she was to be with him, step for step.

"I will—"

"Stay here," he ordered. The words were more a growl than a statement. "You will stay here." It was clear that he didn't intend to argue the point with her.

Very well, she thought, as she folded her arms before her, her eyes smoldering as she watched him go. She would not argue.

But neither would she obey.

Beth waited until they were a little ways from her, and then stealthfully crept after them. The same foliage that sheltered Duncan and Jacob from the thieves' view sheltered Beth from theirs.

She made her way carefully, wanting not to get in the way, but wanting to be there should another hand be needed. He could not deny her that, just because her skin was softer than his. Just because she was not a man. She could not stay behind, to wait and worry and watch. That was for the faint-hearted, not her.

Duncan motioned for Jacob to position himself on one side of the encampment while he rounded to the other. Armed with his sword, his dagger, and most important, the courage that had seen him through so much, Duncan softly crept up on the circle of men. He thanked the powers which watched over him that he was down-wind of the camp. The horses couldn't scent him approaching. One of the men was off to the side, tending to the animals.

Luck and skill were with him.

Duncan surprised the man by pulling him into the brush. The man struggled, but had no chance. Duncan was the more skillful. Swiftly, Duncan ran his adversary through with his sword.

The man did not go to his maker silently. The scream that left his lips was like that of an animal being slaughtered. It instantly alerted the others to the presence of intruders.

"Now we're in for it," Jacob cried, leaping into the camp, his sword drawn and at the ready.

"How was I to know he'd yell like a woman?" Duncan retorted.

The battle was swift and bloody.

Having tasted victory by being among those who had burned down the estate, the three in the camp were still in the grip of the frenzy that had seized them all. They fought like men possessed. Duncan matched swords with first one, then two, as Jacob met the third. The sound of clashing steel rang in the air that was fouled with curses which neither Duncan nor Jacob understood.

Beth abandoned her stealthy path upon hearing the first cry. She broke into a run, reaching the camp in time to see Duncan propel an evil-looking, wiry man away from him. The man had a scar that ran the length of his face and a voice that rattled the gates of heaven as he screamed obscenities at Duncan.

Crashing to the ground, his body arching over the untended campfire, he came down hard on top of the pistol he had stolen from the estate. His eyes glittered as he raised it now and aimed at Duncan's back.

"Duncan!" Beth screamed.

The death rattle from the thief's throat had a fearsome sound. A startled look had entered his eyes as he'd pitched forward a moment after the sound of a discharging pistol exploded. The ball tore a hole in the middle of his forehead.

Beth's scream had Duncan jerking around. He turned in time to see the man with the scar falling not far from him, his hand still gripping the silent pistol. The next moment, his attention perforce returned to the man he was dueling with. He was a younger man who obviously had some training with a sword. Twice he had nearly sliced Duncan's shoulder and he had nicked his arm once.

Her heart hammering wildly in her throat, Beth scrambled forward to seize the pistol from the dead man's hand. She had never killed anyone before, and the realization that she had made her ill and almost dizzy. She forced the feelings away. This was no time to be weak.

With the weapon in her hands, she rose and looked first to Duncan, then to Jacob. Both battles were going strong. Jacob looked more than well matched.

"Halt," Beth shouted in French. "Or I shall fire at the head of the next man who moves."

Neither Duncan nor Jacob understood her, but the two men did. They had but to look at their fallen comrade to know that the woman meant what she said. Each fearing to be her next victim, they put up their swords, cursing her soul to hell.

Duncan was quick to cleave to Beth's side. He threw his arm about her shoulders and pulled her to him, a hearty laugh echoing in the air.

"By God, woman, but you are a constant source of surprise to me."

"As it should be."

Jacob stood slightly apart, looking from the dead man to Beth. He had never known a woman who behaved in this manner and was clearly more and more in awe of her.

Beth looked at the two men who stood quaking before them, their hands raised high. Jacob hurriedly relieved them of their swords. He stripped the dead man of his shirt, and using his dagger, tore it into strips to use as binding. He and Duncan quickly tied the men's hands and feet, then bound them tightly together, back to back.

Hatred shone in her eyes as Beth watched, the pistol still ready in her hands lest one of them moved. She prayed one of them would resist. These were the men who helped destroy a proud old woman's home. Her hand tightened on the pistol.

Done, Duncan rose and laid a hand on hers. It was the one with the pistol in it. He gently forced it down. Beth looked at him in surprise.

"Beth, we need to ask them questions. I know how

you must feel, but killing them won't resurrect your house, or, more importantly, lead us to your father."

She nodded. He was right. As always.

She sheathed the pistol in the waistband of her britches. For the moment, she sealed the ache in her heart away as well and thought only of what she had to do: save her father.

She stepped forward and looked from one man to the other. There was nothing behind their eyes save hatred. They hated her as much as she hated them. And before the hour, they had never even set eyes on one another.

It was the madness that fouled the air.

"Does either of you know where Philippe Beaulieu is?" she asked them, in French.

The smaller of the two men spat on the ground by her boot, but neither answered.

Duncan drew out his sword and rested the tip against the throat of the man who spat. "I know you don't understand a word I say, but I'd answer her if I were you, you bastard, lest you look forward to having your head separated from your body."

Duncan punctuated his statement by pressing the tip of his sword further against the trembling white flesh at the man's neck.

The sneering bravery fled, to be replaced with terror as the eyes grew huge in the dirtied face.

"Once more," Beth repeated in French, her agitation rising in her voice. She bent closer, though the stench of fire clung to the man's clothes. "Do you know where they are keeping Philippe Beaulieu?"

At first, the man could not answer. When Duncan pressed the sword further and a trickle of blood emerged, the man cried out, nearly swallowing his own tongue.

"No, no, I don't know. I swear it, I don't know," he babbled to Beth.

His feet scraping madly against the ground, he tried to scramble back, but there was nowhere to go. His way was blocked by his comrade's back.

"I am just a lowly farmer. They tell me nothing. But—but he knows." He jerked his head toward the man tied to him.

"Coward," the second man shouted. "Traitor! The committee will hear about this and take their revenge on your miserable hide."

Beth watched as the first man shook. He was of no use to her, but the second one was.

"The committee," Beth told him evenly, a malevolent note entering her voice, "is not here." Calmly she drew out her pistol and aimed at his barrel chest. Her eyes were flat and her hand steady as she looked down at him. "I am. Tell me where they are keeping him."

Duncan exchanged looks with Jacob. The look on Beth's face was deadly. This was not a woman to be taken lightly, but he was afraid that she would be driven to kill the man on the ground before they learned what they needed to know. That would be a waste. If need be, there were methods he had learned that would separate a man from any knowledge he had. Duncan could readily employ those methods.

"It's a lovely sounding language, but for the life of me I haven't a clue as to what's going on. Is he going to tell you?"

She nodded her head slightly, her eyes never leaving the Frenchman's face. "Or meet the devil today." She repeated her phrase in French for the man's benefit, her voice eerily calm.

Duncan saw that Jacob hardly blinked as he watched

Beth in silence. "You are a fearsome wench, Beth. Remind me never to anger you."

A half smile raised one corner of her mouth as she continued to keep her eyes on the men on the ground.

"Don't worry, I shall." The smile left abruptly as her eyes narrowed. "Well?" She cocked the trigger slowly. Sweat was pouring from the man's brow. "Are you prepared to die for the information you have?"

It was not worth it. At all costs, he wanted to survive. Hatred glowed on his face as he told her.

"They are bringing Beaulieu to the Bastille today, him and several of the other aristocrat pigs the Friends of the People have herded together."

She thought of the imposing edifice that had been the scene of so much misery. To think of her father there ripped her heart in two.

"The Bastille?"

The man raised his head contemptuously. "We have enough men to take it and free our own." He would have spit at her if he had not been afraid that the big man would cut his tongue out for it. "Yours will go in their stead. To be buried alive, the way ours were."

It was hard to restrain her emotions as she looked down upon the naked face of hate. Once more Beth's hand tightened on the pistol. All that was needed was one simple movement to discharge it and rid herself and France of this vermin.

"Who gave you the right to play God?" she demanded in a hoarse whisper.

"The right of the people," the man cried. A look akin to insanity glowed in his eyes as he strained against his ties. "The same God you thought was smiling over you, you aristocratic bitch."

"That one," Duncan said evenly, though the smile on

his lips was tight, "I understand." He moved his sword so that it cut a long, thin jagged line just below the man's throat. The man gasped. "Mind your mouth. The next cut will be deeper."

Though the Frenchman understood not a word, he understood the language of the sword. Bravado fled as the man looked at Duncan in abject terror.

Beth laid her hand on Duncan's arm. The urgency of her touch took his attention away from the prisoner.

"We have to go to Paris quickly." She nodded at the man she had questioned. "That one said that they're bringing my father to the Bastille today."

Tears suddenly sprang, unbidden to her eyes. Had they been alone, she would have thrown herself into his arms and wept for joy. "Duncan, he's alive. My father is still alive!"

"Aye." He sheathed his sword once more, though he indicated for Jacob to keep his out. "And we must see what we can do to have him remain that way." He glanced at the two men huddled against one another, their bravery vanished, now that there were consequences to be paid. "What do you want to do with them?"

She hadn't thought that Duncan would leave it up to her to decide. "I?"

He spread his hands wide. "They're your prisoners." Though he would rather not have witnessed it, he knew that she had a right to her vengeance, a right to kill the men, if she chose. It went beyond the laws of man, to the one that nature had inscribed eons ago.

The temptation to order their deaths was great and the words hovered on her lips.

But in the next moment, Beth let go of the madness

she felt surging within her before it consumed her as it had others before her. Killing solved nothing.

"Leave them tied here. We have the horses. If they free themselves, then it's the wish of Providence." She looked at them one last time, then dismissed their existence from her mind. "If they don't, then God has other plans for them."

"Done," Duncan laughed and motioned Jacob to follow them. He laid a hand across her shoulders as he led her off to the horses.

Behind them, the men railed and sent a shower of vilifications that only Beth understood. And chose not to hear.

Chapter Thirty-Three

The streets of Paris were alive with excitement and anticipation. The feeling pulsed in the air like an invisible being, consuming everything and everyone in its path. And growing larger by the moment.

The dogs of the Revolution had been let loose into the winds of war.

Beth looked about the faces of the people who were pouring into the city, drawn by a force that spoke to a different level within them than decency and respect thrived upon. As she, Duncan, and Jacob approached, the paths became thick with travelers.

Everyone wanted to take part. Everyone wanted to be in the center of the city.

Beth felt afraid when she looked at their faces. There was something not quite human about the look in these people's eyes. It was as if they weren't people any longer, but more like wolves that had gotten a taste of blood and craved more.

They wanted to feast on the not yet dead carcass of the monarchy.

Taking care, Duncan guided them to what appeared to be a lesser traveled road. Paths were not converging here, as they were elsewhere. They dismounted and held their horses fast. Thieves overran the streets to a far greater degree now than ever before.

Duncan looked around. A little ways beyond, they could hear the collective roar of the mob as it swelled, its number ever growing. He shook his head as he looked at Beth.

"I wish I hadn't brought you here." The mood of a mob was difficult to gauge, and like cows and sheep that could stampede with the slightest noise, he knew that a mob could easily turn on any one of its number.

And they were in its number.

"You forget," Beth reminded him in a stilled voice, struggling to keep her fear from resounding clearly, " 'Tis I who brought you."

There was no time to debate the merits of their opposing points of view. He wanted to get them in and out quickly. With luck, they would learn something useful. Perhaps what those thieves had testified to was true. The Bastille was to fall during this hot July day. It would certainly seem so, by the looks of the mob.

Once again, Duncan looked about the streets. At least for the moment, they stood away from the focal point of the mob.

"We need to safeguard the horses somewhere before they are stolen from us. There's a high premium on horseflesh these days, both for riding and for eating."

He saw the horror register on Jacob's face. It was better the lad was aware of the extent of things, Duncan thought grimly.

"There!" Duncan pointed to an alley.

The next moment, he hurried toward it, the others following in his wake. The path into the alley was heavily littered with rotting vegetables and meats that had been cast there. It was almost thigh deep, but that made it so much the better for their purposes, Duncan thought. People would not be drawn to meander here. Jacob would be safe for the time they required.

"The stench will give them a moment's pause before they enter," Duncan assured Jacob, hastily bringing his horse to the rear of the narrow passageway.

There was but one way out: the way they had entered. A wall of mortar and stone blocked the forging of any other route.

Duncan thrust his reins into Jacob's hand, as did Beth. "Jacob, I need not tell you how important these horses are to us."

Jacob wound all the reins about his large hand. "I'll guard them with my life," he swore solemnly.

Duncan clasped a hand on the other man's shoulder. "No, *you* are more important to me than they." Duncan began to back out of the alleyway. "See that it doesn't come down to that. If you are not here when we return," he called over his shoulder, his words hanging in the air moist, hot air, "we'll search for you."

"I'll be here," Jacob promised, with the surety of the simple of heart.

He waved before he sank down on his haunches to wait out the time. His eyes, ever alert, remained on the alley entrance.

It was but a few moments before Duncan and Beth found themselves increasingly surrounded by peasants. The crowd seemed to multiply. Tired-faced people whose eyes glittered with purpose, hope, and something far more deadly swelled the ranks all around them.

"Stay close," Duncan instructed Beth, as he took her hand in his.

She walked quickly, matching her gait to his. "I was

about to say the same to you. Remember, you don't know the language."

Duncan slanted a look at a group of men hurrying not far from him. He had seen pirates with a gentler look about them. "And you have no idea what men like this can be like."

He took her arm instead now, grateful once more that she had thought to take Tommy's clothing with her rather than her own. Upon a cursory examination, Beth looked like a young boy.

But anything closer would yield the truth.

Duncan hoped that there were too many people upon the streets for any to take proper notice. Every variation from the norm now roused deep suspicion, and if some in the mob thought Beth to be disguised, they would want to know to what purpose.

It would not be a difficult matter to guess.

The swell of the crowd took them almost against their wills. Duncan held tightly to Beth's arm, thinking that if they but followed, they would arrive at the source of the excitement.

And perhaps have their questions answered.

It was not long before they found themselves in the center of the city, before a dark fortress that was imposing and awesome in its solemnity. The history of the structure was fearsome and bloody. It was not one to be thought of with pride.

By now the crowd seemed to be roaring about them, shouting encouragements and cheering the men that stood before the towering building of stone.

Beth recognized the fortress as the Bastille. The fear in her heart grew.

Duncan inclined his head toward Beth. "Do you have any idea what's going on?" He whispered the question, afraid that someone might overhear his native tongue and realize that it was different from theirs.

The very breath within her breast had halted, trapped there by fear.

"What those thieves told me is true." Her head ached from the very thought of it. "Look, look!" she hissed in his ear urgently.

She pointed with disbelief as the gates of the Bastille were suddenly thrown open like the rusty jaws of hell. Her view abruptly obscured, Beth began to push and shove, but to no avail.

Beth turned toward him. "Duncan, I must see. Please," she implored.

He nodded and began to push his way forward, careful to continue holding tightly to her hand. He managed to gain several yards.

Though still at a distance, Beth could see all plainly now.

A human wave of people surged through the newly parted gates, prisoners escaping their doom as they fled from the Bastille. Cries of greeting and thanksgiving littered the air.

The army that was to have guarded the Bastille were now all prisoners of the mob and the mob's leaders.

The cheers of the mob became deafening.

And then, the man at the center of the hurricane leaped atop a cart and raised his hands for silence. As if by magic, the noise abated, like the tide going out, leaving the shore.

Robespierre commanded respect from the beast he had helped create and unleash. As yet, it obeyed. The time when it outgrew its master had not yet come.

There was pride in his face and an arrogance that was

frightening to all who looked upon it. None, Beth thought, would cross this man or disobey him.

And his madness would destroy them all.

"And now, my brothers, we have freed the last of ours." Cheers greeted the words. Again he called for silence. "In their place will go the real criminals and thieves, the real rapists of our land, our women and children." He beckoned to his second in command as regally as any of the kings he'd denounced. "Bring them forth."

Beth's grip on Duncan's hand grew so tight, she nearly cleaved it in two. The very blood left her fingers, as well as her face. Her eyes were frozen on the sight of the men and women who were being brought before the mob in chains, so many clustered to a cart like animals marked for slaughter.

"These," Robespierre cried, "these will finally be made to atone for what they have done to us lo these many, many years." He looked at the people in the carts contemptuously, the devil about to collect the souls whose signatures he held in his hand. "These will be made to suffer and quake while they wait for Monsieur Guillotine," his mouth curved malevolently in rapturous anticipation, "to listen to their final pleas and pitiful screams for mercy."

With each word, the mob became more and more incensed and unruly.

Beth watched as the carts were led, one by one, way into the Bastille. She felt her eyes moisten at the heart-wrenching sight and upbraided herself. She could not allow herself the luxury of crying for these poor souls. If she were seen crying, it would be the end of her.

None could suspect her feelings at this time for the

crowd that swelled and swirled around her could easy tear her in half.

"Death, death to them all," the crowd began to chant, their voices rising and blending as if one. The demand throbbed like the beat of wild drums.

Duncan tugged on her hand. She looked at him and saw that his lips were moving, as if he, too, were repeating the words, though he understood them not. His message was clear. To stay undetected, they perforce had to appear to be one with the mob.

Mimicking him, Beth moved her lips, though not a single sound came forth. She could not bear to utter the words, she could not bear to force them from her mouth, even to save her own life.

But to save Duncan's, for she knew he would die defending her, she pretended to chant the blood lust cries of the crazed mob.

"Death, death to them all."

And then her heart froze within her breast and she gave up the pretense.

Duncan saw the look of horror that overcame her. He looked from Beth toward the carts. In the midst of the last one stood a tall, thin man, patrician in appearance, even though his clothes were in tatters. He wore a small, graying beard, and even at this distance, Duncan could see the shape of Beth's face repeated on the man's.

"Death! Death to them all!"

Duncan leaned down to be close to Beth's ear. "Is that—?"

She did not answer him. Instead, her fingers slackened within his and suddenly he realized that she had let go. Duncan knew her intent immediately.

Beth was pushing her way forward, trying to get to the cart.

Damn the woman, did she think she could rescue her father single-handedly while all the citizens of Paris looked on?

Beth gasped as she felt the strong arm surround her waist and pull her back, lifting her off her feet. The scream she uttered dissolved, unheard, into the mob.

She looked up into Duncan's face. Before she could say a single word of reproof to him, he clamped his hand over her mouth.

"Not now," he hissed. "Not here."

No one within the frenzied mob took any notice of them. Their eyes were on the symbols of their misery: the people in the carts.

The people they had condemned to die, if not today, then tomorrow, and the more painfully, the more degradingly, the better.

Chapter Thirty-four

Somehow, though he was not certain how, as inconspicuously as possible, Duncan managed to get Beth away from the mob. Slowly they made their way back to where they had left Jacob waiting with the horses.

Duncan waited until they were clear of the rabble before he said anything to her. If he waited until his temper cooled, it would have taken too long.

"What possible good did you think you could accomplish by rushing up there?" Duncan demanded.

Though she struggled, he kept a tight hold around her waist. He half dragged, half carried her as they hurried from there. He was afraid that if he released her, she would run back.

"I could have let him see me. Let him see that all was not lost," she insisted.

How could Duncan be so heartless? Couldn't he empathize with what her father must be experiencing? Didn't he understand what it was like, to be vilified before a mob, to be degraded? Her father needed to know that there was help for him.

Where was her mind? "It would have been, if he had seen you. Do you think he would be happy to know his daughter is in danger? Or if he had been so stripped of thought that his face lit to see you, do you think that would have gone unnoticed by that arrogant devil officiating over the whole thing?" An angry cry strangled in his throat. "You would have been as good as dead."

She softened, her anger cooling. Duncan had only been thinking of her.

"I couldn't stand to see him like that, Duncan. In chains." She pressed her lips together to keep the sob back. "There were bruises. Even at that distance, I saw them. They've been beating him."

He knew what she was feeling, but he had to think on a larger scale than immediate action and reaction. It would take a plan to free Dr. Beaulieu, not reckless behavior.

"Bruises will heal, Beth. We will save him, this I promise you. But it will take time. Be patient a little longer."

Her sigh was ragged. "If he has a little longer," she murmured under her breath.

As they approached, Jacob started, his hands tightening about the reins he still held in one hand and the pistol he brandished in the other. When he saw that it was them, he sagged against the wall, as if the air had suddenly left his body.

"Thank God it's you, Duncan." He straightened again, knowing what was expected of him. He had been too long with Duncan not to. One was never lax in the camp of the enemy. "I don't like it here. There's a smell of death and madness to this city." When he realized the import of his words, he flushed and looked at Beth apologetically. They were not here to pass the time, but to find her father. "Did you find your father, mistress?"

Beth's voice was hardly above a whisper. "Aye, we found him."

Jacob narrowed his eyes as he looked beyond them toward the entrance. "Where is he?"

Beth exchanged looks with Duncan. Everything that Duncan had said was true, but still, she could not help the feeling she had. If there had just been some way she could have sent her father a sign, she knew that both of them would feel better for it.

"Imprisoned in the Bastille," she answered. *Awaiting execution* . . .

The name was familiar to Jacob. He looked at Duncan for confirmation. "That big old castle we saw yesterday?"

Had it really been that short a while? Duncan wondered. It felt as if a lifetime had gone by since then. So much had happened to them. To Beth.

"Fortress," Duncan corrected.

Duncan placed his hand on Beth's shoulder, afraid to break contact with her even now. He did not know the extent of her emotions, nor how they had affected her. He'd seen women swoon at far less. But then, he had seen Beth kill a man in order to save him, so perhaps she was made of sterner stuff, as he'd believed.

He looked into her eyes and had his answer. Slowly he withdrew his hand.

"Now that we know where he is, we have to find a way to get him out." Restless, he stroked the hilt of his sword as he cast about for some plan.

For Jacob, the straightest route between two points was always the simplest. He raised the pistol Duncan had entrusted him with.

"We could fight our way in."

Duncan gently redirected the pistol's muzzle until it

pointed to the ground. He laughed indulgently at Jacob's suggestion. His manner did not belittle Jacob, which was what he wanted. Jacob had a good heart and a loyal soul; it was only his mind that was a little slow.

"For that, we would need a score of you, Jacob. And even then, I'd wager," he glanced at Beth, "there'd be no getting out, once we were in. No, stealth will be necessary in this case. Stealth, and someone on the inside we could trust. Or bribe." He blew out a breath. "Preferably both."

Had this been London, the matter would have been settled in a trice. He knew many palms he had but to cross with gold in London to get his way. But Paris was a different matter entirely.

He looked to Beth, but she only shook her head helplessly. She slapped the reins against her hand in frustration. "I don't know anyone here who could help."

He had thought as much, or she'd have volunteered the information long before now. Duncan rubbed his hand along the back of his neck, thinking. "We need time to plan and think."

"Time is short," Beth reminded him. Robespierre looked as if he could arouse the crowd at any time to murder all the people he held prisoner. He needed but a whim; he already possessed the excuse.

"Without a plan," Duncan countered, "it would be endless."

Beth pressed her lips together, suppressing the desire to scream.

"We can go to the house of the old man Therese mentioned," she remembered suddenly, her eyes brightening. Perhaps they would learn something useful there. There was always hope. She saw a dubious look arise on Duncan's face. "She thought we might be safe there," she reminded him.

Duncan thought her suggestion over for a moment. "I don't believe that we will be safe anywhere in this city, but going there is the only course open to us at the moment. We cannot remain in this alley indefinitely." He glanced at the stone wall. "And I have never cared for places that have but one way out."

He took the lead. "Do you recall the directions, Beth?"

"As easily as my own name," she answered.

"You are a treasure," he murmured softly, as they left the shelter of the alley behind them.

The man who opened the door to them upon Beth's knock looked as if he weighed less than she did. He was stoop shouldered, with a face that had long since grown to look soured on life. There were a few wisps of brown hair dancing riotously upon his head, like feathers the wind had blown astray. They swayed with every movement he made. A tiny fringe encircled his head by his ears. He wore spectacles and looked over them at the three who stood before his house with deep suspicion.

They had left their horses at the rear of the hovel. For the moment, they were safe. "Louis, Therese sent us," Beth whispered.

He looked surprised that she knew his name. Still he stood here, his darkly spotted hands clutching the splintered wooden door to his chest as if it were a shield that would protect him against them. One kick from Duncan's boot could easily have separated the door from its hinges, but the man seemed not to think on that.

He squinted until his tiny eyes all but disappeared completely.

"Why?" he rasped, in a voice that had been long since been erased by whisky. "Why would she do that?"

Duncan felt helpless as this exchange went on. He caught only names and a word now and then. Their fate lay in Beth's hand. A hand governed by an unsettled mind, but a worthy one, too.

Beth saw doubt enter the man's eyes. Therese had said Louis had been the groundskeeper at the estate. He had been one of the servants who had fled when Robespierre had come to take her father prisoner. Ashamed of his cowardice, Louis had tried in his own small, frightened way to make amends by providing a little shelter for fleeing aristocrats. But never for long.

Beth pressed on. "She thought we might be safe here. The city is in upheaval, and she was worried about us." Beth paused. "She sends you greetings from the mademoiselle. Madam is dead."

She said it solemnly, but with no feeling. Beth knew if she gave vent to any, all would spill out, and she could not let herself give in to it. Duncan was right. Cool heads would prevail here, not hot blood.

Louis stepped back, though the suspicion did not leave his face entirely. Quickly they hurried inside. Louis bolted the door closed once more, then turned and regarded the three in the dim light of his tiny home.

"You cannot stay," he informed them, not realizing that only Beth understood him.

"We want but an hour or two here," Beth assured him. "Perhaps even less."

There was a time for trust and a time for secrecy, but Beth knew that risks had to be taken if her father was to be freed. She had to trust this man, though she did not feel comfortable doing so.

"What we need is information." It was a handy word to cover a myriad of things. She had no idea what it was they needed, beyond a miracle. "There is someone in the Bastille, someone we must free."

"You?" Louis looked at the men with her, and then at Beth once more. "We'd likely see the Second Coming before you three could manage to free someone from those jaws of death. If he or she is in the Bastille, then they are as good as dead now."

He turned from them and went to poke at the fire that did not seem to want to rise. Even on such a hot day, he wanted to keep a fire going. It was the only thing he had to keep the demons at bay.

Embers glowed and hissed at him, as if angered by the poker's disturbance.

"We want to save Philippe Beaulieu," she said to the man's back.

The poker fell. A moment later, Louis turned around again. He squinted at her face. "I thought you had the look about you."

"He is my father." Beth grasped Louis's hand, imploring the man now. "Please, if there is some way we could get in—"

But Louis shook his head, genuinely sorry now. "No, none. For that, you would need someone great on your side. Perhaps even the sword of Lafayette himself."

The name of the ex-patriot had her eyes widening. "Lafayette?" she repeated. "Is he here? Is he in Paris somewhere?" A shred of hope began to grow.

Louis shook his head. "No."

Beth fought to keep from throwing something in utter frustration.

"What's the matter, Beth?" Duncan took her arm. "What is he saying?"

"I thought we had found a way out." Beth suddenly felt drained to the core. Louis looked at her, confused by the fact that she was speaking another language. "They are English," she explained wearily, in French. "Here to help me rescue my father." *Which is becoming less and less of a possibility* . . .

"Lafayette is not here," Louis repeated, eager to correct the misunderstanding. "But he is close by. He is camped on the outskirts of the city, perhaps a half day's ride from here. Rumors have it," Louis qualified.

Beth didn't understand. "Why would he be camped beyond the city?"

Louis spread his hands as he lifted his shoulders. "Where else would the new Commander of the National Guard be? It is said he is coming to guard the city. Though whether he comes to guard us from them or them from us, I fear I do not know."

"Dear God," Beth whispered.

Duncan saw all the color wash out of Beth's face. He grabbed her, prepared to break her fall, should she collapse. She had the look of one about to faint.

"What?" Duncan demanded, frustrated that he couldn't follow what was being said. "You look as if you've seen an apparition."

"Almost." Her mouth felt dry, and she tried to lick her lips. There was no way to describe how she felt. "He's on the other side." She looked at Duncan, trying to make him understand the import of her words. "Lafayette is with the mob."

There was something in her voice that caught his attention. "You speak as if you know him."

"I do. I did," she corrected. She began to roam about

the tiny table, trying to organize thoughts that were completely scattered, like leaves in the wind. "I met him once, as a child."

She turned on her heel and looked at Duncan. This had to be their key to her father's cell. There was no other available.

"The important thing is that he fought beside my father in the Revolution." She stared into the embers that wouldn't catch hold. "It would seem that he developed a taste for battle and wished for more." She raised her eyes suddenly to Duncan. "We have to go to him. I have to talk to him. He's our only hope. If he allows my father to go free—"

But Duncan was far more of a realist than Beth. "Why would he do that?"

"Because he is a decent man." She said the words fiercely, as if to convince herself as well as Duncan. "Or was." Helpless, she lifted her shoulders and let them fall again. "Because I can think of nothing else and as you said, we cannot fight our way in." She shut her eyes to squeeze back tears.

Taking a deep breath to steady herself, Beth turned toward Louis. "Can you help us find him?"

Louis shrank into the shadows, as if hoping they would somehow blot him out from her view. "I am only an old man—"

Incensed, Beth grasped the frayed ends of his vest, holding him fast.

"I need you to help me save another man, a man you know to be good and kind and decent. Tell me all you know about Lafayette and where he is camped." Beth's voice grew in agitation, if not in volume. "Tell me exactly, or tell me where to find someone who knows."

They had no time to ride about, scouring the country-side. Every minute was vital now.

For a brief moment, Louis hesitated, torn between his desire to help and his desire to live out the remainder of his days untroubled by either side.

After a moment, he fell back and opened the door to the tiny room in the rear.

A horrible stench rose from the room. There was but one window and precious little light within the room. And death had come to hover there as well.

On a pallet lay a young man, no more than twenty or so. His right leg had been removed at the knee. The bandages about his stump were old and filthy. He looked at the people in the doorway with the eyes of bitterness.

"Take them away, old man," he cried, rancor in every syllable.

Louis left the door open, though his heart seem to shrivel in his chest to do so.

"My grandson Marcus was a soldier with Lafayette. They sent him home a week ago. He is not expected to live." The words came heavily. Louis could not bring himself to look at the bandaged limb. "The gangrene has spread too far."

Beth could tell by the smell rising from the limb that Louis was right. Though her heart grieved to see such suffering, there was nothing she could do for Marcus. Curbing her sorrow, she forced herself to enter the air-less room. She waved for Duncan and Jacob to remain outside with Louis.

"I need to see Lafayette," she told Marcus softly. "I have urgent business with him."

Marcus shifted the body that was all but shriveled now on the filthy pallet.

"Are you his whore?" he spat out.

She didn't take offense. It was bitterness at life's cruelty that made him say the words.

"No, that is not my business with him. He knows my father, and I am looking for him," she fabricated. She had no idea if the boy was secretly loyal to the Crown or to Robespierre, or to no one. "I need to find where Lafayette is camped."

It made no difference to Marcus whether she did or not. If he did not answer, she would continue to plague him with questions and noise. So he told her. "The encampment is fifteen miles southwest of Paris. He was to leave for Paris tomorrow."

Marcus turned his face to the wall. "God willing, it will all burn down to the ground soon, and me with it," he whispered to himself.

But Beth heard.

She backed away and slowly closed the door. Beth looked at the old man. There were tears shining in the small eyes. "Godspeed, sir." She shook Louis's hand. "And thank you."

"For what?" Louis asked, his lip curling in a cynical sneer. "I've undoubtedly sent you to your deaths, only faster than you could get there yourselves."

But Beth did not hear. The old man and his grandson had lost all their hope, but she hadn't.

She grasped Duncan's hand. "I know where Lafayette is. We have to hurry."

They left the hovel quickly and rode from the city as fast as they were able.

Chapter Thirty-five

The camp was not located where Marcus had said it would be. Rather than fifteen, it was more than twenty miles from the city outskirts.

Beth had begun to despair in her heart that they would never find Lafayette's camp. But then, just as Duncan was about to suggest that they turn back, they saw it, a huge encampment located just beyond a ridge, far closer to Versailles than to Paris.

The soldiers' tents were scattered about in the distance like so many lily pads upon the water. But unlike the green pads, what thrived within the tents was deadly.

"Thank God," Beth murmured. "I was beginning to give up hope."

She was about to give her horse its rein, but Duncan caught them in his hand, forcing her to remain where she was. Beth looked at him quizzically.

The thought of entering a camp with so many armed men gave Duncan pause.

"Beth, are you sure about this?"

They'd come so far to see Lafayette. How could Duncan possibly question her like this now? "Yes, I'm sure. 'Tis the only way."

Still he kept the reins in his hand, hesitating because he feared for her safety. "But you yourself said that Lafayette is now on a different side. He's on the side of the rebellion."

She had tried not to dwell on that on the long ride here, trusting, instead, to what her father had told her about the man.

"He is a fair and reasonable man. A man of honor," she insisted heatedly, as if saying it aloud would make it so. Beth bit her lip. She had no right to drag Duncan into this, nor Jacob, either. Her eyes washed over them both. "You may retreat if you wish."

Retreating wasn't the point. He was no coward. But not a fool, either, except, it seemed, where she was concerned.

"What I wish is to keep you safe." Duncan nodded toward the encampment in the distance. "This isn't the best way to do it."

To his surprise, she yanked the reins from his hands. "I cannot stay here and debate this with you any longer, Duncan."

Beth kicked her heels into the horse's flanks. The horse immediately responded and galloped quickly down the incline toward the encampment.

"Now we look as if we're chasing her," Duncan bit off as he urged his stallion on. Jacob's bay was right behind him. "Wonderful. The soldiers will all see and fire on us. The gods have visited a plague upon me, and its name is Elizabeth."

Hearing him, Beth pulled on her reins and slowed her horse. She turned in her saddle, waiting for them to join her.

Guilt pricked at her conscience once more.

"You needn't come, if you don't want to," she repeated, aware that the color in Duncan's eyes had grown dark. "I'll understand. This is not your affair."

Jacob was first to reach her. "I shall accompany you, mistress."

He was eager to serve, if not so eager to ride into a camp full of soldiers. A camp of soldiers, any soldiers, made Jacob decidedly uneasy. His conscience was not so clear that he could walk freely around enforcers of the law and feel no anxiety.

Duncan let out a breath as he pulled up beside Beth's horse.

"We both will, though heaven have mercy on our souls." He gestured toward the camp. "Because *they* very well may not."

Summoning all the bravado he had at his disposal, he rode beside Beth into the camp. To all who looked upon him, Duncan gave the appearance of a man who was accustomed to having his wishes carried out.

Soldiers trickled out from the tents. Others were in the open, practicing maneuvers, and turned to watch. Some looked at the incoming three with mild interest, while others regarded them with marked suspicion in their eyes.

Duncan cautioned Beth and Jacob to look neither to the left nor the right, merely ahead, toward their destination—the only tent within the camp that had two guards posted before it.

But as they approached the tent, a lieutenant emerged from within, summoned by the call of one of the guards. Young, brash, and full of the authority of the uniform he wore, he was quick to grab the bit on Beth's horse.

"Hold, Duncan," Beth hissed, without turning around. There was no need to. She knew that Duncan had his hand on his sword, ready to leap to her defense.

The lieutenant regarded her with dark blue eyes that had no feeling behind them. "What business do you have in this camp?"

She matched his arrogant tone. "I am here to see Lafayette."

The men at the tent's entrance exchanged knowing looks at the sound of her voice. The lieutenant's face remained impassive.

"There are many who wish to see the commander. Take your grievances elsewhere." He turned his back, ready to dismiss her.

Her voice stopped him from leaving. "They are not grievances."

He turned slowly around. "Pleasures, then?" A smile slid over his face like a snake slithering along the ground. He approached and rested his hand on Beth's thigh. "Perhaps I should test them first for him. Great men in history had food tasters. Why not a whore taster as well?" He leered at her.

Beth's heart quickened, knowing that Duncan did not understand the words, but could easy comprehend the intent behind them. Her eyes narrowed as she looked down at the officer.

"Lafayette would cut your heart out." She said the words quietly and with such conviction that the man feared the risk in attempting to prove her wrong.

Uttering a curse, he dropped his hand and became formal once more as he drew his shoulders back. Behind him, Beth saw the two guards attempting not to laugh.

"I am afraid that I cannot—"

Beth wouldn't let him finish. With the air of someone born to authority, she charged him to, "Tell Commander

Lafayette that Elizabeth Beaulieu requests an audience with him."

For a moment the lieutenant stood there, balancing his weight on his toes as he seemed to debate whether or not to allow himself to be intimidated. The look Beth gave him never wavered. Finally, he turned on his heel and grudgingly withdrew.

Duncan looked around them uneasily. They were obviously the center of attention. All eyes seemed to be focused on the ragtag threesome on horseback. Duncan wondered if they were going to have to fight their way out.

"Why couldn't your father have been taken to the Tower of London instead of the Bastille?" Duncan complained to her under his breath. "Then at least I could understand what was being said, instead of enduring all this foreign babble."

Beth smiled at his choice of words. "Here, Duncan, you are the foreign one."

In the next moment, the tent flap flew back once again, this time with a vengeance. The lieutenant stepped forward. It was plain to see by his expression that he was not happy about the situation. He would much rather have sent her swiftly on her way.

"The commander will see you." He took a step forward when all three began to dismount. "Only you," he cautioned Beth pointedly.

Beth looked over her shoulder at Jacob and Duncan. Not for the world would she take the risk of leaving them outside. There was no way to foretell what might happen to them.

"They come with me," Beth informed the lieutenant, leaving no room for him to argue with her. "You may enter and protect your commander, if you fear us." Her mouth momentarily curved in amusement, and she saw that her words had rankled him. So much the better. "We mean no one any harm. We come with an entreaty that only Lafayette is able to help us with."

Stiffly, the lieutenant pulled aside the flap and let them enter, his face a mask of contempt and anger.

Here was one, Beth thought, who gladly fought in this revolution. She prayed God the same couldn't be said for Lafayette.

Beth entered and saw the newly appointed Commander of the National Guard standing over a table, studying several maps that were spread out over the rough-hewn surface.

At thirty-two, the former darling of the American Revolution and Washington's personal favorite had seen two insurrections and successfully survived the first. He felt extremely wearied by the world in which he found himself living. Where once the issues were crystal clear, like a mountain stream, now they had gotten obscured, as muddied as the banks of the River Seine. As the new commander, he sought for a peaceful transfer of power from the aristocracy to the bourgeoisie, but in his heart he knew this was not to be, and his choice bedeviled him.

He looked up as Beth and the others entered. There was no recognition in his eyes as he quickly took account of her. There was only a dark suspicion.

He was not the smiling, handsome youth she remembered, the one who had made her very young heart flutter when, though wounded, he'd taken her hand in his and politely kissed it. With that one action he had forever endeared himself to her.

Though there were lines now about his face, and he

had filled out his uniform more aptly, he was still quite attractive.

But much, much sadder in appearance.

Lafayette blew out an impatient breath. His days and nights were filled with complaints and his dreams were filled with the cries of unavenged gentry, mingled with the entreaties of his ancestors. He constantly fought the war without and struggled with the war within. He stood now just a step beyond a crossroads, and though he had chosen a path for himself, he did not know if it was the right one.

He would have sold his soul to know.

It was all he could do to keep his indecision from his men. A leader could not afford to be thought of as vacillating. What's more, he feared himself at the helm of a ship that would not go where he steered it.

Lafayette stepped forward, studying Beth's face now as intently as he had studied the maps a moment ago.

"Do I know you, Mademoiselle?" Lafayette asked, in French.

"We met once," Beth replied in English. "In America. At a plantation owned by my father." She watched him struggle with a memory, attempting to bring it to the fore. "You were very handsome and very brave. Washington couldn't sing your praises enough," she remembered with a smile. The smile reached her eyes as she added, "You were very kind to an eleven-year-old girl."

She knew the exact moment he remembered. The evidence was in his eyes.

Lafayette nodded, vaguely envisioning her the way she had been. A very young girl with laughing eyes and skillful hands she had inherited from her father. The circumstances returned slowly to him. He remembered that he had been wounded and Beaulieu had taken him into his own home to see to his care.

"You have grown up."

She inclined her head. "And you have grown more powerful."

It wasn't a mantle he wore with delight. But it was necessary. "Power seems to be the only way to make things right."

She wondered if he really believed that. Something in his eyes, a glimmer, told her he didn't. At least, not completely.

"Not always, Commander."

He thought of the monarchy and of the men who had seized power in their stead. Sometimes he wondered which was the worse.

"No," he agreed quietly. "Not always. But you did not come all this way to debate philosophies with me, am I correct?"

He wanted her to be gone, she thought, digging in. "I will be brief. I know you are very busy." She looked down at the maps and wondered if there was some strategy he was mounting, and against whom. Was he to officiate at the executions? She felt her heart in her throat and glanced at Duncan for courage. "My father returned to France to see if he could be of some aid."

So this was about the doctor, Lafayette thought. He saw his lieutenant watching him, a serpent ready to strike at the slightest opportunity. "Which side did he take?"

He was more concerned with sides and not with right, she thought, her heart sinking.

Beth's voice took on a formal edge. "The side of humanity, sir. Wherever there were sick and wounded. His first duty is to his oath as a physician."

"I see."

Lafayette's eyes looked cold, she thought, desperate for a way to break through to him. "For his trouble, he has been arrested and is being held in the Bastille."

Lafayette had recrossed to his maps. He leaned forward, his hands on the table, his eyes on Beth's face. He saw her anguish, but his hands were tied.

"And you wish me to free him."

"Yes." Passion rang out in the single word.

Lafayette shook his head as he straightened. "I cannot."

She stared at him in horror, unable to believe what he was saying to her. "You can't mean that."

He wished it might be otherwise, but it wasn't. Beaulieu had known this when he had gotten involved. "On the contrary, I do."

Beth grasped his arm. "But you fought together, side by side. He saved your life. You lived in my home. How can you just abandon him like this?" She didn't understand how a man could turn his back on all that.

Lafayette waved a hand in the air. "That was a different time, Mademoiselle Beaulieu. We are now apparently on opposite sides, your father and I." There was an abysmal sorrow in his eyes. "All revolutions have sacrifices, all are written in blood."

He was distancing himself from her though he took not a step. It was something he had learned how to do in the last few years. There was no other way to withstand the horrors that surrounded him.

"This is no different than the other." Lafayette inclined his head, already returning to his maps. "You have come all this way for nothing, I am afraid. Now, if you will excuse me—"

"No," Beth cried, catching his arm again. "No, I will not excuse you."

The lieutenant drew his sword with the full intent of driving Beth off. Just as quickly, Duncan and Jacob shield her on both sides with their bodies, their swords at the ready.

Chapter Thirty-six

Tensions sizzled within the tent as swords and sides were crossed. Tempers were frayed, and Lafayette knew how easily lives could be lost because of that one simple factor. He was quick to step between the two opponents.

His eyes were on his lieutenant. Of the three, Lafayette reasoned that he was the most dangerous, though he would not be quick to turn his back on the taller man with Elizabeth. The man had the raw look of courage about him, and the courageous were known to do daring deeds, even when the odds were against them.

"Put up your sword, Maximillien."

The lieutenant looked as if his very honor had been ripped from him. The dark blue eyes grew wide with indignation. He grasped his sword more firmly as a challenge rose to his lips.

"But—"

The expression on Lafayette's face hardened. He would brook no insubordination. He knew the avalanche that would quickly follow.

"I said put up your sword."

Hatred shimmered, barely contained, in the blue eyes

as the lieutenant shoved his sword back into the scabbard. Only after he did so did Duncan and Jacob sheathed their weapons as well.

"What good is the blood of one innocent man on your hands?" Duncan asked, as Lafayette turned toward them once more.

Lafayette regarded the other man in silence for a moment. "You refer to yourself?"

Duncan shook his head. "To Doctor Beaulieu."

Lafayette shrugged helplessly. "If I make an exception here," he began with regret, "I must make exceptions everywhere."

He would be inundated with pleas within a matter of weeks, each one undoubtedly more heart wrenching than the last.

But Beth refused to be put off. "What does your heart tell you?"

A bittersweet smile barely grazed his lips. "I have no heart, Mademoiselle. It was cut out years ago while I watched my beloved country being plunged into poverty and despair by a feeble-minded monarch who indulged a coldblooded queen."

Beth couldn't accept his reasoning. "Is that an excuse to execute so many? To execute my father, who came here only to help, just as you came to America?"

The agony of his decision was there in his eyes for her to see. And take heart from. She would not give up her assault as long as there was a shred of a chance she could persuade him to change his position.

Lafayette turned from her, wanting to close out the sound of her voice, the sound of her argument. It echoed in his mind nonetheless. "Then he should have joined the right side."

Duncan had heard those same arguments before, on the lips of other men.

"Victories decide which side is right. Later, those labels become history." Duncan measured the man before them and found him to be as Beth had said. A good man. A man trapped in an unspeakable position. "Whether a man is a hero or an outlaw depends on the outcome of certain circumstances."

Beth saw that Lafayette was weakening and quickly attempted to widen the opening. "You said all revolutions were the same."

"They are," Lafayette agreed, without feeling.

Beth shook her head, her hair whipping about her face. "During the American Revolution, soldiers fought man to man. There was no talk of public executions of innocent children and women, no atonement sought for grievances that were decades old. No thought of penance for the sins of the fathers."

She laid a hand imploringly on his arm. "Don't you see? This revolution is *not* like the other was. There the people wanted their freedom. Here they want vengeance."

She wasn't reaching him, she realized. Lafayette's expression was stony and unapproachable. He had made his decision and wouldn't allow anything to convince him to change it.

Beth dropped her hand from his arm.

Her voice was weary and full of pity for him when she spoke again.

"My father always spoke highly of you. He said if he did nothing else worthwhile, he had saved your life, and for that, history would thank him." She felt tears gathering in her eyes and her voice shook with feeling. "Too bad it turned out to be at his own expense."

She turned her back on him and began to walk away. The lieutenant smirked as he drew aside the tent flap for her so she might pass.

"Wait."

She thought she would sink to her knees at the sound of the command. Instead, she managed to turn around once more. Thank God, she thought. Thank God.

"Yes, Commander?"

The lieutenant was eying him contemptuously, Lafayette thought. He would have to find a way to have the man transferred, and soon, though Maximillien had been with the guard a long time. If he didn't, the man would either have his job, or his head. Neither could be allowed to happen.

"Maximillien, wait outside," he ordered.

"Commander, I hardly think—"

The look on Lafayette's face darkened. "I said, wait outside."

The lieutenant turned as stiffly as if a bayonet had been pressed between his shoulder blades.

As soon as the man was gone, Lafayette began to write something hastily. He signed his name with a flourish, then dipped his signet ring into red wax. He pressed the wax to the folded letter.

He raised his eyes to Beth's and saw her thanks there. "Here, take this to the captain of the guards at the Bastille. He will recognize my seal."

Beth pressed the letter to her breast, gratitude flooding through her veins.

"Your father is free," Lafayette pronounced. "Tell him the debt is repaid." A smile curved his mouth, one of the few he allowed himself these days. "And that he has a daughter who would have made a worthy soldier had she but been born a man."

Duncan laughed, remembering the way Beth had handled a pistol when she'd saved his life. "You don't know the half of it, Commander. You don't even know the half of it."

"I would have enjoyed finding out." But that was for other men, Lafayette thought sadly. Men who did not find themselves thrust into the midst of arranging their country's destiny.

For the moment, Beth tucked the letter inside her waistband. She would place it securely inside her saddlebags at the first opportunity. Beth took his hand into hers. There were no proper words she could offer. "I cannot begin to thank you."

Lafayette extricated himself. "Then do not even waste the time, for it is precious. I am told that Robespierre wants the executions to begin at dawn."

A chill ran over her heart. She remembered what Marcus had said: that the National Guard was coming to Paris. "You will be there to watch?"

He had no stomach for the guillotine. "No, there's need of my men at Orleans instead. Farewell, Mademoiselle. And Godspeed to us both."

"Godspeed," she echoed.

Duncan took her arm and they hurried out.

Their horses were just as they had left them, tethered before the tent. Though the guards looked upon them as a curiosity, obviously falling into the realm of their commander's favor, the lieutenant stood back and made no effort to hide his dislike.

"I'm glad we're leaving that one behind," Jacob said in a whisper as they rode from the camp.

"You're not the only one," Duncan agreed.

* * *

They were within three miles of Paris when the incident happened.

One moment they were on the road, the next, they were beset on two sides by marauders. Though it was reported that roving bands roamed the countryside, using the revolution as an excuse to plunder and steal, it all happened so quickly, Beth and the men were completely unprepared.

It was suddenly raining men from the very trees and the bushes. There were four, perhaps five. Duncan could not count them, they moved so swiftly.

"Ambush, Beth. *Run!*" He leaned to slap the rump of her horse, but it was too late.

There were hands grabbing at her reins and more grabbing for her legs. Someone pulled her from her horse and Beth hit the ground with a thud that stunned her almost senseless.

Something warm seemed to be oozing just over her eye. The next moment Beth screamed as she felt hot, rancid breath on her face and a man's filthy hands groping hungrily over her body.

"Hey!" the man crowed. In a lumbering movement, he straddled her body in glee. "This one's soft. It's a female!"

He laughed, and the very sound drove bits of glass through her body.

"I'll be well rewarded for my trouble." A mouth with rotting teeth grinned macabrely over her. "Don't worry, your death'll be quick, but first my pleasure."

He began to rip her clothing as another man held her hands above her head. Beth bucked and cursed, but it was to no avail. She couldn't move him off her.

Suddenly, she heard Duncan's outraged cry. It sounded

only half human. The next moment, the man fell over to the side, his blood spurting from the wound in his back. Duncan had buried his sword into the would-be rapist up to the hilt.

Duncan pulled his sword out again and turned on the other man above Beth. The latter scrambled back, yelling in fear. But Jacob caught him with the point of his sword and ran him through.

A third man flew at them, a broken sword raised. Beth pulled her pistol and fired at him. He fell where he had run. Duncan turned to deflect a sword from yet another marauder and quickly did away with him. Two more fled, knowing when all was lost.

It was over as quickly as it had begun. Four lay dead upon the ground beside the very people they wished to rob and kill.

Duncan scanned the area swiftly to make certain that there were no others left who would attack them. But there were none.

Satisfied, he turned to Beth just in time to catch her as she sagged.

"Are you all right?" he asked.

Of course she wasn't all right, he thought, impotent anger and helplessness knitting together. She'd almost been senselessly violated. What woman would be all right under those circumstances?

Beth ran a shaky hand over her body. She pulled closed her rented shirt and made an attempt to tuck it back into her britches. She looked up at Duncan. If it hadn't been for him . . .

She couldn't even bear to think on it. "Yes. Thanks to you," she said softly.

For a moment, all he wanted to do was just hold her

against him. To feel her warm and safe. "God, Beth, when I saw his hands on you—"

She could feel his heart pounding wildly against his ribs. She blinked the moisture from her eyes.

"But you saved me," she whispered. "And that is all that matters."

Leaving them alone, Jacob silently examined each man on the ground to assure himself that they were truly dead. He held a dagger ready in his hands, just in case. There wasn't a breath of life left within the lot of them.

Duncan looked down and saw a fresh red stain on his chest where Beth's head had been only a moment ago. Cupping her chin in his hand, he examined her face closely. It was just as he'd feared.

"That's a nasty gash you have on your head." Duncan felt around it gingerly. The area would swell and bruise soon, he thought. Right now, he wanted to stop the bleeding.

Beth pulled away. "We've no time to waste now. We have to ride into Paris. Lafayette said the executions begin tomorrow at dawn. There isn't much time left, if that is true. We have to free my father before then."

But as she took a step away from Duncan, she tottered and nearly sank to her knees.

Duncan grabbed her arm to steady her. "For God sakes, Beth, you are only human." Holding her firmly by the arm, he looked at Jacob. "Jacob, fetch me your water pouch."

Jacob was quick to obey.

Carefully, Duncan poured a little water upon his handkerchief and used it to clean her wound.

Beth shifted where she stood. "There's no time to fuss," she implored.

"Correction, there's no time to watch you bleed to death. God, you make an awful patient." He tied the handkerchief about her head as best he could, hoping that the bleeding would cease soon.

"I'm fine, fine." She pushed away his hand and rose. This time, she gained her legs more steadily. "I don't need to be treated like a child."

His eyes narrowed. Though she didn't wish it, he took her arm again, lest she fall. He'd rather have her pride hurt than her body.

"If that were the case, you'd have been over my knee a long time ago."

It would have been easy to take offense and rail at him, but she knew that she owed Duncan a debt she could not hope to repay.

"I'm sorry."

He smiled at her and touched her cheek with the back of his hand. "Apology accepted."

Beth looked around. Panic began to mount within her. "Where's my horse?"

They all turned to look now, but there were only the two horses. Beth's was gone.

"Duncan." She clutched at his arm. "That man, he took my horse."

It was a loss, he admitted, but not a fatal one. They still had two left, thank the gods. He gave her an encouraging look.

"We'll ride double." And perhaps they could find someone to sell them a third. They would have need of the horse once Beth's father was freed.

He didn't understand, she thought, almost beside herself. It was difficult keeping the hysteria out of her voice.

"The letter, Duncan." He looked at her as the reason for her distress became apparent. "Lafayette's letter was in the saddlebag, as was half the gold we brought to ransom my father!"

Chapter Thirty-seven

It seemed to Beth that no sooner had she realized that her horse had been stolen, and with it, Lafayette's precious letter, than more trouble was suddenly looming on the horizon.

Jacob tugged urgently on Duncan's arm.

"Duncan, look. To the east." Agitated by the battle that had just passed, Jacob drew his sword out quickly, ready to defend Beth to the death, if need be. "More men coming."

One hand protectively thrown out before Beth, Duncan swung around to look up. Approaching them swiftly were four men on horseback.

"Damn this countryside, it's crawling with cutthroats and murderers, and I can't understand a word any of them says." He looked quickly over his shoulder to Jacob. "Quick, take her to the horses. You stand a chance of outriding them."

But Jacob stood fast for a moment, puzzled. "With two on a horse?"

Duncan shook his head. "No, you take Beth. I'll stand here and hold them off as long as I can. Hurry, there's not much time before—"

Jacob had his hand on Beth's arm, about to obey Duncan's order. But Beth pulled free, her eyes on Duncan.

"The devil you will," Beth shouted at him. "We all go, or we all stay. I am *not* leaving you behind."

Biting off an oath, Duncan looked up again to see how far away the riders were now.

"Woman, you are—" His voice abruptly trailed off as he tried to make out the face of the leader. "Jacob." He beckoned to the other man. "Look at those men again. The tall one in front, the one with the long, flowing brown hair." He looked at Jacob to see if there was any recognition. "Christian?"

Jacob squinted. He leaned forward, like a bird regarding his reflection on a pond. A grin spread over his lips. "Aye."

Beth fisted her hands at her waist. Had they gone mad? "What does it matter what religion they are?"

Duncan laughed at her question, realizing what she must have thought. He took another look at the leader, who was now only a few yards away, and confirmed his original supposition.

"No, not his religion, Beth, his name: Christian. Jacques Christian."

"What ho, pilgrims. Are you in any sort of trouble?" the man Duncan knew as Jacques Christian called to them in French.

Duncan had no idea what Jacques asked, but he cupped his hands and shouted back. "We certainly don't need any help from any black-hearted, seafaring pirates like you, Christian."

Surprised to be addressed by name, the tall, proud-looking man pulled up his horse for a moment in order to focus better. Recognition followed instantly as he took a good look at the man who had shouted out his name. Jacques urged his horse forward until he reached the three people standing in the midst of a circle of dead men.

Jacques swung his leg over the pommel and slid off his horse with the grace and agility that was the demarcation of everything he did and touched. His sensual mouth curved over two rows of perfectly formed white teeth as he grinned his obvious delight.

"Duncan! Duncan Fitzhugh! I thought the devil had long ago called you home."

"Not yet," Duncan testified, relieved finally to see a familiar face.

The man clasped Duncan to his chest. Duncan returned the fierce hug. Of the two, Duncan knew that he was the happier to see an old friend.

Jacques held Duncan at arm's length, as if unable to believe that he was actually here on this side of the Channel. "What matter of booty brings you to France? I've heard no talk of secret treasures."

Jacques was not so taken with Duncan's unexpected appearance that he missed the fact that Duncan had a woman with him, as well as one of his companions from their seafaring days.

His smile broadened. "But then, I see you have brought your own treasure with you. You always did have excellent taste."

With a hearty laugh, he shook Jacob's hand in greeting, but his eyes were still on Beth.

Behind Jacques, his men had ridden up and remained on their horses, looking at the reunion with mild interest. Duncan recognized none of their faces.

Jacques released Jacob's hand and took a step back as

he looked at the two men. "It has been what, five years, since our paths have crossed?"

"Seven," Duncan corrected. It had been that long since he had left the sea behind and last seen Jacques Christian.

Jacques took a long look at the bodies strewn around them on the ground. Humor touched his mouth.

"I see you have not lost your touch, my friend." Thinking he knew one man, Jacques turned him over with the toe of his boot. But he didn't recognize the man's face. "From the looks of them, France will not be the worse off for their demise. I would even say that you have done her a service."

Beth looked uncertainly from Jacques to Duncan. She was relieved that they were not about to be beset again by thieves, but she was anxious to attempt to recover her stolen mount.

"Duncan, shouldn't we try to find the man who stole my horse?"

Jacques dark eyes shifted to Beth's face. He took quick appraisal of her and found that what he saw pleased him.

"Well, are you going to introduce me to the lovely lady, or do you wish to keep her to yourself?" A knowing look slid over his face. "You always were a greedy bast—scoundrel," he amended at the last moment, for Beth's benefit.

Though he counted Jacques as a friend, Duncan still knew the limits of that friendship. He placed a proprietary hand on Beth's shoulder as he made the introductions. "Elizabeth Beaulieu, I'd like you to meet Jacques Christian."

There was a familiar, cocky manner to the way the man stood before her. It mirrored Duncan's as easily as if one had been the shadow of the other. "Another privateer?" Beth asked.

Jacques laughed, delighted at her question. There was neither contempt nor fear in her eyes. He slanted a look toward Duncan.

"Ah, so she knows about you, does she?" Taking her hand in his, he bowed low and kissed it. "I am your humble servant, mademoiselle." He raised his eyes to her face. A woman of substance, he thought in open admiration. "Beaulieu," he repeated, rolling the name about his tongue. "You are French?"

"American," she corrected. "But my father was born here, as were his people." As she spoke, she felt herself relaxing. There was something about the man, despite the devil in his eyes, that she trusted.

Jacques considered her words. Surely she wasn't traveling through just now. He regarded her clothing. An odd choice of apparel for a visitor.

"It is not an advisable time to be traveling aboard." He looked questioningly at Duncan, waiting for an explanation to be tendered.

When they looked back at it later, both Duncan and Beth thought of Jacques's appearance that day as a godsend.

"Jacques," Duncan began, as he placed his arm about the man's broad shoulders, "I think I'm about to say something to you that I never thought I would."

The dark crescents rose in an arch above expressive, dark eyes. "And that is—?"

Duncan exchanged looks with Beth. She nodded. It was another time to trust blindly, as she had with Lafayette. "We need your help."

Jacques laughed, though his eyes had grown serious. He motioned his men from their horses, then turned to look at his friend. "As it so happens, my friend, I have the afternoon free."

He quickly introduced his men, Henri, Sebastian, and Pierre. As the latter two stood guard, Christian took a seat on a fallen log. He waited until Beth and Duncan joined him. Jacob stood not far away, tending to their horses and keeping a watchful eye out of his own.

"Tell me what you wish of me, my friend," Jacques encouraged. "My right arm is yours."

He looked at Duncan significantly, wondering if Duncan remembered the incident on the *Black Death* when Duncan saved him from having his arm severed by pirates that had boarded.

The smile on Duncan's face told Jacques he did.

As succinctly as possible, Duncan and Beth explained the circumstances of what had brought them to Paris.

Jacques listened in silence, interjecting not one word. He stroked his chin thoughtfully. The look in his eyes told them, as if they did not already know, that what they were about was dangerous.

When Duncan finished, Jacques smiled.

"The Bastille," he repeated slowly. There was no reverence in his voice, but no intimidation, either. "This is clearly a challenge. And as you know, my friend, I dearly love challenges." He thought of the uprising he had witnessed yesterday. And the needless bloodshed that had followed shortly thereafter. "I do not, however, dearly love Robespierre. He is a madman."

Beth studied Jacques's face. There was no way to gauge his loyalties. "Are you a royalist?"

"Perish the thought." He placed his hands on his knees and rose. Beth and Duncan followed suit. "I am Jacques Christian, and that is enough for me and my men." He turned and looked toward the city that lay not far beyond. Plans began to form.

"I might know of someone who could help us." In fact, he was certain of it, but it would not do to say too much too soon. Easily, he laid a hand on Beth's arm and ushered her toward Jacob and the horses. "Come with me, my friends. I have a place where you can remain safe while I make inquiries."

Paris was as crowded today as it had been the day before. They drew no undue attention as they passed through the streets. There were too many people about for anyone to be singled out. People were sitting, huddled or sleeping, in doorways and alleys, awaiting the continuation of the celebration.

And waiting for the executions to begin.

Beth saw men, women, and children all eagerly gathered for the bloodletting that was to come.

She understood her grandmother's despair. That such a beautiful land could be brought so low was unthinkable. She couldn't wait to be gone from this wretched place.

Jacques brought them to an inn with no name. Years before, the sign had been struck down by lightning. The innkeeper, a superstitious man, took it to be an omen. The sign was never put up again and the name never repeated. It was merely known as "the inn."

The innkeeper, a heavyset man who sampled his own wares with relish, was a friend, Jacques assured them. And one who could be trusted to hold his tongue. Securing a room for Duncan, Beth, and Jacob, Jacques left them, promising to return as soon as there was news.

* * *

That had been several hours ago.

Duncan paced the length of the room as he had been doing for the last hour. His restlessness grew rather than diminished.

"I don't like small places," Duncan explained, when Beth looked at him quizzically. "They make me feel as if I was in a coffin."

She felt as restless as he did, but for far different reasons. And she didn't understand his reaction. "You were at sea. There were long months when you had but a small cabin to retreat to."

Duncan shook his head as he crossed the room once more. "The sea is vast, as are the stars overhead. And I had the entire ship at my disposal, not a tiny room."

He glanced at Jacob. The latter sat on the floor, his lank body leaned comfortably against the wall, content to wait.

"That one would be comfortable sitting on the points of a fence." He envied Jacob that trait. The young man was never impatient, as if he felt that there was time enough for everything.

Jacob merely grinned his acknowledgment.

Beth took care as she looked out the window, afraid to be seen. The rear of the inn faced an alley. Beyond it was a clear view of the Bastille.

Where was her father this moment? she wondered. Were they beating him? Was he fed? Was he frightened and in the throes of despair?

She turned back to face Duncan. "Do you think he can help us? Your friend Jacques?"

Duncan didn't want to make promises he had no control over. But he had faith in Christian. "Jacques is a very crafty scoundrel."

Jacob looked up at the comment. "He said the same of you, once," he recalled.

Duncan laughed. "And an intelligent man as well." Crossing to her in a few steps, Duncan gathered Beth into his arms. "Don't worry, Beth; if there is a way, we'll find it."

Beth laid her head against his chest. She took such comfort in his warmth, in his words, this man she had not even known existed a month ago. She felt that if he told her it was so, it would be so, though she had nothing to base her faith on.

But Duncan would not lie.

The next moment, before she could respond to Duncan, the door opened. Jacob leaped to his feet, but it was only Jacques.

He eyed the two in the center of the room as he slipped in quietly and shut the door behind him. He grinned broadly at them.

"Oh, forgive me for breaking up such a touching scene." Jacques closed the door firmly behind him before continuing. "But I've news."

Afraid to hope, afraid that it might be something she didn't want to hear, Beth still flew to him. She grabbed ahold of his arm with both hands.

"Tell me."

The fear pulsed in her voice. Jacques was glad to be the bearer of good news. He lay a gentling hand on the two that gripped his arm.

"For the moment, your father is still alive, mademoiselle."

Self-consciously, Beth released Jacques's arm. "Thank God."

"For the moment," Jacques repeated. "They will be transporting him from the Bastille to the guillotine for execution tomorrow." A mirthless smile lifted his lips, though the turn of events was fortunate for them. "It seems their docket is filled today. There are only so many they can dispose of in a day."

Beth closed her eyes, heartsick over his words. Heartsick for the people who were to die today. She wished she could save them all.

"Tomorrow." Duncan nodded thoughtfully. "Then I have a plan."

"Somehow, I knew you would." A smile played on Jacques's lips as he straddled a chair to listen. "Tell me, my friend, what is on that crafty mind of yours, and I will see what can be arranged."

Chapter Thirty-eight

It was a simple plan that required a minimum of information and a maximum of courage to execute.

After listening to Duncan and offering a few of his own suggestions, Jacques dispatched Henri to acquaint himself with the route taken by the carts when they left the Bastille for the execution site. Sebastian was sent to purchase an extra horse to replace the one stolen from Beth. Pierre was told to secure a wagon.

Duncan doled out the gold coins that were in his saddlebags.

"You'll have need of that to buy the silence of whomever you deal with," Jacques cautioned his men. "No one can know the purpose behind these purchases. And I want the wagon filled with straw," he told Pierre. "We shall need plenty of straw to conceal the good doctor from prying eyes." He smiled encouragingly at Beth.

As his men were sent about their different tasks, Jacques remained with Duncan, Jacob, and Beth. They lingered not far from the gates of the Bastille. It was important to familiarize themselves with procedures and to be there in the event that plans were changed for some reason and her father was transported earlier than originally scheduled.

Jacques reclined indolently against a wall not far from his horse. To the passing eye, he appeared to be but one of hundreds who had come to cheer the departure of the filled carts as they took their human cargo to slaughter. The man's bearing gave no indication of the passionate fighter who existed beneath.

He shifted his eyes toward Beth and Duncan. Beth was dressed in the peasant garb he had obtained for her from one of the many women he'd visited when nights were too long. Yvette had never looked like that in them, he mused with a critical eye. He wished, however, that Beth's eyes were not so bright. Fear could be seen glowing in them. Fear and sympathy.

He hoped no one would notice.

"My friend inside the walls," Jacques said softly, as he nodded toward the Bastille, "said that it would not be until dawn tomorrow, but one's friends tend to be forgetful, or they make mistakes. It's best if we see for ourselves. At least, until Henri returns to us."

Beth scarcely heard what he was saying. She was watching the procession. It broke her heart to see the opened carts slowly pass on the cobblestones. Some of the people within them sat and cried; others stood, meeting their fate with dignity. Still others looked too weak to stand.

The crowd gathered around each cart as it emerged from the fortress, shouting and spitting on the occupants who, because of the whims of fate, had been born on a different side than they.

She thought her heart was breaking.

Beth laid her hand on Duncan's arm as if to draw

strength from him. Strength to endure this horrible scene.

"Oh, Duncan," she whispered, when she saw a mother within one of the carts holding her child to her breast.

The woman was bedraggled and far removed from any hope. Her eyes were vacant as she looked straight ahead. It was as if she had already passed on to another world and knew not of this one, save for the baby that cried pitifully at her breast.

The woman was younger than she, Beth realized.

For one instant, their eyes met, Beth's full of pity, the woman's empty.

Beth knew she had looked into the face of death.

Duncan could sense what she was thinking. He leaned over so that only she might hear. "Beth, we can't save them. If we risk doing something now, we won't be able to save your father when the times comes."

She knew he was right, and yet somehow it did not seem right. She turned from the sight before her tears could spill. Her eyes caught Jacques's.

By his pose and his manner, Jacques appeared unaffected. But Beth could see that the feelings within her breast beat in his as well.

But there was nothing any of them could do.

Jacques moved closer to his friends. "It is a page of our history that will be too black to read."

He turned his back on them and the carts, and pretended for the moment to be so bored that he slept. If his eyes were shut, the tears could not come.

Because of their effort and Jacques's precautions, they blended in well with the crowd who had gathered to cheer the carts on their way. Looking upon them, no one would have suspected that they were there to stay the hand of the avenging angel from the depths of hell that Robespierre had summoned.

The time passed slowly.

Beth thought she would go mad with the waiting. The carts had ceased departing on their macabre journey and there was nothing to do except wait for the dawn.

Henri returned to eagerly inform them that there was a point in the journey from the fortress to the guillotine that provided them with a good opportunity to take possession of the cart. Pleased with the information, Jacques instructed Henri to show them.

Henri led them to a desolate part of the city, one that was unsavory and not frequently traversed by citizens who did not wish to risk their lives.

Jacques looked about, satisfied. "I know this place."

They came from the same background, he and Jacques. "Somehow, I thought you might," Duncan commented.

Jacques laughed in response. "The people who live here are the citizens of the damned. They have no care who is on the throne or if it is vacant. All they want is to be left alone. If someone sees us through the window," he pointed in the distance, "it will not make a difference," he assured them.

The streets were perfect for a wagon, Beth thought, as she surveyed her surroundings. The houses that were clustered here had the sad-eyed appearance of neglect and despair. Beth blotted out the sense of desolation they created within her.

The pieces came together.

Pierre returned with a wagon, pulled by a sorry-looking horse and filled to the brim with straw. Sebastian was posted on the western outskirts of the city with the horse he had "found." Sebastian returned the gold to Duncan, who told him to keep it as payment for finding the horse. Sebastian laughed and did so gladly.

Henri was left to stand watch at the Bastille and alert them when Philippe Beaulieu was being transported. Beth had given Henri a detailed description of her father and had entrusted Jacques's man with her most cherished possession, a miniature of her parents that had been painted on their wedding day.

Henri had eyed the miniature dubiously as he'd held it in his hand, but swore he would know when he saw the original.

All there was left for them to do was wait.

It felt to Beth as if she was lying beneath a boulder, watching it totter precariously overhead, waiting for it to fall.

Duncan felt her tension as they stood there in the predawn hours. It matched his own. "I would rather that you had remained near the Bastille to confirm your father's appearance for us, or better yet, waited for us at the inn."

He knew it was futile to mention it, but he had to voice his thoughts.

She looked at him as she blew out an impatient breath. Her impatience was with time, not with him.

"There will be no opportunity to return to the inn," she pointed out. "Once we have him, there is no turning back for us."

She wondered if Jacques knew how much he might be risking, helping them.

Jacques broke the tension. "So tell me, my friend,

how did someone as ugly as you wind up with such a beautiful companion?" He smiled at Beth, hoping to set her at ease in this deathwatch in which they were engaged.

It seemed as if it had happened in another lifetime.

"I rescued her from a highwayman and got shot in the process." He glanced at his shoulder, remembering the way she had ministered to him, and the way she had looked that night he'd thought he dreamed her.

What kind of fool was he for allowing her to endanger herself this way? But then, he knew she had no choice in the matter.

The look Jacques gave Beth was full of appreciation. "It would seem that your wound was well worth it."

"I have my own opinion about that," Duncan replied.

It was an oddly closed-mouth comment for him, and Jacques looked at the man he saw rarely but would regard as a friend years from now with his last breath.

He saw in his eyes what Duncan was not yet consciously aware of. Jacques smiled to himself.

Well, well well. It would seem that the falcon has been tethered ...

The sound of pounding hooves broke the stillness in the early morning air. The four looked at one another, immediately alerted. A moment later, Henri came riding up, his horse in a dead run.

He slid off the animal before it had come to a full stop.

"I saw him." Henri held up the miniature. "I saw the old man she described. They are coming this way. Ten, perhaps fifteen minutes behind. He is in the very first cart. The second one has not been dispatched yet. They will arrive some time apart, to facilitate the executions."

Beth took her miniature from Henri and quickly slipped it into her pouch. She would never forgive herself if she lost it.

"Good work." Jacques nodded. "Positions, everyone."

The wagon was led out into the street, directly in what would be the path of the oncoming cart. Jacob, purposely slouched shoulder and sleepy-eyed, sat on the seat with the reins in his hand. The worn animal that Pierre had brought with the wagon had been replaced with Jacob's bay, Megan. Megan was as fleet-footed as she was strong.

There would be a need to flee almost instantly.

Beth, still dressed in her peasant garb, stood to the rear of the wagon, prepared to stop the cart's driver and plead for help in moving the stubborn animal attached to her wagon.

Jacques and his men, as well as Duncan were hidden from view for the moment, ready to spring out once the driver was distracted.

Duncan took one moment to hug Beth to him. "Take care," he whispered to her, then brushed his lips over hers.

"You needn't worry." But in her heart, she was glad that he did.

She pushed him away when she heard the sound of the cart approaching. The mournful wailing that preceded it froze her heart. One of the occupants of the cart was keening. She could not distinguish whether it was a man or a woman.

Dear God, what if it was her father?

Beth swallowed her fear.

As the cart with its doomed cargo approached, a

guard at its side, Beth ran out before them. Her hands were raised in supplication.

"Help, oh help me, messieurs," she begged tearfully. "My horse has gone lame, and it cannot pull my wagon." She pointed toward it. "My brother knows not what to do to get her to move out of the way."

The man raised his whip, ready to strike Beth. "Stupid girl, do I look as if I had the time to help you? I'm on official business." He turned to the guard. "Shoot the horse and get them out of the way," he ordered. "If they give you any trouble, shoot them as well. We cannot keep Robespierre waiting."

"No, please, sir, you can't—"

"Oh, can't I?" The driver stood up in his seat, his whip raised high.

He never had the opportunity to strike.

The next moment, Duncan and the others charged the cart from both sides as well as the rear. The guard was immediately engulfed and pulled from his horse. He was dead before he could reach for his musket.

The driver tried to urge his horse on, ready to trample Beth in his path, but Duncan fired and the man pitched forward, dead. The horse reared, his nostrils flaring as he pawed the air wildly. Jacob jumped from the wagon. Running, he grabbed for the reins, stopping the animal before it collided with the wagon.

The three people in the cart appeared dazed and almost beyond comprehending what was happening around them. Beth was the first to climb into the cart. She threw her arms around the battered body of her father. He was so pitifully thin, she could have cried.

But he was alive. Still alive.

"Father," Beth cried. "Father, don't you know me?"

Eyes that had lived so long in the dark and could now barely focus squinted at her face.

"Beth?" He whispered the name in disbelief. "Elizabeth?"

"Yes, Father, it's me."

Only then did she realize that his hands were tied behind his back. As if he could use them to harm anyone, she thought with hot indignation. She tried to pull the ropes loose.

Duncan was in the wagon now. "There's no time, Beth, we have to move quickly." Even now, he thought the others might be coming.

If not now, then soon.

Even so, Beth took a moment to pull the dagger from her boot and sliced the ropes from her father's hands. "Yes, we have to hurry, Father." She began to usher him from the cart.

But he resisted. "Wait, the boy." Philippe pointed to the fragile body next to him. "I cannot leave without Andre."

Beth looked down at the boy, not more than sixteen, lying in the straw, too weak to stand. She looked toward Duncan. "Duncan."

There was no need to say more. Duncan scooped the boy up in his arms. He was hardly more than skin and bones. "I have him."

"And Violet," Dr. Beaulieu urged.

Jacques shook his head as he raised the woman's limp hand in his. "This one is dead. It is as if her heart gave out. Such a pity." She couldn't have been more than thirty, he estimated.

The next moment, Jacques buried his feelings and looked around at the people surrounding him. "Hurry, my friends, hurry. There will be others following them, and soon, I assure you."

Duncan carried the boy to the wagon as Philippe Beaulieu leaned on Jacques and Beth, trying to make his battered legs move. With their arms around his waist, they managed to get him to the wagon.

The two were quickly covered with straw and cautioned against making noise. Jacob clutched the reins of the wagon in his hands, more than ready to leave.

"Not too quickly," Jacques warned him, as Beth scrambled up on the seat beside Jacob. "We want no suspicions aroused." He mounted his horse and fell into step beside the wagon for a moment. "I shall ride with you until the outskirts of town. Sebastian has extra horses waiting there."

Even as they left, they heard the approach of another cart.

Beth looked at Jacob. "If they see the empty cart and dead driver, they'll be on our trail in an instant. Drive quickly."

Jacob looked over his shoulder at Jacques. "But he said—"

"Jacob, drive," Beth ordered.

Jacob needed no other entreaty. He snapped the reins in his hands, sending a message to the horse he had trained from a foal. "Run, Megan, run."

The bay seemed to come to life. Pulling the cart, she trotted quickly from the heart of the city.

Beth's heart beat fast as they managed to go unnoticed by the patrols that were in the city. No one seemed to care about a sleepy-eyed driver and the tired-looking, dirty woman beside him.

Duncan and Jacques matched the path of the wagon,

step for step a few yards away, watching for any signs of trouble.

For once, the gods were with them and the winds were clean, Duncan thought. They reached the edge of Paris without incident.

Chapter Thirty-nine

As promised, Sebastian was waiting for them on the outskirts of town. He had with him two horses instead of just the one, as if some instinct had prompted him to "find" another along the way.

It was a fortuitous instinct.

Like a man with the devil snapping at his heels, Jacob pulled the wagon to a halt and leaped from the driver's seat. Working swiftly, he removed the harness from his horse.

Behind him, Beth, Duncan, and Jacques were helping Philippe and Andre from the cart. Neither could really walk very far. Andre was close to being delirious and could not stand. Though Philippe fared slightly better, he was consumptively weak.

Beth looked at Duncan, concerned, as between them they took Andre from the wagon. "I don't know if either one of them can ride."

There was no choice in the matter. "They'll have to. The wagon is too slow, and the further we are from Paris, the better for all involved. The wagon might attract unwanted attention. Megan is swift, but she can't outrun pursuers while pulling a wagon with four people in it. This is for the best."

Philippe, leaning heavily against Jacques, attempted to smile at his daughter, but the effort was far from complete. "I can ride, Beth. Don't concern yourself."

Beth frowned. Her father didn't look as if he could even sit in the saddle. And there was no question that Andre couldn't. "They'll both fall."

"He'll double with me," Duncan told Beth. "Jacob, you ride with the boy." Duncan glanced at Beth. "We'll take the extra horse with us." She could hold onto its reins as they rode.

"I do not mean to rush you, my friends, but we must hurry," Jacques urged. He had Henri watching the road for any sign of someone approaching.

Duncan nodded. Between the two of them, he and Jacques managed to seat Philippe in the saddle. Duncan swung on behind the rail-thin man, placing his arms around the skeletal body.

Jacques and Sebastian helped Jacob with Andre. But as Duncan, Beth, and Jacob prepared to leave, Jacques remained standing on the ground. He held the reins of his horse fast in his hand.

"This is where we part company, my friends," he told them. He swung into his saddle and joined his men. "It is best if my men and I don't know where you are going." He smiled at Duncan as they exchanged knowing looks. "Just in case."

Duncan understood. No man knew what he might reveal under torture. Each man had his limits, and each man's was different. He would not want Jacques tested for his, if it came to that.

With one arm around Philippe and the reins, Duncan

leaned and reached for Jacques's hand. He clasped it tightly for a moment.

"I don't know what we would have done without you and your men, Jacques."

Jacques was not a vain man, but he let himself bask a moment in Duncan's gratitude. Then he lifted a shoulder carelessly.

"As always, you would have managed." A smile creased his lips. "But it would have taken you a little longer, perhaps."

"Time was what we didn't have," Beth interjected. He turned to look at her. Gratitude shone in her eyes like shimmering beacons. "There's no way I can thank you for all you have done." And all that he risked for them, she added silently.

He allowed himself a moment to look at her one last time. Fitzhugh was a lucky man. "Your smile is payment enough, mademoiselle. Now go, quickly. Revenge flies on swift wings."

With that, Jacques and his men turned and rode away, back into Paris and the chaos that was abounding there. There were others to help.

Jacob looked from Beth to Duncan. He pressed the sagging boy against his chest. "Where do we go?" he wanted to know.

"To the harbor," Duncan urged. But Beth shook her head.

"No. Back to Therese's," she cried. When Duncan looked at her, mystified, she reminded him of her reason. "My great-aunt is still there. We can't just leave her here. She has to come with us."

Duncan's arm tightened about the man who nodded before him. Philippe was unconscious. Duncan didn't bother to argue with Beth. He had known from the first that they would have to return for the woman. He had only forgotten that in the excitement of the flight.

Duncan motioned for Jacob to be off. "You heard the lady. Let's go to Therese's."

On horseback, the journey to the cottage nestled on the perimeter of the forest was swift.

The pace was quick, but Beth feared what the ride might do to her father's broken health. Not to mention what it must have been doing for Andre's. But again, they had no choice. Every moment held the threat of discovery and capture. This time, there would be no one to rescue them, no way to escape.

With a watchful eye for roving bands, they arrived at Therese's just as the late-afternoon sun cast its light along the land.

Beth uttered a cry of relief as the cottage came into view. To her it was as if they had arrived at a haven. They needed to rest the horses, but more than that, they needed a momentary respite for both her father and the young boy they'd rescued with him.

"Wait," Duncan cautioned, his hand raised for silence. He looked around, his eyes alert.

Beth had brought her horse to a halt and was about to dismount. She looked at Duncan quizzically, not understanding his somber expression. She looked about. Nothing seemed amiss.

"Why?" she asked.

His eyes caught her. "Listen."

She did, then shrugged, still not comprehending. "I don't hear anything."

"That's just it. Why isn't the dog barking? He was wild when we approached the last time." Agitated, a horrific thought forming in his mind, Duncan handed the reins to Beth and eased himself from the saddle. The doctor was slumped forward over the pommel. "Watch him," he cautioned Beth.

Beth laid a hand on her father to secure him where he was. "Duncan."

He turned to look at her.

Beth pressed her lips together, a strange unease slipping through her. "Take care."

He nodded and silently approached the cottage. Crouching, he took care to stay within the shelter of the trees until he had made his way to the side. Only when he was beneath the window did he attempt to rise and look in. By then, he was out of sight of the others.

The moments trickled by slowly. With each second, Beth could feel herself growing more and more anxious, as if she was a ball of yarn being wound too tightly. Her throat felt dry and parched, and it wasn't thirst that was making it so.

It was fear.

She turned toward Jacob. "What's taking him so long?" she whispered.

Jacob was used to waiting. Duncan always returned, no matter where he went. "Perhaps it isn't safe to enter yet. Duncan doesn't like to take unnecessary chances."

Then what's he doing here? Beth pulled a hand through her hair. She saw her father slip a little and she muttered an oath at her own carelessness. She steadied him, then looked toward Jacob. This couldn't continue. She couldn't take much more waiting.

"If he doesn't return in another minute, I am going to see what's keeping him."

Jacob looked distressed and torn between loyalties. "Duncan wouldn't like that."

Beth blew out a long breath. The devil take what Duncan liked.

"Well, I don't like sitting here and waiting. Worrying," she added in a whisper. Enough was enough. She leaned toward Jacob, the reins to all three horses in her hand. "Jacob, hold the reins—"

Reluctantly, Jacob reached over to accept them. He bit his lower lip, knowing this was wrong. The next moment he started as a figure emerged from the trees to their right.

Duncan.

But a Duncan he had never seen before. There was a look in his eyes that had Jacob shrinking back without realizing it.

Duncan swung up onto his horse. "Give her back the reins, Jacob, we're leaving."

Beth stared at him. What was he saying? "But my great-aunt—"

He took the reins of his horse from her. "We cannot take her with us." Thank God the man was past hearing, he thought.

But Beth wouldn't leave. Stubbornly she remained where she was. "Why?"

He turned to look at her then, and she saw it, the look of death in his eyes. The same look that had been in the woman's eyes yesterday. The one on the cart holding the infant.

"Don't ask me questions, Beth. Let's go," he growled out the order.

But before he could kick his heels into the horse's flanks, she placed her hand on his. "Duncan, what did you see?"

He closed his eyes then, and for a moment, he thought he was going to weep. "A sight I shall forever be glad you didn't see with me."

Horror consumed her like a never satiated monster. "She is dead?" The words spilled from her numbed lips.

Duncan gave one short nod. "Someone must have informed on Therese." His breathing grew quick and shallow as indignation beat in his breast. "Robespierre's vengeance is not pretty."

Tears fought to gain the surface. Somehow, she managed to repress them. She looked over her shoulder at the cottage, then grabbed Duncan's arm. "We can't just leave them. We have to bury them."

He didn't want to tell her, but if he didn't, she'd go back herself. He knew her. And he couldn't allow her to see what he had seen.

"There isn't enough left to bury, Beth." He saw the shock wash over her face. "I'm sorry," he whispered. "Let's go."

Beth nodded and kicked her heels into the horse's flanks.

She thought she was going to be ill, but the will to live, to bring her father to safety, strengthened her resolve and kept her in the saddle as they rode, relentlessly, to the harbor.

They stopped only once to rest the horses. Duncan helped Philippe and Andre down and leaned each against the trunk of a tree for support.

He looked at the way Andre sat slumped against the bark. Duncan shook his head. "I don't know if he can make it," he told Beth.

Philippe accepted the water pouch Jacob urged on him. He took but a few sips, knowing he could not sate his thirst quickly. It was a thirst that had been weeks in the making. He looked toward Duncan.

"He will make it," Philippe told him weakly. "He is a strong boy." He shut his eyes wearily, only vaguely aware that Beth had sunk down beside him. He felt her hand on his arm. Philippe fought against the tears of a broken man. "Oh God, Beth, the things I have seen. They will stay with me forever."

When he opened his eyes, he had the look of a man who had aged a decade. "I want nothing more than to leave this Godforsaken land and forget I was ever French. I cannot believe you saved me. My beautiful daughter."

She closed her hand over his. "I couldn't let anything happen to you, Father. We will be away from here soon, I promise."

He had come along blindly, too weak to even form questions. But they came to him now.

"But how did you get here? Why did your mother allow you to come?" His eyes searched her face for answers. "And who are they—?"

There was so much to tell him, but now was not the time. They had to be off again. "All in good time, Father, when you are better. For now, you are safe and we must get to the harbor."

Beth rose as Duncan brought the horses over once more.

The captain of the *Silver Ram* looked at the bedraggled group before him with scorn. His ship was set to sail within the next twenty-four hours, and he had no time to waste with beggars.

"I make no charity runs." Contempt hummed in his voice as he attempted to push them out of his way.

Duncan's temper was at its very end. "What the bloody hell is he saying, Beth, and quickly, before I feed his teeth to him one at a time."

He looked prepared to do it, she thought. They were all tired and angry, but this was not the way to get on board. She laid a hand on his.

"His men," she cautioned Duncan, "whether they like him or not, will avenge him. You should know that better than anyone."

He knew, but that didn't cool his temper.

Beth turned her eyes on the captain. He was regarding her with open curiosity now, and a goodly amount of interest. He was always willing to avail himself of a little pleasure, and she looked ripe for the taking, despite the condition of her clothing.

Beth cut off his path with her body. "We ask for no charity, only that you take us aboard. You will be paid."

The smile that sliced his face was oily and made her want to wash. "I will see this payment now."

She knew exactly what he was asking for, and refrained from translating for Duncan. Instead, she beckoned for Jacob to step forward.

"Jacob, the saddlebag."

Jacob handed it to her. She held it out and opened one side, allowing the captain a look inside. There were still gold coins left within, far more than necessary to secure passage for five people and two horses.

Gold was far more profitable than a few minutes lost in the arms of pleasure. The captain placed his hand on the saddlebag. "I will just take—"

"—Us to Dover," Beth concluded with a smile.

The captain's eyes grew wide as he realized that beneath the saddlebag there was a dagger pointed at him and it was close to piercing his skin.

He saw by the look on the tall one's eyes that he was the one who held it.

Duncan smiled easily. "Tell him it's pointed at his belly and if he wants to ever feel it filled with rum again, he had better set sail." Duncan held the man's eyes prisoner. "Now."

There was an urgency to the last word. This much the captain understood.

Beth relayed the message quickly in French. The captain turned pale and trembled. He nodded as he backed away from the point of the dagger. Quickly, he gave the order to his men to cast off.

The sailors upon the deck looked at him quizzically, but they knew better than to question the captain.

Duncan and Jacob led Philippe and Andre on board while Beth took the horses.

"Not the animals," the captain cried in disgust. He saw Duncan rest his hand upon the hilt of his sword. Duncan tossed the captain another gold coin, which the latter caught handily.

With a shake of his head, the captain retreated.

The *Silver Ram* put out to sea within the quarter of the hour.

Chapter Forty

Beth spent the journey back to Dover below deck, tending to her father and Andre. She cared for both of them as tenderly as if they were but children and she the mother.

Both were weak from starvation, their bodies nearly broken from the torture to which they had been subjected. There were welts upon her father's back and chest that brought hot, angry tears to Beth's eyes.

"In the past, Beth," her father whispered, slipping in and out of consciousness, though he fought hard to stay awake. "It's all in the past. There is the future still before us."

Beth clung to that, for both of them.

Andre fell into a fever. She did what she could for him and perforce left the rest up to God.

And all the while, she thought of what Duncan wouldn't tell her, of the horrible death her proud great-aunt had met. It was hard for Beth to keep hope in her heart with thoughts of all she had just seen lurking in the back of her mind like a festering, dark secret that threatened to overwhelm her.

* * *

Through the daylong journey across the Channel, Duncan remained on deck and on his guard. Though they had more than paid their way, Duncan wanted to ensure that the captain would not attempt to exact revenge on them for the way they had gained his acquiescence.

It would not have been a difficult matter to turn the ship around and head back to France.

Duncan kept his eye on the ship's wheel and his hand on the hilt of his sword.

The captain needed no more than Duncan's presence to understand the silent message being given him. Though in his heart, he would have enjoyed handing his passengers over to the new order that haunted the realm in France, he knew that he would not live out the day such an occurrence came to pass.

He took them to Dover. And lived.

When he saw the English coastline shimmering on the horizon like a woman waiting for her man to return from the sea, his heart was filled with joy. Duncan hurried below deck and knocked on Beth's cabin door.

She was quick to open it. Her apprehensive look softened slightly when she saw his expression. "What's wrong?"

"Nothing, I want you to see something with me." Taking her hand, he led her topside to the deck. Positioning her against the railing, he placed his hands on her shoulders. "Look," he pointed. "There. England." There was a proud echo in his voice.

Tears glistened in her eyes and spilled freely down her cheeks as she looked.

He heard the change in her breathing and turned her around to see for himself. He thought she'd be happy. "Beth, what's the matter?"

"I never thought I would be so grateful to see English soil." She covered her mouth to keep back the sob of relief that welled in her throat.

He laced his arm around her in silent comfort. Yes, he thought, he had forgotten how much she'd disliked the British and how she had initially felt about the things that had stood between them.

There was a world of difference between them. And half a world that would yet come.

But now was not the time to think on that, though the emotion tugged at him both urgently and sadly.

They were the first to disembark from the ship, getting off before the cargo was unloaded and only moments after the ship had docked at the harbor. The captain stood off to the side and glared as he watched them leave his vessel.

"We could stop at the inn," Duncan suggested, though he would have preferred to be on his way.

Beth was of the same mind as he.

"No, I want to get to Shalott as quickly as possible," Beth told him. She looked at her father and Andre. "They need bed rest." She raised her eyes to Duncan's. "Duncan, can we get a coach?"

A coach would be slower, but he doubted that the boy would survive another long ride on horseback. And it would be easier to transport her father inside a coach as well.

"Jacob, stay with her. I'll see what I can do about getting us a coach."

He was back within the half-hour, riding beside a coach driven by a small man with flaming red hair. He looked more like a gnome than a man. His shoulders were hunched as if he were perpetually seeking shelter from the cold. He looked pleased for the business and guaranteed them a ride, "as soft as if you were being cradled to your mother's bosom."

It was argument enough for Beth.

She rode within the coach with her father and Andre as Jacob rode alongside and Duncan rode on top, with the driver. Duncan's horse was tied to the back. Beth heard the endless murmur of the driver's high voice and didn't envy Duncan the position he had chosen.

She smiled to herself, thinking of the care he had given her and everything he had done. She could not wait to put all this behind her and pick up the thread of the new life she had found, a life with him.

All he need do, she thought, was ask her.

Two days later, they came to the outskirts of Shalott. As they approached the manor, word spread quickly from cottage to cottage that Duncan had returned. It was, Beth thought, as she watched people in the fields wave at them as they passed, a little like being in the company of returning royalty. Despite the goings-on she had endured, the notion made her smile.

Duncan watched as he saw the manor rise up before him. A feeling tugged at his gut and he recognized it for what it was: a feeling of homecoming. He was home.

Shalott was home now, far more than any other place had ever been. Even more than the sea. And as long as Sin-Jin remained in America, it would remain so for him and his family.

It was a good feeling, and he cherished it the way only an orphan could. He thought of the boy within the coach and wondered if Andre would wish to remain here with him.

It was a foregone conclusion that the others would be leaving. But Duncan chose not to dwell on that now. It would distill the joy he was experiencing.

Samuel was at the coach before the horses had been brought to a complete stop. His small eyes glowed with relief and happiness as he looked up at Duncan. "You made it back."

Duncan leaped gracefully from the driver's seat to the ground just as Jacob pulled up behind him. "I told you I would, old man." He laughed heartily to see that nothing had changed. God, but it felt wonderful to be here. "Have I ever lied to you?"

Samuel pretended to look at him somberly. "More times than there are fingers and toes in Shalott."

"Now who lies, you old bastard?" With a cry of joy, Duncan found himself engulfed in a bearhug, though he was by far the larger of the two.

"Good to see you, boy," Samuel murmured, his voice getting lost against Duncan's brawn. It was just as well. It was in danger of cracking, he thought. "Good to see you." He released Duncan. "And even you." Samuel laughed as he turned to Jacob.

The old man looked up just as Beth stepped down from the coach. He was quick to present his hand to her. "Mistress, did you—?" Samuel raised tufted eyebrows to silently end his question.

Beth nodded. "We did."

She looked about at the smiling faces and felt the same odd tug at her heart that Duncan had. Sylvia stood sobbing her relief in the doorway.

Same old Sylvia, she thought with amusement.

Her attention returned to Samuel. "We need a litter, or some way to carry him inside."

Samuel was already turning on his heel.

"Forget the litter, Samuel," Duncan called.

Duncan nudged Beth aside. Reaching within the carriage, he took her father gently into his arms. He instructed Jacob to take the boy.

Duncan looked down into her face. "All you ever need, Beth," he told her quietly as he turned on his heel, "is me."

Beth looked at Duncan's departing back and her heart quickened.

I know.

With Amy's good food and her tender care, her father and Andre mended far more quickly than Beth thought it was possible. The very fact that they were free of the shadow of the Bastille did much to aid their recovery.

Time seemed to pass her on winged feet as she saw to their care.

It was the other matter that troubled her. It seemed that ever since their return, Duncan had gone out of his way to avoid her. For three days he was not to dinner when she came down, or in his room when she went to speak to him.

Everywhere she was, he was not—by design, she both sensed and feared.

A chill began to cover her heart.

So on the eve of the fifth day, when she heard his voice coming from the study, Beth was quick to enter. She did so without knocking, fearing that if she hesitated, she would lose her courage. The courage that was quickly waning.

Duncan looked surprised to see her and immediately restless, as if he wanted to be gone.

What happened? she wondered. This wasn't the man who had held her in his arms, or ridden at her side in France. What had happened since they had docked on this English soil?

She measured her words and her steps as she entered. "Hello, Duncan. We seem to be missing one another these days."

Duncan dismissed Hank. "I'll talk to you presently," he said. The lanky man swept from the room, though his eyes remained on Beth until he was out in the hall.

Beth laced her hands together, suddenly feeling afraid, though there was no name to her fear. "We'll be leaving soon."

She watched for a sign that the news disturbed him, but her words seemed to have no effect on him.

Don't you care?

"My mother has been living in hell all these long months, worried about my father. I want to set her mind at ease."

He looked at her and told himself that she was just another thing he could not have. It should not make a difference. He did not even come close to convincing himself. "I'd imagine that she is worried about you as well."

Words were difficult now between them. Why? They never had been before. *Is it so hard to speak to me,*

Duncan? Have I displeased you somehow? "Yes, I suppose there is that, too."

He looked at her, as if to memorize each feature, each expression and press them between the pages of a book within his mind. "You'll be happy to go."

Beth stared at him, wondering if he was attempting to put into her mouth the words that he wanted to hear. Was he sending her away? Was it just a matter of sharing her bed a few times and then being done with her?

Or had all the dangers they had been through left a bitter taste in his mouth, after all?

But if that wasn't the case, why wasn't he asking her to remain? He had but to say it, to ask. She couldn't very well throw herself at him. Not if the chance existed that he didn't want her.

Because he couldn't resist, Duncan allowed himself the pleasure of touching her once more. Very lightly, he sifted her hair through his fingers and watched the moonlight cast it in gold as it rained down.

Moved, it was on the very tip of his tongue to ask her to remain with him. To beg her to stay, the way he had never allowed himself to beg for anything before.

But what could he give her?

For the first time in his life, his legacy and his heritage, or rather the very lack of it, stared him in the face.

She was descended from bluebloods and he was the son of a stablemaster's daughter and a bastard to boot. She was returning with her father to a vast plantation, while he had nothing to call his own but the loyalty of his men. And while he was rich in that, rich in spirit, he was poor in everything else. In all the things she had flowered into womanhood enjoying.

What could he offer her in place of a life at Eagle's Nest? A home in some other man's manor?

It wasn't enough for someone like Beth.

Feeling increasingly more awkward, she looked at the floor. "It will be good to see my mother and my sisters again."

She was anxious to leave, and who could blame her? "So when will you leave?"

Are you that anxious to see me go? Very well then, I shall.

"I thought, perhaps, tomorrow . . ." Her voice trailed off as she looked up, hoping to see something within his eyes that asked her to stay. "Or the day after."

There was nothing there. His eyes were flatter than the piece of paper she had seen Duncan looking at when she entered.

He nodded. "I'll have some of my men take you and your father to the harbor."

"And the boy," she told him. He raised his brow. "Andre. He's coming with us."

This was news. He had just assumed that the boy would remain here with him, to fit in as best he could. "You're taking him?"

Beth moved restlessly around the room, as restless now as she had been in that tiny room at the inn in Paris, but for an entirely different reason.

"My father has adopted him in a manner of speaking. The boy is an orphan with no family left now." Beth shivered though the room was warm. She ran her hands along her arms. "Robespierre thought to break the line that came down from King Louis himself."

There it was again: lineage. All his life, Duncan had hated the class system, and now he found himself trapped by it, for she belonged on one side of it and he on the other. And he knew that better than she.

"Now it won't be broken." He moved away from her

as if standing so close was painful to him. "Well, I've some things to see to."

She had hoped that perhaps they could walk in the moonlight one last time. Even this was denied to her, she thought. "So late?"

"Yes," he snapped.

The frustration of wanting her and knowing that for her own good, he could not have her, was rubbing him raw. He had forgotten himself and his station. He had enjoyed her body, not knowing that he would fall in love with the rest of her as well.

Duncan knew he could not bring her down to his level. And someday she would thank him for it. Though right now, he damned the God who'd made him for that very thing.

Beth stood in the study and watched him leave her. She had thought, would have sworn, that he cared for her. That he loved her the way she loved him.

It was a mistake.

An illusion.

She pressed her lips together. It had been her mistake, not his. A mistake that had driven a dagger through her heart. She could feel it bleeding even now.

Well, she wasn't a fool; at least, not completely. She would not let him see her cry for him. If he didn't want her, then it was his loss and he the fool, not she.

Very carefully she retraced her steps and went to her room, where she spent the night crying.

Chapter Forty-one

Sylvia approached quietly behind Amy in the kitchen. The cook set the tray she had carried upstairs two hours ago angrily on the long wooden table.

Hardly anything had been touched.

Sylvia glanced at it and shook her head. This could not keep up, she thought sadly. Since her wedding to Samuel more than a month ago, she had blossomed, cocooned in the folds of her happiness and newfound love. It distressed her doubly so to see anyone else's misery, especially when it was tied to affairs of the heart.

As Duncan's plainly was.

Since Beth had left, he had become a changed man. He never laughed heartily the way he had before, and his eyes were preoccupied, as if his mind was somewhere else. He was still a fair man, but he had given himself up to brooding the way he never had before. Samuel was clearly worried about him.

Sylvia cleared her throat and Amy turned to look at her. Sylvia touched the tray shyly. "How is he today?"

Amy shrugged her wide shoulders in disgust, then sighed.

"Same as yesterday. Same as all the other days since

she left." She cleared the dishes from the shield she still used as a tray. "I've never seen him so disagreeable." Amy turned to look at Sylvia. She pressed the shield to her breast with both hands as she confided. "He like to bit Hank's head off the other day for forgetting to cut wood for me. Hank's a lazy lout, but still . . ."

The older woman shook her head as she laid the shield aside. "He apologized, of course, but that doesn't go changing the fact that he just isn't our Duncan anymore."

Amy continued talking aloud, more to herself than to Sylvia. She never even noticed when Sylvia left the kitchen.

Sylvia slipped from the room, lacing and unlacing her hands as she labored over a thought.

She was not a brave soul, she never had been, but someone had to speak with Duncan. It seemed that everyone at the manor was tiptoeing around the subject that was weighing so heavily on his heart.

Who better to raise it than someone who knew Beth?

She caught sight of herself in the reflecting glass of the window as she passed and braced her shoulders. Who better, indeed?

Gathering her courage to her like a threadbare, invisible cloak, Sylvia marched to the library where Duncan buried himself these days and knocked on the door. At first she knocked timidly, but when that received no answer, she knocked harder.

"Go away. I'm busy."

The words were growled so deeply, Sylvia almost retreated. Then, placing a hand over her fluttering heart, she opened the door and forced her feet to enter. Dark, brooding eyes looked up at her.

"This will take but a moment, sir." Her voice squeaked in the middle of the sentence.

He sighed and slammed the account book shut. It wasn't making much sense to him at the moment anyway. At *any* moment. These days, he couldn't read, couldn't eat, couldn't think.

And it was all her fault.

Damn that woman for ever appearing in his life. He had never been this way before. No woman had *ever* bedeviled him, ever haunted his nights and echoed about the corners of his days before.

It was like a sickness, one he couldn't seem to recover from.

He'd even gone to the town, seeking out Elaine at the tavern. But when she pressed herself to him, eager to please, eager to couple with him once more, he had pushed away her firm, supple body, made some excuse like some wet-behind-the-ears urchin and left her naked and cursing in her room.

Beth.

Every thought was Beth, every breath was Beth, every prayer was Beth.

There was no one for him but her.

And she was not here.

He dragged both hands through his hair and looked at the wide-hipped, good-natured woman before him. She had been a blessing for Samuel, a gift from the gods in his old age. For that Duncan was grateful to her. But he did not feel like being charitable toward anyone right now. He felt more like a bear who had been mortally wounded trying to gather honey.

"If it is some complaint about the way Samuel is treating you—" Duncan began wearily, not wanting to hear it.

Her eyes grew wide in surprise. "Oh, no," Sylvia assured Duncan quickly. A smile rose to her lips, and there were stars in her eyes. "Samuel and I are very happy. I have never been so happy."

At least someone is. "That is good." Duncan opened his book and realized that it had been upside down all this time. "Then there is no reason for you to seek me out." He pretended to look engrossed in his work.

It was clearly a dismissal, but Beth would not be dismissed. She took a step forward, though she kept the desk between them. "Oh, but that is *just* the reason to seek you out."

Typical woman: she made no sense like the rest of her breed, he thought in exasperation. Duncan strove for patience.

Samuel and Jacob had attempted to talk to him, as had John at the very beginning. He had tersely ordered them all from his business. But politeness kept him from employing the same means to disengage himself from Sylvia.

"Yes?"

She saw no other way to say it. She looked at Duncan, her eyes urgent. "Go to her, sir."

Very quietly, he closed the book once more and raised his eyes to hers. His men knew enough to retreat when faced with that black look. Sylvia quaked, but remained where she was.

"To whom?"

Her throat felt dried and parched, but she forced the name out. "Beth."

Manners only went so far. "Madam, I believe you overstep yourself."

She had come this far, ventured this much; she had to continue until it was done.

"No, I do not. Everyone else in this household is afraid to tell you, or perhaps they feel if they say nothing, this will all pass." The soft dark eyes, filled with compassion, met his and held. "But your agony grows each day, festering like some sort of poison in your body."

Genteel woman or not, he would not sit here and be lectured to by someone who had no idea what he was going through.

"It is none of—"

"My business?" she concluded. "No, but seeing your pain is, especially when there is such an easy solution to it."

This time she moved behind the desk, empowered with the strength of her feelings and beliefs.

"Go to her," Sylvia entreated. "She loves you."

For a moment he stared at her, dumbfounded. "She told you?"

Sylvia smiled and shook her head. "Beth is not so open-mouthed. You know that yourself."

She had lost him. He narrowed his eyes. "Then what are you saying?"

Sylvia had grown much since the first time she had lain in Samuel's strong arms. It was as if there had been blinders on her eyes until then.

"That there are ways to hear things without words being said. It was there, in her voice. And I saw it in her eyes whenever she looked at you. Even from the very beginning, when she tended to your wound, it was there. Beth loves you, sir."

These were the fanciful imaginings of an old woman, Duncan thought. He rose and crossed to the sleeping fireplace. He wanted no cheer, no warmth about him when his heart felt so cold.

"If this is true, then why did she leave?"

It was so simple, she couldn't understand why he didn't see. "Did you ask her to stay?"

Duncan threw up his hands in exasperation. It hadn't been his place to ask, to beg. "No, but—"

Sylvia drew herself up to her full height. For a moment, she took on the bearing of the teacher she had once been, leading a child into enlightenment.

"Sir, as much as she might love you, a woman cannot very well throw herself at a man. Not even Beth." She raised her brows. "What if, she fears, he does not want to catch her? Then she falls and more than her heart is bruised."

Sylvia leaned forward. "I am not very wise, sir, but I have known her since she was a child. I know her loyalties and her emotions. When she feels strongly, it is always there in her eyes." She smiled. "As it was when she looked at you."

Because he was silent, Sylvia hesitantly continued. "Samuel tells me that you keep strict accounts for the earl."

"Yes."

"And that the earl resides now in Virginia." Her eyes filled with sympathy. "Is in fact, a neighbor to the Beaulieus."

Their eyes met and held. "Yes."

Slowly Sylvia trailed her finger along the outer rim of the account book. "Would it not be possible to perhaps bring him the annual reports yourself, rather than to send them to him by some sort of courier?"

She did not wait for him to answer. Instead, she merely smiled as she left the room.

Her suggestion lingered in the air long after she had closed the door.

Duncan stared at the book before him. He began to thumb through the last report, the one he had taken far too long to finish. He saw not a line, not a single word that he had penned.

Without thinking, he closed his hand over the pouch at his waist. He felt the shape of the ring that Cosette had entrusted him with. Beth's grandmother's wedding ring. Beth's ring now.

And he had it.

The stupidity of his decision to nobly let Beth go shimmered before him, like heat rising from the cobblestones of London on a scorching summer's day. He had always hated the class system that had frowned on him since the moment of his birth, that choked society as he knew it. He had fought his way above it, like a sailor outswimming a shark bent on having him for supper.

And now, when it involved the most important aspect of his life, he had allowed himself to be mired by it once again. And by his own volition. He had allowed the class system to doom his and Beth's relationship by agreeing to have his mind and his soul shackled by it.

He who had always been so free.

Well, no more. No more.

"Jacob," he shouted as he strode into the hall, "pack your things. We are going to Virginia."

When the halls echoed with whoops of joy and relief, he realized that Sylvia had not been alone in her feelings in the matter.

"Mother, you have to do something about Beth." Mary pouted, as she flounced down upon the settee in the morning room. "She was always headstrong, but she has become utterly impossible." Mary rushed to continue, lest her mother take up Beth's case. "I know she rescued Father and was very brave and all," she said the words as if she was reciting a boring lesson, "but she has become a veritable hellion since she returned."

Dorothy laid down the needlepoint she had been working on so diligently and sighed. Of all her children, it was Beth who had always given her concern. Still, a little leeway was allowed, given the circumstances. Philippe had only hinted at the atrocities that had befallen him, but it was enough to make her mother's heart congeal with cold.

For now, Beth needed an extra dose of understanding. Dorothy patted her daughter's hand in mute sympathy.

Philippe, however, was a little less tolerant. He overheard Mary's words as he walked in. "Now, Mary, that is no way to speak about your sister."

She had not seen him, or else she would have kept her silence. Mary curtsied deeply.

"A thousand pardons, Father, but I am only giving voice to what everyone else is saying." She turned her eyes toward her mother, waiting for the woman to come to her support. "Even Mother knows it to be true."

Dorothy spread her hands helplessly, torn between duty and feeling. "Philippe, I could never speak to the girl. If you would but say a word."

Philippe smiled indulgently. "Perhaps more than a word is necessary." He believed he knew what was troubling his oldest daughter's heart. "But I shall do what I can."

Mary beamed. "Thank you, Father."

Philippe found Beth in the garden. He had but to follow the tail of resounding oaths. Beth's skirt had gotten snagged on one of the bushes, and she was swearing both impatiently and royally at the bush, the thorns, the roses, and everything else in her path.

"Elizabeth!" Philippe chided, but his heart was clearly not in it. Beth had gone through a great deal in order to rescue him and deserved more than her share of understanding, at least for a while. Everyone tiptoed about him and Andre, but no one seemed to comprehend what Beth had been through as well.

She turned and flushed, embarrassed at being discovered this way. Her words rang out childish and petulant to her ear. It was a sentiment worthy of Mary, not of her.

She managed to pull her skirt free. "Sorry, Father, I'm not myself today."

"You have not been so since we set sail from England." He lowered himself onto the marble bench before the azaleas and patted the place beside him. "Do you miss him that much?"

Beth took the place, but appeared to perch, like a sparrow ready to take flight at the least provocation. "Miss who, Father?"

He drew his brows together. "There have never been secrets between us before."

Beth looked away, not wanting to meet his eyes. She didn't want to talk of what was ripping her heart into tiny pieces. What good would it do? The bastard didn't care. "There is none now."

Philippe nodded slowly. "Then there is a secret between you and your heart." He placed his hand over hers and drew her eyes to him. "Why did you not remain in England, Beth?"

"My home is here, and I belong with you and the others," she replied quickly. She looked down at the ground and sighed deeply. "And he did not ask me to remain," she added in a small voice.

He had been ill then, but not too ill to see the way Duncan looked at his daughter. Not so ill that he didn't understand the depth of the passion that was there. Duncan had bidden them goodbye at the manor, refusing to ride with them to the ship. And Philippe had seen the ache in the man's eyes. He had not realized at the time that it mirrored the one in his daughter's soul.

"His eyes did."

Her father was fantasizing, she thought. "Then you saw more clearly than I." She refused to delude herself any longer. The love that beat in her breast had no twin. "No, I looked for signs, Father. He was glad to see me leave." She blinked, refusing to cry over the likes of Duncan. He didn't deserve any more of her tears.

"Men like Duncan Fitzhugh are not tied to a single woman. Not when there are so many to choose from." She lifted her head, suddenly realizing how sharply she had spoken. "I am sorry if I have offended you."

Philippe laced his hand over hers. "You could never offend me, Beth. But it makes my heart heavy to see you so sad."

Beth lifted her chin. "Then I shall strive to be happier." She rose to her feet. "Come, join me in a walk, Father, and I shall school myself to be more even tempered for everyone's sake."

"No, Beth, for your own sake, never anyone else's. Remember—"

"To thine own self be true," she said, her voice blending with his. She laughed, though the sound echoed with sadness. "I shall try, Father. I shall truly try."

Chapter Forty-two

When she saw him standing there, amid the roses, broad-shouldered and larger than life, Beth thought her heart would stop.

Her hand tightened on her father's.

"Father, I think I need to lie down," she whispered hoarsely, her eyes fastened to Duncan's form. He was dressed like one of the gentlemen who frequented her mother's salon and was as far in appearance from the Duncan she knew as the sun was from the earth. "I am seeing things."

The sight of Duncan made Philippe Beaulieu's heart glad. From the corner of his eyes he saw his wife and daughters hanging back. They had obviously shown him in and directed Duncan to the gardens.

"If that is the case, I am as ill as you, Beth, for I see the same apparition."

Taking her hand from his arm, Philippe strode forward until he was before the uncertain-looking man. Oh, to be that young again, he thought fondly. And that much in love. He shook his hand warmly.

"Mr. Fitzhugh, is it really you?"

Duncan felt like a fool in these stiff clothes, standing

here with people gawking at him. He had left Jacob at
Sin-Jin's and made the journey here at Sin-Jin's and Rachel's urgings.

And at the intense urgings of his own heart.

But now that he was here, he wished it was in his
own clothing, as his own man. These were Sin-Jin's,
pressed upon him in the belief that clothes made the
man.

It was the other way around, Duncan thought.

He felt as nervous as a bridegroom just looking at
her. God, but she was even more beautiful than he remembered.

"Yes, Doctor Beaulieu, it is I." He licked his lips and
fumbled. "I have come to see Sin-Jin." Perhaps he
ought not to call Sin-Jin by name in formal society.
"The earl, I mean, I brought his reports to him. I—damn
it, sir, excuse me."

Duncan gave up all attempt at pretense. He strode
past the man toward the woman he had spent a month
and a half at sea for. No words were necessary as he enfolded Beth in his arms.

She felt as if she had died. Died and walked through
the gates of heaven.

There would be no other way that this could be happening, no other reason to see him, to feel his arms
around her once more. Like a frozen waif warming herself by the fire at long last, Beth rose up on her toes and
lost herself in his embrace.

And when he lowered his mouth to hers, she gave up
a small cry of joy as rapture filled her, pushing through
and lighting every desolate corner of her soul.

She had no notion that her sisters and mother had followed the handsome young stranger to the garden after

admitting him in, or that they were watching now, along with her father, as she kissed Duncan.

The whole world could have watched and she would not have cared. All that mattered to her at this very moment was Duncan.

"Scandalous," Mary murmured reprovingly, her eyes nearly falling from her head.

But there was a longing sigh in her voice. She had never seen anyone kiss that way before, and it made her very soul burn with secret yearning.

Dorothy blushed deeply and looked away. Such behavior belonged between a husband and wife, and perhaps not even then. But it was not in her to deny her daughter this, not while her father looked on this way with approval.

"Under the circumstances," Dorothy announced quietly to her shoes, unable to raise her eyes, "I think perhaps it is forgivable."

Anne sniffed haughtily and raised her chin. "You'd never catch me kissing anyone so shamelessly."

Kate merely laughed, knowing the way of her sister's envy. "Then it would be your loss, Sister. I sincerely hope someone kisses me that way someday."

Kate sighed as she watched and vicariously felt the warmth of the stranger's mouth and the eagerness of his ardor. She cast a covert look toward Andre, who was in the house, and dreamed.

The murmur of voices in the not too distant background penetrated some layer of Beth's mind. She pulled back, thoroughly shaken. She stared at Duncan, still not completely convinced that she hadn't fallen into some fever or was dreaming.

She remembered with sudden clarity the sullen way

he had looked as she had taken her leave. Obviously, he had changed his mind on the subject.

The bastard!

Did he think her some puppet on a string to be yanked back and forth at will? "Why are you here?"

It was past the time for lies and for excuses. Past the time for trying to save his pride. If he had wanted that preserved, he would have remained on Shalott. Duncan placed his hands on her shoulders. Her eyes darkened. God, but he did love her eyes.

"Because I cannot function properly when my heart has been ripped out of my very chest."

Oh, no, he was not going to blame that on her. "It was not ripped," she retorted, fisting her hands at her waist. "You let it fall out."

He knew that light which came into her eyes and would not let himself be trapped in a senseless debate. "Beth, I did not travel over a month and a half with only Jacob as my companion to argue with you now."

"Jacob is here?" She looked around.

He cupped her chin and brought her attention back to him. "Jacob is with Sin-Jin. *I* am here."

Beth balanced her weight on her toes as she looked up at him, unafraid of the stern note in his voice. She would not be shouted at or bullied in her own home. Or anywhere else. "All right, *why* did you travel all this way?"

"Because I—"

Duncan looked toward Philippe, wondering if the man was going to be offended by what he proposed. And then, the next moment, he damned himself for his vacillation and for even the very existence of the question that echoed in the chambers of his mind. This very feeling was what had caused him to lose Beth in the first place—this feeling that he was not good enough for her. His heart was, and that was all that mattered.

"Because I love you, headstrong, stubborn, and annoying though you are." One of the girls in the background uttered a cry at his words, but he knew not which and cared less. It was Beth's reaction he was interested in.

Did he think he could just walk in and kiss her, after all the agony he had caused her, and then fling insults at her? Did he think the single word "love" would completely blot out the rest?

"I will not stand here and be insulted."

She turned to go, but he grasped her hand.

Dorothy looked questioningly at her husband, but he merely shook his head. This was between the young people, and he would give them their privacy.

Beth looked accusingly at Duncan.

"Then we shall go somewhere else, and I shall do it in private," he told her.

Beth swallowed, knowing that if they were alone together, it would not be insults that they were trading, but something far more heated. And intimate. She could not resist him for long if they were alone.

Still holding Beth, Duncan turned to face Philippe. "Doctor Beaulieu, I am a simple man, and I have nothing to offer Beth that can compare with what she will be leaving behind. But I request your permission to take her hand in marriage."

Beth stared at Duncan, stunned and completely speechless.

Philippe heard his wife gasp behind him and attempted to keep a straight face as he looked upon Duncan. But his gratitude and admiration for the man overpowered any whimsical momentary wish to appear stern. He was too glad of the event.

"Not only her hand, but the rest of her as well." Philippe's eyes twinkled whimsically. "And I would say that what you have to offer her far exceeds what I have." He laid a paternal hand upon Duncan's shoulder. "You give her a strong, loving heart within the chest of a man who is fearless and compassionate. I could not have wished for a better man to ask for my daughter's hand than if I had asked God to create you upon request."

Withdrawing his hand from Duncan's shoulder, he clasped Duncan's hand between his own. "You gave me back my life, I give you my daughter. I do not have to ask if she goes willing. It is there, in her eyes."

Philippe looked from one to the other and was pleased with what he saw. "I have but one request."

"Name it," Duncan said eagerly.

He had always wanted a son, Philippe thought. And now, in his later years, God had granted him not one, but two. "That the wedding take place here, so I might see the fulfillment of Beth's joy. And that you return to visit me once in a while." He looked at Beth and smiled, though a bittersweetness tugged at his heart. "For I shall miss her dearly."

Beth bit her lower lip, which had begun to tremble. "Father—"

But he would not allow her to interrupt him. "It is a father's greatest wish to see his daughter on the arm of a man who would treat her in the same fashion as he had." He took a deep breath, then, placing a hand on either of them, he urged them toward one another. "You have my blessings and my permission. And my heartfelt wish for your lasting joy. May the love I see here now exist for the rest of your days."

He turned on his heel and saw the other women in his life still clustered in the doorway. Philippe stepped forward and herded them back.

"Let them have a few moments alone," he instructed his daughters gently. "Before you swallow the man up completely."

"Father!" Mary cried, shocked.

"You only wish that someone looked at you that way," Anne snipped, and she flounced through the doorway ahead of the others.

Kate smiled prettily into her older sister's face as she followed Anne. "Or kissed *you* that way."

Philippe merely shook his head as he hurried them on their way. His wife took his arm, though there was a hesitant look upon her face as she looked back.

"Philippe, do you think it wise to leave them alone like this?"

He laughed softly at her question. "I assure you, dear wife, that nothing will happen now between them that has not happened before." Walking into the house, he did not look back.

Whether or not he was finally here, he still had a debt he owed her. Beth glared at him, remembering the many nights she had suffered because of him, the tears she had shed, the sorrow she had felt. He could easily have spared her everything.

She wheeled on her heel as soon as the others had left. "So, you think you can come here and just take me? That I would be sitting here like some pining, love-sick idiot, waiting for you?"

He liked the light that entered her eyes when she took

on this way. He leaned down, his face an inch away from hers, his mouth curved sensuously.

"Yes."

Her mouth fell open. How dared he? Beth's hand flew back, ready to strike the smirk from his face. "You arrogant son of a—"

He caught her wrist and held it captive. The smile never wavered, though there was a slight edge to it. Very quietly, he slipped her grandmother's ring upon her hand. "Careful, woman, you are talking about the father of your future children."

The smile that rose to her lips came slowly and flowered like a sunrise reaching its zenith. Love radiated from it, as well as from her eyes. She looked down upon the ring and watched it catch the sun. It was time to accept it, she thought. The ring and her love.

"Yes, I suppose I am, aren't I?"

It was then that he saw it. His salvation. She was his salvation, redeeming him from the depths of the hell where life had cast him. And he would never take that for granted.

He took both her hands in his. "Beth, the last two and a half months were the worst I have ever spent, even worse than the two weeks I languished in the Tower, waiting to be hanged."

"You never did tell me how you came to be there," she reminded him.

He kissed the top of her head. "Another time, when we are lying in one another's arms and the night that stretches out before us is long. The point is, my own men were about to hang me if I didn't come here to you."

So it hadn't been his idea, but someone else's? No, she thought, no one could make Duncan do what he chose not to do. Still, she could not resist teasing a little. "So they are to blame for your being here?"

He shook his head and said solemnly, "No, Beth, that blame lies with you."

"With me?" She laid her hand on his chest and felt his heart beat beneath her fingers. Warmth began to curl through her. "How am I the cause of your long travels?"

He took her once more into his arms and swore he would never let her free as long as he lived.

"For being everything I never believed existed. For haunting my days and my nights for wanting you. What I told your father was true. I am a poor man on my own. Save for the money I have put by, what I have belongs to Sin-Jin."

She knew Sin-Jin and knew that he would never force Duncan to leave his land. But that had never been the point.

She slowly shook her head. "No, that is not true." When he raised his brow questioningly, she explained. "I don't belong to Sin-Jin, and you have me. You have always had me."

Duncan's heart felt as if it would surely burst in its joy. "Then I truly am the richest man on the face of the earth."

She could feel the heat of his body as it spoke to hers. She smiled at him invitingly and looked over her shoulder. There were none watching now. She blessed her father for that.

Beth twined her fingers with Duncan's.

"Come, there is a back way to my room that only I know of." Her smile grew as mischief entered her eyes. "Perhaps you would like to sift your newly regained treasure through your hands."

"Eagerly."

Her expression grew serious for a moment before she led him inside. "It's been too long since you touched me, Duncan, and my body cries for yours."

"No more than mine does for you, Beth. No more than mine does for you."

It was some time before they emerged again to speak with her father. And none went to look for them.

None would have dared.